Silas K. Ho

CW00449288

The Squire's Daughter

outlook

Silas K. Hocking

The Squire's Daughter

1st Edition | ISBN: 978-3-75232-839-4

Place of Publication: Frankfurt am Main, Germany

Year of Publication: 2020

Outlook Verlag GmbH, Germany.

Reproduction of the original.

THE SQUIRE'S DAUGHTER

BY SILAS K. HOCKING

CHAPTER I

AN IMPERIOUS MAIDEN

The voice was soft and musical, but the tone was imperative.

"I say, young man, open that gate."

The young man addressed turned slowly from the stile on which he had been leaning, and regarded the speaker attentively. She was seated on a high-stepping horse with that easy grace born of long familiarity with the saddle, and yet she seemed a mere girl, with soft round cheeks and laughing blue eyes.

"Come, wake up," she said, in tones more imperious than before, "and open the gate at once."

He resented the tone, though he was charmed with the picture, and instead of going toward the gate to do her bidding he turned and began to climb slowly over the stile.

She trotted her horse up to him in a moment, her eyes flashing, her cheeks aflame. She had been so used to command and to prompt obedience that this insubordination on the part of a country yokel seemed nothing less than an insult.

"You dare disobey me?" she said, her voice thrilling with anger.

"Of course I dare," he answered, without turning his head. "I am not your servant."

The reply seemed to strike her dumb for a moment, and she reined back her horse several paces.

He turned again to look at her, then deliberately seated himself on one of the posts of the stile.

There was no denying that she made a pretty picture. With one foot on the top rung of the stile he was almost on a level with her, and he was near enough to see her bosom heave and the colour come and go upon her rounded cheeks.

His heart began to beat uncomfortably fast. He feared that he had played a churlish part. She looked so regal, and yet so sweet, that it seemed almost as if Nature had given her the right to command. And who was he that he should resent her imperious manner and refuse to do her bidding?

He had gone too far, however, to retreat. Moreover, his dignity had been touched. She had flung her command at him as though he were a serf. Had she asked him to open the gate, he would have done so gladly. It was the imperious tone that he resented.

"I did not expect such rudeness and incivility here of all places," she said at length in milder tones.

His cheeks flamed at that, and an angry feeling stole into his heart. Judged by ordinary standards, he had no doubt been rude, and her words stung him all the more on that account. He would have played a more dignified part if he had pocketed the affront and opened the gate; but he was in no mood to go back on what he had done.

"If I have been rude and uncivil, you are to blame as much as I—and more," he retorted angrily.

"Indeed?" she said, in a tone of lofty disdain, and an amused smile played round the corners of her mouth. She was interested in the young man in spite of his incivility. Now that she had an opportunity of looking more closely at him, she could not deny that he had no common face, while his speech was quite correct, and not lacking in dignity.

"I hope I am not so churlish as not to be willing to do a kindness to anybody," he went on rapidly, "but I resent being treated as dirt by such as you."

"Indeed? I was not aware——" she began, but he interrupted her.

"If you had asked me to open the gate I would have done so gladly, and been proud to do it," he went on; "but because I belong to what you are pleased to call the lower orders, you cannot ask; you command, and you expect to be obeyed."

"Of course I expect to be obeyed," she said, arching her eyebrows and smiling brightly, "and I am surprised that you——"

"No doubt you are," he interrupted angrily. "But if we are lacking in good manners, so are you," and he turned and leaped off the stile into the field.

"Come back, you foolish young man."

But if he heard, he did not heed; with his eyes fixed on a distant farmhouse, he stalked steadily on, never turning his head either to the right or the left.

For a moment or two she looked after him, an amused smile dimpling her cheeks; then she turned her attention to the gate.

"I wonder what I am to do now?" she mused. "I cannot unfasten it, and if I get off, I shall never be able to mount again; on the other hand, I hate going back through the village the way I came. I wonder if Jess will take it?" and she rode the mare up to the gate and let her smell at the rungs.

It was an ordinary five-barred gate, and the ground was soft and springy. The road was scarcely more than a track across a heathery common. Beyond the gate the road was strictly private, and led through a wide sweep of plantation, and terminated at length, after a circuit of a mile or two, somewhere near Hamblyn Manor.

Jess seemed to understand what was passing through her mistress's mind, and shook her head emphatically.

"You can do it, Jess," she said, wheeling the mare about, and trotting back a considerable distance. "I know you can," and she struck her across the flank with her riding crop.

Jess pricked up her ears and began to gallop toward the gate; but she halted suddenly when within a few feet of it, almost dislodging her rider.

The young lady, however, was not to be defeated. A second time she rode back, and then faced the gate once more.

Jess pricked up her ears, and shook her head as if demanding a loose rein, and then sprang forward with the swiftness of a panther. But she took the gate a moment too soon; there was a sharp crash of splintered wood, a half-smothered cry of pain, and horse and rider were rolling on the turf beyond.

Ralph Penlogan caught his breath and turned his head suddenly. The sound of breaking wood fell distinctly on his ear, and called him back from his not over-pleasant musings. He was angry with himself, angry with the cause of his anger. He had stood up for what he believed to be his rights, had asserted his opinions with courage and pertinacity; and yet, for some reason, he was anything but satisfied. The victory he had won—if it was a victory at all—was a barren one. He was afraid that he had asserted himself at the wrong time, in the wrong place, and before the wrong person.

The girl to whom he had spoken, and whose command he had defied, was not responsible for the social order against which he chafed, and which pressed so hardly on the class to which he belonged. She was where Providence had placed her just as much as he was, and the tone of command she had assumed was perhaps more a matter of habit than any assumption of superiority.

So within three minutes of leaving the stile he found himself excusing the fair creature to whom he had spoken so roughly. That she had a sweet and winning face there was no denying, while the way she sat her horse seemed to him the embodiment of grace.

Who she was he had not the remotest idea. To the best of his recollection he had never seen her before. That she belonged to what was locally termed the gentry there could be no doubt—a visitor most likely at one or other of the big houses in the neighbourhood.

Once the thought flashed across his mind that she might be the daughter of Sir John Hamblyn, but he dismissed it at once. In the first place, Sir John's daughter was old enough to be married—in fact, the wedding day had already been fixed—while this young lady was a mere girl. She did not look more than seventeen if she looked a day. And in the second place, it was inconceivable that such a mean, grasping, tyrannical curmudgeon as Sir John could be the father of so fair a child.

He had seen Dorothy Hamblyn when she was a little girl in short frocks, and his recollection of her was that she was a disagreeable child. If he remembered aright, she was about his own age—a trifle younger.

"Why, I have turned twenty," he mused. "I am a man. She's only a girl."

So he dismissed the idea that she was Sir John's daughter who returned from school only about six months ago, and who was going to marry Lord Probus forthwith.

Suddenly he was recalled from his musings by the crash of the breaking gate. Was that a cry also he heard? He was not quite sure. A dozen vague fears shot through his mind in a moment. For a second only he hesitated, then he turned swiftly on his heel and ran back the way he had come.

The field was a wide one, wider than he had ever realised before. He was out of breath by the time he reached the stile, while his fears had increased with every step he took.

He leaped over the stile at a bound, and then stood still. Before him was the broken gate, and beyond it——

For a moment a mist swam before his eyes, and the ground seemed to be slipping away from beneath his feet. Vague questions respecting his responsibility crowded in upon his brain; the harvest of his churlishness had ripened with incredible swiftness. The word "guilty" seemed to stare at him from every point of the compass.

With a strong effort he pulled himself together, and advanced toward the prostrate figure. The horse stood a few paces away, trembling and bleeding from the knees.

He was almost afraid to look at the girl's face, and when he did so he gave a loud groan. There was no movement, nor any sign of life. The eyes were closed, the cheeks ghastly pale, while from underneath the soft brown hair there ran a little stream of blood.

CHAPTER II

APPREHENSIONS

Sir John Hamblyn was walking up and down in front of his house, fuming, as usual, and with a look upon his face that betokened acute anxiety. Why he should be so anxious he hardly knew. There seemed to be no special reason for it. Everything appeared to be moving along satisfactorily, and unless the absolutely unexpected happened, there was no occasion for a moment's worry.

But it was just the off-chance of something happening that irritated him. The old saying, "There's many a slip 'twixt cup and lip," kept flitting across his brain with annoying frequency. If he could only get another month over without accident of any kind he would have peace; at least, so he believed.

Lord Probus was not the man to go back on his word, and Lord Probus had promised to stand by him, provided he became his—Sir John's—son-in-law.

It seemed a little ridiculous, for Lord Probus was the older man of the two, and to call a man his son-in-law who was older than himself was not quite in harmony with the usual order of things. But then, what did it matter? There were exceptions to every rule, and such exceptions were of constant occurrence.

When once the marriage knot was tied, a host of worries that had harassed him of late would come to an end. He had been foolish, no doubt. He ought to have lived within his income, and kept out of the way of the sharks of the Turf and the Stock Exchange. He had a handsome rent-roll, quite sufficient for his legitimate wants; and if things improved, he might be able to raise rents all round. Besides, if he had luck, some of the leases might fall in, which would further increase his income. But the off-chance of these things was too remote to meet his present needs. He wanted immediate help, and Lord Probus was his only hope.

Fortunately for him, Dorothy was not old enough to see the tragedy of such an alliance. She saw only the social side—the gilt and glitter and tinsel. The appeal had been made to her vanity and to her love of pretty and costly things. To be the mistress of Rostrevor Castle, to bear a title, to have a London house, to have any number of horses and carriages, to go to State functions, to be a society dame before she was twenty—all these things appealed to her girlish pride and vanity, and she accepted the offer of Lord Probus with alacrity, and with scarcely a moment's serious thought.

No time was lost in hurrying forward arrangements for the wedding. The sooner the contract was made secure the better. Any unnecessary delay might give her an excuse for changing her mind. Sir John felt that he would not breathe freely again until the wedding had taken place.

Now and then, when he looked at his bright-eyed, happy, imperious girl, his heart smote him. She had turned eighteen, but she was wonderfully girlish for her years, not only in appearance but in manner, and in her outlook upon life. She knew nothing as yet of the ways of the world, nothing of its treachery and selfishness. She had only just escaped from the seclusion of school and the drudgery of the classroom. She felt free as a bird, and the outlook was just delightful. She was going to have everything that heart could desire, and nothing would be too expensive for her to buy.

She was almost as eager for the wedding to take place as was her father; for directly the wedding was over she was going out to see the world—France, Switzerland, Italy, Greece, Egypt. They were going to travel everywhere, and travel in such luxury as even Royalty might envy. Lord Probus had already given her a foretaste of what he would do for her by presenting her with a beautiful mare. Jess was the earnest of better things to come.

If Dorothy became imperious and slightly dictatorial, it was not to be wondered at. Nothing was left undone or unsaid that would appeal to her vanity. She was allowed her own way in everything.

Sir John was desperately afraid that the illusions might fade before the wedding day arrived. Financially he was in the tightest corner he had ever known, and unless he could tap some of Lord Probus's boundless wealth, he saw before him long years of mean economies and humiliating struggles with poverty. He saw worse—he saw the sale of his personal effects to meet the demands of his creditors, he saw the lopping off of all the luxuries that were as the breath of life to him.

Hence, though deep down in his heart he loathed the thought of his little girl marrying a man almost old enough to be her grandfather, he was sufficiently cornered in other ways to be intensely anxious that the wedding should take place. Lord Probus was the head of a large brewery and distilling concern. His immense and yearly increasing revenues came mainly from beer. How rich he was nobody knew. He hardly knew himself. He had as good as promised Sir John that if the wedding came off he would hand over to him sufficient scrip in the great company of which he was head to qualify him—Sir John—for a directorship. The scrip could be paid for at Sir John's convenience. The directorship should be arranged without undue delay. The work of a director was not exacting, while the pay was exceedingly generous.

Sir John had already begun to draw the salary in imagination, and to live up to it. Hence, if anything happened now to prevent the wedding, it would be like knocking the bottom out of the universe.

In the chances of human life, it did not seem at all likely that anything would happen to prevent what he so much desired. It seemed foolish to worry himself for a single moment. And yet he did worry. There was always that off-chance. Nobody could ward off accidents or disease.

Dorothy had gone out riding alone. She refused to have a groom with her, and, of course, she had to have her own way; but he was always more or less fidgety when she was out on these expeditions.

And yet it was not the fear of accidents that really troubled him. What he feared most was that she might become disillusioned. As yet she had not awakened to the meaning and reality of life. She was like a child asleep, wandering through a fairyland of dreams and illusions. But she might awake at any moment—awake to the passion of love, awake to the romance as well as the reality of life.

The appeal as yet had been to her vanity—to her sense of self-importance. There had been no appeal to her heart or affections. She did not know what love was, and if she married Lord Probus it would be well for her if she never knew. But love might awake when least expected; her heart might be stirred unconsciously. Some Romeo might cross her path, and with one glance of his eyes might change all her life and all her world; and a woman in love was more intractable than a comet.

Sir John would not like to be brought into such a position that he would have to coerce his child. Spendthrift that he was, and worse, with a deep vein of selfishness that made him intensely unpopular with all his tenants, he nevertheless loved Dorothy with a very genuine affection. Geoffrey, his son and heir, had never appealed very strongly to his heart. Geoffrey was too much like himself, too indolent and selfish. But Dorothy was like her mother, whose passing was as the snapping of a rudder chain in a storm.

The gritting of wheels on the gravel caused Sir John to turn suddenly on his heel, and descending the steps at the end of the terrace, he walked a little distance to meet the approaching carriage.

Lord Probus was not expected, but he was not the less welcome on that account.

"The day is so lovely that I thought I would drive across to have a peep at you all," Lord Probus said, stepping nimbly out of the landau.

He was a dapper man, rather below the medium height, with a bald head and iron-grey, military moustache. He was sixty years of age, but looked ten years younger.

"I am delighted to see you," Sir John said, with effusion, "and I am sure Dorothy will be when she returns."

"She is out, is she?"

"She is off riding as usual. Since you presented her with Jess, she has spent most of her time in the saddle."

"She is a good horsewoman?"

"Excellent. She took to riding as a duck takes to water. She rode with the hounds when she was ten."

"I wish I could ride!" Lord Probus said, reflectively. "I believe horse exercise would do me good; but I began too late in life."

"Like skating and swimming, one must start young if he is to excel," Sir John answered.

"Yes, yes; and youth passes all too quickly." And his lordship sighed.

"Well, as to that, one is as young as one feels, you know." And Sir John led the way into the house.

Lord Probus followed with a frown. Sir John had unwittingly touched him on a sore spot. If he was no younger than he felt, he was unmistakably getting old. He tried to appear young, and with a fair measure of success; tried to persuade himself that he was still in his prime; but every day the fact was brought painfully home to him that he had long since turned the brow of the hill, and was descending rapidly the other side. Directly he attempted to do what was child's play to him ten years before, he discovered that the spring had gone out of his joints and the nerve from his hand.

He regretted this not only for his own sake, but in some measure for Dorothy's. He never looked into her fresh young face without wishing he was thirty years younger. She seemed very fond of him at present. She would sit on the arm of his chair and pat his bald head and pull his moustache, and call him her dear, silly old boy; and when he turned up his face to be kissed, she would kiss him in the most delightful fashion.

But he could not help wondering at times how long it would last. That she was fond of him just now he was quite sure. She told him in her bright, ingenuous way that she loved him; but he was not so blind as not to see that there was no passion in her love. In truth, she did not know what love was.

He was none the less anxious, however, on that account, to make her his wife, but rather the more. The fact that the best part of his life was gone made him all the more eager to fill up what remained with delight. He might reckon upon another years of life, at least, and to possess Dorothy for ten years would be worth living for—worth growing old for.

"You expect Dorothy back soon?" Lord Probus questioned, dropping into an easy-chair.

"Any minute, my lord. In fact, I expected her back before this."

"Jess has been well broken in. I was very careful on that point." And his lordship looked uneasily out of the window.

"And then, you know, Dorothy could ride an antelope or a giraffe. She is just as much at ease in a saddle as you are in that easy-chair."

"Do you know, I get more and more anxious as the time draws near," his lordship said absently. "It would be an awful blow to me if anything should happen now to postpone the wedding."

"Nothing is likely to happen," Sir John said grimly, but with an apprehensive look in his eyes. "Dorothy is in the best of health, and so are you."

"Well, yes, I am glad to say I am quite well. And Dorothy, you think, shows no sign of rueing her bargain?"

"On the contrary, she has begun to count the days." And Sir John walked to the window and raised the blind a little.

"I shall do my best to make her happy," his lordship said, with a smile. "And, bachelor as I am, I think I know what girls like."

"There's no doubt about that," was the laughing answer. "But who comes here?" And Sir John ran to the door and stepped out on the terrace.

A boy without coat, and carrying his cap in his hand, ran eagerly up to him. His face was streaming with perspiration, and his eyes ready to start out of their sockets.

"If you please, sir," he said, in gasps, "your little maid has been and got killed!"

"My little maid?" Sir John questioned. "Which maid? I did not know any of the servants were out."

"No, not any servant, sir; but your little maid, Miss Dorothy."

"My daughter!" he almost screamed. And he staggered up against the porch and hugged one of the pillars for support.

"Thrown from her horse, sir, down agin Treliskey Plantation," the boy went

11

on. "Molly Udy says she reckons her neck's broke."

Sir John did not reply, however. He could only stand and stare at the boy, half wondering whether he was awake or dreaming.

CHAPTER III

A NEW SENSATION

Ralph Penlogan's first impulse was to rush off into St. Goram and rouse the village; but on second thoughts he dropped on his knees by the side of the prostrate girl, and placed his ear close to her lips. For a moment or two he remained perfectly still, with an intent and anxious expression in his eyes; then his face brightened, and something like a smile played round the corners of his lips.

"No, she is not dead," he said to himself. And he heaved a great sigh of relief.

But he still felt doubtful as to the best course to take. To leave the unconscious girl lying alone by the roadside seemed to him, for some reason, a cruel thing to do. She might die, or she might return to consciousness, and find herself helpless and forsaken, without a human being or even a human habitation in sight.

"Oh, I hope she will not die," he said to himself, half aloud, "for if she does I shall feel like a murderer." And he put his ear to her lips a second time.

No, she still breathed, but the rivulet of blood seemed to be growing larger.

He raised her gently and let her head rest against his knee while he examined the wound underneath her auburn hair. He tried his best to repress a shudder, but failed. Then he pulled a handkerchief from his pocket, and proceeded to bind it tightly round her head. How pale her face was, and how beautiful! He had never seen, he thought, so lovely a face before.

He wondered who she was and where she lived.

The horse whinnied a little distance away, and again the question darted through his mind, What was he to do? If he waited for anyone to pass that way he might wait a week. The road was strictly private, and there was a notice up that trespassers would be prosecuted. It had been a public road once —a public road, indeed, from time immemorial—but Sir John had put a stop to that. In spite of protests and riots, and threatened appeals to law, he had won the day, and no man dared walk through the plantation now without first asking his consent.

"She can't be very heavy," Ralph thought, as he looked down into her sweet, colourless face. "I'll have to make the attempt, anyhow. It's nearly two miles to St. Goram; but perhaps I shall be able to manage it."

A moment or two later he had gathered her up in his strong arms, and, with her bandaged head resting on his shoulder, and her heart beating feebly against his own, he marched away back over the broken gate in the direction of St. Goram. Jess gave a feeble whinny, then followed slowly and dejectedly, with her nose to the ground.

Half a mile away the ground dipped into a narrow valley, with a clear stream of water meandering at the bottom.

Ralph laid down his burden very gently and tenderly close to the stream, with her head pillowed on a bank of moss. He was at his wits' end, but he thought it possible that some ice-cold water sprinkled on her face might revive her.

Jess stood stock-still a few yards away and watched the operation. Ralph sprinkled the cold water first on her face, then he got a large leaf, and made a cup of it, and tried to get her to drink; but the water trickled down her neck and into her bosom.

She gave a sigh at length and opened her eyes suddenly. Then she tried to raise her head, but it fell back again in a moment.

Ralph filled the leaf again and raised her head.

"Try to drink this," he said. "I'm sure it will do you good." And she opened her lips and drank.

He filled the leaf a third time, and she followed him with her eyes, but did not attempt to speak.

"Now, don't you feel better?" he questioned, after she had swallowed the second draught.

"I don't know," she answered, in a whisper. "But who are you? And where am I?"

"You have had an accident," he said. "Your horse threw you. Don't you remember?"

She closed her eyes and knitted her brows as if trying to recall what had happened.

"It was close to Treliskey Plantation," he went on, "and the gate was shut. You told me to open it, and I refused. I was a brute, and I shall never forgive myself so long as I live."

"Oh yes; I remember," she said, opening her eyes slowly, and the faintest suggestion of a smile played round her ashen lips. "You took offence because _____"

"I was a brute!" he interjected.

14

"I ought not to have spoken as I did," she said, in a whisper. "I had no right to command you. Do—do you think I shall die?"

"No, no!" he cried, aghast. "What makes you ask such a question?"

"I feel so strange," she answered, in the same faint whisper, "and I have no strength even to raise my head."

"But you will get better!" he said eagerly. "You must get better—you must! For my sake, you must!"

"Why for your sake?" she whispered.

"Because if you die I shall feel like a murderer all the rest of my life. Oh, believe me, I did not mean to be rude and unkind! I would die for you this very moment if I could make you better! Oh, believe me!" And the tears came up and filled his eyes.

She looked at him wonderingly. His words were so passionate, and rang with such a deep note of conviction, that she could not doubt his sincerity.

"It was all my fault," she whispered, after a long pause; then the light faded from her eyes again. Ralph rushed to the stream and fetched more water, but she was quite unconscious when he returned.

For a moment or two he looked at her, wondering whether her ashen lips meant the approach of death; then he gathered her up in his arms again and marched forward in the direction of St. Goram.

The road seemed interminable, while his burden hung a dead weight in his arms, and grew heavier every step he took. He was almost ready to drop, when a feeble sigh sounded close to his ear, followed by a very perceptible shudder.

He was afraid to look at her. He had heard that people shuddered when they died. A moment or two later he was reassured. A soft voice whispered—

"Are you taking me home?"

"I am taking you to St. Goram," he answered "I don't know where your home is."

She raised herself suddenly and locked her arms about his neck, and at the touch of her hands the blood leaped in his veins and his face became crimson. He no longer felt his burden heavy, no longer thought the way long. A new chord had been struck somewhere, which sang through every fibre of his being. A new experience had come to him, unlike anything he had ever before felt or imagined.

He raised her a little higher in his arms, and pressed her still closer to his heart. He was trembling from head to foot; his head swam with a strange intoxication, his heart throbbed at twice its normal rate. He had suddenly got into a world of enchantment. Life expanded with a new meaning and significance.

It did not matter for the moment who this fair creature was or where she lived. He had got possession of her; her arms were about his neck, her head rested on his shoulder, her face was close to his, her breath fanned his cheek, he could feel the beating of her heart against his own.

He marched over the brow of the hill and down the other side in a kind of ecstasy.

He waited for her to speak again, but for some reason she kept silent. He felt her fingers clutch the back of his neck, and every now and then a feeble sigh escaped her lips.

"Are you in pain?" he asked at length.

"I think I can bear it," she answered feebly.

"I wish I could carry you more gently," he said, "but the ground is very rough."

"Oh, but you are splendid!" she replied. "I wish I had not been rude to you."

He gave a big gulp, as though a lump had risen in his throat.

"Don't say that again, please," he said at length. "I feel bad enough to drown myself."

She did not reply again, and for a long distance he walked on in silence. He was almost ready to drop, and yet he was scarcely conscious of fatigue. It seemed to him as though the strength of ten men had been given to him.

"We shall be in the high road in a few minutes now," he said at length; but she did not reply. Her hands seemed to be relaxing their hold about his neck again; her weight had suddenly increased.

He staggered hurriedly forward to the junction of the roads, and then sat down suddenly on a bank, still holding his precious charge in his arms. He shifted her head a little, so that he could look at her face. She did not attempt to speak, though he saw she was quite conscious.

"There's some kind of vehicle coming along the road," he said at length, lifting his head suddenly.

She did not reply, but her eyes seemed to search his face as though something perplexed her.

"Are you easier resting?" he questioned.

She closed her eyes slowly by way of reply; she was too spent to speak.

"You have not yet told me who you are," he said at length. All thought of rank and station had passed out of his mind. They were on an equality while he sat there folding her in his arms.

She opened her eyes again, and her lips moved, but no sound escaped them.

In the distance the rattle of wheels sounded more and more distinct.

"Help is coming," he whispered. "I'm sure it is."

Her eyes seemed to smile into his, but no other answer was given.

He looked eagerly toward the bend of the road, and after a few minutes a horse and carriage appeared in sight.

"It's Dr. Barrow's carriage," he said half aloud. "Oh, this is fortunate!"

He raised a shout as the carriage drew near. The coachman saw that something had happened, and pulled up suddenly. The doctor pushed his head out of the window, then turned the door-handle and stepped out on to the roadside.

"Hello, Ralph Penlogan!" he said, rushing forward, "what is the meaning of this?"

"She got thrown from her horse up against Treliskey Plantation," he answered. "Do you know who she is?"

"Of course I know who she is!" was the quick reply. "Don't you know?"

"No. I never saw her before. Do you think she will recover?"

"Has she been unconscious all the time?" the doctor asked, placing his fingers on her wrist.

"No; she's come to once or twice. I thought at first she was dead. There's a big cut on her head, which has bled a good deal."

"She must be got home instantly," was the reply. "Help me to get her into the carriage at once!"

It was an easy task for the two men. Dorothy had relapsed into complete unconsciousness again. Very carefully they propped her up in a corner of the brougham, while the doctor took his place by her side.

Ralph would have liked to ride with them. He rather resented Dr. Barrow taking his place. He had a notion that nobody could support the unconscious girl so tenderly as himself.

There was no help for it, however. He had to get out of the carriage and leave the two together.

"Tell William," said the doctor, "to drive round to the surgery before going on to Hamblyn Manor."

"To Hamblyn Manor?" Ralph questioned, with a look of perplexity in his eyes as he stood at the carriage door.

"Why, where else should I take her?"

"Is she from up the country?"

"From up the country—no. Do you mean to say you've lived here all your life and don't know Miss Hamblyn?"

"But she is only a girl," Ralph said, looking at the white face that was leaning against the doctor's shoulder.

"Well?"

"Miss Hamblyn is going to bemarried!"

The doctor's face clouded in a moment.

"I fear this will mean the postponement of the marriage," he said.

Ralph groaned inwardly and turned away.

"The doctor says you must drive round to the surgery before going on to Hamblyn Manor," he said, speaking to the coachman, and then he stood back and watched the carriage move away.

It seemed to him like a funeral, with Jess as the mourner, limping slowly behind. The doctor hoped to avoid attracting attention in St. Goram. He did not know that Jess was following the carriage all the way.

It was the sight of the riderless horse that attracted people's attention. Then, when the carriage pulled up at the doctor's door, someone bolder than the rest looked in at the window and caught a glimpse of the unconscious figure.

The doctor's anger availed him nothing. Other people came and looked, and the news spread through St. Goram like wildfire, and in the end an enterprising lad took to his heels and ran all the distance to Hamblyn Manor that he might take to Sir John the evil tidings.

18

CHAPTER IV

A BITTER INTERVIEW

Dr. Barrow remained at the Manor House most of the night. It was clear from his manner, as well as from the words he let fall, that he regarded Dorothy's case as serious. Sir John refused to go to bed.

"I shall not sleep in any case," he said. "And I prefer to remain downstairs, so that I can hear the latest news."

Lord Probus remained with him till after midnight, though very few words passed between them. Now and then they looked at each other in a dumb, despairing fashion, but neither had the courage to talk about what was uppermost in their thoughts.

Just as the daylight was struggling into the room, the doctor came in silently, and dropped with a little sigh into an easy-chair.

"Well?" Sir John questioned, looking at him with stony eyes.

"She is a little easier for the moment," was the quiet, unemotional answer.

"You think she will pull through?"

"I hope so, but I shall be able to speak with more confidence later."

"The wound in her head is a bad one?"

The doctor smiled. "If that were all, we would soon have her on her feet again."

"But what other injuries has she sustained?"

"It is impossible to say just at present. She evidently fell under the horse. The wonder is she's alive at all."

"I suppose nobody knows how it happened?" Sir John questioned after a pause.

"Well, I believe nobody saw the accident, though young Ralph Penlogan was near the spot at the time—and a fortunate thing too, or she might have remained where she fell till midnight."

"You have seen the young man?"

"He had carried her in his arms from Treliskey Plantation to the junction of the high road."

"Without assistance?"

"Without assistance. What else could he do? There was not a soul near the spot. Since you closed the road through the plantation, it is never used now, except by the few people to whom you have granted the right of way."

"So young Penlogan was in the plantation, was he?"

"I really don't know. He may have been on the common."

Sir John frowned. "Do you know," he said, after a pause, "that I dislike that young man exceedingly."

"Indeed?"

"He is altogether above his station. I believe he is clever, mind you, and all that, but what does a working-man's son want to bother himself with mechanics and chemistry for?"

"Why not?" the doctor asked, with slightly raised eyebrows.

"Why? Because this higher education, as it is called, is bringing the country to the dogs. Get an educated proletariat, and the reign of the nobility and gentry is at an end. You see the thin end of the wedge already. Your Board-school boys and girls are all cursed with notions; they are too big for their jackets, too high for their station; they have no respect for squire or parson, and they are too high and mighty to do honest work."

"I cannot say that has been my experience," the doctor said quietly; and he rose from his chair and began to pull on his gloves.

"You are not going?" Sir John questioned anxiously.

"For an hour or two. I should like, with your permission, to telegraph to Dr. Roscommon. You know he is regarded now as the most famous surgeon in the county."

"But surely, doctor——" Sir John began, with a look of consternation in his eyes.

"I should like to have his opinion," the doctor said quietly.

"Of course—of course! Get the best advice you can. No expense must be spared. My child must be saved at all costs."

"Rest assured we shall do our best," the doctor answered, and quietly left the room.

For the best part of another hour Sir John paced restlessly up and down the room, then he dropped into an easy-chair and fell fast asleep.

He was aroused at length by a timid knock at the door.

"Come in!" he answered sleepily, fancying for a moment that he was in bed, and that his servant had brought him his shaving-water.

The next moment he was on his feet, with an agitated look in his eyes.

A servant entered, followed by Ralph Penlogan, who looked as if he had not slept for the night.

Instead of waiting to know if Sir John would see him, Ralph had stalked into the room on the servant's heels. He was too anxious to stand on ceremony, too eager to unburden his mind. He had never had a moment's peace since his meeting with Dorothy Hamblyn the previous afternoon. He felt like a criminal, and would have given all he possessed if he could have lived over the previous afternoon again.

Sir John recognised him in a moment, and drew himself up stiffly. He never felt altogether at ease in the presence of the Penlogans. He knew that he had "done" the father, driven a most unfair bargain with him, and it is said a man never forgives a fellow-creature he has wronged.

"I have come to speak to you about the accident to your daughter," Ralph said, plunging at once into the subject that filled his mind.

"Yes, yes; I am glad you have called," Sir John said, walking to the mantelpiece and leaning his elbow on it.

"I hope she is better?" Ralph went on. "You think she will recover?"

"I am sorry to say she is very seriously injured," Sir John answered slowly; "but, naturally, we hope for the best."

Ralph dropped his eyes to the floor, and for a moment was silent.

"Dr. Barrow tells me that you were near the spot at the time of the accident," Sir John went on; "for that reason I am glad you have called."

"There isn't much to tell," Ralph answered, without raising his eyes, "but I am anxious to tell what there is."

"Ah!" Sir John gasped, glancing across at his visitor suspiciously.

"After what has happened, you can't blame me more than I blame myself," Ralph went on; "though, of course, I never imagined for a moment that she would attempt to leap the gate."

"I don't quite understand," Sir John said stiffly.

"Well, it was this way. I was leaning on the stile leading down into Dingley Bottom, when someone rode up and ordered me to open the gate leading into

Treliskey Plantation. If the lady had asked me to open the gate I should have done it in a minute."

"So you refused to do a neighbourly act, did you?"

"I told her I was not her servant, at which she got very indignant, and ordered me to do as I was told."

"And you refused a second time?"

"I did. In fact, I felt very bitter. People in our class suffer so many indignities from the rich that we are apt to be soured."

"Soured, indeed! Your accursed Board-school pride not only makes cads of you, but criminals!" And Sir John's eyes blazed with passion.

"I am not going to defend myself any further," Ralph said, raising his eyes and looking him full in the face. "I am sorry now that I did not open the gate —awfully sorry. I would give anything if I could live over yesterday afternoon again!"

"I should think so, indeed!" Sir John said, in his most biting tones. "And understand this, young man, if my daughter dies I shall hold you responsible for her death!"

Ralph's face grew very white, but he did not reply.

Sir John, however, was in no mood to be silent. He had a good many things bottled up in his mind, and Ralph's visit gave him an excuse for pulling the cork out.

"I want to say this also to you," he said, "now that you have given me an opportunity of opening my mind—that I consider young men of your stamp a danger and a menace to the neighbourhood!"

Ralph looked at him without flinching, but he did not speak.

"There was a time," Sir John went on, "when people knew how to respect their betters, when the working classes kept their place and did not presume, and when such as you would never have ventured into this house by the front door!"

"I came by the nearest way," Ralph answered, "and did not trouble to inquire which door it was."

"Your father no doubt thinks he has been doing a wise thing in keeping himself on short commons to give you what he foolishly imagines is an education."

"Excuse me, but we are all kept on short commons because you took advantage of my father's ignorance. If he had had a little better education he would not have allowed himself to be duped by you!" And he turned and made for the door.

But Sir John intercepted him, with flashing eyes and passion-lined face.

"Have you come here to insult me?" he thundered. "By Heaven, I've a good mind to call my servants in and give you a good horsewhipping!"

Ralph stood still and scowled angrily.

"I neither came here to insult you nor to be insulted by you! I came here to express my regret that I did not pocket my pride and open the gate for your daughter. I have made the best amends in my power, and now, if you will let me, I will go home."

"I am not sure that I will let you!" Sir John said angrily. "It seems to me the proper thing would be to send for the police and get you locked up. How do I know that you did not put something in the way to prevent my daughter's horse clearing the gate? I know that you hate your betters—like most of your class, alas! in these times——"

"We should not hate you if you dealt justly by us!" Ralph retorted.

"Dealt justly, indeed!" Sir John sneered. "It makes me ill to hear such as you talking about justice! You ought to be thankful that you are allowed to live in the parish at all!"

"We are. We are grateful for the smallest mercies—grateful for room to walk about."

"That's more than some of you deserve," Sir John retorted angrily. "Now go home and help your father on the farm. And, by Jove, tell him if he's behind with his ground rent this year I'll make him sit up."

Ralph's eyes blazed in a moment. That ground rent was to him the sum of all iniquity. It represented to him the climax of greed and injustice. The bitterness of it had eaten out all the joy of his father's life and robbed his mother of all the fruits of her thrift and economy.

Ralph's face was toward the door; but he turned in a moment, white with passion.

"I wonder you are not ashamed to speak of that ground rent," he said slowly, and with biting emphasis. "You, who took advantage of my father's love for his native place, and of his ignorance of legal phraseology—you, who robbed a poor man of his savings, and cheated his children out of their due. Ground rent, indeed! I wonder the word does not stick in your throat and choke you." And before Sir John could reply he had pulled open the door and passed out into the hall.

He walked home by the forbidden path through the plantation, feeling more reckless and defiant than he had ever felt before. He was in the mood to run his head against any brick wall that might stand in his way; he almost hoped that a keeper would cross his path and arrest him. He wanted to have another tilt with Sir John, and show him how lightly he regarded his authority.

No keeper, however, showed his face. He was left in undisturbed possession of field and fell. He whistled loudly and defiantly, as he strutted through the dim aisles of the plantation, and tried to persuade himself that he was not a bit sorry that Sir John at that moment was suffering all the tortures of suspense. He would have persuaded himself, if he could, that he did not care whether Dorothy Hamblyn lived or died; but that was altogether beyond his powers. He did care. Every fibre of his being seemed to plead for her recovery.

He came at length upon the scene of the previous day's accident. To all appearances no one had visited it. The broken gate had not been touched. On the ground was a dark stain which had been crimson the day before, but no one would notice it unless it were pointed out; for the rest, Nature showed no regard for human pain or grief.

It was a glorious morning in late summer. The woods were at their best; the fields were yellowing in all directions to the harvest. High in the blue heavens the larks were trilling their morning song, while in the banks and hedges the grasshoppers were whirring and chattering with all their might. It was a morning to inspire the heart with confidence and hope, to cleanse the eyes from the dust of doubt, and to uplift the spirit from the fogs of pessimism and despair.

And yet Ralph Penlogan heard no song that morning, nor even saw the sunshine. A dull weight was pressing on his heart which he had no power to lift. Anger and regret struggled within him for the mastery, while constantly a new emotion—which he did not understand as yet—ran through his veins like liquid fire.

When he reached the stile he rested for a few moments, and recalled the scene of the previous day. It was not difficult. The face of the fair horsewoman he would never forget; the soft, imperious voice rang through his brain like the sound of evening bells. Her smile was like sunshine on waving corn.

Then in his fancy he saw Jess dart forward, and then came the sickening sound of splintering wood. What happened after that he knew all too well.

It would be a cruel thing for death to blot out a smile so sweet, and the grave to hide a face so fair. While there were so many things in the world that were neither lovely nor useful nor inspiring, it would seem like a sin against Nature to blot out and destroy so sweet a presence. Let the weeds be plucked up, let the thorns be burned; but the flowers should be allowed to remain to brighten the world and gladden the hearts of men.

He sprang over the stile at length, and strode away in the direction of Dingley Bottom with a scowl upon his face.

What right had he to be thinking about the squire's daughter? Did he not despise the class to which she belonged? Did he not hate her father because, having a giant's strength, he used it like a giant? Had not the justice of the strong become a byword and a loathing? Had he not sworn eternal enmity to the oppressor and all who shared his gains?

On the brow of the next low hill he paused again. Before him, in a little hollow, lay the homestead his father had built; and spread out on three sides were the fields he had reclaimed from the wilderness.

It had been a hard and almost heartbreaking task, for when he commenced the enterprise he had but a faint idea what it would cost. It seemed easy enough to root up the furze bushes and plough down the heather, and the soil looked so loamy and rich that he imagined a heavy crop would be yielded the first year.

And yet it was not to make money that David Penlogan had leased a portion of Polskiddy Downs, and built a house thereon. It was rather that he might have a quiet resting-place in the evening of his life, and be able to spend his days in the open air—in the wind and sunshine—and be set free from the perils that beset an underground captain in a Cornish mine.

With what high hopes he embarked upon the enterprise none but David knew. It was his one big investment. All the savings of a lifetime went into it. He took his hoarded sovereigns out of the bank without misgiving, and felt as happy as a king, while he toiled like a slave.

His neighbours stared and shook their heads when it leaked out on what terms he had taken the lease.

"Sir John has been too many for you, David," an old farmer said to him one day. "You might as well empty your purse in his pocket right off. You'll not have money enough to buy a coffin with when he's finished with you."

But David knew better, or fancied he did, which is much the same thing.

He hired horses and ploughs and stubbers and hedgers and ditchers, and masons and carpenters, and for a year that corner of Polskiddy Downs was alive with people.

The house was built from plans David prepared himself. Barn and cowsheds were erected at a convenient distance. Hedges were carried in straight lines across the newly cultivated fields. A small orchard was planted beyond the kitchen garden, and everything, to David's hopeful eyes, looked promising for the future.

That was twelve years ago, and in those years David had grown to be an old man. He had spent his days in the open air, it is true—in the wind and sunshine, and in the rain and snow—and he had contracted rheumatism and bronchitis, and all the heart had gone out of him in the hopeless struggle.

As Ralph looked out over the not too fruitful fields which his father had reclaimed from the waste with such infinite toil, and at the sacrifice of all his savings, he forgot the fair face of Dorothy Hamblyn, which had been haunting him all the way back, and remembered only the iron hand of her father.

CHAPTER V

THE CHANCES OF LIFE

Ralph had started so early that morning that he had had no time to get breakfast. Now he began to feel the pangs of hunger most acutely.

"I expect mother will have kept something for me," he said to himself, as he descended the slope. "I hope she is not worrying about what has become of me."

He looked right and left for his father, expecting to find him at work in the fields, but David was nowhere in evidence.

Ralph made a bee-line across the fields, and was soon in the shelter of the little homestead. He found his father and mother and his sister Ruth still seated at the breakfast-table. Ruth pushed back her chair at the sound of his footsteps and rose to her feet.

"Why, Ralph," she said, "where have you been? Mother's been quite worried about you."

"If that's all she has to worry her, she needn't worry much," he said, with a laugh. "But has anything happened? You all look desperately sober."

"We've heard some news that has made us all feel very anxious," David answered wearily. "We've sat here talking about it for the last half-hour."

"Then the news concerns us all?" Ralph questioned, with a catch in his voice.

"Very closely, my boy—very closely. The truth is, Julian Seccombe has got wounded out in Egypt."

"And he's the last life on the farm?" Ralph questioned, with a gasp.

"That is so, my boy. It seems strange that I should be so unfortunate in the choice of lives, and yet I could not have been more careful. Who could have thought that the parson's boy would become a soldier?"

"Life is always uncertain," Ralph answered, with a troubled look in his eyes, "whether a man is a soldier or a farmer."

"That is so," David answered reflectively. "Yet my father held his little place on only two lives, and one of them lived to be seventy-five."

"But, even then, I've heard you say the lease ran only a little over sixty years. It's a wicked gamble, is this leasehold system, with the chances in favour of the landlord."

"Why a gamble in favour of the landlord, my boy?" David questioned, lifting his mild eyes to his son's face.

"Why, because if all the 'lives' live out their threescore years and ten, the lease is still a short one; for you don't start with the first year of anyone's life."

"That is true," David answered sadly. "The parson's boy was ten, which I thought would be balanced by the other two."

"And the other two did not live ten years between them."

"Of course, nobody could foresee that," David answered sadly. "They were both healthy children. Our little Billy was three, and the healthiest baby of the lot."

"But with all the ailments of children in front of him?"

"Well, no. He had had whooping-cough, and got through it easily. It was the scarlet fever that carried him off. Poor little chap, he was gone in no time."

"And so, within a year, and after you had spent the greater part of your money, your farm hung upon two lives," Ralph said bitterly.

"But, humanly speaking, they were good lives. Not lives that would be exposed to much risk. Lawyer Doubleday told me that he intended to bring up his boy to the same profession, and Parson Seccombe told me he had dedicated Julian to the Church in his infancy. What better lives, humanly speaking, could you get? Neither parsons nor lawyers run any risks to speak of."

"Yes; that's true enough. The system being what it is, you did the best you could, no doubt."

"Nobody could foresee," David said sadly, "that Doubleday's boy would go and get drowned. I nearly fainted when I heard the news."

"And now you say that young Seccombe has got shot out in Egypt."

"I don't know as to his being shot; but Tom Dyer, who was here this morning, said that he had just seen the parson, who was in great trouble, news having reached him last evening that Julian was wounded."

"Then if the parson's in great trouble, the chances are he's badly wounded."

"I don't know. I thought of walking across to St. Goram directly, and seeing the parson for myself; but I'm almost afraid to do so, lest the worst should be true."

"We shall have to face it, whatever it is," Ralph said doggedly.

"But think of what it would mean to us if the parson's son should die! Poor mother is that troubled that she has not been able to eat a mouthful of breakfast!"

"She seems scarcely able to talk about it," Ralph said, glancing at the door through which his mother and Ruth had disappeared.

"She's a little bit disposed to look on the dark side of things generally," David said slowly. "For myself, I keep hoping for the best. It doesn't seem possible that God can strip us of everything at a blow."

"It doesn't seem to me as though God had any hand in the business," Ralph answered doggedly.

"Hush, Ralph, my boy! The issues of life and death are in His hands."

"And you believe also that He is the author of the leasehold system that obtains in this country?"

"I did not say that, Ralph; but He permits it."

"Just as He permits lying and theft, and murder and war, and all the other evil things there are in the world. But that is nothing to the point. You can't make me believe that the Almighty ever meant a few people to parcel out the world among themselves, and cheat all the rest out of their rights."

"The world is what it is, my boy, and neither you nor I can alter it."

"And you think it is our duty to submit quietly and uncomplainingly to whatever wrong or injustice is heaped upon us?"

"We must submit to the law, my boy, however hardly it presses upon us."

"But we ought to try, all the same, to get bad laws mended."

"You can't ladle the sea dry with a limpet-shell, Ralph, nor carry off a mountain in your pocket. No, no; let us not talk about the impossible, nor give up hope until we are forced to. Perhaps young Seccombe will recover."

"But if he should die, father. What would happen then?"

"I don't know, my boy, and I can't bear to think."

"But we'd better face the possibility," Ralph answered doggedly, "so that, if the worst should come to the worst, we may know just where we are."

"'Sufficient unto the day is the evil thereof,'" David answered, with a far-away look in his eyes. And he got up from his seat and walked slowly out of the house.

Ralph sat looking out of the window for several minutes, and then he went off in search of his mother and Ruth.

"Do you know, mother," he said, as cheerily as he could, "that I have had no breakfast yet? And, in spite of the bad news, I am too hungry for words."

"Had no breakfast?" she said, lifting up her hands in surprise. "I made sure you got something to eat before you went out."

"Well, then, you were wrong for once," he said, laughing. "Now, please put me out of my misery as quickly as possible."

"Ah, Ralph," she answered, with a sigh, "if we had no worse misery than hunger, how happy we should be!"

"That is so, mother," he said, with a laugh. "Hunger is not at all bad when you have plenty to eat."

She sighed again.

"It is well that you young people don't see far ahead of you," she said plaintively. "But come here and get your breakfast."

Two hours later, when in the home close hoeing turnips, he lifted his head and saw his father coming across the fields from the direction of St. Goram, he straightened his back at once and waited. He knew that he had been to see the parson to get the latest and fullest news. David came slowly on with his eyes upon the ground, as if buried in profound thought.

"Well, father, what news?" Ralph questioned, when his father came within speaking distance.

David started as though wakened out of a reverie, and came to a full stop. Then a pathetic smile stole over his gentle face, and he came forward with a quickened step.

"I waited for the parson to get a reply from the War Office, or I should have been home sooner," he said, bringing out the words slowly and painfully.

"Well?" Ralph questioned, though he felt sure, from his father's manner, what the answer would be.

"The parson fears the worst," David answered, bringing out the words in jerks. "Poor man! He's in great trouble. I almost forgot my own when I thought of his."

"But what was the news he got from the War Office?" Ralph questioned.

"Not much. He's on the list of the dangerously wounded, that's all."

"But he may recover," Ralph said, after a pause.

"Yes, he may," David answered, with a sigh. "God alone knows, but the parson gave me no comfort at all."

"How so?"

"He says that the swords and spears of the dervishes are often poisoned; then, you see, water is scarce, and the heat is terrible, so that a sick man has no chance like he has here."

Ralph did not reply. For a moment or two he looked at his father, then went on with his hoeing. David walked by his side between the rows of turnips. His face was drawn and pale, and his lips twitched incessantly.

"The world seems terribly topsy-turvy," he said at length, as if speaking to himself. "I oughtn't to be idling here, but all the heart's gone out of me somehow."

"We must hope for the best," Ralph said, without raising his head.

"The parson's boy is the last 'life,'" David went on, as though he had not heard what Ralph had said. "The last life. Just a thread, a feeble little thread. One little touch, and then——"

"Well, and what then?" Ralph questioned.

"If the boy dies, this little farm is no longer ours. Though I have reclaimed it from the waste, and spent on it all my savings, and toiled from dawn to dark for twelve long years, and built the house and the barn and the cowsheds, and gone into debt to stock it; if that boy dies it all goes."

"You mean that the squire will take possession?"

"I mean that Sir John will claim it as his."

Ralph did not speak again for several moments, but he felt his blood tingling to his finger-tips.

"It's a wicked, burning shame," he jerked out at length.

"It is the law, my boy," David said sadly, "and you see there's no going against the law."

Ralph hung his head, and began hoeing vigorously his row.

"Besides," David went on, "you see I was party to the arrangement—that is, I accepted the conditions; but the luck has been on Sir John's side."

"He took a mean advantage of you, father, and you know it, and he knows it," Ralph snapped.

"He knew that I had set my heart on a bit of land that I could call my own;

that I wanted a sort of resting-place in my old age, and that I desired to end my days in the parish in which I was born."

"And so he put the screw on. It's always been a wonder to me, since I could think about it at all, that you accepted the conditions. I would have seen Sir John at the bottom of the sea first."

"I did try to get better terms," David answered, looking wistfully across the fields, "and I mentioned ninety-nine years as the term of the lease, and he nearly turned me out of his office. 'Three lives or nothing,' he snarled, 'and be quick about it.' So I had to make up my mind there and then."

"You'd have been better off, father, if you'd dropped all your money down a mine shaft, and gone to work on a farm as a day labourer," Ralph said bitterly.

"I shouldn't have had to work so hard," David assented.

"And you would have got more money, and wouldn't have had a hundredth part of the anxiety."

"You see, I thought the land was richer than it has turned out to be, and the furze roots have kept sprouting year after year, and that has meant ploughing the fields afresh. And the amount of manure I have had to put in has handicapped me terribly. But I have kept hoping to get into smooth waters by and by. The farm is looking better now than ever it did before."

"But the ground rent, father, is an outrage. Did you really understand how much you were paying?"

"He wouldn't consent to any less," David said wistfully. "You see things were good with farmers at the time, and rents were going up. And then I thought I should be allowed to work the quarry down in the delf, and make some money out of the stone."

"And you were done in that as in other things?"

"Well, yes. There's no denying it. When I got to understand the deed—and it took me a goodish time to riddle it out—I found out that I had no right to the stone or the mineral, or the fish in the stream, or to the trees, or to the game. Do you know he actually charged me for the stone dug out of my own farm to build the house with?"

"And ever since has been working the quarry at a big profit, which would never have been unearthed but for you, and destroying one of your fields in the process?"

"I felt that about the quarry almost more than anything," David went on. "But he's never discovered the tin lode, and I shall never tell him."

"Is there a tin lode on the farm?" Ralph questioned eagerly.

"Ay, a beauty! It must be seven years ago since I discovered it, and I've kept it to myself. You see, it would ruin the farm to work it, and I should not get a penny of the dues; they'd all go to the squire."

"Everything gets back to the rich in the long-run," Ralph said bitterly. "There's no chance for the poor man anywhere."

"Oh, well, in a few years' time it won't matter to any of us," David said, looking with dreamy eyes across the valley to the distant range of hills. "In the grave we shall all be equal, and we shall never hear again the voice of the oppressor."

"That does not seem to me anything to the point," Ralph said, flashing out the words angrily. "We've got as good a right to live as anybody else. I don't ask favours from anybody, but I do want justice and fair play."

"It's difficult to know what justice is in this world," David said moodily. "But there, I've been idling long enough. It's time I went back and fetched my hoe and did a bit of work." And he turned slowly on his heel and walked away toward the house.

Ralph straightened his back and looked after him, and as he did so the moisture came into his eyes.

"Poor old father!" he said to himself, with a sigh. "He's feeling this much more deeply than anyone knows. I do hope for all our sakes that Julian Seccombe will recover."

For the rest of the day Ralph's thoughts hovered between the possible loss of their farm and the chances of Dorothy Hamblyn's recovery. He hardly knew why he should worry himself about the squire's daughter so much. Was it solely on the ground that he had refused to open the gate, or was it because she was so pretty?

He felt almost vexed with himself when this thought suggested itself to his mind. What did it matter to him whether she was fair or plain? She was Sir John Hamblyn's daughter, and that ought to be sufficient for him. If there was any man on earth he hated and despised it was John Hamblyn; hence to concern himself about the fate of his daughter because she was good to look upon seemed the most ridiculous folly.

It must surely be the other consideration that worried him. If he had opened the gate the accident would not have happened; but neither would it if she had ridden home the other way. She was paying the penalty of her own wilfulness and her own imperiousness. He was not called on to be the hack of anybody.

But from whatever cause his anxiety might spring, it was there, deep-rooted and persistent.

He was glad when night came, so that he might forget himself, forget the world, and forget everybody in it in the sweet oblivion of sleep.

He hoped that the new day would bring better news, but in that he was disappointed. The earlier part of the day brought no news at all, and neither he nor his father went to seek it. But as the afternoon began to wane, a horse-dealer from St. Goram left word that the parson's son was dead, and that the squire's daughter was not likely to get better.

CHAPTER VI

WAITING FOR THE BLOW TO FALL

David Penlogan was not the man to cry out when he was hurt. He went about his work in dumb resignation. The calamity was too great to be talked about, too overwhelming to be shaped into words. He could only shut his teeth and endure. To discuss the matter, even with his wife, would be like probing a wound with a red-hot needle. Better let it be. There are times when words are like a blister on a burn.

What the future had in store for him he did not know, and he had not the courage to inquire. One text of Scripture he repeated to himself morning, noon, and night, "Sufficient unto the day is the evil thereof," and to that he held. It was his one anchor. The rope was frayed, and the anchor out of sight —whether hooked to a rock or simply embedded in the sand he did not know —but it steadied him while the storm was at its worst. It helped him to endure.

Harvest was beginning, and the crop had to be gathered in—gathered in from fields that were no longer his, and that possibly he would never plant again. It was all very pathetic. He seemed sometimes like a man preparing for his own funeral.

"When next year comes——" he would say to himself, and then he would stop short. He had not courage enough yet to think of next year; his business was with the present. His first, and, as far as he could see, his only duty was to gather in the crops. Sir John had not spoken to him yet. He was too concerned about his daughter to think of so small a matter as the falling-in of a lease. Strange that what was a mere trifle to one man should be a matter of life and death to another.

It was a sad and silent harvest-tide for the occupants of Hillside Farm. The impending calamity, instead of drawing them more closely together, seemed to separate them. Each was afraid of betraying emotion before the rest. So they avoided each other. Even at meal-times they all pretended to be so busy that there was no time to talk. The weather was magnificent, and all the cornfields were growing ripe together. This was true of nearly every other farm in the parish. Hence hired labour could not be had for love or money. The big farmers had picked up all the casual harvesters beforehand. The small farmers would have to employ their womenfolk and children.

Ralph and his father got up each morning at sunrise, and, armed with reaping-hooks, went their ways in different directions. Ralph undertook to cut down the barley-field, David negotiated a large field of oats. They could not talk while they were in different fields. Moreover, neither was in the mood for company. Later on they might be able to talk calmly and without emotion, but at present it would be foolish to make the attempt.

Every day they expected that Sir John Hamblyn or his steward would put in an appearance; that would bring things to a head, and put an end to the little conspiracy of silence that had now lasted nearly a week. But day after day passed away, and the solemn gloom of the farm remained unbroken.

Ralph kept doggedly to his work. Work was the best antidote against painful thoughts. Since the morning he walked across to Hamblyn Manor, in order to ease his conscience by making a clean breast of it, he had never ventured beyond his own homestead. He tried to persuade himself it was no concern of his what happened, and that if Dorothy Hamblyn died it would be a just judgment on Sir John for his grasping and oppressive ways.

But his heart always revolted against such reasoning. Deep down in his soul he knew that, for the moment, he was more concerned about the fate of Dorothy than anything else, and that it would be an infinite relief to him to hear that she was out of danger. Try as he would, he could not shake off the feeling that he was more or less responsible for the accident.

But day by day the news found its way across to the farm that "the squire's little maid," as the villagers called her, was no better. Sometimes, indeed, the news was that she was a good deal worse, and that the doctors held out very little hope of her recovery.

Ralph remained as silent on this as on the other subject. He had never told anyone but Sir John that he had refused to open the gate. It had seemed to him, while he sat on the stile and faced the squire's daughter, a brave and courageous part to take, but he was ashamed of it now. It would have been a far more heroic thing to have pocketed the affront and overcome arrogance by generosity.

But vision often comes too late. We see the better part when we are no longer able to take it.

Sunday brought the family together, and broke the crust of silence that had prevailed so long.

It was David's usual custom on a Sunday morning to walk across the fields to his class-meeting, held in the little Methodist Chapel at Veryan. But this particular Sunday morning he had not the courage to go. If he could not open his heart before the members of his own family, how could he before others?

Besides, his experience would benefit no one. He had no tale to tell of faith triumphing over despondency, and hope banishing despair. He had come nearer being an infidel than ever before in his life. It is not every man who can see that Providence may be as clearly manifested in calamity as in prosperity.

So instead of going to his meeting, David went out for a quiet walk in the fields. He could talk to himself, if he had not the courage to talk to others. Besides, Nature was nearly always restful, if not inspiring.

Ralph came down to breakfast an hour later than was his custom. He was so weary with the work of the week that he was half disposed to lie in bed till the following morning. He found his breakfast set for him in what was called the "living-room," but neither Ruth nor his mother was visible. He ate his food without tasting it. His mind was too full of other things to trouble himself about the quality of his victuals. When he had finished he rose slowly from his chair, took a cloth cap from a peg, and went through the open door into the garden. Plucking a sprig of lad's-love, he stuck it into the buttonhole of his jacket, then climbed over the hedge into an adjoining field.

He came face to face with his father ten minutes later, and stared at him in surprise.

"Why, I thought you had gone to your meeting!" he said, in a tone of wonderment.

"I don't feel in any mood for meetings," David answered gloomily. "I reckon I'm best by myself."

"I fancy we've all been thinking the same thing these last few days," Ralph answered, with a smile. "I'm not sure, however, that we're right. We've got to talk about things sooner or later."

"Yes; I suppose that is so," David answered wearily. "But, to tell you the truth, I haven't got my bearings yet."

"I reckon our first business is to try to keep afloat," Ralph answered. "If we can do that, we may find our bearings later on."

"You will find no difficulty, Ralph, for you are young, and have all the world before you. Besides, I've given you an education. I knew it was all I could give you."

"I'm afraid it won't be of much use to me in a place like this," Ralph answered, with a despondent look in his eyes.

"There's no knowing, my boy. Knowledge, they say, is power. If you are thrown overboard you will swim; but with mother and me it is different.

We're too old to start again, and all our savings are swallowed up."

"Not all, surely, father! There are the crops and cattle and implements."

David shook his head.

"Over against the crops," he said, "are the seed bills, and the manure bills, and the ground rent, and over against the cattle is the mortgage. I never thought of telling you, Ralph, for I never reckoned on this trouble coming. But when I started I thought the money I had would be quite enough not only to build the house and outbuildings, and bring the farm under cultivation, but to stock it as well. But it was a much more expensive business than I knew."

"And so you had to mortgage the farm?"

"No, my lad. Nobody would lend money on a three-life lease."

"And yet you risked your all on it?"

"Ah, my boy, I did it for the best. God knows I did! I wanted to provide a nest for our old age."

"No one will blame you on that score," Ralph answered, with tears in his eyes; "but the best ships founder sometimes."

"Yes. I have kept saying to myself ever since the news came that I am not the only man who has come to grief, and yet I don't know, my boy, that that helps me very much."

Ralph was silent for several minutes; then he said—

"Is this mortgage or note of hand or bill of sale—or whatever it is—for a large amount?"

"Well, rather, Ralph. I'm afraid, if we have to shift from here, there'll be little or nothing left."

"But if you are willing to remain as tenant, Sir John will make no attempt to move you?"

"I'm not so sure, my son. Sir John is a hard man and a bitter, and he has no liking for me. At the last election I was not on his side, as you may remember, and he never forgets such things."

Ralph turned away and bit his lip. The memory of what the squire said to him a few days previously swept over him like a cold flood.

"I'm inclined to think, father," he said at length, "that we'd better prepare for the worst. It'll be better than building on any consideration we may receive from the squire."

"I think you are right, my boy." And they turned and walked toward the house side by side.

They continued their talk in the house, and over the dinner-table. Now that the ice was broken the stream of conversation flowed freely. Ruth and Mrs. Penlogan let out the pent-up feelings of their hearts, and their tears fell in abundance.

It did the women good to cry. It eased the pain that was becoming intolerable. Ralph talked bravely and heroically. All was not lost. They had each other, and they had health and strength, and neither of them was afraid of hard work.

By tea-time they had talked each other into quite a hopeful frame of mind. Mrs. Penlogan was inclined to the belief that Sir John would recognise the equity of the case, and would let them remain as tenants at a very reasonable rent.

"Don't let us build on that, mother," Ralph said. "If he foregoes the tiniest mite of his pound of flesh, so much the better; but to reckon on it might mean disappointment. We'd better face the worst, and if we do it bravely we shall win."

In this spirit they went off to the evening service at the little chapel at Veryan. The building was plain—four walls with a lid, somebody described it—the service homely in the extreme, the singing decidedly amateurish, but there were warmth and emotion and conviction, and everybody was pleased to see the Penlogans in their places.

At the close of the service a little crowd gathered round them, and manifested their sympathy in a dozen unspoken ways. Of course, everybody knew what had happened, and everybody wondered what the squire would do in such a case. The law was on his side, no doubt, but there ought to be some place for equity also. David Penlogan had scarcely begun yet to reap any of the fruit of his labour, and it would be a most unfair thing, law or no law, that the ground landlord should come in and take everything.

"Oh, he can't do it," said an old farmer, when discussing the matter with his neighbour. "He may be a hard man, but he'd never be able to hold up his head again if he was to do sich a thing."

"It's my opinion he'll stand on the law of the thing," was the reply. "A bargain's a bargain, as you know very well, an' what's the use of a bargain ef you don't stick to 'un?"

"Ay, but law's one thing and right's another, and a man's bound to have some regard for fair play."

39

"He ought to have, no doubt; but the squire's 'ard up, as everybody knows, and is puttin' on the screw on every tenant he's got. My opinion is he'll stand on the law."

No one said anything to David, however, about what had happened, except in the most indirect way. Sunday evening was not the time to discuss secular matters. Nevertheless, David felt the unspoken sympathy of his neighbours, and returned home comforted.

The next week passed as the previous one had done, and the week after that. The squire had not come across, nor sent his steward. David began to fear that the long silence was ominous. Mrs. Penlogan held to the belief that Sir John meant to deal generously by them. Ralph kept his thoughts to himself, but on the whole he was not hopeful.

The weather continued beautifully fine, and all hands were kept busy in the fields. Except on Sundays they scarcely ever caught a glimpse of their neighbours. No one had any time to pay visits or receive them. The harvest must be got in, if possible, before the weather broke, and to that end everyone who could help—little and big, young and old—was pressed into the service.

On the big farms there was a good deal of fun and hilarity. The village folk—lads and lasses alike—who knew anything about harvest work, and were willing to earn an extra sixpence, were made heartily welcome. Consequently there was not a little horse-play, and no small amount of flirtation, especially after night came on, and the harvest moon began to climb up into the heavens.

Then, when the field was safely sheafed and shocked, they repaired to the farm kitchen, where supper was laid, and where ancient jokes were trotted out amid roars of laughter, and where the hero of the evening was the man who had a new story to tell. Supper ended, they made their way home through the quiet lanes or across the fields. That, to some of the young people, seemed the best part of the day. They forgot the weariness engendered by a dozen hours in the open air while they listened to a story old as the human race, and yet as new to-day as when syllabled by the first happy lover.

But on the small farms, where no outside help was employed, there was very little mirth or hilarity. All the romance of harvest was found where the crowd was gathered. Young people sometimes gave their services of an evening, so that they could take part in the fun.

As David Penlogan and his family toiled in the fields in the light of the harvest moon they sometimes heard sounds of merry-making and laughter floating across the valley from distant farmsteads, and they wondered a little bit sadly where the next harvest-time would find them.

On the third Saturday night they stood still to listen to a familiar sound in that part of the country.

"Listen, Ralph," Ruth said, "they're cutting neck at Treligga."

Cutting neck means cutting the last shock of the year's corn, and is celebrated by a big shout in the field, and a special supper in the farmer's kitchen.

Ralph raised himself from his stooping posture, and his father did the same. Ruth took her mother's hand in hers, and all four stood and listened. Clear and distinct across the moonlit fields the words rang—

"What have 'ee? What have 'ee?"

"A neck! A neck!"

"Hoorah! Hoorah! Hoorah!"

Slowly the echoes died over the hills, and then silence reigned again.

Ralph and David had also cut neck, but they raised no shout over it. They were in no mood for jubilation.

Sir John Hamblyn had not spoken yet, nor had his steward been across to see them. Why those many days of grace, neither David nor Ralph could surmise.

It was reported that the squire's daughter was slowly recovering from her accident, but that many months would elapse before she was quite well and able to ride again.

"We shall not have to wait much longer, depend upon it," David said, on Monday morning, as he and Ralph went out in the fields together; and so it proved. About ten o'clock a horseman was seen riding up the lane toward the house. David was the first to catch sight of him.

"It's the squire himself," he said.

CHAPTER VII

DAVID SPEAKS HIS MIND

Sir John alighted from his horse and threw the reins over the garden gate, then he walked across the stockyard, and looked at the barn and the cowsheds, taking particular notice of the state of repair they were in. After awhile he returned to the dwelling-house and walked round it deliberately, looking carefully all the time at the roof and windows, but he did not attempt to go inside.

David and Ralph watched him from the field, but neither attempted to go near him.

"He'll come to us when he has anything to say," David said, with a little catch in his voice.

Ralph noticed that his father trembled a good deal, and that he was pale even to the lips.

The squire came hurrying across the fields at length, slapping his leg as he walked with his riding-crop. His face was hard and set, like a man who had braced himself to do an unpleasant task, and was determined to carry it through. Ralph watched his face narrowly as he drew near, but he got no hope or inspiration from it. The squire did not notice him, but addressed himself at once to David.

"Good-morning, Penlogan!" he said. "I see you have got down all your corn."

"Yes, sir, we cut neck on Saturday night."

"And not a bad crop either, by the look of it."

"No, sir, it's pretty middling. The farm is just beginning to show some fruit for all the labour and money that have been spent on it."

"Exactly so. Labour and manure always tell in the end. You know, of course, that the lease has fallen in?"

"I do, sir. It's hard on the parson at St. Goram, and it's harder lines on me."

"Yes, it's rough on you both, I admit. But we can't be against these things. When the Almighty does a thing, no man can say nay."

"I'm not so sure that the Almighty does a lot of those things that people say He does."

42

"You're not?"

"No, sir. I don't see that the parson's son had any call to go out to Egypt to shoot Arabs, particularly when he knew that my farm hung on his life."

"He went at the call of duty," said the squire unctuously; "went to defend his Queen and country."

"Don't believe it," said David doggedly. "Neither the Queen nor the country was in any danger. He went because he had a roving disposition and no stomach for useful ways."

"Well, anyhow, he's dead," said the squire, "and naturally we are all sorry—sorry for his father particularly."

"I suppose you are not sorry for me?" David questioned.

"Well, yes; in some respects I am. The luck has gone against you, there's no denying, and one does not like to see a fellow down on his luck."

"Then in that case I presume you do not intend to take advantage of my bad luck?"

The squire raised his eyebrows, and his lip curled slightly.

"I don't quite understand what you mean," he said.

"Well, it's this way," David said mildly. "According to law this little farm is now yours."

"Exactly."

"But according to right it is not yours—it is mine."

"Oh, indeed?"

"You need not say, 'Oh, indeed.' You can see it as clearly as I do. I've made the farm. I reclaimed it from the waste. I've fenced it and manured it, and built houses upon it. And what twelve years ago was a furzy down is now a smiling homestead, and you have not spent a penny piece on it, and yet you say it is yours."

"Of course it is mine."

"Well, I say it isn't yours. It's mine by every claim of equity and justice."

"I'm not talking about the claims of equity and justice," the squire said, colouring violently. "I take my stand on the law of the country; that's good enough for me. And what's good enough for me ought to be good enough for you," he added, with a snort.

"That don't by any means follow," David answered quietly. "The laws of the land were made by the rich in the interests of the rich. That they're good for you there is no denying; but for me they're cruel and oppressive."

"I don't see it," the squire said, with an impatient shrug of his shoulders. "You live in a free country, and have all the advantages of our great institutions."

"I suppose you call the leasehold system one of our great institutions?" David questioned.

"Well, and what then?"

"I don't see much advantage in living under it," was the reply.

"You might have something a great deal worse," the squire said angrily. "The high-and-mighty airs some of you people take on are simply outrageous."

"We don't ask for any favours," David said meekly. "But we've a right to live as well as other people."

"Nobody denies your right, that I know of."

"But what am I to do now that my little farm is gone? All the savings of a lifetime, and all the toil of the last dozen years, fall into your pocket."

"I grant that the luck has been against you in this matter. But we have no right to complain of the ways of Providence. The luck might just as easily have gone against me as against you."

"I don't believe in mixing luck and Providence up in that way," David answered, with averted eyes. "But, as far as I can see, what you call luck couldn't possibly have gone against you."

"Why not?"

"Because you laid down the conditions, and however the thing turned out you would stand to win."

"I don't see it."

"You don't?" And David gave a loud sniff. "Why, if all the 'lives' had lived till they were eighty, I and mine would not have got our own back."

"Stuff and nonsense!" the squire said angrily. "Besides, you agreed to the conditions."

"I know it," David answered sadly. "You would grant me no better, and I was hopeful and ignorant, and looked at things through rose-coloured glasses."

"I'm sure the farm has turned out very well," the squire replied, with a hurried glance round him.

"It's just beginning to yield some little return," David said, looking off to the distant fields. "For years it's done little more than pay the ground rent. But this year it seems to have turned the corner. It ought to be a good little farm in the future." And David sighed.

"Yes, it ought to be a good farm, and what is more, it is a good farm," the squire said fiercely. "Upon my soul, I believe I've let it too cheap!"

"You've done what, sir?" David questioned, lifting his head suddenly.

"I said I believed I had let it too cheap. It's worth more than I am going to get for it."

"Do you mean to say you have let it?" David said, in a tone of incredulity.

"Of course I have let it. I could have let it five times over, for there's no denying it's an exceedingly pretty and compact little farm."

At this point Ralph came forward with white face and trembling lips.

"Did I hear you tell father that you had let this farm?" he questioned, bringing the words out slowly and with an effort.

"My business is with your father only," the squire said stiffly, and with a curl of the lip.

"What concerns my father concerns me," Ralph answered quietly, "for my labour has gone into the farm as well as his."

"That's nothing to the point," the squire answered stiffly. And he turned again to David, who stood with blanched face and downcast eyes.

"I want to make it as easy and pleasant for you as possible," the squire went on. "So I have arranged that you can stay here till Michaelmas without paying any rent at all."

David looked up with an expression of wonder in his eyes, but he did not reply.

"Between now and Michaelmas you will be able to look round you," the squire continued, "and, in case you don't intend to take a farm anywhere else, you will be able to get your corn threshed and such things as you don't want to take with you turned into money. William Jenkins, I understand, is willing to take the root crops at a valuation, also the straw, which, by the terms of your lease, cannot be taken off the farm."

"So William Jenkins is to come here, is he?" David questioned suddenly.

"I have let the farm to him," the squire replied pompously, "and, as I have before intimated, he will take possession at Michaelmas."

"It is an accursed and a cruel shame!" Ralph blurted out vehemently.

The squire started and looked at him.

"And why could you not have let the farm to me?" David questioned mildly, "or, at any rate, given me the refusal of it? You said just now that you were sorry for me. Is this the way you show your sorrow? Is this doing to others as you would be done by?"

"I have surely the right to let my own farm to whomsoever I please," the squire said, in a tone of offended dignity.

"This farm was not yours to start with," Ralph said, flinging himself in front of the squire. "Before you enclosed it, it was common land, and belonged to the people. You had no more right to it than the man in the moon. But because you were strong, and the poor people had no power to oppose you, you stole it from them."

"What is that, young man?" Sir John said, stepping back and striking a defiant attitude.

"I said you stole Polskiddy Downs from the people. It had been common land from time immemorial, and you know it." And Ralph stared him straight in the eyes without flinching. "You took away the rights of the people, shut them out from their own, let the land that did not belong to you, and pocketed the profits."

"Young man, I'll make you suffer for this insult," Sir John stammered, white with passion.

"And God will make you suffer for this insult and wrong to us," Ralph replied, with flashing eyes. "Do you think that robbing the poor, and cheating honest people out of their rights, will go unpunished?"

Sir John raised his riding-crop suddenly, and struck at Ralph with all his might. Ralph caught the crop in his hand, and wrenched it from his grasp, then deliberately broke it across his knee and flung the pieces from him.

**"SIR JOHN RAISED HIS HUNTING-CROP, AND STRUCK AT RALPH WITH
ALL HIS MIGHT."**

For several moments the squire seemed too astonished either to speak or
move. In all his life before he had never been so insulted. He glowered at
Ralph, and looked him up and down, but he did not go near him. He was no
match for this young giant in physical strength.

David seemed almost as much astonished as the squire. He looked at his son,
but he did not open his lips.

The squire recovered his voice after a few moments.

"If I had been disposed to deal generously with you——" he began.

"You never were so disposed," Ralph interposed bitingly. "You did your worst before you came. We understand now why you kept away so long. I wonder you are not ashamed to show your face here now."

"Cannot you put a muzzle on this wild beast?" the squire said, turning to David.

"He has not spoken to you very respectfully," David replied slowly, "but there's no denying the truth of much that he has said."

"Indeed! Then let me tell you I am glad you will have to clear out of the parish."

"You would have been glad if I could have been cleared out of the parish before the last election," David said insinuatingly.

"I have never interfered with your politics since you came."

"You had no right to; but you've intimidated a great many others, as everybody in the division knows."

Sir John grew violently red again, and turned on his heel. He had meant to be conciliatory when he came, and to prove to David, if possible, that he had dealt by him very considerately, and even generously. But the tables had been turned on him unexpectedly, and he had been insulted to his face.

"This is the result of the Board schools," he reflected to himself angrily. "I always said that education would be the ruin of the working classes. They learn enough to make them impertinent and discontented, and then they are flung adrift to insult their betters and undermine our most sacred institutions. That young fellow will be a curse to society if he's allowed to go on. If I could have my way, I'd lock him up for a year. He's evidently infected his father with his notions, and he'll go on infecting other people." And he faced round again, with an angry look in his eyes.

"I'm sorry I took the trouble to come and speak to you at all," he said. "I did it in good part, and with the best intentions. I wanted to show you that my action is strictly within the law, and that in letting you remain till Michaelmas I was doing a generous thing. But clearly my good feeling and good intentions are thrown away."

"Good feelings are best shown in kind deeds," David said quietly. "If you had come to me and said, 'David, you are unfortunate, but as your loss is my gain, I won't insist on the pound of flesh the law allows me, but I'll let you have the farm for another eight or ten years on the ground rent alone, so that you can recoup yourself a little for all your expenditure'—if you had said that, sir, I should have believed in your good feelings. But since you have let the little place over my head, and turned me out of the house I built and paid for out of

48

my own earnings, I think, sir, the less said about your good feelings the better."

"As you will," the squire replied stiffly, and in a hurt tone. "As you refuse to meet me in a friendly spirit, you must not be surprised if I insist upon my own to the full. My agent will see you about putting the place in proper repair. I notice that one of the sheds is slated only about half-way up, the remainder being covered with corrugated iron. You will see to it that the entire roof is properly slated. The stable door is also worn out, and will have to be replaced by a new one. I noticed, also, as I rode along, that several of the gates are sadly out of repair. These, by the terms of the lease, you will be required to make good. If I mistake not, also the windows and doors of the dwelling-house are in need of a coat of paint. I did not go inside, but my agent will go over the place and make an inventory of the things requiring to be done."

"He may make out twenty inventories if he likes," David said angrily, "but I shan't do a stitch more to the place than I've done already."

"Oh, well, that is not a point we need discuss," the squire said, with a cynical smile. "The man who attempts to defy the law soon discovers which is the stronger." And with a wave of the hand, he turned on his heel and strode away.

David stood still and stared after him, and after a few moments Ralph stole up to his side.

"Well, Ralph, my boy," David said at length, with a little shake in his voice, "he's done his worst."

"It's only what I expected," Ralph answered. "Now, we've got to do our best."

David shook his head.

"There's no more best in this world for me," he said.

"Don't say that, father. Wherever we go we shan't work harder than we've done on the farm."

"Ah, but here I've worked for myself. I've been my own master, with no one to hector me. And I've loved the place and I've loved the work. And I've put so much of my life into it that it seems like part of myself. Boy, it will break my heart!" And the tears welled suddenly up into his eyes and rolled down his cheeks.

Ralph did not reply. He felt that he had no word of comfort to offer. None of them as yet felt the full weight of the blow. They would only realise how much they had lost when they had to wander forth to a strange place, and see strangers occupying the home they loved.

CHAPTER VIII

CONFLICTING EMOTIONS

Two days later Sir John's agent came across to Hillside Farm, and made a careful inspection of the premises, after which he made out a list of repairs that needed doing, and handed it to David.

"What is this?" David asked, taking the paper without looking at it.

"It is a list of repairs that you will have to execute before leaving the place."

"Oh, indeed!" And David deliberately tore the paper in half, then threw the pieces on the ground and stamped upon them.

"That's foolish," the agent said, "for you'll have to do the repairs whether you like it or no."

"I never will," David answered vehemently. And he turned on his heel and walked away.

In the end, the agent got the repairs done himself, and distrained upon David's goods for the amount.

By Michaelmas Day David was ready to take his departure. Since his interview with the squire he had never been seen to smile. He made no complaint to anyone, neither did he sit in idleness and mope. There was a good deal to be done before the final scene, and he did his full share of it. The corn was threshed and sold. The cattle were disposed of at Summercourt Fair. The root crops and hay were taken at a valuation by the incoming tenant. The farm implements were disposed of at a public auction, and when all the accounts had been squared, and the mortgage cleared off, and the ground rent paid, David found himself in possession of his household furniture and thirty pounds in hard cash.

David's neighbours sympathised with him greatly, but none of them gave any more for what they bought than they could help. They admitted that things went dirt cheap, that the cattle and implements were sold for a great deal less than their real value; but that was inevitable in a forced sale. When the seller was compelled to sell, and there was no reserve, and the buyers were not compelled to buy, and there was very little competition, the seller was bound to get the worst of it.

David looked sadly at the little heap of sovereigns—all that was left out of the savings of a lifetime. He had spent a thousand pounds on the farm, and, in addition, had put in twelve years of the hardest work of his life, and this was all that was left. What he thought no one knew, not even his wife, for he kept his thoughts and his feelings to himself.

The day before their departure, David took Ralph for a walk to the extreme end of the farm.

"I have something to tell you, my boy, and something to show you."

Ralph wondered what there was to see that he had not already seen, but he asked no questions.

"You may remember, Ralph," David said, when they had got some distance from the house, "that I told you once that I had discovered a tin lode running across the farm?"

"Yes, I remember well," Ralph answered, looking up with an interested light in his eyes.

"I want to show it to you, my boy."

"Why, what's the use?" Ralph questioned, after a momentary pause. "If it were a reef of gold it would be of no value to us."

"Yes, that seems true enough now," David answered sadly, "but there's no knowing what may happen in the future."

"I don't see how we can ever benefit by it, whatever may happen."

"I am not thinking of myself, Ralph. My day's work is nearly over. But new conditions may arise, new discoveries may be made, and if you know, you may be able to sell your knowledge for something."

Ralph shook his head dubiously, and for several minutes they tramped along side by side in silence.

Then David spoke again.

"It is farewell to-day, my boy. We shall toil in these fields no more."

"That fact by itself does not trouble me," Ralph said.

"You do not like farming," his father answered. "You never did; and sometimes I have felt sorry to keep you here, and yet I could not spare you. You have done the work of two, and you have done it for your bare keep."

"I have done it for the squire," Ralph answered, with a cynical laugh.

"Ah, well, it is over now, my boy, and we know the worst. In a few years nothing will matter, for we shall all be asleep."

Ralph glanced suddenly at his father, but quickly withdrew his eyes. There was a look upon his face that hurt him—a look as of some hunted creature that was appealing piteously for life.

For weeks past Ralph had wished that his father would get angry. If he would only storm and rave at fortune generally, and at the squire in particular, he believed that it would do him good. Such calm and quiet resignation did not seem natural or healthy. Ralph sometimes wondered if what his father predicted had come true—that the loss had broken his heart.

They reached the outer edge of the farm at length, and David paused in the shadow of a tree.

"Come here, my boy," he said. And Ralph went and stood by his side. "You see the parlour chimney?" David questioned.

"Yes."

"Well, now draw a straight line from this tree to the parlour chimney, and what do you strike?"

"Well, nothing except a gatepost over there in Stone Close."

"That's just it. It was while I was digging a pit to sink that post in that I struck the back of the lode."

"And you say it's rich in tin?"

"Very. It intersects the big Helvin lode at that point, and the junction makes for wealth. There'll be a fortune made out of this little farm some day—not out of what grows on the surface, but out of what is dug up from underground."

"And in which direction does the lode run?"

"Due east and west. We are standing on it now, and it passes under the house."

"Then it passes under Peter Ladock's farm also?" Ralph questioned. And he turned and looked over the boundary hedge across their neighbour's farm.

"Ay; but the lode's no use out there," David said.

"Why?"

"Well, you see, 'tisn't mineral-bearing strata, that's all. I dug a pit just where you are standing, and came upon the lode two feet below the surface. But there's no tin in it here scarcely. It's the same lode that the spring comes out of down in the delf, and I've sampled it there. But all along that high ridge where it cuts through the Helvin it's richer than anything I know in this part of the county."

"But the tin might give out as you sink."

"It might, but it would be something unheard of, if it did. If I know anything about mining—and I think I know a bit—that lode will be twenty per cent. richer a hundred fathoms down than it is at the surface."

"Oh, well!" Ralph said, with a sigh, "rich or poor, it can make no difference to us."

"Perhaps not—perhaps not," David said wistfully. "But it may be valuable to somebody some day. I have passed the secret to you. Some day you may pass it on to another. The future is with God," and he drew a long breath, and turned his face toward home, which in a few hours would be his home no more.

Ralph turned his face in another direction.

"I think I will go on to St. Goram," he said, "and see how they are getting on with the cottage. You see we have to move into it to-morrow."

"As you will," David answered, and he strode away across the stubble.

Ralph struck across the fields into Dingley Bottom, and then up the gentle slant toward Treliskey Plantation. When he reached the stile he rested for several minutes, and recalled the meeting and conversation between Dorothy Hamblyn and himself. How long ago it seemed, and how much had happened since then.

Though he loathed the very name of Hamblyn, he was, nevertheless, thankful that the squire's daughter was getting slowly better. She had been seen once or twice in St. Goram in a bath-chair, drawn by a donkey. "Looking very pale and so much older," the villagers said.

By all the rules of logic and common sense, Ralph felt that he ought not only to hate the squire, but everybody belonging to him. Sir John was the tyrant of the parish, the oppressor of the poor, the obstructor of everything that was for the good of the people, and no doubt his daughter had inherited his temper and disposition; while as for the son, people said that he gave promise of being worse than his father.

But for some reason Ralph was never able to work up any angry feeling against Dorothy. He hardly knew why. She had given evidence of being as imperious and dictatorial as any autocrat could desire. She had spoken to him as if he were her stable boy.

And yet——

He recalled how he had rested her fair head upon his lap, how he had carried her in his arms and felt her heart beating feebly against his, how he had given her to drink down in the hollow, and when he lifted her up again she clasped her arms feebly about his neck, and he felt her cheek almost close to his.

It is true he did not know then that she was the squire's daughter, and so he let his sympathies go out to her unawares. But the curious thing was he had not been able to recall his sympathy, though he had discovered directly after that she was the daughter of the man he hated above all others.

As he made his way across the broad and billowy common towards the high road, he found himself wondering what Lord Probus was like. By all the laws and considerations of self-interest, he ought to have been wondering how he and his father were to earn their living—for, as yet, that was a problem that neither of them had solved. But for a moment it was a relief to forget the sorrowful side of life, and think of something else. And, as he had carried Dorothy Hamblyn in his arms every step of the way down the high road, it was the most natural thing in the world that his thoughts should turn in her direction, and from her to the man she had promised to marry.

For some reason or other he felt a little thrill of satisfaction that the wedding had not taken place, and that there was no prospect of its taking place for several months to come.

Not that it could possibly make any difference to him; only he did not see why the rich and strong should always have their heart's desire, while others, who had as much right to live as they had, were cheated all along the line.

Who Lord Probus was Ralph had not the slightest idea. He was a comparatively new importation. He had bought Rostrevor Castle from the Penwarricks, who had fallen upon evil times, and had restored it at great expense. But beyond that Ralph knew nothing.

That he was a young man Ralph took for granted. An elderly bachelor would not want to marry, and a young girl like Dorothy Hamblyn would never dream of marrying an elderly man.

To Ralph Penlogan it seemed almost a sin that a mere child, as Dorothy seemed to be, should think of marriage at all. But since she was going to get married, it was perfectly natural to assume that she was going to marry a young man.

He reached the high road at length, and then hurried forward with long strides in the direction of St. Goram.

The cottage they had taken was at the extreme end of the village, and, curiously enough, was in the neighbouring parish of St. Ivel.

CHAPTER IX

PREPARING TO GO

Almost close to St. Goram were the lodge gates of Hamblyn Manor. The manor itself was at the end of a long and winding avenue, and behind a wide belt of trees. As Ralph reached the lodge gates he walked a little more slowly, then paused for a moment and looked at the lodge with its quaint gables, its thatched roof and overhanging eaves. Beyond the gates the broad avenue looked very majestic and magnificently rich in colour. The yellow leaves were only just beginning to fall, while the evergreens looked all the greener by contrast with the reds and browns.

He turned away at length, and came suddenly face to face with "the squire's little maid." She was seated in her rubber-tyred bath-chair, which was drawn by a white donkey. By the side of the donkey walked a boy in buttons. Ralph almost gasped. So great a change in so short a time he had never witnessed before. Only eight or nine weeks had passed since the accident, and yet they seemed to have added years to her life. She was only a girl when he carried her from Treliskey Plantation down to the high road. Now she was a woman with deep, pathetic eyes, and cheeks hollowed with pain.

Ralph felt the colour mount to his face in a moment, and his heart stabbed him with a sudden poignancy of regret. He wished again, as he had wished many times during the last two months, that he had pocketed his pride and opened the gate. It might be quite true that she had no right to speak to him as she did, quite true also that it was the most natural and human thing in the world to resent being spoken to as though he were a serf. Nevertheless, the heroic thing—the divine thing—would have been to return good for evil, and meet arrogance with generosity.

He would have passed on without presuming to recognise her, but she would not let him.

"Stop, James," she called to the boy; and then she smiled on Ralph ever so sweetly, and held out her hand.

For a moment a hot wave of humiliation swept over him from head to foot. He seemed to realise for the first time in his life what was meant by heaping coals of fire on one's head. He had the whole contents of a burning fiery furnace thrown over him. He was being scorched through every fibre of his being.

At first he almost resented the humiliation. Then another feeling took possession of him, a feeling of admiration, almost of reverence. Here was nobleness such as he himself had failed to reach. Here was one high in the social scale, and higher still in grace and goodness, condescending to him, who had indirectly been the cause of all her suffering. Then in a moment his mood changed again to resentment. This was the daughter of the man who had broken his father's heart. But a moment ago he had looked into his father's hopeless, suffering eyes, and felt as though it would be the sweetest drop of his life if he could make John Hamblyn and all his tribe suffer as he had made them suffer.

But even as he reached out his hard brown hand to take the pale and wasted one that was extended to him, the pendulum swung back once more; the better and nobler feeling came back. The large sad eyes that looked up into his had in them no flash of pride or arrogance. The smile that played over her wan, pale face seemed as richly benevolent as the sunshine of God. Possibly she knew nothing of the calamity that had overtaken him and his, a calamity that her father might have so wonderfully lightened, and at scarcely any cost to himself, had he been so disposed. But it was not his place to blame the child for what her father had done or left undone.

The soft, thin fingers were enveloped in his big strong palm, and then his eyes filled. A lump came up into his throat and prevented him from speaking. Never in all his life before had he seemed so little master of himself.

Then a low, sweet voice broke the silence, and all his self-possession came back to him.

"I am so glad I have met you."

"Yes?" he questioned.

"I wanted to thank you for saving my life."

He dropped his eyes slowly, and a hot wave swept over him from head to foot.

"Dr. Barrow says if you had not found me when you did I should have died." And she looked at him as if expecting an answer. But he did not reply or even raise his head.

"And you carried me such a long distance, too," she went on, after a pause; "and I heard Dr. Barrow tell the nurse that you bound up my head splendidly."

"You were not much to carry," he said, raising his head suddenly. "But—but you are less now." And his voice sank almost to a whisper.

"I have grown very thin," she said, with a wan smile. "But the doctor says I shall get all right again with time and patience."

"I hoped you would have got well much sooner," he said, looking timidly into her face. "I have suffered a good deal during your illness."

"You?" she questioned, raising her eyebrows. "Why?"

"Because if I had not been surly and boorish, the accident would not have happened. If you had died, I should never have forgiven myself."

"No, no; it was not your fault at all," she said quickly. "I have thought a good deal about it while I have been ill, and I have learnt some things that I might never have learnt any other way, and I see now that—that——" And she dropped her eyes to hide the moisture that had suddenly gathered. "I see now that it was very wrong of me to speak to you as I did."

"You were reared to command," he said, ready in a moment to champion her cause, "and I ought to have considered that. Besides, it isn't a man's place to be rude to a girl—I beg your pardon, miss, I mean to a——"

"No, no," she interrupted, with a laugh; "don't alter the word, please. If I feel almost an old woman now, I was only a girl then. How much we may live in a few weeks! Don't you think so?"

"You have found that out, have you?" he questioned. And a troubled look came into his eyes.

"You see, lying in bed, day after day and week after week, gives one time to think——"

"Yes?" he questioned, after a brief pause.

She did not reply for several seconds; then she went on as if there had been no break. "I don't think I ever thought seriously about anything before I was ill. I took everything as it came, and as most things were good, I just enjoyed myself, and there seemed nothing else in the world but just to enjoy one's self ——"

"There's not much enjoyment for most people," he said, seeing she hesitated.

"I don't think enjoyment ought to be the end of life," she replied seriously. Then, suddenly raising her eyes, she said—

"Do you ever get perplexed about the future?"

"I never get anything else," he stammered. "I'm all at sea this very moment."

"You? Tell me about it," she said eagerly.

He shrugged his shoulders, and looked along the road toward the village. Should he tell her? Should he open her eyes to the doings of her own father?

Should he point out some of the oppressive conditions under which the poor lived?

For a moment or two there was silence. He felt that her eyes were fixed intently on his face, that she was waiting for him to speak.

"I suppose your father has never told you that we have lost our little farm?" he questioned abruptly, turning his head and looking hard at her at the same time.

"No. How have you lost it? I do not understand."

"Well, it was this way." And he went on to explain the nature of the tenure on which his father leased his farm, but he was careful to avoid any mention of her father's name.

"And you say that in twelve years all the three 'lives' have died?"

"That is unfortunately the case."

"And you have no longer any right to the house you built, nor to the fields you reclaimed from the downs?"

"That is so."

"And the lord of the manor has taken possession?"

"He has let it to another man, who takes possession the day after to-morrow."

"And the lord of the manor puts the rent into his own pocket?"

"Yes."

"And your father has to go out into the world and start afresh?"

"We leave Hillside to-morrow. I'm going to St. Goram now, to see if the little cottage is ready. After to-morrow father starts life afresh, in his old age, having lost everything."

"But wasn't your father very foolish to risk his all on such a chance? Life is always such an uncertain thing."

"I think he was very foolish; and he thinks so now. But at the time he was very hopeful. He thought the cost of bringing the land under cultivation would be much less than it has proved to be. He hoped, too, that the crops would be much heavier. Then, you see, he was born in the parish, and he wanted to end his days in it—in a little home of his own."

"It seems very hard," she said, with a distant look in her eyes.

"It's terribly hard," he answered; "and made all the harder by the landlord letting the farm over father's head."

"He could have let you remain?"

"Of course he could, if he had been disposed to be generous, or even just."

"I've often heard that Lord St. Goram is a very hard man."

He started, and looked at her with a questioning light in his eyes.

"He needn't have claimed all his pound of flesh," she went on. "Law isn't everything. Nobody would have expected that all three 'lives' would have died in a dozen years."

"I believe the law of average works out to about forty-seven years," he said.

"In which case your father ought to have his farm another thirty-five years."

"He ought. In fact, no lease ought to be less than ninety-nine years. However, the chances of life have gone against father, and so we must submit."

"I don't understand any man exacting all his rights in such a case," she said sympathetically. "If only people would do to others as they would be done unto, how much happier the world would be!"

"Ah, if that were the case," he said, with a smile, "soldiers and policemen and lawyers would find all their occupations gone."

"But, all the same, what's religion worth if we don't try to put it into practice? The lord of the manor has, no doubt, the law on his side. He can legally claim his pound of flesh, but there's no justice in it."

"It seems to me the strong do not often know what justice means," he said, with an icy tone in his voice.

"No; don't say that," she replied, looking at him reproachfully. "I think most people are really kind and good, and would like to help people if they only knew how."

"I'm afraid most people think only of themselves," he answered.

"No, no; I'm sure——" Then she paused suddenly, while a look of distress or of annoyance swept over her face. "Why, here comes Lord Probus," she said, in a lower tone of voice, while the hot blood flamed up into her pale cheeks in a moment.

Ralph turned quickly round and looked towards the park gates.

"Is that Lord Probus?" he asked.

"Yes."

"Good——" But he did not finish the sentence. She looked up into his face, and saw that it was dark with anger or disgust. Then she glanced again at the approaching figure of her affianced husband, then back again to the tall, handsome youth who stood by her side, and for a moment she involuntarily contrasted the two men. The lord and the commoner; the rich brewer and the poor, ejected tenant.

"Please pardon me for detaining you so long," he said hurriedly.

"You have not detained me at all," she replied. "It has been a pleasure to talk to you, for the days are very long and very dull."

"I hope you will soon be as well as ever," he answered; and he turned quickly on his heel and strode away.

"And I hope your father will soon——" But the end of the sentence did not reach his ears. For the moment he was not concerned about himself. The tragedy of his own life seemed of small account. It was the tragedy of her life that troubled him. It seemed a wicked thing that this fragile girl—not yet out of her teens—should marry a man old enough almost to be her grandfather.

What lay behind it, he wondered? What influences had been brought to bear upon her to win her consent? Was she going of her own free will into this alliance, or had she been tricked or coerced?

He recalled again the picture of her when she sat on her horse in the glow of the summer sunshine. She was only a girl then—a heedless, thoughtless, happy girl, who did not know what life meant, and who in all probability had never given five minutes' serious thought to its duties and responsibilities. But eight or nine weeks of suffering had wrought a great change in her. She was a woman now, facing life seriously and thoughtfully. Did she regret, he wondered, the promise she had made? Was she still willing to be the wife of this old man?

Ralph felt the blood tingling to his finger-tips. It was no business of his. What did it matter to him what Sir John Hamblyn or any of his tribe did, or neglected to do? If Dorothy Hamblyn chose to marry a Chinaman or a Hindoo, that was no concern of his. He had no interest in her, and never would have.

He pulled himself up again at that point. He had no interest in her, it was true, and yet he was interested—more interested than in any other girl he had ever seen. So interested, in fact, that nothing could happen to her without it affecting him.

He reached the cottage at length at the far end of the village. It was but a tiny crib, but it was the best they could get at so short a notice, and they would not have got that if Sir John Hamblyn could have had his way.

Ralph could hardly repress a groan when he stepped over the threshold. It was so painfully small after their roomy house at Hillside. The whitewashers and paperhangers had just finished, and were gathering up their tools, and a couple of charwomen were scouring the floors.

A few minutes later there was a patter on the uncarpeted stairs, and Ruth appeared, with red eyes and dishevelled hair.

"There seems nothing that I can do," he said, without appearing to notice that she had been crying.

"Not to-day," she answered, looking past him; "but there will be plenty for you to do to-morrow."

Half an hour later they walked away together toward Hillside Farm, but neither was in the mood for conversation. Ralph looked up the drive towards Hamblyn Manor as they passed the park gates, but no one was about, and the name of Hamblyn was not mentioned.

During the rest of the day all the Penlogans were kept busy getting things ready for the carts on the morrow. To any bystander it would have been a pathetic sight to see how each one tried to keep his or her trouble from the rest, and even to wear a cheerful countenance.

Neither talked of the past, nor uttered any word of regret, but they planned where this piece of furniture should be placed in the new house, and where that, and speculated as to how the wardrobe should be got up the narrow stairs, and in which room the big chest of drawers should be placed.

David seemed the least interested of the family. He sat for the most part like one dazed, and watched the others in a vague, unseeing way. Ruth and her mother bustled about the house, pretending to do a dozen things, and talked all the while about the fittings and curtains and pictures.

When evening came on, and there was no longer any room for pretence, they sat together in the parlour before a fire of logs, for the air was chilly, and the wind had risen considerably. No one attempted to break the silence, but each one knew what the others were thinking about. The wind rumbled in the chimney and whispered through the chinks of the window, but no one heeded it.

This was to be their last evening together in the old home, which they had learned to love so much, and the pathos of the situation was too deep for words. They were silent, and apparently calm, not because they were resigned, but because they were helpless. They had schooled themselves not to resignation, but to endurance. They could be silent, but they could never approve. The loathing they felt for John Hamblyn grew hour by hour. They could have seen him gibbeted with a sense of infinite satisfaction.

The day faded quickly in the west, and the firelight alone illumined the room. Ralph, from his corner by the chimney-breast, could see the faces of all the others. Ruth looked sweeter and almost prettier than he had ever seen her. The chastening hand of sorrow had softened the look in her dark-brown eyes and touched with melancholy the curves of her rich, full lips. His mother had aged rapidly. She looked ten years older than she did ten weeks ago. Trouble had ploughed its furrows deep, and all the light of hope had gone out of her eyes. But his father was the most pathetic figure of all. Ralph looked across at him every now and then, and wondered if he would ever rouse himself again. He looked so worn, so feeble, so despairing, it would have been a relief to see him get angry.

Ruth had got up at length and lighted the lamp and drew the blind; then, without a word, sat down again. The wind continued to rumble in the chimney and sough in the trees outside; but, save for that, no sound broke the silence. There were no sheep in the pens, no cows in the shippen, no horses in the stable, and no neighbour came in to say good-bye.

The evening wore away until it grew late. Then David rose and got the family Bible and laid it on the table, so that the light of the lamp fell upon its pages.

Drawing up his chair, he sat down and began to read—

"'I will lift up mine eyes unto the hills, from whence cometh my help.'"

His voice did not falter in the least. Quietly, and without emphasis, he read the psalm through to the end; then he knelt on the floor, with his hands on the chair, the others following his example. His prayer was very simple that night. He made no direct allusion to the great trouble that was eating at all their hearts. He gave thanks for the mercies of the day, and asked for strength to meet the future.

"Now, my dears," he said, as he rose from his knees, "we had better get off to bed." And he smiled with great sweetness, and Ruth recalled afterwards how he kissed her several times.

But if he had any premonition of what was coming, he did not betray it by a single word.

CHAPTER X

RALPH SPEAKS HIS MIND

It was toward the dawn when Ralph was roused out of a deep sleep by a violent knocking at his bedroom door.

"Yes," he called, springing up in bed and staring into the semi-darkness.

"Come quickly; your father is very ill!" It was his mother who spoke, and her voice was vibrant and anxious.

He sprang out of bed at once, and hurriedly got into his clothes. In a few moments he was by his father's bedside.

At first he thought that his mother had alarmed herself and him unnecessarily. David lay on his side as if asleep.

"I cannot rouse him," she said in gasps. "I've tried every way, but he doesn't move."

Ralph laid his hand on his father's shoulder and shook him, but there was no response of any kind.

"He must be dead," his mother said.

"No, no. He breathes quite regularly," Ralph answered, and he took the candle and held it where the light fell full on his father's eyelids. For a moment there was a slight tremor, then his eyes slowly opened, and a look of infinite appeal seemed to dart out of them.

"He has had a stroke," Ralph answered, starting back. "He is paralysed. Call Ruth, and I will go for the doctor at once."

Twenty-four hours later David was sufficiently recovered to scrawl on a piece of paper with a black lead pencil the words—

"I shall die at home. Praise the Lord!"

He watched intently the faces of his wife and children as they read the words, and a smile played over his own. It seemed to be a smile of triumph. He was not going to live in the cottage after all. He was going to end his days where he had always hoped to do, and no one could cheat him out of that victory.

Ralph sat down by the bedside and took his father's hand. The affection between the two was very tender. They had been more than father and son, they had been friends and comrades. Ruth and her mother ran out of the room to hide their tears. They did not want to distress the dying man by obtruding their grief.

For several minutes Ralph was unable to speak. David never took his eyes from his face. He seemed waiting for some assurance that his message was understood.

"We understand, father," Ralph said at length. "No one can turn you out now."

David smiled again. Then the tears filled his eyes and rolled down his cheeks.

"You always wanted to end your days here," Ralph went on, "and it looks as if you were going to do it."

David raised the hand that was not paralysed and pointed upward.

"There are no leasehold systems there, at any rate," Ralph said, with a gulp. "The earth is the landlord's, but heaven is God's."

David smiled again, and then closed his eyes. Three hours later a second stroke supervened, and stilled his heart for ever.

Ralph walked slowly out of the room and into the open air. He felt thankful for many reasons that his father was at rest. And yet, in his heart the feeling grew that John Hamblyn had killed him, and there surged up within him an intense and burning passion to make John Hamblyn suffer something of what he himself was suffering. Why should he go scot free? Why should he live unrebuked, and his conscience be left undisturbed?

For a moment or two Ralph stood in the garden and looked up at the clouds that were scudding swiftly across the sky. Then he flung open the gate and struck out across the fields. The wind battered and buffeted him and almost took his breath away, but it did not weaken his resolve for a moment. He would go and tell John Hamblyn what he had done—tell him to his face that he had killed his father; ay, and tell him that as surely as there was justice in the world he would not go unpunished.

Over the brow of the hill he turned, and down into Dingley Bottom, and then up the long slant toward Treliskey Plantation. He scarcely heeded the wind that was blowing half a gale, and appeared to be increasing in violence every minute.

The gate that Dorothy's horse had broken had been mended long since, and the notice board repainted:

"Trespassers will be Prosecuted."

He gritted his teeth unconsciously as the white letters stared him in the face. He had heard his father tell that from time immemorial here had been a public thoroughfare, till Sir John took the law into his own hands, and flung a gate across it and warned the public off with a threat of prosecution.

But what cared he about the threat? John Hamblyn could prosecute him if he liked. He was going to tell him what he thought of him, and he was going the nearest way.

He vaulted lightly over the gate, and hurried along without a pause. In the shadow of the trees he scarcely felt the violence of the wind, but he heard it roaring in the branches above him, like the sound of an incoming tide.

He reached the manor, and pulled violently at the door bell.

"Is your master at home?" he said to the boy in buttons who opened the door.

"Yes——"

"Then tell him I want to see him at once," he went on hurriedly, and he followed the boy into the hall.

A moment later he was standing before Sir John in his library.

The baronet looked at him with a scowl. He disliked him intensely, and had never forgiven him for being the cause—as he believed—of his daughter's accident. Moreover, he had no proper respect for his betters, and withal possessed a biting tongue.

"Well, young man, what brought you here?" he said scornfully.

"I came on foot," was the reply, and Ralph threw as much scorn into his voice as the squire had done.

"Oh, no doubt—no doubt!" the squire said, bridling. "But I have no time to waste in listening to impertinences. What is your business?"

"I came to tell you that my father is dead."

"Dead!" Sir John gasped. "No, surely? I never heard he was ill!"

"He was taken with a stroke early yesterday morning, and he died an hour ago."

"Only an hour ago? Dear me!"

"I came straight away from his deathbed to let you know that you had killed him."

"That I had killed him!" Sir John exclaimed, with a gasp.

"You might have seen it in his face, when you told him that you had let the farm over his head, and that he was to be turned out of the little home he had built with his own hands."

"I gave him fair notice, more than he could legally claim," Sir John said, looking very white and distressed.

"I am not talking about the law," Ralph said hurriedly. "If you had behaved like a Christian, my father would have been alive to-day. But the blow you struck him killed him. He never smiled again till this morning, when he knew he was dying. I am glad he is gone. But as surely as you punished us, God will punish you."

"What, threatening, young man?" Sir John replied, stepping back and clenching his fists.

"No, I am not threatening," Ralph said quietly. "But as surely as you stand there, and I stand here, some day we shall be quits," and he turned on his heel and walked out of the room.

Outside the wind was roaring like an angry lion and snapping tree branches like matchwood. A little distance from the house he met a gardener, who told him there was no road through the plantation. But Ralph only smiled at him and walked on.

He was feeling considerably calmer since his interview with Sir John. It had been a relief to him to fling off what was on his mind. He was conscious that his heart was less bitter and revengeful. He only thought once of Dorothy, and he quickly dismissed her from his mind. He wished that he could dismiss her so effectually that the thought of her would never come back. It was something of a humiliation that constantly, and in the most unexpected ways, her face came up before him, and her sweet, winning eyes looked pleadingly and sometimes reproachfully into his.

But he was master of himself to-day. At any rate he was so far master of himself that no thought of the squire's "little maid" could soften his heart toward the squire. He hurried back home at the same swinging pace as he came. It was a house of mourning to which he journeyed, but his mother and Ruth would need him. He was the only one now upon whom they could lean, and he would have to play the man, and make the burden for them as light as possible.

He scarcely heeded the wind. His thoughts were too full of other things. In the heart of the plantation the branches were still snapping as the trees bent before the fury of the gale. He rather liked the sound. Nature was in an angry mood, and it accorded well with his own temper. It would have been out of place if the wind had slept on the day his father died.

He was hardly able to realise yet that his father was dead. It seemed too big and too overwhelming a fact to be comprehended all at once. It seemed impossible that that gentle presence had gone from him for ever. He wondered why he did not weep. Surely no son ever loved a father more than he did, and yet no tear had dimmed his eyes as yet, no sob had gathered in his throat.

Over his head the branch of a tree flew past that had been ripped by the gale from its moorings.

"Hallo," he said, with a smile. "This is getting serious," and he turned into the middle of the road and hurried on again.

A moment or two later a sudden blow on the head struck him to the earth. For several seconds he lay perfectly still just where he fell. Then a sharp spasm of pain caused him to sit up and stare about him with a bewildered expression in his eyes. What had happened he did not know. He raised his right hand to his head almost mechanically—for the seat of the pain was there—then drew it slowly away and looked at it. It was dyed red and dripping wet.

He struggled to his feet after a few moments, and tried to walk. It was largely an unconscious effort, for he did not know where he was, or where he wanted to go to; and when he fell again and struck the hard ground with his face, he was scarcely aware that he had fallen.

In a few minutes he was on his feet again, but the world was dark by this time. Something had come up before his eyes and shut out everything. A noise was in his ears, but it was not the roaring of the wind in the trees; he reeled and stumbled heavily with his head against a bank of heather. Then the noise grew still, and the pain vanished, and there was a sound in his ears like the ringing of St. Goram bells, which grew fainter till oblivion wrapped him in its folds.

CHAPTER XI

UNCONSCIOUS SPEECH

Ralph had scarcely left the house when Dorothy sought her father in the library. He was walking up and down with his hands in his pockets, and a troubled expression in his eyes. He was much more distressed than he liked to own even to himself. To be told to his face that he had caused the death of one of his tenants would, under some circumstances, have simply made him angry. But in the present case he felt, much more acutely than was pleasant, that there was only too much reason for the contention.

That David Penlogan had loved his little homestead there was no doubt whatever. He had poured into it not only the savings of a lifetime and the ungrudging labour of a dozen years, but he had poured into it the affection of a generous and confiding nature. There was something almost sentimental in David's affection for his little farm, and to have to leave it was a heavier blow than he was able to bear. That his misfortune had killed him seemed not an unreasonable supposition.

"But I am not responsible for that," Sir John said to himself angrily. "I had no hand in killing off the 'lives.' That was a decree of Providence."

But in spite of his reasoning, he could not shake himself free from an uneasy feeling that he was in some way responsible.

Legally, no doubt, he had acted strictly within his rights. He had exacted no more than in point of law was his due, but might there not be a higher law than the laws of men? That was the question that troubled him, and it troubled him for the first time in his life.

He was a very loyal citizen. He had been taught to regard Acts of Parliament as something almost as sacred as the Ark of the Covenant, and the authority of the State as supreme in all matters of human conduct. Now for the first time a doubt crept into his mind, and it made him feel decidedly uncomfortable. Man-made laws might, after all, have little or no moral force behind them. Selfish men might make laws just to protect their own selfish interests.

Legally, man's law backed him up in the position he had taken. But where did God's law come in? He knew his Bible fairly well. He was a regular church-goer, and followed the lessons Sunday by Sunday with great diligence. And he felt, with a poignant sense of alarm, that Jesus Christ would condemn what he had done. There was no glimmer of the golden rule to be discerned in his conduct. He had not acted generously, nor even neighbourly. He had extorted the uttermost farthing, not because he had any moral claim to it, but because laws which men had made gave him the right.

He was so excited that his mind worked much more rapidly than was usual with him. He recalled again Ralph Penlogan's words about God punishing him and their being quits. He disliked that young man. He ought to have kicked him out of the house before he had time to utter his insults. But he had not done so, and somehow his words had stuck. He wished it was the son who had died instead of the father. David Penlogan, in spite of his opinions and politics, was a mild and harmless individual; he would not hurt his greatest enemy if he had the chance. But he was not so sure of the son. He had a bolder and a fiercer nature, and if he had the chance he might take the law into his own hands.

The door opened while these thoughts were passing through his mind, and his daughter stood before him. He stopped suddenly in his walk, and his hard face softened.

"Oh, father, I've heard such a dreadful piece of news," she said, "that I could not help coming to tell you!"

"Dreadful news, Dorothy?" he questioned, in a tone of alarm.

"Well, it seems dreadful to me," she went on. "You heard about the Penlogans being turned out of house and home, of course?"

"I heard that he had to leave his farm," he said shortly.

"Well, the trouble has killed him—broken his heart, people say. He had a stroke yesterday morning, and now he's dead."

"Well, people must die some day," he said, with averted eyes.

"Yes, that is true. But I think if I were in Lord St. Goram's place I should feel very unhappy."

"Why should Lord St. Goram feel unhappy?"

"Well, because he profited by the poor man's misfortune."

"What do you know about it?" he snapped almost angrily.

"Only what Ralph Penlogan told me."

"What, that young rascal who refused to open the gate for you?"

"That was just as much my fault as his, and he has apologised very handsomely since."

"I am surprised, Dorothy, that you condescend to speak to such people," he said severely.

"I don't know why you should, father. He is well educated, and has been brought up, as you know, quite respectably."

"Educated beyond his station. It's a mistake, and will lead to trouble in the long-run. But what did he say to you?"

"I met him as he was walking into St. Goram, and he told me how they had taken a little cottage, and were going to move into it next day—that was yesterday. Then, of course, all the story came out, how the vicar's son was the last 'life' on their little farm, and how, when he died, the farm became the ground landlord's."

"And what did he say about the ground landlord?" he questioned.

"I don't remember his words very well, but he seemed most bitter, because he had let the farm over their heads, without giving them a chance of being tenants."

"Well?"

"I told him I thought it was a very cruel thing to do. Law is not everything. David Penlogan had put all his savings into the farm, had reclaimed the fields from the wilderness, and built the house with his own money, and the lord of the manor had done nothing, and never spent a penny-piece on it, and yet, because the chances of life had gone against David, he comes in and takes possession—demands, like Shylock, his pound of flesh, and actually turns the poor man out of house and home! I told Ralph Penlogan that it was wicked—at least, if I did not tell him, I felt it—and, I am sure, father, you must feel the same."

Sir John laughed a short, hard laugh.

"What is the use of the law, Dorothy," he said, "unless it is kept? It is no use getting sentimental because somebody is hanged."

"But surely, father, our duty to our neighbour is not to get all we can out of him?"

"I'm inclined to think that is the general practice, at any rate," he said, with a laugh.

She looked at him almost reproachfully for a moment, and then her eyes fell. He was quick to see the look of pain that swept over her face, and hastened to reassure her.

"You shouldn't worry yourself, Dorothy, about these matters," he said, in

71

gentler tones. "You really shouldn't. You see, we can't help the world being what it is. Some are rich and some are poor. Some are weak and some are strong. Some have trouble all the way, and some have a good time of it from first to last, and nobody's to blame, as far as I know. If luck's fallen to our lot, we've all the more to be grateful for, don't you see. But the world's too big for us to mend, and it's no use trying. Now, run away, that's a good girl, and be happy as long as you can."

She drew herself up to her full height, and looked him steadily in the eyes. She had grown taller during her illness, and there was now a look upon her face such as he had never noticed before.

"I do wish, father," she said slowly, "that you would give over treating me as though I were a child, and had no mind of my own."

"Tut, tut!" he said sharply. "What's the matter now?"

"I mean what I say," she answered, in the same slow and measured fashion. "I may have been a child up to the time of my illness, but I have learned a lot since then. I feel like one who has awaked out of a sleep. My illness has given me time to think. I have got into a new world."

"Then, my love, get back into the old world again as quickly as possible. It's not a bit of use your worrying your little head about matters you cannot help, and which are past mending. It's your business to enjoy yourself, and do as you are told, and get all the happiness out of life that you can."

"There's no getting back, father," she answered seriously. "And there's no use in pretending that you don't feel, and that you don't see. I shall never be a little girl again, and perhaps I shall never be happy again as I used to be; or, perhaps, I may be happy in a better and larger way—but that is not the point. You must not treat me as a child any longer, for I am a woman now."

"Oh, nonsense!" he said, in a tone of irritation.

"Why nonsense?" she asked quickly. "If I am old enough to be married, I am old enough to be a woman——"

"Oh, I am not speaking of age," he interjected, in the same irritable tone. "Of course you are old enough to be married, but you are not old enough—and I hope you never will be—to worry yourself over other people's affairs. I want my little flower to be screened from all the rough winds of the world, and I am sure that is the desire of Lord Probus."

"There you go again!" she said, with a sad little smile. "I'm only just a hothouse plant, to be kept under glass. But that is what I don't want. I don't want to be treated as though I should crumple up if I were touched—I want to do my part in the world."

"Of course, my child, and your part is to look pretty and keep the frowns away from your forehead, and make other folks happy by being happy yourself."

"But really, father, I'm not a doll," she said, with just a touch of impatience in her voice. "I'm afraid I shall disappoint you, but I cannot help it. I've lived in dreamland all my life. Now I am awake, and nothing can ever be exactly the same again as it has been."

"What do you mean by that, Dorothy?"

"Oh, I mean more than I can put into words," she said, dropping her eyes slowly to the floor. "Everything is broken up, if you understand. The old house is pulled down. The old plans and the old dreams are at an end. What is going to take their place I don't know. Time alone will tell." And she turned slowly round and walked out of the room.

An hour later she got into her bath-chair, and went out for her usual airing.

"I think, Billy," she said to her attendant, "we will drive through the plantation this afternoon. The downs will be too exposed to this wind."

"Yes, miss."

"In the plantation it will be quite sheltered—don't you think so?"

"Most of the way it will," he answered; "but there ain't half as much wind as there was an hour ago."

"An hour ago it was blowing a gale. If it had kept on like that I shouldn't have thought of going out at all."

"Which would have been a pity," Billy answered, with a grin, "for the sun is a-shinin' beautiful."

Two or three times Billy had to stop the donkey, while he dragged large branches out of the way. They were almost on the point of turning back again when Dorothy said—

"Is that the trunk of a tree, Billy, lying across the road?"

"Well, miss, I was just a-wonderin' myself what it were. It don't look like a tree exactly."

"And yet I cannot imagine what else it can be."

"Shall we drive on that far and see, miss?"

"I think we had better, Billy, though I did not intend going quite so far."

A few minutes later Billy uttered an exclamation.

"Why, miss, it looks for all the world like a man!"

"Drive quickly," she said; "I believe somebody's been hurt!"

It did not take them long to reach the spot where Ralph Penlogan was lying. Dorothy recognised him in a moment, and forgetting her weakness, she sprang out of her bath-chair and ran and knelt down by his side.

He presented a rather ghastly appearance. The extreme pallor of his face was accentuated by large splotches of blood. His eyelids were partly open, showing the whites of his eyes. His lips were tightly shut as if in pain.

Dorothy wondered at her own calmness and nerve. She had no disposition to faint or to cry out. She placed her ear close to Ralph's mouth and remained still for several seconds. Then she sprang quickly to her feet.

"Unharness the donkey, Billy," she said, in quick, decided tones, "and ride into St. Goram and fetch Dr. Barrow!"

"Yes, miss." And in a few seconds Billy was galloping away as fast as the donkey could carry him.

Dorothy watched him until he had passed beyond the gate and was out on the common. Then she turned her attention again to Ralph. That he was unconscious was clear, but he was not dead. There were evidences also that he had scrambled a considerable distance after he was struck.

For several moments she stood and looked at him, then she sat down by his side. He gave a groan at length and tried to sit up, and she got closer to him, and made his head comfortable on her lap.

After a while he opened his eyes and looked with a bewildered expression into her face.

"Who are you?" he asked abruptly, and he made another effort to sit up.

"You had better lie still," she said gently. "You have got hurt, and Dr. Barrow will be here directly."

"I haven't got hurt," he said, in decided tones, "and I don't want to lie still. But who are you?"

"Don't you remember me?" she questioned.

"No, I don't," he said, in the same decisive way. "You are not Ruth, and I don't know who you are, nor why you keep me here."

"I am not keeping you," she answered quietly. "You are unable to walk, but I have sent for the doctor, and he will bring help."

For a while he did not speak, but his eyes searched her face with a puzzled and baffled look.

"You are very pretty," he said at length. "But you are not Ruth."

"No; I am Dorothy Hamblyn," she answered.

He knitted his brows and looked at her intently, then he tried to shake his head.

"Hamblyn?" he questioned slowly. "I hate the Hamblyns—I hate the very name! All except the squire's little maid," and he closed his eyes, and was silent for several moments. Then he went on again—

"I wish I could hate the squire's little maid too, but I can't. I've tried hard, but I can't. She's so pretty, and she's to marry an old man, old enough to be her grandfather. Oh, it's a shame, for he'll break her heart. If I were only a rich man I'd steal her."

"Hush, hush!" she said quickly. "Do you know what you are saying?"

He opened his eyes slowly and looked at her again, but there was no clear light of recognition in them. For several minutes he talked incessantly on all sorts of subjects, but in the end he got back to the question that for the moment seemed to dominate all the rest.

"You can't be the squire's little maid," he said, "for she is going to marry an old man. Don't you think it is a sin?"

"Hush, hush!" she said, in a whisper.

"I think it's a sin," he went on. "And if I were rich and strong I wouldn't allow it. I wish she were poor, and lived in a cottage; then I would work and work, and wait and hope, and—and——"

"Yes?" she questioned.

"We would fight the world together," he said, after a long pause.

She did not reply, but a mist came up before her eyes and blotted out the surrounding belt of trees, and the noise of the wind seemed to die suddenly away into silence, and a new world opened up before her—a land where springtime always dwelt, and beauty never grew old.

Ralph lay quite still, with his head upon her lap. He appeared to have relapsed into unconsciousness again.

She brushed her hand across her eyes at length and looked at him, and as she did so her heart fluttered strangely and uncomfortably in her bosom. A curious spell seemed to be upon her. Her nerves thrilled with an altogether new sensation. She grew almost frightened, and yet she had no desire to break the spell; the pleasure infinitely exceeded the pain.

She felt like one who had strayed unconsciously into forbidden ground, and yet the landscape was so beautiful, and the fragrance of the flowers was so sweet, and the air was so soft and cool, and the music of the birds and the streams was so delicious, that she had neither the courage nor the inclination to go away.

She did not try to analyse this new sensation that thrilled her to the finger-tips. She did not know what it meant, or what it portended.

She took her pocket-handkerchief at length and began to wipe the bloodstains from Ralph's face, and while she did so the warm colour mounted to her own cheeks.

There was no denying that he was very handsome, and she had already had proof of his character. She recalled the day when she lay in his strong arms, with her head upon his shoulder, and he carried her all the way down to the cross roads. How strange that she should be performing a similar service for him now! Was some blind, unthinking fate weaving the threads of their separate lives into the same piece?

The colour deepened in her cheeks until they grew almost crimson. The words to which she had just listened from his lips seemed to flash upon her consciousness with a new meaning, and she found herself wondering what would happen if she had been only a peasant's child.

A minute or two later the sound of wheels was heard on the grass-grown road. Ralph turned his head uneasily, and muttered something under his breath.

"Help is near," she whispered. "The doctor is coming."

He looked up into her eyes wonderingly.

"Don't tell the squire's little maid that I love her," he said slowly. "I've tried to hate her, but I cannot."

She gave a little gasp, and tried to speak, but a lump rose in her throat which threatened to choke her.

"But her father," he went on slowly, "he's a—a——" but he did not finish the sentence.

When the doctor reached his side he was quite unconscious again.

CHAPTER XII

DOROTHY SPEAKS HER MIND

Dorothy—to quote her father's words—had taken the bit between her teeth and bolted. The squire had coaxed her, cajoled her, threatened her, got angry with her, but all to no purpose. She stood before him resolute and defiant, vowing that she would sooner die than marry Lord Probus.

Sir John was at his wits' end. He saw his brightest hopes dissolving before his eyes. If Dorothy carried out her threat, and refused to marry the millionaire brewer, what was to become of him? All his hopes of extricating himself from his present pecuniary embarrassments were centred in his lordship. But if Dorothy deliberately broke the engagement, Lord Probus would see him starve before raising a finger to help him.

Fortunately, Lord Probus was in London, and knew nothing of Dorothy's change of front. He had thought her somewhat cool when he went away, but that he attributed to her long illness. Warmth of affection would no doubt return with returning health and strength. Sir John had assured him that she had not changed towards him in the least.

Dorothy's illness had been a great disappointment to both men. All delays were dangerous, and there was always the off-chance that Dorothy might awake from her girlish day-dream and discover that not only her feeling toward Lord Probus, but also her views of matrimony, had undergone an entire change.

Sir John had received warning of the change on that stormy day when Ralph Penlogan had visited him to tell him that his father was dead. But he had put her words out of his mind as quickly as possible. Whatever else they might mean, he could not bring himself to believe that Dorothy would deliberately break a sacred and solemn pledge.

But a few weeks later matters came to a head. It was on Dorothy's return from a visit to the Penlogans' cottage at St. Goram that the truth came out.

Sir John met her crossing the hall with a basket on her arm.

"Where have you been all the afternoon?" he questioned sharply.

"I have been to see poor Mrs. Penlogan," she said, "who is anything but well."

"It seems to me you are very fond of visiting the Penlogans," he said crossly.

"I suppose that lazy son is still hanging on to his mother, doing nothing?"

"I don't think you ought to say he is lazy," she said, flushing slightly. "He has been to St. Ivel Mine to-day to try to get work, though Dr. Barrow says he ought not to think of working for another month."

"Dr. Barrow is an old woman in some things," he retorted.

"I think he is a very clever man," she answered; "and we ought to be grateful for what he did for me."

"Oh, that is quite another matter. But I suppose you found the Penlogans full of abuse still of the ground landlord?"

"No, I did not," she answered. "Lord St. Goram's name was never mentioned."

"Oh!" he said shortly, and turned on his heel and walked away.

"She evidently doesn't know yet that I'm the ground landlord," he reflected. "I wonder what she will say when she does know? I've half a mind to tell her myself and face it out. If I thought it would prevent her going to the Penlogans' cottage, I would tell her, too. Curse them! They've scored off me by not telling the girl." And he closed the library door behind him and dropped into an easy-chair.

He came to the conclusion after a while that he would not tell her. All things considered, it was better that she should remain in ignorance. In a few weeks, or months at the outside, he hoped she would be Lady Probus, and then she would forget all about the Penlogans and their grievance.

He took the poker and thrust it into the fire, and sent a cheerful blaze roaring up the chimney. Then he edged himself back into his easy-chair and stared at the grate.

"It's quite time the wedding-day was fixed," he said to himself at length. "Dorothy is almost as well as ever, and there's no reason whatever why it should be any longer delayed. I hope she isn't beginning to think too seriously about the matter. In a case like this, the less the girl thinks the better."

The short November day was fading rapidly, but the fire filled the room with a warm and ruddy light.

He touched the bell at length, and a moment or two later a servant stood at the open door.

"Tell your young mistress when she comes downstairs that I want to see her."

"Yes, sir." And the servant departed noiselessly from the room.

Sir John edged his chair a few inches nearer the fire. He was feeling very nervous and ill at ease, but he was determined to bring matters to a head. He knew that Lord Probus was getting impatient, and he was just as impatient himself. Moreover, delays were often fatal to the best-laid plans.

Dorothy came slowly into the room, and with a troubled look in her eyes.

"You wanted to see me, father?" she questioned timidly.

"Yes, I wanted to have a little talk with you. Please sit down." And he continued to stare at the fire.

Dorothy seated herself in an easy-chair on the other side of the fireplace and waited. If he was nervous and ill at ease, she was no less so. She had a shrewd suspicion of what was coming, and she dreaded the encounter. Nevertheless, she had fully made up her mind as to the course she intended to take, and she was no longer a child to be wheedled into anything.

Sir John looked up suddenly.

"I have been thinking, Dorothy," he said, "that we ought to get the wedding over before Christmas. You seem almost as well as ever now, and there is no reason as far as I can see why the postponed ceremony should be any longer delayed."

"Are you in such a great hurry to get rid of me?" she questioned, with a pathetic smile.

"My dear, I do not want to get rid of you at all. You know the old tag, 'A daughter's a daughter all the days of her life,' and you will be none the less my child when you are the mistress of Rostrevor Castle."

"I shall never be the mistress of Rostrevor Castle," she replied, with downcast eyes.

"Never be the mistress of—never? What do you mean, Dorothy?" And he turned hastily round in his chair and stared at her.

"I was only a child when I promised," she said timidly, "and I did not know anything. I thought it would be a fine thing to have a title and a house in town, and everything that my foolish heart could desire, and I did not understand what marriage to an old man would mean."

"Lord Probus is anything but an old man," he said hastily. "He is in his prime yet."

"But if he were thirty years younger it would be all the same," she answered quietly. "You see, father, I have discovered that I do not love him."

"And you fancy that you love somebody else?" he said, with a sneer.

"I did not say anything of the kind," she said, raising her eyes suddenly to his. "But I know I don't love Lord Probus, and I know I never shall."

"Oh, this is simple nonsense!" he replied angrily. "You cannot play fast and loose in this way. You have given your solemn promise to Lord Probus, and you cannot go back on it."

"But I *can* go back on it, and I will!"

"You mean that you will defy us both, and defy the law into the bargain?"

"There is no law to compel me to marry a man against my will," she said, with spirit.

"If there is no law to compel you, there's a power that can force you to keep your promise," he said, with suppressed passion.

"What power do you refer to?" she questioned.

"The power of my will," he answered. "Do you think I am going to allow a scandal of this kind to take place?"

"It would be a greater scandal if I married him," she replied.

"Look here, Dorothy," he said. "We had better look at this matter in the light of reason and common sense——"

"That is what I am doing," she interrupted. "I had neither when I gave my promise to Lord Probus. I was just home from school; I knew nothing of the world; I had scarcely a serious thought in my head. My illness has given me time to think and reflect; it has opened my eyes——"

"And taken away your moral sense," he snarled.

"No, father, I don't think so at all," she answered mildly. "Feeling as I do now, it would be wicked to marry Lord Probus."

He rose to his feet and faced her angrily.

"Look here, Dorothy," he said. "I am not the man to be thwarted in a thing of this kind. My reputation is in a sense at stake. You have gone too far to draw back now. We should be made the laughing-stock of the entire county. If you had any personal objection to Lord Probus, you should have discovered it before you promised to marry him. Now that all arrangements are made for the wedding, it is too late to draw back."

"No, father, it is not too late; and I am thankful for my illness, because it has opened my eyes."

"And all this has come about through that detestable young scoundrel who refused to open a gate for you."

In a moment her face flushed crimson, and she turned quickly and walked out of the room.

"By Jove, what does this mean?" Sir John said to himself angrily when the door closed behind her. "What new influences have been at work, I wonder, or what quixotic or romantic notions has she been getting into her head? Can it be possible—but no, no, that is too absurd! And yet things quite as strange have happened. If I find—great Scott, won't we be quits!" And Sir John paced up and down the room like a caged bear.

He did not refer to the subject again that day, nor the next. But he kept his eyes and ears open, and he drew one or two more or less disquieting conclusions.

That a change had come over Dorothy was clear. In fact, she was changed in many ways. She seemed to have passed suddenly from girlhood into womanhood. But what lay at the back of this change? Was her illness to bear the entire responsibility, or had other influences been at work? Was the romantic notion she had got into her mind due to natural development, or had some youthful face caught her fancy and touched her heart?

But during all those long weeks of her illness she had seen no one but the doctor and vicar and Lord Probus, except—and Sir John gave his beard an impatient tug.

By dint of careful inquiry, he got hold of the entire story, not merely of Dorothy's accident, but of the part she had played in Ralph Penlogan's accident.

"Great Scott!" he said to himself, an angry light coming into his eyes. "If, knowingly or unknowingly, that young scoundrel is at the bottom of this business, then he can cry quits with a vengeance."

The more he allowed his mind to dwell on this view of the case, the more clear it became to him. There was no denying that Ralph Penlogan was handsome. Moreover, he was well educated and clever. Dorothy, on the other hand, was in the most romantic period of her life. She had found him in the plantation badly hurt, and her sympathies would go out to him in a moment. Under such circumstances, and in her present mood, social differences would count for nothing. She might lose her heart to him before she was aware. He, of course, being inherently bad—for Sir John would not allow that the lower orders, as he termed them, possessed any sense of honour whatever—would take advantage of her weakness and play upon the romantic side of her nature to the full, with the result that she was quite prepared to fling over Lord Probus, or to pose as a martyr, or to pine for love in a cottage, or do any other idiotic thing that her silly and sentimental heart might dictate.

As the days passed away Sir John had very great difficulty in being civil to his daughter. Also, he kept a strict watch himself on all her movements, and put a stop to her playing my Lady Bountiful among the sick poor of St. Goram.

He hoped in his quieter moments that it was only a passing madness, and that it would disappear as suddenly as it came. If she could be kept away from pernicious and disquieting influences for a week or two she might get back to her normal condition.

Sir John was debating this view of the question one evening with himself when the door was flung suddenly open, and Lord Probus stood before him, looking very perturbed and excited.

The baronet sprang out of his chair in a moment, and greeted his guest effusively. "My dear Probus," he said, "I did not know you were in the county. When did you return?"

"I came down to-day," was the answer. "I came in response to a letter I received from your daughter last night. Where is she? I wish to see her at once."

"A moment, sir," the baronet said appealingly. "What has she been writing to you?"

"I hardly know whether I should discuss the matter with you until I have seen her," was the somewhat chilly answer.

"She has asked to be released from her engagement," Sir John said eagerly. "I can see it in your face. The truth is, the child is a bit unhinged."

"Then she has spoken to you?" his lordship interrupted.

"Well, yes, but I came to the conclusion that it was only a passing mood. She has not picked up her strength as rapidly as I could have desired, but, given time, and I have little doubt she will be just the same as ever. I am sorry she has written to you on the matter."

"I noticed a change in her before I went away. In fact, she was decidedly cool."

"But it will pass, my lord. I am sure it will. We must not hurry her. Don't take her 'No' as final. Let the matter remain in abeyance for a month or two. Now I will ring for her and leave you together. But take my advice and don't let her settle the matter now."

Sir John met Dorothy in the hall, and intimated that Lord Probus was waiting for her in the library. She betrayed no surprise whatever. In fact, she expected he would hurry back on receipt of her letter, and so was quite ready for the interview.

They did not remain long together. Lord Probus saw that, for the present at any rate, her mind was absolutely made up. But he was not prepared, nevertheless, to relinquish his prize.

She looked lovelier in his eyes than she had ever done before. He felt the charm of her budding womanhood. She was no longer a schoolgirl to be wheedled and influenced by the promise of pretty things. Her eyes had a new light in them, her manner an added dignity.

"Be assured," he said to her, in his most chivalrous manner, "that your happiness is more to me than my own. But we will not regard the matter as settled yet. Let things remain in abeyance for a month or two."

"It is better we should understand each other once for all," she said decisively, "for I am quite sure time will only confirm me in my resolution."

"No, no. Don't say that," he pleaded. "Think of all I can give you, of all that I will do for you, of all the love and care I will lavish upon you. You owe it to me not to do this thing rashly. Let us wait, say, till the new year, and then we will talk the matter over again." And he took her hand and kissed it, and then walked slowly out of the room.

CHAPTER XIII

GATHERING CLOUDS

The following afternoon Sir John went for a walk in the plantation alone. He was in a very perturbed and anxious condition of mind. Lord Probus had taken his advice, and refused to accept Dorothy's "No" as final; but that by no means settled the matter. He feared that at best it had only postponed the evil day for a few weeks. What if she continued in the same frame of mind? What if she had conceived any kind of romantic attachment for young Penlogan, into whose arms she had been thrown more than once?

Of course, Dorothy would never dream of any alliance with a Penlogan. She was too well bred for that, and had too much regard for the social order. But all the same, such an attachment would put an end to Lord Probus's hopes. She would be eternally contrasting the two men, and she would elect to remain a spinster until time had cured her of her love-sickness. In the meanwhile he would be upon the rocks financially, or in some position even worse than that.

"It is most annoying," he said to himself, with knitted brows and clenched hands, "most confoundedly annoying, and all because of that young scoundrel Penlogan. If I could only wring his neck or get him clear out of the district it would be some satisfaction."

The next moment the sound of snapping twigs fell distinctly on his ear. He turned suddenly and caught a momentary glimpse of a white face peering over a hedge.

"By Heaven, it's that scoundrel Penlogan!" was the thought that darted suddenly through his mind. The next moment there was a flash, a report, a stinging pain in his left arm and cheek, and then a moment of utter mental confusion.

He recovered himself in a moment or two and took to his heels. He had been shot, he knew, but with what effect he could not tell. His left arm hung limply by his side and felt like a burning coal. His cheek was smarting intolerably, but the extent of the damage he had no means of ascertaining. He might be fatally hurt for all he knew. Any moment he might fall dead in the road, and the young villain who had shot him might go unpunished.

"I must prevent that if possible," he said to himself, as he kept running at the top of his speed. "I must hold out till I get home. Oh, I do hope my strength will not fail me! It's a terrible thing to be done to death in this way."

The perspiration was running in streams down his face. His breath came and went in gasps, but he never slackened his pace for a moment; and still as he ran the conviction grew and deepened in his mind that a deliberate attempt had been made to murder him.

He came within sight of the house at length, and began to shout at the top of his voice—

"Help! help! Murder! Be quick——"

The coachman and the stable boy, who happened to be discussing politics in the yard at the moment, took to their heels and both ran in the same direction. They came upon their master, hatless and exhausted, and were just in time to catch him in their arms before he sank to the ground.

"Oh, I've been murdered!" he gasped. "Think of it, murdered in my own plantation! Carry me home, and then go for the doctor and the police. That young Penlogan shall swing for this."

"But you can't be murdered, master," the coachman said soothingly, "for you're alive and able to talk."

"But I'm nearly done for," he groaned. "I feel my life ebbing away fast. Get me home as quickly as you can. I hope I'll live till the policeman comes."

The two men locked hands, and made a kind of chair for their master, and then marched away towards the house.

Sir John talked incessantly all the distance.

"If I die before I get home," he said, "don't forget what I am telling you. Justice must be done in a case like this. Won't there be a sensation in the county when people learn that I was deliberately murdered in my own plantation!"

"But why should Ralph Penlogan want to murder you?" the coachman queried.

"Why? Don't ask me. He came to the house the day his father died and threatened me. I saw murder in his eyes then. I believe he would have murdered me in my own library if he had had the chance. But make haste, for my strength is ebbing out rapidly."

"I don't think you are going to die yet, sir," the coachman said cheerfully.

"Oh, I don't know! I feel very strange. I keep praying that I may live to get home and give evidence before the proper authorities. It seems very strange that I should come to my end this way."

85

"But you may recover, sir," the stable boy interposed. "There's never no knowing what may happen in this world."

"Please don't talk to me," he said petulantly. "You are wasting time while you talk. I want to compose my mind. It's an awfully solemn thing to be murdered, but he shall swing for it as sure as I'm living at this moment! Don't you think you can hurry a little faster?"

Sir John had considerably recovered by the time they reached the house, and was able to walk upstairs and even to undress with assistance.

While waiting for the doctor, Dorothy came and sat by his side. She was very pale, but quite composed. Hers was one of those natures that seemed to gather strength in proportion to the demands made upon it. She never fainted or lost her wits or became hysterical. She met the need of the moment with a courage that rarely failed her.

"Ah, Dorothy," he said, in impressive tones, "I never thought I should come to this, and at the hands of a dastardly assassin."

"But are you sure it was not an accident, father?" she questioned gently.

"Accident?" he said, and his eyes blazed with anger. "Has it come to this, that you would screen the man who has murdered your father?"

"Let us not use such a word until we are compelled," she replied, in the same gentle tones. "You may not be hurt as much as you fear."

"Whether I am hurt much or little," he said, "the intention was there. If I am not dead, the fault is not his."

"But are you sure it was he who fired at you?"

"As sure as I can be of anything in this world. Besides, who else would do it? He threatened me the day his father died."

"Threatened to murder you?"

"Not in so many words, but he had murder in his eyes."

"But why should he want to do you any harm? You never did any harm to him."

For a moment or two Sir John hesitated. Should he clench his argument by supplying the motive? He would never have a better opportunity for destroying at a single blow any romantic attachment that she may have cherished. Destroy her faith in Ralph Penlogan—the handsome youth with pleasant manners—and her heart might turn again to Lord Probus.

But while he hesitated the door opened, and Dr. Barrow came hurriedly into

86

the room, followed by a nurse.

Dorothy raised a pair of appealing eyes to the doctor's face, and then stole sadly down to the drawing-room to await the verdict.

As yet her faith in Ralph Penlogan remained unshaken. She had seen a good deal of him during the last few weeks, and the more she had seen of him the more she had admired him. His affection for his mother and sister, his solicitude for their comfort and welfare, his anxiety to take from their shoulders every burden, his impatience to get well so that he might step into his dead father's place and be the bread-winner of the family, had touched her heart irresistibly. She felt that a man could not be bad who was so good to his mother and so kind and chivalrous to his sister.

Whether or no she had done wisely in going to the Penlogans' cottage was a question she was not quite able to answer. Ostensibly she had gone to see Mrs. Penlogan, who had not yet recovered from the shock caused by her husband's death, and yet she was conscious of a very real sense of disappointment if Ralph was not visible.

That she should be interested in him was the most natural thing in the world. They had been thrown together in no ordinary way. They had succoured each other in times of very real peril—had each been the other's good angel. Hence it would be folly to pretend the indifference of absolute strangers. Socially, their lives lay wide as the poles asunder, and yet there might be a very true kinship between them. The only drawback to any sort of friendship was the confession she had unwittingly listened to while he lay dazed and unconscious in the plantation.

How much it amounted to she did not know. Probably nothing. It was said that people in delirium spoke the exact opposite of what they meant. Ralph had reiterated that he hated her father. Probably he did nothing of the kind. Why should he hate him? At any rate, since he began to get better he had said nothing, as far as she was aware, that would convey the remotest impression of such a feeling. His words respecting herself probably had no more meaning or value, and she made an honest effort to forget them.

She had questioned him as to what he could remember after the branch of the tree struck him. But he remembered nothing till the following day. For twenty-four hours his mind was a complete blank, and he was quite unsuspicious that he had spoken a single word to anyone. And yet, try as she would, whenever she was in his presence, his words kept recurring to her. There might be a worse tragedy in his life than that which had already occurred.

These thoughts kept chasing each other like lightning through her brain, as she sat waiting for the verdict of the doctor.

He came at length, and she rose at once to meet him.

"Well, doctor?" she questioned. "Let me know the worst."

She saw that there was a perplexed and even troubled look in his eyes, and she feared that her father was more seriously hurt than she had imagined.

"There is no immediate danger," he said, taking her hands and leading her back to her seat. They were great friends, and she trusted him implicitly.

She gave a little sigh of relief and waited for him to speak again.

"The main volume of the charge just missed him," he went on, after a pause. "Had he been an inch or two farther to the left, the chances are he would never have spoken again."

"But you think that he will get better?"

"Well, yes. I see no cause for apprehension. His left shoulder and arm are badly speckled, no doubt, but I don't think any vital part has been touched."

Dorothy sighed again, and for a moment or two there was silence. Then she said, with evident effort—

"But what about—about—young Penlogan?"

"Ah, that I fear is a more serious matter," he answered, with averted eyes. "I sincerely trust that your father is mistaken."

"You are not sure that he is?"

"It seems as if one can be sure of nothing in this world," he answered slowly and evasively, "and yet I could have trusted Ralph Penlogan with my life."

"Does father still persist that it was he?"

"He is quite positive, and almost gets angry if one suggests that he may have been mistaken."

"Well, doctor, and what will all this lead to?" she questioned, making a strong effort to keep her voice steady.

"For the moment I fear it must lead to young Penlogan's arrest. There seems no way of escaping that. Your father's depositions will be taken as soon as Mr. Tregonning arrives. Then, of course, a warrant will be issued, and most likely Penlogan will spend to-night in the police-station—unless——" Then he paused suddenly and looked out of the window.

"Unless what, doctor?"

"Well, unless he has tried to get away somewhere. It will be dark directly, and under cover of darkness he might get a long distance."

"But that would imply that he is guilty?"

"Well—yes. I am assuming, of course, that he deliberately shot at your father."

"Which I am quite sure he did not do."

"I have the same conviction myself, and yet he made no secret of the fact that he hated your father."

"But why should he hate my father?"

"You surely know——" Then he hesitated.

"I know nothing," she answered. "What is the ground of his dislike?"

"Ah, here is Mr. Tregonning's carriage," he said, in a tone of relief. "Now I must run away. Keep your heart up, and don't worry any more than you can help."

For several moments she walked up and down the room with a restless yet undecided step. Then she made suddenly for the door, and three minutes later she might have been seen hurrying along the drive in the swiftly gathering darkness as fast as her feet could carry her.

"I'll see him for myself," she said, with a resolute light in her eyes. "I'll get the truth from his own lips. I'm sure he will not lie to me."

It was quite dark when she reached the village, save for the twinkling lights in cottage windows.

She met a few people, but no one recognised her, enveloped as she was in a heavy cloak. For a moment or two she paused before the door of the Penlogans' cottage. Her heart was beating very fast, and she felt like a bird of evil omen. If Ralph was innocent, then he knew nothing of the trouble that was looming ahead, and she would be the petrel to announce the coming storm.

She gave a timid rat-tat at the door, and after a moment or two it was opened by Ruth.

"Why, Miss Dorothy!" And Ruth started back in surprise.

"Is your brother at home?" Dorothy questioned, with a little gasp.

"Why, yes. Won't you come in?"

"Would you mind asking him to come to the door. I have only a moment or two to spare."

"You had better come into the passage," Ruth said, "and I will go at once and tell him you are here."

Dorothy stepped over the threshold and stood under the small lamp that lighted the tiny hall.

In a few moments Ralph stood before her, his cheeks flushed, and an eager, questioning light in his eyes.

She looked at him eagerly for a moment before she spoke, and could not help thinking how handsome he looked.

"I have come on a strange errand," she said, speaking rapidly, "and I fear there is more trouble in store for you. But tell me first, have you ever lifted a finger against my father?"

"Never, Miss Dorothy! Why do you ask?"

"And you have never planned, or purposed, or attempted to do him harm?"

"Why, no, Miss Dorothy. Why should you think of such a thing?"

"My father was shot this afternoon in Treliskey Plantation. He saw a face for a moment peering over a hedge; the next moment there was a flash and a report, and a part of the charge entered his left arm and shoulder. He is in bed now, and Mr. Tregonning is taking his depositions. He vows that it was your face that he saw peering over the hedge—that it was you who shot him."

Ralph's face grew ashen while she was speaking, and a look almost of terror crept into his eyes. The difficulty and peril of his position revealed themselves in a moment. How could he prove that Sir John Hamblyn was mistaken?

"But you do not believe it, Miss Dorothy?" he questioned.

"You tell me that you are innocent?" she asked, almost in a whisper.

"I am as innocent as you are," he said; and he looked frankly and appealingly into her eyes.

For a moment or two she looked at him in silence, then she said in the same low tone—

"I believe you." And she held out her hand to him, and then turned towards the door.

He had a hundred things to say to her, but somehow the words would not come. He watched her cross the threshold and pass out into the darkness, and he stood still and had not the courage to follow her. It would have been at least a neighbourly thing to see her to the lodge gates, for the night was unillumined by even a star, but his lips refused to move. He stood stock-still, as if riveted to the ground.

How long he remained there staring into the darkness he did not know. Time and place were swallowed up and lost. He was conscious only of the steady approach of an overwhelming calamity. It was gathering from every point of the compass at the same time. It was wrapping him round like a sable pall. It was obliterating one by one every star of hope and promise.

Ruth came to look for him at length, and she uttered a little cry when she saw him, for his face was like the face of the dead.

CHAPTER XIV

THE STORM BURSTS

"Why, Ralph, what is the matter?" And Ruth seized one of his hands and stared eagerly and appealingly into his face.

He shook himself as if he had been asleep, then closed the door quietly and followed her into the living-room.

"Are you not well, Ralph?" Ruth persisted, as she drew up his chair a little nearer the fire. Mrs. Penlogan laid her knitting in her lap, and her eyes echoed Ruth's inquiry.

"I've heard some bad news," he said, speaking with an effort, and he dropped into his chair and stared at the fire.

"Bad news!" both women echoed. "What has happened, Ralph?"

He hesitated for a moment, then he told them the story as Dorothy had told it to him.

"But why should you worry?" Ruth questioned quickly. "You were nowhere near the plantation."

"But how am I to prove it?" he questioned.

"Have you been alone all the afternoon?"

"Absolutely."

"But you have surely seen someone?"

"As bad luck would have it, I have not seen a soul."

"But some people may have seen you."

"That is likely enough. Twenty people in the village looking from behind their curtains may have seen me walk out with a gun under my arm."

"And it's the first time you've carried a gun since we left Hillside."

"The very first time, and it looks as if it will be the last."

"But surely, Ralph, no one would believe for a moment that you could do such a thing?" his mother interposed. "It's been some awkward accident, you may depend. It will all come out right in the morning."

"I'm very sorry for you, mother," he said slowly. "You've had trouble enough lately, God knows. We all have, for that matter. But it is of no use shutting our eyes to the fact that this is a very awkward business, and while we should hope for the best, we should prepare for the worst."

"What worst do you refer to, Ralph?" she asked, a little querulously. "You surely do not think——"

"I hardly know what to think, mother," he interrupted, for it was quite clear she did not realise yet the gravity of the situation. "It may mean imprisonment and the loss of my good name, which would mean the loss of everything and the end of the world for me."

"Oh no; surely not," and the tears began to gather in her eyes.

"The trouble lies here," he went on. "Everybody knows that I hate the squire. We all do, for that matter, and for very good reasons. As it happens, I have been out with a gun this afternoon, and have brought home a couple of rabbits. I shot them in Dingley Bottom, but no one saw me. Somebody trespassing in the plantation came upon the squire. He was climbing over a hedge, and very likely in drawing back suddenly something caught the trigger and the gun went off. Now unless that man confesses, what is to become of me?"

"But he will confess. Nobody would let you be wrongfully accused," she interrupted.

He shook his head dubiously. "Most people are so anxious to save their own skin," he said, "that they do not trouble much about what becomes of other people."

"But if the worst should come to the worst, Ralph," Ruth questioned timidly, "what would it mean?"

"Transportation," he said gloomily.

Mrs. Penlogan began to cry. It seemed almost as if God had forsaken them, and her faith in Providence was in danger of going from her. She and Ruth had been bewailing the hardness of their lot that afternoon while Ralph was out with his gun. The few pounds saved from the general wreck were nearly exhausted. When the funeral expenses had been paid, and the removal accounts had been squared, there was very little left. To make matters worse, Ralph's accident had to be added to their calamities. He was only just beginning to get about again, and when the doctor's bill came in they would be worse than penniless, they would be in debt.

And now suddenly, and without warning, this new trouble threatened them. A trouble that was worse than poverty—worse even than death. Their good name, they imagined, was unassailable, and if that went by the board, everything would be lost.

Ralph sat silent, and stared into the fire. In the main his thoughts were very bitter, but one sweet reflection came and went in the most unaccountable fashion. One pure and almost perfect face peeped at him from between the bars of the grate and vanished, but always came back again after a few minutes and smiled all the more sweetly, as if to atone for its absence.

Why had Dorothy Hamblyn taken the trouble to interview him? Why was she so interested in his fate? How was it that she was so ready to accept his word? To give any rational answer to these questions seemed impossible. If she felt what he felt, the explanation would be simple enough; but since by no exercise of his fancy or imagination could he bring himself to that view of the case, her conduct—her apparent solicitude—remained inexplicable.

Nevertheless, the thought of Dorothy was the one sweet drop in his bitter cup. The why and wherefore of her interest might remain a mystery, yet the fact remained that of her own free will she had come to see him that she might get the truth from his own lips, and without any hesitation she had told him that she believed his word. Sir John might hunt him down with all the venom of a sleuth hound, but he would always have this crumb of consolation, that the Squire's daughter believed in him still.

He had given up trying to hate her. Nay, he accepted it as part of the irony of fate that he should do the other thing. He could not understand why destiny should be so relentlessly cruel to him, why every circumstance and every combination of circumstances should unite to crush him. But he had to accept life as he found it. The world seemed to be ruled by might, not by justice. The strong worked their will upon the weak. It was the fate of the feeble to go under; the helpless cried in vain for deliverance, the poor were daily oppressed.

He found his youthful optimism a steadily diminishing quantity. His father's fate seemed to mock the idea of an over-ruling Providence. If there was ever a good man in the parish, his father was that man. No breath of slander had ever touched his name. Honest, industrious, pure-minded, God-fearing, he lived and wrought with all his might, doing to others as he would they should do to him. And yet he died of a broken heart, defeated and routed in the unequal contest, victimised by the uncertain chances of life, ground to powder by laws he did not make, and had no chance of escaping. And in that hour of overwhelming disaster there was no hand to deliver him save the kindly hand of death.

"And what is there before me?" he asked himself bitterly. "What have I to live for, or hope for? The very springs of my youth seem poisoned. My love is a cruel mockery, my ambitions are frost-nipped in the bud."

For the rest of the evening very little was said. Supper was a sadly frugal meal, and they ate it in silence. Ruth and her mother could not help wondering how long it would be ere they would have no food to eat.

Ralph kept listening with keen apprehension for the sound of a measured footstep outside the door. At any moment he might be arrested. Sir John was one of the most important men in St. Goram, hence the law would be swift to take its course. The policemen would be falling over each other in their eagerness to do their duty.

The tall grandfather's clock in the corner beat out the moments with loud and monotonous click. The fire in the grate sank lower and lower. All the village noises died down into silence. Mrs. Penlogan's chin, in spite of her anxiety, began to droop upon her bosom.

"I think we shall be left undisturbed to-night," Ralph said, with a pathetic smile. "Perhaps we had better get off to bed."

Mrs. Penlogan rose at once and fetched the family Bible and handed it on to Ruth. It fell open at the 23rd Psalm: "The Lord is my Shepherd, I shall not want."

Ruth read it in a low, even voice. It was her father's favourite portion—his sheet-anchor when the storms of life raged most fiercely. Now he was beyond the tempest and beyond the strife.

For the first time Ralph felt thankful that he was dead.

"Dear old father," he said to himself. "He has got beyond the worry and the pain. His heart will ache no more for ever."

They all knelt down when the psalm ended; but no one prayed aloud.

Ralph remained after the others had gone upstairs. It seemed of little use going to bed, he felt too restless to sleep.

Ever since Dorothy went away he had been expecting Policeman Budda to call with a warrant for his arrest. Why he had not come he could not understand. He wondered if Dorothy had interceded with her father, and his eyes softened at the thought.

He did not blame himself for loving her in a restrained and far-off way. She was so fair and sweet and generous. That she was beyond his reach was no fault of his—that he had carried her in his arms and pressed her to his heart was the tragedy as well as the romance of his life. That she had watched by him and succoured him in the plantation was only another cord that bound his heart to her. That he should love her was but the inevitable sequence of events.

It was foolish to blame himself. He would be something less than man if he did not love her. He had tried his hardest not to—had struggled with all his might to put the memory of her out of his heart. But he gave up the struggle weeks ago. It was of no use fighting against fate. It was part of the burden he had been called upon to bear, and he would have to bear it as bravely and as patiently as he knew how.

He was not so vain as to imagine that she cared for him in the smallest degree —or ever could care. Moreover, she was engaged to be married, and would have been married months ago but for her accident.

Ralph got up from his chair and began to walk about the room. Dorothy Hamblyn was not for him, he knew well enough, and yet whenever he thought of her marrying Lord Probus his whole soul revolted. It seemed to him like sacrilege, and sacrilege in its basest form.

It was nearly midnight when he stole silently and stealthily to his little room, and soon after he fell fast asleep.

When he opened his eyes again the light of a new day filled the room, and a harsh and unfamiliar voice was speaking rapidly in the room below. Ralph leaned over the side of his bed for a moment or two and listened.

"It's Budda's voice," he said to himself at length, and he gave a little gasp. If Dorothy had interceded for him, her intercession had failed. The law would now have to take its course.

He dressed himself carefully and with great deliberation. He would not show the white feather if he could help it. Besides, it was just possible he might be able to clear himself. He would not give up hope until he was compelled to.

Budda was very civil and even sympathetic. He sat by the fire while Ralph ate his breakfast, and retailed a good deal of the gossip of the village so as to lessen the strain of the situation. Ralph replied to him with an air of well-feigned indifference and unconcern. He would rather die than betray weakness before a policeman.

Mrs. Penlogan and Ruth moved in and out of the room with set faces and dry eyes. They knew how to endure silently. So many storms had beaten upon them that it did not seem to matter much what came to them now. Also they knew that the real bitterness would come when Ralph's place was empty.

Budda appeared to be in no hurry. It was all in his day's work, and since Ralph showed no disposition to bolt, an hour sooner or later made no difference. He read the terms of the warrant with great deliberation and in his most impressive manner. Ralph made no reply. This was neither the time nor the place to protest his innocence.

Breakfast over, Ralph stretched his feet for a few moments before the fire. Budda talked on; but Ralph said nothing. He sprang to his feet at length and got on his hat and overcoat, while his mother and Ruth were out of the room.

"Now I am ready," he said; and Budda at once led the way.

He met his mother and sister in the passage and kissed them a hurried good-morning, and almost before they knew what had happened the door closed, and Ralph and the policeman had disappeared.

On the following morning he was brought before the magistrates and remanded for a week, bail being refused.

It was fortunate for him that in the solitude of his cell he had no conception of the tremendous sensation his arrest produced. There had been nothing like it in St. Goram for more than a generation, and for a week or two little else was talked about.

Of course, opinions varied as to the measure of his guilt or innocence. But, in the main, the current of opinion went strongly against him. When a man is down, it is surprising how few his friends are. The bulk of the St. Goramites were far more ready to kick him than defend him. Wiseacres and busybodies told all who cared to listen how they had predicted some such catastrophe. David Penlogan was a good man, but he had not trained his children wisely. He had spent more on their education than his circumstances warranted, with the result that they were exclusive and proud, and discontented with the station in life to which Providence had called them.

Ralph would have been infinitely pained had he known how indifferent the mass of the people were to his fate, and how ready some of those whom he had regarded as his friends were to listen to tales against him. Even those who defended him, did it in a very tepid and half-hearted way; and the more strongly the current ran against him, the more feeble became his defence.

At the end of a week Ralph was brought up and remanded again. Sir John Hamblyn was still confined to his bed, and the doctor could not say when he would be well enough to appear and give evidence.

So time after time he was dragged into the dock, only to be hustled after a few minutes back into his cell.

But at length, after weary weeks of waiting, Sir John appeared at the court-house with his arm in a sling. The bench was crowded with magistrates, all of whom were loud in their expressions of sympathy and emphatic in their denunciation of the crime that had been committed.

Sir John being a baronet and a magistrate, and a very considerable landowner, was accommodated with a cushion, and allowed to sit while he gave evidence. The court-room was packed, and the crowd outside was considerably larger than that within.

Ralph was led into the dock looking but a ghost of his former self. The long weeks of confinement—following upon his illness—the scanty prison fare in place of nourishing food, had wasted him almost to a shadow. He stood, however, erect and defiant, and faced the bench of country squires with a fearless light in his eyes. They might have the power to shut him up within stone walls, but they could not break his spirit.

CHAPTER XV

SIR JOHN GETS ANGRY

It was remarked that Sir John never looked at the prisoner all the time he was giving evidence. He was, however, perfectly at home before his brother magistrates, and showed none of that nervousness and restraint which ordinary mortals feel in similar circumstances. The story he told was simple and straightforward. He had not an enemy in the parish, as far as he knew, except the prisoner, who had made no secret of his hatred and of his desire for revenge.

He admitted that fortune had been unkind to the elder Penlogan, but in the chances of life it was inevitable that some should come out at the bottom. As the ground landlord, he had acted with every consideration, and had given David Penlogan plenty of time to realise to the best advantage. Hence he felt quite sure that their worships would acquit him of any intention of being either harsh or unjust.

A general nodding of heads on the part of the magistrates satisfied him on that point.

He then went on to tell the story of the prisoner's visit to Hamblyn Manor, and how he had the effrontery to charge him with killing his father.

"Gentlemen, he had murder in his eyes when he came to see me; but, fortunately, he had no opportunity of doing me harm."

Sir John waved his right hand dramatically when he uttered these words, the effect of which—in the language of the local reporter—was "Sensation in Court."

He then went on to describe the events of the afternoon when the shot was fired.

He was not likely to be mistaken in the prisoner's face. He had no wish to take an oath that it was the prisoner, but he was morally certain that it was he.

Then followed a good deal of collateral evidence that the police had gathered up and spliced together. The prisoner had been seen by a number of people that afternoon with a gun under his arm. He wore a cloth cap, such as Sir John had described. He had been seen crossing Polskiddy Downs, which, as everyone knew, abutted on Treliskey Plantation. He had expressed himself very bitterly on several occasions respecting Sir John, and had talked vaguely about being quits with him some day. Footprints near the hedge behind which the shot was fired tallied with a pair of boots in the prisoner's house; also, the prisoner returned to his own house within an hour of the shot being fired.

The magistrates looked more and more grave as the chain of evidence lengthened out, though most of them had quite made up their minds before the proceedings began.

Ralph, in spite of all advice to the contrary, pleaded "not guilty," and being allowed to speak in his own defence, availed himself of the opportunity.

"Why should I want to kill the squire?" he said, in a tone of scorn. "God will punish him soon enough." (More sensation in court.) "That he has behaved badly to us," Ralph went on, "no unprejudiced person will deny, though you, being landowners yourselves, approve. I don't deny that he acted within his legal rights. So did Shylock. But had he the heart of a savage, to say nothing of a Christian, he could not have acted more oppressively. I told him that he killed my father—and I repeat it to-day!" (Renewed sensation.) "I did go out shooting on that day in question. My gun licence has not expired yet. Mr. Hooker told me I could shoot over Dingley Bottom any time I liked, and I was glad of the opportunity, for our larder was not overstocked, as you may imagine. I crossed Polskiddy Downs, I admit—it is the one bit of common land that you gentry have not filched from us——" (Profound sensation, during which the chairman protested that if prisoner did not keep himself strictly to his defence, the privilege of speaking further would be taken from him.) "As you will, gentlemen," Ralph said indifferently. "I do not expect justice or a fair hearing in a court of this kind."

"Order, order!" shouted the magistrates' clerk. The chairman intimated, after a few moments of silence, that the prisoner might proceed if he would promise not to insult the Bench.

"I have very little more to add," Ralph went on, quite calmly. "Unfortunately, no one saw me in Dingley Bottom, and yet I went straight there from home, and came straight back again. I did not go within half a mile of Treliskey Plantation. Moreover, if I wanted to meet Sir John, I should go to his house, as I have done more than once, and not wander through miles of wood on the off-chance of meeting him. Nor is that all. If I wanted to kill the gentleman, I should have killed him, and not sprinkled a few shots on his coat sleeve. I have two barrels to my gun, and I do not often miss what I aim at. If I had intended to murder him, do you think I should have been such a fool as to first show my face and then let him escape? I went out in broad daylight; I returned in broad daylight. Is it conceivable that if I intended to shoot the gentleman I should have been seen carrying a gun? or that, having done the deed, I should have returned in sight of all the village? It has been suggested that, having been caught trespassing in the plantation, I was seized with a sudden desire for revenge. If that had been the case, do you think I would have half completed the task? As all the parish can testify, I am no indifferent shot. If I was alone in the plantation with him, and wanted to kill him, I could have done it. But, gentlemen, I swear before God I was not in the plantation, nor even near it. I have never lifted a finger against this man, nor would I do it if I had the opportunity. That he has treated me and mine with cruel oppression is common knowledge. But vengeance is God's, and I have no desire, nor ever had any desire, to take the law into my own hands."

Many opinions were expressed afterwards as to the effect produced by Ralph's speech, but the general impression was that he did no good for himself. The Bench was by no means impressed in his favour. They detected a socialistic flavour in some of the things he flung at them. He had not been respectful—indeed, in plain English, he had been insulting. They would not have tolerated him, only he was on his trial, and they were anxious to avoid any suspicion of unfairness. They flattered themselves afterwards that they displayed a spirit of great Christian forbearance, and as they had almost to a man made up their minds beforehand, they had no hesitation in committing him to take his trial at the next Assizes on the charge of shooting at Sir John Hamblyn with intent to do him grievous bodily harm.

The question of bail was not mentioned, and Ralph went back to his cell to meditate once more on the tender mercies of the rich and the justice of the strong.

Sir John returned to his home very well pleased with the result of the morning's proceedings. The decision of the magistrates seemed a compliment to himself. To make it an Assize case indicated a due appreciation of his position and importance.

Also he was pleased because he believed the decision would completely destroy any romantic attachment that Dorothy might cherish for the accused. It had come to his knowledge that at the very time Mr. Tregonning was at his bedside taking his depositions, she was at the cottage of the Penlogans interviewing the accused himself. This knowledge had made Sir John more angry than he had been for a very long time. It was not merely the indiscretion that angered him, it was what the indiscretion implied.

However, he believed that the decision of the magistrates would put an end to all this nonsense, and that in the revulsion of feeling Lord Probus would again have his opportunity.

Dorothy asked him the result of the trial on his return, and when he told her she made no reply whatever. Neither did he enlarge on the matter. He concluded that it would be the wiser policy to let the simple facts of the case make their own impression. Women, he knew, were proverbially stubborn, and not always reasonable, while the more they were opposed, the more doggedly determined they became.

Such fears and suspicions as he had he wisely kept to himself. Dorothy was only a foolish girl, who would grow wiser with time. The teaching of experience and the pressure of circumstances would in the end, he believed, compel her to go the way he wished her to take. In the meanwhile, his cue was to watch and wait, and not too obtrusively show his hand.

Dorothy was as reticent on the matter as her father. That she had become keenly interested in the fate of Ralph Penlogan she did not attempt to hide from herself. That a cruel wrong had been done to him she honestly believed. That her sympathies went out to him in his undeserved sufferings was a fact she had no wish to dispute, and that in some way he had influenced her in her decision not to marry Lord Probus was also, to her own mind, too patent to be contested.

But she saw no danger in any of these simple facts. The idea of being in love with a small working farmer's son did not enter her head. She belonged to a different world socially, and such a proposition would not occur to her. But social position could not prevent her admiring good looks, and physical strength, and manly ways, and a generous disposition, when they were brought under her notice.

On the day following the decision of the magistrates she read a full account of the proceedings in the local newspaper, and for the first time was made aware of the fact that it was not Lord St. Goram who had so unmercifully oppressed the Penlogans, but her own father.

For a few minutes she felt quite stunned.

It had never occurred to her that her father was the lord of the manor. In her mind he was not a lord at all. He was simply a baronet.

How short-sighted she had been! Slowly the full meaning and significance of the fact worked its way into her brain, and her face flushed with shame and indignation. Why had not her father the courage to tell her the truth? Why had he allowed her to wrong Lord St. Goram even in thought? Why was he so relentless in his pursuit of the people he had treated so harshly? Was it true that people never forgave those they had wronged? Then her thoughts turned unconsciously to the Penlogans. How they must hate her father, and yet how sensitive they had been not to hurt her feelings. Even Ralph had allowed her to think that Lord St. Goram was the oppressor.

"He ought not to have deceived me," she said to herself, and yet she liked him all the more for his chivalry.

Her thoughts went back to that first day of their meeting, when she mistook him for a country yokel. Considering the fact that she was a lady, and on horseback, he had undoubtedly been rude to her, and yet he was rude in a manly sort of way. She liked him even then, and liked him all the more because he did not cringe to her.

But since then his every word and act had evinced the very soul of chivalry. In many ways he was much more a gentleman than Lord Probus. Indeed, she was inclined to think that in every way he was more of a gentleman. Lord Probus had wealth—fabulous wealth, it was believed—and a thin veneer of polish. But, stripped of the outer shell, she felt quite certain that the farmer's son was much more the gentleman of the two.

It was inevitable, however, that the subject should sooner or later crop up between the father and daughter, and when it did crop up, Sir John was quite unable to hide the bias of his mind.

"In tracking down a crime," he said, with quite a magisterial air, "the first thing to discover, if possible, is a motive. Given a motive, the rest is often comparatively easy. Now in this case I kept the motive from you, as I had no wish to prejudice the young man in your eyes. But in the preliminary trial, as you will have observed, the motive came out. Why he shot me is clear enough. Why he did not complete the work is due probably to failure of nerve; or possibly he thought I was dead, for I fell to the ground like a log."

"Why, father, you said you took to your heels and ran like the wind, and so got out of his reach."

"That was after I recovered myself, Dorothy. I admit I ran then."

"And you still believe that it was he who fired the shot?"

"Why, of course I do."

"With intent to kill?"

"There is not the least doubt of it."

"You think he had good reason for hating you?"

"From his point of view he may think that I ought to have foregone my rights."

"He thinks you ought not to have pushed them to extremes, as you did. It was a cruel thing to do, father, and you know it."

"The Penlogans have never been desirable people. They have never known their place, or kept it. I wouldn't have leased the downs to them if I had known their opinions. No man did so much to turn the last election as David Penlogan."

"I suppose he had a perfect right to his opinions?"

"And I have the right to exercise any influence or power I possess in any way I please," he retorted angrily. "And if I chose to accept a more suitable tenant for one of my farms, that's my business and no one else's."

"I have no wish to argue the question, father," she answered quietly.

"But I suppose you will own that the fellow is guilty?"

"No, father. I am quite sure that he is no more guilty than I am."

"What folly!" he ejaculated angrily.

"I do not think it is folly at all. I know Ralph Penlogan better than you do, and I know he is incapable of such a thing. At the Assizes you will be made to look incredibly foolish."

"What? what?" he ejaculated.

"Here, all the magistrates belong to your set. They had made up their minds beforehand. No unprejudiced jury in the world would ever convict on such evidence."

"Child," he said angrily, "you don't know what you are talking about."

"And even if he were convicted," she went on, with flashing eyes, "I should know all the same that he is innocent."

He looked at her almost aghast. This was worse than his worst suspicions.

"Then you have made up your mind," he said, with a brave effort to control himself, "to believe that he is innocent, whatever judge or jury may say?"

"I know he is innocent," she answered quietly.

"You are a little simpleton," he said, clenching and unclenching his hands; "a foolish, headstrong girl. I am grieved at you, ashamed of you! I did expect ordinary common sense in my daughter."

"I am sorry you are angry with me," she said demurely. "But think again. Are you not biased and prejudiced? You are not sure it was his face you saw. In all probability the gun going off was pure accident. Have you not been hard enough on the Penlogans already, that you persist in having this on your conscience also?"

"Silence!" he almost screamed, and he advanced a step towards her with clenched hand. "Go to your room," he cried, "and don't show your face again to-day! To-morrow I will talk to you, and not only talk but act."

CHAPTER XVI

THE BIG HOUSE

It was when Mrs. Penlogan began to dispose of her furniture in order to provide food and fuel that the landlord became alarmed about his rent, and so promptly seized what remained in order to make himself secure.

It was three days after Christmas, and the weather was bitterly cold. Mrs. Penlogan and Ruth looked at each other for a moment in silence, and then burst into tears. What was to be done now she did not know. Ralph was still in prison awaiting his trial, and so was powerless to help them. Their money was all spent. Even their furniture was gone, and they had no friends to whom they could turn for help.

Since Ralph's committal their old friends had fought shy of them. Ruth felt the disgrace more keenly than did her mother. The cold looks of people they had befriended in their better days cut her to the heart. Ruth had tried to get the post of sewing mistress at the day school, which had become vacant, but the fact that her brother was in prison awaiting his trial proved an insuperable barrier. It would never do to contaminate the tender hearts of the young by bringing them into contact with one whose brother had been accused of a terrible crime.

She never realised before how sensitive the public conscience was, nor how jealous all the St. Goramites were for the honour of the community. People whom she had always understood were no better than they ought to be, turned up their noses at her in haughty disdain. But that it was so tragic, she could have laughed at the virtuous airs assumed by people whose private life had long been the talk of the district.

It was a terrible blow to Ruth. The Penlogans, though looked upon as somewhat exclusive, had been widely respected. David Penlogan was a man in a thousand. Mistaken, some people thought, foolish in the investment of his money, and much too trusting where human nature was involved, but his sincerity and goodness no one doubted. The young people had been less admired, for they seemed a little above their station. They spoke the language of the gentry, and kept aloof from everything that savoured of vulgarity. "They were too well educated for their position."

Their sudden and painful fall proved an occasion for much moralising. "Pride goeth before a fall," was a passage of Scripture that found great acceptance. If the Penlogans had not been so exclusive in their better days, they would not have found themselves so destitute of friends now.

Two or three days practically without food or fire reduced Ruth and her mother to a state bordering on despair. If they had possessed any pride in the past it was all gone now. Hunger is a great leveller.

The relieving officer, when consulted, had little in the way of comfort to offer, though he gave much sage advice. He had little doubt that the parish would allow Mrs. Penlogan half a crown a week; that was the limit of outdoor relief. Her husband had paid scores of pounds in the shape of poor rate, but that counted for nothing. The justice of the strong manifests itself in many ways. When a man is no longer able to contribute to the maintenance of paupers in general, he becomes a pauper himself. Cease to pay your poor rate, because you are too old to work, and you cease to be a citizen, your vote is taken away, you are classed among the social rubbish of your generation.

"But what is to become of me?" Ruth asked pitifully.

The relieving officer stroked the side of his nose and considered the question for a moment before he answered.

"I'm afraid," he said, "the law makes no provision for such as you. You see you are a able-bodied young woman. You must earn your own living."

"That is what I have been trying my best to do," she answered tearfully. "But because poor Ralph has been wrongfully and wickedly accused, no one will look at me."

"That, of course, we cannot 'elp," the relieving officer answered.

Ruth and her mother lay awake all the night and talked the matter over. It was clearly beyond the bounds of possibility that two people could live and pay rent out of half a crown a week. What then was to be done? There was only one alternative, and Ruth had not the courage to face it. Her mother was in feeble health, her spirit was broken, and to send her alone into the workhouse would be to break her heart.

The maximum of cruelty with the minimum of charity appears to be the principle on which our poor-law system is based. The sensitive and self-respecting loathe the very thought of it, and no man with a heart in him can wonder.

Mrs. Penlogan, however, had reached the limit of mental suffering. There comes a point when the utmost is reached, when the lash can do no more, when the nerves refuse to carry any heavier burden of pain. To the sad and broken-hearted woman it seemed of little moment what became of her. All that she asked was a lonely corner somewhere in which she might hide herself and die.

She knew almost by instinct what was passing through Ruth's mind. She lay silent, but she was not asleep.

"You are thinking about the workhouse, Ruth?" she said at length.

"They'll not have me there, mother, for I am healthy and able-bodied."

"There'll be something left from the furniture when the rent is paid," Mrs. Penlogan said, after a long pause. "You'll have to take it and face the world. When I am in the workhouse you will be much more free."

"Mother!"

"It's got to come, Ruth. I would much rather go down to St. Ivel and throw myself into a shaft, but that would be self-murder, and a murderer cannot enter into the kingdom of heaven. So I will endure as patiently as I can, and as long as God wills. When it is over, it will seem but a dream. I want to see father again when the night ends. Dear David, I am glad he went when he did."

"If he had lived we should not have come to this," Ruth answered tearfully.

"If he had lived a paralytic, Ruth, our lot would have been even worse. So it is better that God took him before he became a burden to himself."

"And yet but for the cruel laws made by the rich and powerful he would still be with us, and we should not have been turned out of the dear old home."

"That is over and past, Ruth," Mrs. Penlogan answered, with a sigh. "Ah me! if this life were all, it would not be worth the living—at least for the poor and oppressed. But we have to endure as best we may. You can tell Mr. Thomas that I will go to the workhouse whenever he likes to fetch me."

"Do you really mean it, mother?"

"Yes, Ruth. I've thought it all over. It's the only thing left. It wouldn't be right to lie here and die of starvation. Maybe when the storm has spent itself there will come a time of peace."

"Yes, in the grave, mother."

"If God so wills," she answered. "But I would like to live to see Ralph's name cleared before the world."

"I have almost given up hope of that," Ruth answered sadly. "How can the poor defend themselves against the rich? Poor Ralph will stand undefended before judge and jury, and we have seen how easy it is to work up a case and make every link fit into its place."

"Perhaps God will stand by him," Mrs. Penlogan answered, but in doubting tones. "Oh, if I only had faith as I once had! But I seem like a reed that has been broken by the storm. I try my hardest to believe, but doubts will come. And yet, who knows, God may be better than our fears."

"God appears to be on the side of the rich and strong," Ruth answered, a little defiantly. "Why should John Hamblyn be allowed to work his will on everybody? Even his daughter is kept a prisoner at home, lest she should show her sympathy to us."

"That is only gossip, Ruth. She may have no desire to come, or she may not have the courage. She knows now the part her father has played."

To this Ruth made no answer, and then silence fell until it was time to get up.

The day passed for the most part as the night had done, in discussing the situation. The last morsel of food in the house had disappeared, and strict watch was kept that they pawned no more of the furniture.

Mrs. Penlogan never once faltered in her purpose.

"It will be better than dying of starvation," she said. "Besides, it will set you free."

"Free?" Ruth gasped. "It will be a strange kind of freedom to find oneself in a hostile world alone."

"You will be able to defend yourself, Ruth, and I do not think anyone will molest you."

"Please don't imagine that I am afraid," Ruth answered defiantly. "But you, mother, in that big, cheerless house, will break your heart," and she burst into tears.

"No, don't fret, child," the mother said soothingly. "My heart cannot be broken any more than it is already. Maybe I shall grow more cheerful when I've had enough to eat."

On the following day Ruth went with her mother in the workhouse van to the big house. It was the most silent journey she ever took, and the saddest. She would rather have followed her mother to the cemetery—at least, so she thought at the time. There was such a big lump in her throat that she could not talk. Her mother seemed only vaguely to comprehend what the journey meant. Her eyes saw nothing on the way, her thoughts were in some far-distant place. She got out of the van quite nimbly when they reached the end of their journey, and stood for a moment on the threshold as if undecided.

"You had better not come in," she said at length. "We will say good-bye here."

"Do you think you can bear it, mother?" Ruth questioned, the tears welling suddenly up into her eyes.

"Oh yes," she answered, with a pathetic smile. "There'll be nothing to worry about, you know, and I shall have plenty to eat."

Ruth threw her arms about her mother's neck and burst into a passion of tears. "Oh, I never thought we should come to this!" she sobbed.

"Ruth threw her arms about her mother's neck and burst into a passion of tears."

"It won't matter, my girl, when we are in heaven," was the quiet and patient answer.

"But we are not in heaven, mother. We are here on this wicked, cruel earth, and it breaks my heart to see you suffer so."

"My child, the suffering is in the past. The storm has done its worst. I feel as though I couldn't worry any more. I am just going to be still and wait."

"I shall come and see you as often as I can," Ruth said, giving her mother a final hug, "and you'll not lose heart, will you?"

"No. I shall think of you and Ralph, and if there's a ray of hope anywhere I shall cherish it."

So they parted. Ruth watched her mother march away through a long corridor in charge of an attendant, watched her till a door swung and hid her from sight. Then, brushing her hand resolutely across her eyes, she turned away to face the world alone.

CHAPTER XVII

DEVELOPMENTS

The Penlogans' cottage had been empty two full days before the people of St. Goram became aware that anything unusual had happened. That Ruth and her mother were reduced to considerable straits was a matter of common knowledge. People could not dispose of a quantity of their furniture without the whole neighbourhood getting to know, and in several quarters—notably at the Wheat Sheaf, and in Dick Lowry's smithy, and in the shop of William Menire, general dealer—the question was discussed as to how long the Penlogans could hold out, and what would become of them in the end.

To offer them charity was what no one had the courage to do, and for a Penlogan to ask it was almost inconceivable. Since the event which had landed Ralph in prison, Mrs. Penlogan and Ruth had withdrawn themselves more than ever from public gaze. They evidently wanted to see no one, and it was equally clear they desired no one to see them. What little shopping they did was done after dark, and when Ruth went to chapel she stole in late, and retired before the congregation could get a look at her.

Hence for two days no one noticed that no smoke appeared above the chimney of the Penlogans' cottage, and that no one had been seen going in or coming out of the house. On the third day, however, William Menire—whose store they had patronised while they had any money to spend—became uneasy in his mind on account of the non-appearance of Ruth.

His thoughts had been turned in her direction because he had been expecting for some time that she would be asking for credit, and he had seriously considered the matter as to what answer he should make. To trust people who had no assets and no income was, on the face of it, a very risky proceeding. On the other hand, Ruth Penlogan had such a sweet and winning face, and was altogether so good to look upon, that he felt he would have considerable difficulty in saying no to her. William was a man who was rapidly reaching the old age of youth, and so far had resisted successfully all the blandishments of the fair sex; but he had to own to himself that if he were thrown much in the company of Ruth Penlogan he would have to tighten up the rivets of his armour, or else weakly and ignominiously surrender.

While the Penlogans lived at Hillside he knew very little of them. They did not deal with him, and he had no opportunity of making their acquaintance. But since they came to the cottage Ruth had often been in his shop to make some small purchase. He sold everything, from flour to hob nails and from calico to mouse traps, and Ruth had found his shop in this respect exceedingly convenient. It saved her from running all over the village to make her few purchases.

William had been impressed from the first by her gentle ways and her refined manner of speech. She spoke with the tone and accent of the quality, and had he not been informed who she was he would have taken her for some visitor at one of the big houses.

For two days William had watched with considerable interest for Ruth's appearance. He felt that it did him good to look into her sweet, serious eyes, and he had come to the conclusion that if she asked for credit he would not be able to say no. He might have to wait for a considerable time for his money, but after all money was not everything—the friendship of a girl like Ruth Penlogan was surely worth something.

As the third morning, however, wore away, and Ruth did not put in an appearance, William—as we have seen—got a little anxious. And when his mother—who kept house for him—was able to take his place behind the counter, he took off his apron, put on his bowler hat, and stole away through the village in the direction of St. Ivel.

The cottage stood quite alone, just over the boundary of St. Goram parish, and was almost hidden by a tall thorn hedge. As William drew near he noticed that the chimneys were smokeless, and this did not help to allay his anxiety. As he walked up to the door he noticed that none of the blinds were drawn, and this in some measure reassured him.

He knocked loudly with his knuckles, and waited. After awhile he knocked again, and drew nearer the door and listened. A third time he knocked, and then he began to get a little concerned. He next tried the handle, and discovered that the door was locked.

"Well, this is curious, to say the least of it," he reflected. "I hope they are not both dead in the house together."

After awhile he seized the door handle and gave the door a good rattle, but no one responded to the assault, and with a puzzled expression in his eyes William heaved a sigh, and began to retrace his steps towards the village.

"I'll go to Budda," he said to himself. "A policeman ought to know what to do for the best. Anyhow, if a policeman breaks into a house, nobody gets into trouble for it." And he quickened his pace till he was almost out of breath.

As good luck would have it, he met Budda half-way up the village, and at once took him into his confidence.

Budda put on an expression of great profundity.

"I think we ought to break into the house," William said hurriedly.

This proposition Budda negatived at once. To do what anyone else advised would show lack of originality on the part of the force. If William had suggested that they ask Dick Lowry the smith to pick the lock, Budda would have gone at once and battered the door down. Initiative and originality are the chief characteristics of the men in blue.

"Let me see," said Budda, looking wise and stroking his chin with great tenderness, "Amos Bice the auctioneer is the landlord, if I'm not greatly mistook."

"Then possibly he knows something?" William said anxiously.

"Possibly he do," Budda answered oracularly. "I will walk on and see him."

"I will walk along with you," William replied. "I confess I'm getting a bit curious. Everybody knows, of course, that they're terribly hard up, though I must say they've paid cash down for everything got at my store."

"Been disposing of their furniture, I hear," Budda said shortly.

"So it is reported," William replied. "That implies sore straits, and they are not the sort of people, by all accounts, to ask for help."

"Would die sooner," Budda replied laconically.

"Then perhaps they're dead," William said, with a little gasp. "It must be terrible hard for people who have known better days."

Amos Bice looked up with a start when Budda and William Menire entered his small office.

"I have come to inquire," Budda began, quite ignoring his companion, "if you know anything about—well, about what has become of the Penlogans?"

"Well, I do—of course," he said, slowly and reflectively; though why he should have added "of course" was not quite clear.

William began to breathe a little more freely. Budda looked disappointed. Budda revelled in mysteries, and when a mystery was cleared up all the interest was taken out of it.

"Then you know where they are?" Budda questioned shortly.

"I know where the mother is—I am not so sure of the daughter. But naturally it is not a matter that I care to talk about, particularly as they did not wish their doings to be the subject of common gossip."

"May I ask why you do not care to talk about them?" Budda questioned severely.

"Well, it's this way. I'm the owner of the cottage, as perhaps you know. The rent is paid quarterly in advance. They paid their first quarter at Michaelmas. The next was due, of course, at Christmas. Well, you see, I found they were getting rid of their furniture rapidly, and in my own interests I had naturally to put a stop to it. Well, this brought things to a head. You see, the boy is in prison awaiting his trial, the mother is ailing, and the girl has found no way yet of earning her living, or hadn't a week ago. So, being brought to a full stop, they had to face the question and submit to the inevitable. I took all the furniture at a valuation—in fact, for a good deal more than it was worth—and after subtracting the rent, handed them over the balance. Mr. Thomas got an order for the old lady to go into the workhouse, and the girl, as I understand, is going to try to get a place in domestic service."

William Menire almost groaned. The idea of this sweet, gentle, ladylike girl being an ordinary domestic drudge seemed almost an outrage.

"And how long ago is all this?" Budda asked severely.

"Oh, just the day before yesterday. No, let me see. It was the day before that."

"And you have said nothing about it?"

"It was no business of mine to gossip over other people's affairs."

"They seem to have been very brave people," William remarked timidly.

"What some people would call proud," the auctioneer replied. "Not that I object. I like to see people showing a little proper pride. Some people would have boasted that they had heaps of money coming to them, and would have gone into debt everywhere. The Penlogans wouldn't buy a thing they couldn't pay for."

"It's what I call a great come down for them," Budda remarked sententiously; and then the two men took their departure, Budda to spread the news of the Penlogans' last descent in the social scale, and William to meditate more or less sadly on the chances of human life.

Before the church clock pointed to the hour of noon all St. Goram was agog with the news, and for the rest of the day little else was talked about. People were very sorry, of course—at any rate, they said they were; they paid lip service to the god of convention. It was a great come down for people who had occupied a good position, but the ways of Providence were very mysterious, and their duty was to be very grateful that no such calamity had overtaken them.

115

CHAPTER XVIII

A CONFESSION

The vicar was in the throes of a new sermon when the news reached him. He had been at work on the sermon all the day, for its delivery was to be a great effort. Hence, it was long after dark before the tidings filtered through to his study.

Mr. Seccombe laid down his pen, and looked thoughtful. The news sent his thoughts running along an entirely new track. The thread of his sermon was cut clean through, and every effort he made to pick up the ends and splice them proved a dismal failure. From the triumphs of grace his thoughts drifted away to the mysteries of Providence.

He pulled himself up with a jerk at length. How much had God to do, after all, with what men called Providence? Was it the purpose of God that his boy Julian should grow into a fighter? Was it part of the same purpose that he should be killed in a distant land by an Arab's lance; that out of that should grow the commercial ruin of one of the saintliest men in the parish; and that his wife, in the closing years of her life, should be driven into the cold shadow of the workhouse?

John Seccombe got up from his chair and began to pace up and down the study.

He was interrupted in his meditations by a feeble knock on his study door.

"Come in," he said, pausing in his walk; and he waited a little impatiently for the door to open.

"A young man wants to see you, sir," the housemaid said, opening the door just wide enough to show her face.

"Who is he?"

"I don't know, sir. He did not give any name."

"Some shy young man who wants to get married, I expect," was the thought that passed through Mr. Seccombe's mind.

"Show him in," he said, after a pause. And a moment or two later a pale-faced young man came shyly and hesitatingly into the room. He carried a cloth cap in his hand, and was dressed in a badly fitting suit of tweed.

Mr. Seccombe looked at him for a moment inquiringly. He thought he knew,

116

by sight, nearly everybody in the parish, but he was not sure that he had seen this young man before.

"Will you take a seat?" he said, anxious to put the young man at his ease; for he was still convinced that this was a timid bachelor, who wanted to make arrangements for getting married.

"I would prefer to stand, if you don't mind," he answered, toying nervously with his cap.

"As you will," the vicar said, with a smile. "I presume you are about to take to yourself a wife?"

"Me? Oh dear, no. I've something else to think of."

"I beg your pardon," the vicar said, feeling a little confused. "I thought, perhaps——"

"Nothing so pleasant," was the hurried answer. "The fact is, I've come upon a job that—well, I hardly know if I can tell it, now I've come."

The vicar began to feel interested.

"You had better take a seat," he said. "You will feel more comfortable."

The young man dropped into an easy-chair and stared at the fire. He was not a bad-looking young fellow. His face was pale, as though he worked underground, and his cheeks were thin enough to suggest too little nourishing food.

"The truth is, I only made up my mind an hour ago," he said abruptly.

"Yes?" the vicar said encouragingly.

"You have heard of that poor woman being carried off to the workhouse, I expect."

"You mean Mrs. Penlogan?"

"Ay! Well, that floored me. I felt that I could hold out no longer. I meant to have waited to see which way the trial went——"

"Yes?" the vicar said again, seeing he hesitated.

"I've always believed that no jury that wasn't prejudiced would convict him on the evidence."

"You refer to Ralph Penlogan, of course?"

"The young man who's in prison on the charge of shooting Squire Hamblyn. Do you think he's anything like me?"

"You certainly are not unlike him in the general outline of your face. But, of course, anyone who knows young Penlogan——"

"Would never mistake him for me," the other interrupted.

"Well, I should say not, certainly."

"And yet bigger mistakes have been made. But I'd better tell you the whole story. I don't know what'll become of mother and the young ones, but I can't bear it any longer, and that's a fact. When I heard that that poor woman had been took off to the workhouse, I said to myself, 'Jim Brewer, you're a coward.' And that's the reason I'm here——"

"Yes?" said the vicar again, and waited for his visitor to proceed.

"It was I who shot the squire!"

The vicar started, but did not speak.

"I had no notion that he was about, or I shouldn't have ventured into the plantation, you may be quite sure. I was after anything I could get—hare, or rabbit, or pheasant, or barnyard fowl, if nothing else turned up."

"Then you were poaching?" said the vicar.

"Call it anything you like, but if you was in my place, maybe you'd have done the same. There hadn't been a bit of fresh meat in our house for a fortnight, and little Fred, who'd been ill, was just pining away. You see I'd been off work, through crushing my thumb, for a whole month, and we'd got to the end of the tether. Butcher wouldn't trust us no further, and we'd been living on dry bread and a little skimmed milk, with a vegetable now and then. It was terrible hard on us all. I didn't mind myself so much, but to see the little one go hungry——"

"But what does your father do?" the vicar interrupted.

"Father was killed in the mine six years agone, and I've been the only one as has earned anything since. Well, you see, I took the old musket—though I knew, of course, I had no licence—and I went out on the common to shoot anything as came in the way—but nothing turned up. Then I went into the plantation, and as I was getting over a hedge I came face to face with the squire.

"Well, I draws back in a moment, and that very moment something catches the trigger, and off the gun went. A minute after I heard the squire a-howling and a-screaming like mad, and when next I looks over the hedge he was running for dear life and shouting at the top of his voice.

"Well, I just hid myself in the 'browse' till it was dark, and then I creeps home empty-handed and never said a word to nobody. Well, next day, in the mine, I hears as how young Penlogan had been took up on the charge of trying to murder the squire. I never thought nobody would convict him, and if I'd been in the police court when he were sent to the Assizes I couldn't have kept the truth back. But you see I weren't there, and I says to myself that no jury with two ounces of brains will say he's guilty; and so I reckon I'd have held out till the Assizes if I hadn't heard they'd took his poor old mother off to the workhouse. That finished me. I says to myself, 'Jim Brewer, you're a coward,' I says, and I made up my mind then and there to tell the truth. And so I've come to you, being a parson and a magistrate. And the story I've told you is gospel truth, as sure as I'm a living man."

"It seems a very great pity you did not tell this story before," the vicar said reflectively.

"Ay, that's true enough. But I hadn't the courage somehow. You see, I made sure he'd come out all right in the end; and then I thought of mother and little Fred, and Jack and Mary and Peggy, and somehow I couldn't bring myself to face it. It was the poor woman being drove to the workhouse as did it. I think I'd rather die than that my mother should go there."

"I really can't see, for the life of me, why you working people so much object to the workhouse," the vicar said, in a tone of irritation. "It's a very comfortable house; the inmates are well treated in every way, and there isn't a pauper in the House to-day that isn't better off than when outside."

"Maybe it's the name of it, sir," the young man went on. "But I feel terrible bitter against the place. But the point now is, what are we going to do with Ralph Penlogan, and what are you going to do with me?"

"Well, really I hardly know," the vicar said, looking uncomfortable. "You do not own to committing any crime. You were trespassing, certainly—perhaps I ought to say poaching. But—well, I think I ought to consult Mr. Tregonning, and—well, yes—Budda. Would you mind waiting while I send and ask Mr. Tregonning to come on?"

"No; I'll do anything you wish. Now I've started, I want to go straight on to the end."

Mr. Seccombe was back again in a few moments.

"May I ask," he said, with his eyes on the carpet, "if you saw anyone on the afternoon in question, or if anyone saw you?"

"Only Bilkins."

"He's one of Sir John's gardeners, I think."

"Very likely."

"And you were in the plantation when he saw you?"

"Oh no; I was on the common."

"And you were carrying the gun?"

"Well, you see, I pushed it into a furze bush when he come along, for, as I told you, I had no gun licence."

"Did he speak to you?"

"Ay. He passed the time of day, and asked if I had any sport."

"And you saw no one else?"

"Nobody but the squire."

Later in the day Bilkins was sent for, and arrived at the vicarage much wondering what was in the wind. He wondered still more when he was ushered into the vicar's library, and found himself face to face with Budda, Mr. Tregonning, and Jim Brewer, in addition to the vicar. For several moments he looked from one to another with an expression of utter astonishment on his face.

"I have sent for you, Bilkins," said the vicar mildly, "in order to ask you one or two questions that seem of some importance at the present moment."

"Yes, sir," said Bilkins, looking, if possible, more puzzled than before.

"Can you recall the afternoon on which Sir John Hamblyn was shot?"

"Why, yes, sir. Very well, sir."

"Did you cross Polskiddy Downs that afternoon?"

"I did, sir."

"Did you see anybody on the downs?"

"Well, only Jim Brewer. We met accidental like."

"What was he doing?"

"Well, he wasn't doing nothing. He was just standing still with his 'ands in his pockets lookin' round him and whistlin'."

"Was he carrying a gun?"

"Oh no, sir. He had nothin' in his 'ands."

"Did you see a gun?"

Bilkins glanced apprehensively at Jim Brewer, and then at the policeman.

"Well, no," he said, with considerable hesitation. "I didn't see no gun—that is
____."

"Did you see any part of a gun?" Mr. Tregonning interjected.

"Well, sir, I don't wish to do no 'arm to nobody," Bilkins stammered, growing very red, "but I did see somethin' stickin' out of a furze bush as might have been a gun."

"The stock of a gun, perhaps?"

"Well, no; but it might 'ave been the barrel."

"You did not say anything to Brewer?"

"Well, I might, as a kind of joke, 'ave axed him if he 'ad any sport, but it weren't my place to be inquisitive."

"And was this far from the plantation?"

"Oh no; it were almost close."

"Then why, may I ask," interjected the vicar sternly, "did you not volunteer this information when the question was raised as to who shot your master?"

"Never thought on it, sir. Jim Brewer is a chap as couldn't hurt nobody."

"And yet the fact remains that you saw him close to the plantation on the afternoon on which Sir John was shot, and that no one saw Ralph Penlogan near the place."

"Yes, sir," Bilkins said vacantly.

"But what explanation or excuse have you to offer for such dereliction of duty?"

"For what, sir?"

"You must know, surely, that information was sought in all directions that would throw any light on the question."

"No one axed me anything, sir."

"But you might have told what you knew without being asked."

Bilkins looked perplexed, and remained silent.

"Why did you not inform someone of what you had seen?" Mr. Tregonning interposed.

"Well, you see, sir, Sir John had made up his mind as 'twas young Penlogan as shot him. He see'd his face as he was a-climbing over the hedge, an' he ought to know; and besides, sir, it ain't my place to contradict my betters."

"Oh, indeed!" And Mr. Tregonning, as one of his "betters," looked almost as puzzled as Bilkins.

After a few more questions had been asked and answered, there was a general adjournment to Hamblyn Manor.

Sir John was on the point of retiring for the night when he was startled by a loud ringing of the door bell, and a moment or two later he heard the vicar's voice in the hall.

Throwing open the library door, he came face to face with Mr. Seccombe and Mr. Tregonning, two or three shadowy figures bringing up the rear.

"We must ask your pardon, Sir John, for intruding at this late hour," the vicar said, constituting himself chief spokesman, "but Mr. Tregonning and myself felt that the matter was of so much importance that there ought to be not an hour's unnecessary delay."

"Indeed; will you come into the library?" Sir John said pompously, though he felt not a little curious as to what was in the wind.

Standing with his back against the mantelpiece, Sir John motioned his visitors to seats. Budda, however, elected to stand guard over the door.

For several moments there was silence, while the vicar looked at Mr. Tregonning and Mr. Tregonning looked at the vicar.

At last they appeared to understand each other, and the vicar cleared his throat.

"The truth is, Sir John," he began, "I was interrupted in my work this evening by a visit from this young man"—inclining his head toward Brewer—"who informed me that it was he who shot you, accidentally, on the 29th September last——"

"Stuff and nonsense," Sir John snapped, withdrawing his shoulders suddenly from the mantelpiece. "Do you think I don't know a face when I see it?"

"And yet, sir, it were my face you saw," Brewer interposed suddenly.

"Don't believe it," Sir John replied, with a snort.

"You must admit, sir," Mr. Tregonning interposed apologetically, "that this young man is not unlike Ralph Penlogan."

"No more like him than I am," Sir John retorted, almost angrily.

"Anyhow, you had better hear the story from the young man's lips," said the vicar mildly, "then your own man Bilkins will give evidence that he saw him close to the plantation on the afternoon in question."

"Then why did you not say so?" Sir John snarled, glaring angrily at his gardener.

"'Tweren't for the likes of me," Bilkins said humbly, "to say anything as would seem to contradict what you said. I hopes I know my place."

"I hope you do," Sir John growled; and then he turned his attention to the young miner.

Brewer told his story straightforwardly and without any outward sign of nervousness. He had braced himself to the task—his nerves were strung up to the highest point of tension, and he was determined to see the thing through now, cost what it might.

Sir John listened with half-closed eyes and a heavy frown upon his brow. He was far more angry than he would like anyone to know at the course events were taking. He saw clearly enough that, from his point of view, this was worse than a verdict of "not guilty" at the Assizes. This story, if accepted, would clear Ralph Penlogan absolutely. Not even the shadow of a suspicion would remain. Moreover, it would lay him (Sir John) open to the charge of vindictiveness.

As soon as Brewer had finished the story, the squire subjected him to a severe and lengthy cross-examination, all of which he bore with quiet composure, and every question he answered simply and directly.

Then Bilkins was called upon to tell his story, which Sir John listened to with evident disgust.

It was getting decidedly late when all the questions had been asked and answered, and Budda was growing impatient to know what part he was to play in the little drama. He was itching to arrest somebody. It would have been a relief to him if he could have arrested both Brewer and Bilkins.

Sir John and his brother magistrates withdrew at length to another room, while Budda kept guard with renewed vigilance.

"Now," said the vicar, when the door had closed behind the trio, "what is the next step?"

"Let the law take its course," said Sir John angrily.

"It will take its course in any case," said Mr. Tregonning. "The confession of Brewer, and the corroborative evidence of Bilkins, must be forwarded at once to the proper quarter. But the question is, Sir John, will you still hold to the charge of malicious shooting, or only of trespass?"

"If this story is accepted, I'll wash my hands of the whole business—there now!" And Sir John pushed his hands into his pockets and looked furious.

"I don't quite see why you should treat the matter in this way," the vicar said mildly.

"You don't?" Sir John questioned, staring hard at him. "You don't see that it will make fools of the whole lot of us; that it will turn the tide of popular sympathy against the entire bench of magistrates, and against me in particular; that it will do more harm to the gentry than fifty elections?"

"That's a very narrow view to take," the vicar said, with spirit. "We should care for the right and do the right, though the heavens fall."

"That may be all right to preach in church," Sir John said irritably, "but in practical life we do the best we can for ourselves, unless we are fools."

"Then you'll not proceed against this young man for trespass?" Mr. Tregonning inquired.

"I tell you I'll wash my hands of the whole affair, and I mean it. It's bad enough to be made a fool of once, without playing the same game a second time," and Sir John strutted round the room like an angered turkey.

"Then there's no excuse for keeping young Brewer here any longer, or of keeping you out of your bed," said the vicar, and he made for the door, followed by Mr. Tregonning.

Five minutes later the door closed on his guests, and Sir John found himself once more alone.

"Well, this is a kettle of fish," he said to himself angrily, as he paced up and down the room; "a most infernal kettle of fish, I call it. I shouldn't be surprised if before a week is out that young scoundrel will be heralded by a brass band playing 'See the Conquering Hero comes.' And, of course, every ounce of sympathy will go out to him. He'll be a kind of martyr, and I shall be execrated as a kind of Legree and Judge Jeffreys rolled into one. And then, of course, Dorothy will catch the popular contagion, and will interview him if she has the chance; and he'll make love to her—the villain! And here's Lord Probus bullying me, and every confounded money-lending Jew in the neighbourhood dunning me for money, and Geoffrey taking to extravagant ways with more alacrity than I did before him. I wonder if any other man in the county is humbugged as I am?"

Sir John spent the rest of the waking hours of that night in scheming how best he could get and keep Dorothy out of the way of Ralph Penlogan.

CHAPTER XIX

A SILENT WELCOME

If a man is unfortunate enough to find himself in the clutches of what is euphemistically called "the law," the sooner and the more completely he can school himself to patience the better for his peace of mind. Lawyers and legislators do not appear generally to be of a mechanical turn, and the huge machine which they have constructed for the purpose of discovering and punishing criminals is apparently without any reversing gear. The machine will go forward ponderously and cumbrously, but it will not go backward without an infinite amount of toil and trouble. Hence, if a man is once caught in its toils, even though he is innocent, he will, generally speaking, have to go through the mill and come out at the far end. For such a small and remote contingency as a miscarriage of justice there is apparently no provision. If the wronged and deluded man will only have patience, he will come out of the mill in due course; and if he is but civil, he will be rewarded with a free pardon and told not to do it again.

The generosity of the State in compensating those who have been wrongfully convicted and punished has grown into a proverb. In some instances they have been actually released before their time has expired—which, of course, has meant a considerable amount of work for those who had control of the mill; and work to the highly paid officials of the State is little less to be dreaded than the plague.

The whole country had been ringing with Jim Brewer's story for more than a week before the law officers of the Crown condescended to look at the matter at all, and when they did look at it they saw so many technicalities in the way, and so much red tape to be unwound, that their hearts failed them. It seemed very inconsiderate of this Jim Brewer to speak at all after he had kept silent so long, particularly as the Grand Jury would so soon have the case before them.

Meanwhile Ralph was waiting with as much patience as he could command for the day of the trial. That he would be found guilty he could not bring himself to believe. The more he reviewed the case, the more angry and disgusted he felt with the local Solomons who had sat in judgment on him. He was disposed almost to blame them more than he blamed the squire. Sir John might have some grounds for supposing that he (Ralph) had deliberately fired at him. But that the great unpaid of St. Goram and neighbouring parishes could be so blind and stupid filled him with disgust.

For himself, he did not mind the long delay so much; but as the days grew into weeks, his anxiety respecting his mother and Ruth grew into torment. He knew that their little spare cash could not possibly hold out many weeks, and then what would happen?

He had heard nothing from them for a long time, and Bodmin was so far away from St. Goram that they could not visit him. He wondered if they had reached such straits that they could not afford a postage stamp. The more he speculated on the matter the more alarmed he got. The letters he had been allowed to send had received no answer. And it seemed so unlike his mother and Ruth to remain silent if they were able to write.

Of Jim Brewer's story he knew nothing, for newspapers did not come his way, and none of the prison officials had the kindness to tell him. So he waited and wondered as the slow days crept painfully past, and grew thin and hollow-eyed, and wished that he had never been born.

The end came nearly a month after Jim Brewer had told his story. He was condescendingly informed one morning that his innocence having been clearly established, the Crown would offer no evidence in support of the charge, and the Grand Jury had therefore thrown out the bill of indictment. This would mean his immediate liberation.

For several moments he felt unable to speak, and he sat down and hid his face in his hands. Then slowly the meaning of the words he had listened to began to take shape in his mind.

"You say my innocence has been established?" he questioned at length.

"That is so."

"By what means?"

The governor told him without unnecessary words.

"How long ago was this?"

"I do not quite know. Not many weeks I think."

"Not many weeks! Good heavens! You mean that I have been allowed to suffer in this inferno after my innocence was established?"

"With that I have nothing to do. Better quietly and thankfully take your departure."

Ralph raised a pair of blazing eyes, then turned on his heel. He felt as though insult had been heaped upon insult.

His brain seemed almost on fire when at length he stepped through the heavy portal and found himself face to face with William Menire.

Ralph stared at him for several moments in astonishment. Why, of all the people in the world, should William Menire come to meet him? They had never been friends—they could scarcely be called acquaintances.

William, however, did not allow him to pursue this train of thought. Springing forward at once, he grasped Ralph by the hand.

"I made inquiries," he said, speaking rapidly, "and I couldn't find out that anybody was coming to meet you. And I thought you might feel a bit lonely and cheerless, for the weather is nipping cold. So I brought a warm rug with me, and I've ordered breakfast at the King's Arms; for there ain't no train till a quarter-past ten, and we'll be home by——"

Then he stopped suddenly, for Ralph had burst into tears.

The prison fare, the iron hand of the law, the bitter injustice he had suffered so long, had only hardened him. He had shed not a single tear during all the months of his incarceration. But this touch of human kindness from one who was almost a stranger broke him down completely, and he hid his face in his hands, and sobbed outright.

William looked at him in bewilderment.

"I hope I have not said anything that's hurt you?" he questioned anxiously.

"No, no," Ralph said chokingly. "It's your kindness that has unmanned me for a moment. You are almost a stranger, and I have no claim upon you whatever." And he began to sob afresh.

"Oh, well, if that's all, I don't mind," William said, with a cheerful smile. "You see, we are neighbours—at least we were. And if a man can't do a neighbourly deed when he has a chance, he ain't worth much."

Ralph lifted his head at length, and wiped his eyes.

"Pardon me for being so weak," he said. "But I didn't expect——"

"Of course you didn't," William interrupted. "I knew it would be a surprise to you. But hadn't we better be going? I don't want the breakfast at the King's Arms to get cold."

"A word first," Ralph said eagerly. "Are my mother and sister well?"

"Well, your mother is only middling—nothing serious. But the weather's been very trying, and her appetite's nothing to speak of. And, you see, she's worried a good deal about you."

"And my sister?" he interposed.

"She's very well, I believe. But let's get out of sight of this place, or it'll be getting on my nerves."

A quarter of an hour later they were seated in a cosy room before an appetising breakfast of steaming ham and eggs.

Ralph had a difficulty in keeping the tears back. The pleasant room, hung with pictures, the cheerful fire crackling in the grate, the white tablecloth and dainty china and polished knives and forks, the hot, fragrant tea and the delicious ham, were such a contrast from what he had endured so long, that he felt for a moment or two as if his emotion would completely overcome him.

William wisely did not look at him, but gave all his attention to the victuals, and in a few minutes had the satisfaction of seeing his guest doing full justice to the fare.

During the journey home they talked mainly about what had happened in St. Goram since Ralph went away, but William could not bring himself to tell him the truth about his mother. Again and again he got to the point, and then his courage failed him.

At St. Ivel Road, William's trap was waiting for them, and they drove the two miles to St. Goram in silence.

Suddenly Ralph reached out his hand as if to grasp the reins.

"You are driving past our house," he said, in a tone of suppressed excitement.

"Yes, that's all right," William answered, in a tone of apparent unconcern. "They're not there now."

"Not there?" he questioned, with a gasp.

"No. You'll come along with me for a bit."

"But I do not understand," Ralph said, turning eager eyes on William's face.

"Oh, I'll explain directly. But look at the crowd of folk."

William had to bring his horse to a standstill, for the road was completely blocked. There was no shouting or hurrahing; no band to play "See the Conquering Hero comes." But the men uncovered their heads, and tears were running down the women's faces.

Ralph had to get out of the trap to steer his way as best he could to William's store. It was a slow and painful process, and yet it had its compensations. Children tugged at his coat-tails, and hard-fisted men squeezed his hand in silence, and women held up their chubby babies to him to be kissed, and young fellows his own age whispered a word of welcome. It was far more impressive than a noisy demonstration or the martial strains of a brass band. Of the sympathy of the people there could be no doubt whatever. Everybody realised now that he had been cruelly treated—that the suspicion that rested on him at first was base and unworthy; that he was not the kind of man to do a mean or cowardly deed; and that the wrong that was done was of a kind that could never be repaired.

They wondered as they crowded round him whether he knew of the crowning humiliation and wrong. The workhouse was a place that most of them regarded with horror. To become a pauper was to suffer the last indignity. There was nothing beyond it—no further reproach or shame.

It was the knowledge that Ralph's mother was in the workhouse, and that his little home had been broken up—perhaps for ever—that checked the shout and turned what might have been laughter into tears. Any attempt at merriment would have been a mockery under such circumstances. They were glad to see Ralph back again—infinitely glad; but knowing what they did, the pathos of his coming touched them to the quick.

Very few words were spoken, but tears fell like rain. Ralph wondered, as he pressed his way forward toward William Menire's shop, and yet he had not the courage to ask any questions. Behind the people's silent sympathy he felt there was something that had not yet been revealed. But what it was he could not guess. That his mother and Ruth were alive, he knew, for William had told him so. Perhaps something had happened in St. Goram that William had not told him, which affected others more than it affected him.

William went in front and elbowed a passage for Ralph.

"We be fine an' glad to see 'ee 'ome again," people whispered here and there, and Ralph would smile and say "Thank you," and then push on again.

William was in a perfect fever of excitement. He had been hoping almost against hope all the day. Whether his little scheme had succeeded or miscarried, he could not tell yet. He would know only when he crossed his own threshold. What his little scheme was he had confided to no one. If it failed, he could still comfort himself with the thought that he had done his best. But he still hoped and prayed that what he had tried so hard to accomplish had come to pass.

CHAPTER XX

WILLIAM MENIRE'S RED-LETTER DAY

The crowd pressed close to the door of William's shop, but no one dared to enter. Ralph followed close upon his heels, still wondering and fearing. William lifted the flap of his counter and opened the door of the living-room beyond. No sooner had he done so than his heart gave a sudden bound. Ruth Penlogan came forward with pale face and eyes full of tears.

William's little plan had succeeded. Ruth was present to receive her brother. William tried to speak, but his voice failed him, and with a sudden rush of tears he turned back into the shop, closing the door behind him.

Ruth fell on her brother's neck, and began to sob. He led her to a large, antiquated sofa, and sat down by her side. He did not speak. He could wait till she had recovered herself. She dried her eyes at length and looked up into his face.

"You did not expect to see me here?" she questioned.

"No, I did not, Ruth; but where is mother?"

"Has he not told you?"

"Told me? She is not dead, is she?"

"No, no. She would be happier if she were. Oh, Ralph, it breaks my heart. I wish we had all died when father was taken."

"But where is she, Ruth? What has happened? Do tell me."

"She is in the workhouse, Ralph."

He sprang to his feet as though he had been shot.

"Ruth, you lie!" he said, almost in a whisper.

She began to sob again, and he stood looking at her with white, drawn face, and a fierce, passionate gleam in his eyes.

For several moments no other word passed between them. Then he sat down by her side again.

"There was no help for it," she sobbed at length. "And mother was quite content and eager to go."

"And you allowed it, Ruth," he said, in a tone of reproach.

"What could I do, Ralph?" she questioned plaintively. "We had spent all, and the landlord stopped us from selling any more furniture. The parish would allow her half a crown a week, which would not pay the rent, and I could get nothing to do."

He gulped down a lump that had risen in his throat, and clenched his hands, but he did not speak.

"She said there was no disgrace in going into the House," Ruth went on; "that father had paid rates for more than five-and-twenty years, and that she had a right to all she would get, and a good deal more."

"Rights go for nothing in this world," he said bitterly. "It is the strong who win."

"Mrs. Menire told me this morning that her son would have trusted us to any amount and for any length of time if he had only known."

"You did not ask him?"

"Mother would never consent," she replied. "Besides, Mr. Menire is a comparative stranger to us."

"That is true, and yet he has been a true friend to me to-day."

"I hesitated about accepting his hospitality," Ruth answered, with her eyes upon the floor. "He sent word yesterday that he had learned you were to be liberated this morning, and that he was going to Bodmin to meet you and bring you back, and that his mother would be glad to offer me hospitality if I would like to meet you here."

"It was very kind of him, Ruth; but where are you living?"

"I am in service, Ralph."

"No!"

"It is quite true. I was bound to earn my living somehow."

He laughed a bitter laugh.

"Prison, workhouse, and domestic service! What may we get to next, do you think?"

"But we have not gone into debt or cheated anybody, and we've kept our consciences clean, Ralph."

"Yes, ours is a case of virtue rewarded," he answered cynically. "Honesty sent to prison, and thrift to the workhouse."

"But we haven't done with life and the world yet."

"You think there are lower depths in store for us?"

"I hope not. We may begin to rise now. Let us not despair, Ralph. Suffering should purify and strengthen us."

"I don't see how suffering wrongly or unjustly can do anybody any good," he answered moodily.

"Nor can I at present. Perhaps we shall see later on. There is one great joy amid all our grief. Your name has been cleared."

"Yes, that is something—better than a verdict of acquittal, eh?" and a softer light came into his eyes.

"I would rather be in our place, Ralph, bitter and humiliating as it is, than take the place of the oppressor."

"You are thinking of Sir John Hamblyn?" he questioned.

"They say he is being oppressed now," she answered, after a pause.

"By whom?"

"The money-lenders. Rumour says that he has lost heavily on the Turf and on the Stock Exchange—whatever that may be—and that he is hard put to it to keep his creditors at bay."

"That may account in some measure for his hardness to others."

"He hoped to retrieve his position, it is said, by marrying his daughter to Lord Probus," Ruth went on, "but she refuses to keep her promise."

"What?" he exclaimed, with a sudden gasp.

"How much of the gossip is true, of course, nobody knows, or rather how much of it isn't true—for it is certain she has refused to marry him; and Lord Probus is so mad that he refused to speak to Sir John or have anything to do with him."

Ralph smiled broadly.

"What has become of Miss Dorothy is not quite clear. Some people say that Sir John has sent her to a convent school in France. Others say that she has gone off of her own free will, and taken a situation as a governess under an assumed name."

"Are you sure she isn't at the Manor?" he questioned eagerly.

"Quite sure. The servants talk very freely about it. Sir John stormed and swore, and threatened all manner of things, but she held her own. He shouted so loudly sometimes that they could not help hearing what he said. Miss

Dorothy was very calm, but very determined. He taunted her with being in love with somebody else——"

"No!"

"She must have had a very hard time of it by what the servants say. It is to be hoped she has peace now she has got away."

"Sir John is a brute," Ralph said bitterly. "He has no mercy on anybody, not even on his own flesh and blood."

"Isn't it always true that 'with what measure ye mete it shall be measured to you again'?" Ruth questioned, looking up into his face.

"It may be," he answered, "and yet many people suffer injustice who have never meted it out to others."

For a while silence fell between them, then looking up into his face she said—

"Have you any plans for the future, Ralph?"

"A good many, Ruth, but the chances are they will come to nothing. One thing my prison experience has allowed me, and that is time to think. If I can work out half my dreams there will be topsy-turvydom in St. Goram." And he smiled again.

"Then you have not given up hope?"

"Not quite, Ruth. But first of all I must see mother and get her out of the workhouse."

"You will have to earn some money and take a house first. You see, everything has gone, Ralph."

"Which means an absolutely fresh start, and from the bottom," he answered. "But never mind, when you build from the bottom you are pretty sure of your foundation."

"Oh, it does me good to hear you talk like that," she said, the tears coming into her eyes again.

"I hope I'm not altogether a coward, sis," he said, with a smile. "It'll be a hard struggle, I know; but, at any rate, I have something to live for."

"That's bravely said." And she leant over and kissed him.

"Now we must stop talking, and act," he went on. "I must get William Menire to lend me his trap, and I must drive over to see mother."

"That will be lovely, for then I can ride with you, for I must be in by seven o'clock."

"What?"

"This is an extra day off, you know."

"Are you cook, or housemaid, or what?"

"I am sewing maid," she answered. "The Varcoes have a big family of children, you know, and I have really as much as I can do with the making and mending."

"What, Varcoes the Quakers?"

"Yes. And they have really been exceedingly kind to me. They took me without references, and have done their best to make me comfortable. There are some good people in the world, Ralph."

"It would be a sorry world if there weren't," he answered. And then William Menire and his mother entered.

A few minutes later a substantial dinner was served, and for the next hour William fluttered about his guests unmindful of how his customers fared.

Had not Ralph been so busy with his own thoughts, and Ruth so taken up with her brother, they would have both seen in what direction William's inclinations lay. He would gladly have kept them both if he could, and hailed their presence as a dispensation of Providence. Ruth looked lovelier in William's eyes than she had ever done, and to be her friend was the supreme ambition of his life.

He insisted on driving them to St. Hilary, but demanded as a first condition that Ralph should return with him to St. Goram.

"You can stay here," he said, "until you can get work or suit yourself with better lodgings. You can't sleep in the open air, and you may as well stay with me as with anybody else."

This, on the face of it, seemed a reasonable enough proposition, and with this understanding Ralph climbed into the back of the trap, Ruth riding on the front seat with William.

Never did a driver feel more proud than William felt that afternoon. It was not that he was doing a kindly and neighbourly deed; there was much more in his jubilation than that. He had by his side, so he believed, the fairest girl in the three parishes. William watched with no ordinary interest and curiosity the face of everyone they met, and when he saw some admiring pairs of eyes resting upon his companion, his own eyes sparkled with a brighter light.

William thought very little of Ralph, who was sitting at his back, and who kept up a conversation with Ruth over his left shoulder. It was Ruth who filled his thoughts and awakened in his heart a new and strange sensation. He did not talk himself. He was content to listen, content to catch the sweet undertone of a voice that was sweeter and softer than St. Goram bells on a stormy night; content to feel, when the trap lurched, the pressure of Ruth's arm against his own.

He did not drive rapidly. Why should he? This was a red-letter day in the grey monotony of his life, a day to be remembered when business was bad and profits small, and his mother's temper had more rough edges in it than usual.

So he let his horse amble along at its own sweet will. They would return at a much smarter pace.

William pulled up slowly at the workhouse gates. He would have helped Ruth down if there had been any excuse or opportunity. He was sorry the journey had come to an end. It might be long before he looked into those soft brown eyes again. He suppressed a sigh with difficulty when Ralph sprang out behind and helped his sister down. How much less clumsily he could have done it himself, and how he would have enjoyed the privilege!

"I'll put the horse up at the Star and Garter," he said, adjusting the seat to the lighter load, "and will be waiting round there till you're ready."

Then Ruth came up and stood by the shafts.

"I shall not see you again," she said, raising grateful eyes to his. "But I should like to thank you very much for your kindness."

"Please don't say a word about it," he answered, blushing painfully. "The pleasure's been on my side." And he reached down and grasped Ruth's extended hand with a vigour that left no doubt as to his sincerity.

He did not drive away at once. He waited till Ralph and Ruth had disappeared within the gloomy building, then, heaving a long-drawn sigh, he touched his horse with his whip, and drove slowly down the hill toward the Star and Garter.

"It's very foolish of me to think about women at all," he mused, "especially about one woman in particular. I'm not a woman's man, and never was, and never shall be. Besides, she's good enough for the best in the land."

And he plucked at the reins and started the horse into a trot.

"If I were ten years younger and handsome," he went on, "and didn't keep a shop, and hadn't my mother to keep, and—and——But there, what's the use of saying 'if' this and 'if' that? I'm just William Menire, and nobody else, and there ain't her equal in the three parishes. No, I'd better be content to jog along quietly as I've been doing for years past. It's foolish to dream at my time of life—foolish—foolish!" And with another sigh he let the reins slacken.

But, foolish or not, William continued to dream, until his dreams seemed to him the larger part of his life.

CHAPTER XXI

A GOOD NAME

In a long, barrack-like room, with uncarpeted floor and whitewashed walls, Ralph and Ruth found their mother. She was propped up with pillows in a narrow, comfortless bed. Her hands lay listless upon the coarse coverlet, her eyes were fixed upon the blank wall opposite, her lips were parted in a patient and pathetic smile.

She did not see the wall, nor feel the texture of the bedclothes, nor hear the sound of footsteps on the uncarpeted floor. She was back again in the old days when husband and children were about her, and hope gladdened their daily toil, and love glorified and made beautiful the drudgery of life. She tried not to think about the present at all, and in the main she succeeded. Her life was in the past and in the future. When she was not wandering through the pleasant fields of memory, and plucking the flowers that grew in those sheltered vales, she was soaring aloft into those fair Elysian fields which imagination pictured and faith made real—fields on which the blight of winter never fell, and across which storms and tempests never swept.

She had lost all count of days, lost consciousness almost of her present surroundings. Every day was the same—grey and sunless. There were no duties to be done, no meals to prepare, no butter to make, no chickens to feed, no husband to greet when the day was done, no hungry children to come romping in from the fields.

There were old people who had been in the workhouse so long that they had accommodated their life to its slow routine, and who found something to interest them in the narrowest and greyest of all worlds. But Mary Penlogan had come too suddenly into its sombre shadow and had left too many pleasant things behind her.

She did not complain. There were times when she did not even suffer. The blow had stunned her and numbed all her sensibilities. Now and then she awoke as from a pleasant dream, and for a moment a wave of horror and agony would sweep over her, but the tension would quickly pass. The wound was too deep for the smart to continue long.

She seemed in the main to be wonderfully resigned, and yet resignation was scarcely the proper word to use. It was rather that voiceless apathy born of despair. For her the end of the world had come; there was nothing left to live for. Nothing could restore the past and give her back what once she had prized so much, and yet prized all too little. It was just a question of endurance until the Angel of Death should set her free.

She conformed to all the rules of the House without a murmur, and without even the desire to complain. She slept well, on the whole, and tried her best to eat such fare as was considered good enough for paupers. If she wept at all she wept in secret and in the night-time; she had no desire to obtrude her grief upon others. She even made an earnest effort to be cheerful now and then. But all the while her strength ebbed slowly away. The springs of her life had run dry.

The workhouse doctor declared at first that nothing ailed her—nothing at all. A week later he spoke of a certain lack of vitality, and wrote an order for a little more nourishing food. A fortnight later he discovered a certain weakness in the action of the heart, and wrote out a prescription to be made up in the dispensary.

Later still he had her removed to the sick-ward and placed under the care of a nurse. It was there Ralph and Ruth found her on the afternoon in question.

She looked up with a start when Ralph stopped at the foot of her bed, then, with a glad cry, she reached out her wasted arms to him. He was by her side in a moment, with his arms about her neck, and for several minutes they rocked themselves to and fro in silence.

Ruth came up on the other side and sat down on a wooden chair, and for awhile her presence was forgotten.

"My dear, darling old mother!" Ralph said, as soon as he had recovered himself sufficiently to speak. "I did not think it would have come to this."

She made no reply, but continued to rock herself to and fro.

He drew himself away after a while and took her thin, wrinkled hands in his.

"You must get better now as soon as ever you can," he said, trying to speak cheerfully, though every word threatened to choke him.

She shook her head slowly and smiled.

"When we get you back to St. Goram," he went on, "you'll soon pick up your strength again, for it is only strength you need."

She turned her head and looked up into his face and smiled pathetically.

"If it is God's will that I should get strong again I shall not complain," she answered, "but I would rather go Home now I am so near."

"Oh no, we cannot spare you yet," he replied quickly; and he gulped down a big lump that had risen in his throat. "I'm going to work in real earnest and build a new home. I've lots of plans for the future."

"My poor boy," she said gently, and she tapped the back of his hand with the tips of her wasted fingers, "even if your plans succeed, life will be a hard road still."

"Yes, yes, I know that, mother. But to have someone to live for and care for will make it easier." And he bent his head and kissed her.

"God alone can tell that, my boy," she said wistfully. "But oh, you've been a long time coming to me."

"I wonder if it has seemed so long to you as to me?" he questioned.

"But why did they not release you sooner?" she asked. "Oh, it seems months ago since they told me that Jim Brewer had confessed."

"Can anybody tell why stupid officialism ever does anything at all?" he questioned. "Liberty is a goddess bound, and justice is fettered and cannot run."

"I know nothing about that," she answered slowly, "but it seemed an easy thing to set you free when your innocence had been proved."

"No, mother; nothing is easy when you are caught in the blind and blundering toils of the law."

"But what is the law for, my boy?"

He laughed softly and yet bitterly.

"Chiefly, it seems," he said, "to find work for lawyers; and, secondly, to protect the interests of those who are rich enough to pay for it."

"Oh, my boy, the bitterness of the wrong abides with you still, but God will make all things right by and by."

"Some things can never be made right, mother; but let us not talk of that now. I want you to get better fast, and think of all the good times we shall have when we get a little home of our own once more."

"Your father will not be there," she answered sadly; "and I want to be with him."

"But you should think of us also, mother," he said, with a shake in his voice.

"I do—I do," she answered feebly and listlessly. "I have thought of you night and day, and have never ceased to pray for you since I came here. But you can do without me now."

"No, no. Don't say that!" he pleaded.

139

"I should have feared to leave you once," she answered; "but not now."

"Why not now?" he questioned.

"Ah, Ralph, my boy"—and she smoothed the back of his hand slowly and gently—"you will never forget your father and the good name he bore. That name is your inheritance. It is better than money—better than houses and lands. He was one of the good men of the world—not great, nor successful, nor even wise, as the world counts wisdom. But no shadow of wrong, Ralph, ever stained his life. He walked with God. You will think of this, my son, in the days that are to come. And if ever you should be tempted to sin, the memory of your father will be like an anchor to you. You will say to yourself, 'He bore unstained for nearly sixty years the white flag of a blameless life, and I dare not lower it now into the dust.'"

"God help me, mother!" he choked.

"God will help you, my boy. As He stood by your father and has comforted me, so will He be your strength and defence. You and Ruth will fight all the better for not having the burden of my presence."

"Mother, mother, how can you say so?" Ruth interposed, with streaming eyes.

"I may be permitted to watch you from the hills of that Better Country," she went on, "I and your father. But in any case, God will watch over you."

This was her benediction. They went away at length, sadly and silently, but not till they reached the outer air did either of them speak. It was Ruth who broke the silence.

"She will never get better, Ralph."

"Oh, nonsense, sis. She is overcome to-day, but she will pick up again to-morrow."

"She has been gradually failing ever since we left Hillside, and she has never recovered any ground she lost."

"But the spring is coming, and once we have got her out of that dismal and depressing place, her strength will come back."

But Ruth shook her head.

"I don't want to discourage you," she said, "but I have watched the gradual loosening of her hold upon life. Her heart is in heaven, Ralph, that is the secret of it. She is longing to be with father again."

They walked on in silence till they reached Mr. Varcoe's house, then Ralph spoke again.

"We must get mother out of the workhouse, and at once, whatever happens," he said.

"How?" she asked.

"I don't know yet. But think of it, if she should die in the workhouse."

"She has lived in it," Ruth answered.

"Yes, yes; but the disgrace of it if she should end her days there."

"If there is any disgrace in poverty, we have suffered it to the full," Ruth answered. "Nothing that can happen now can add to it."

For a moment he stood silent. Then he kissed her and walked away.

He found William Menire waiting for him at the street corner, a few yards from the Star and Garter.

"I haven't harnessed up yet," he said. "I thought perhaps you might like a cup of tea or a chop before we returned. Your sister, I presume, has gone back to her—to her place?"

"Yes, I saw her home before I came on here."

William sighed and waited for instructions. He was willing to be servant to Ralph for Ruth's sake.

"I should like a cup of tea, if you don't mind," Ralph said at length, and he coloured painfully as he spoke. He was living on charity, and the sting of it made all his nerves tingle.

"There's a confectioner's round the corner where they make capital tea," William said cheerfully. And he led the way with long strides.

The moon was up when they started on their homeward journey, and the air was keen and frosty. Neither of them talked much. To Ralph the day seemed like a long and more or less incoherent dream. He had dressed that morning in the dim light of a prison cell—it seemed like a week ago. He felt at times as though he had dreamed all the rest.

William was dreaming of Ruth, and so did not disturb his companion. The horse needed no whip, he seemed the most eager of the three to get home. The fields lay white and silent in the moonlight. The bare trees flung ghostly shadows across the road. The stars twinkled faintly in the far-off depths of space, now and then a dove cooed drowsily in a neighbouring wood.

At length the tower of St. Goram Church loomed massively over the brow of the hill, and a little later William pulled up with a jerk at his own shop door.

Mrs. Menire had provided supper for them. Ralph ate sparingly, and with many pauses. This was not home. He was a stranger in a stranger's house, living on charity. That thought stung him constantly and spoiled his appetite.

He tried to sleep when he got to bed, but the angel was long in coming. His thoughts were too full of other things. The fate of his mother worried him most. How to get her out of the workhouse and find an asylum for her somewhere else was a problem he could not solve. He had been promised work at St. Ivel Mine before his arrest, and he had no doubt that he would still be able to obtain employment there. But no wages would be paid him till the end of the month, and even then it would all be mortgaged for food and clothes.

He slept late next morning, for William had given orders that he was not to be disturbed. He came downstairs feeling a little ashamed of himself. If this was his new start in life, it was anything but an energetic beginning.

William was on the look-out for him, and fetched the bacon and eggs from the kitchen himself.

"We've had our breakfast," he explained. "You won't mind, I hope. We knew you'd be very tired, so we kept the house quiet. I hope you've had a good night, and are feeling all the better. Now I must leave you. We're busy getting out the country orders. You can help yourself, I know." And he disappeared through the frosted glass door into the shop.

He came back half an hour later, just as Ralph was finishing his breakfast, with a telegram in his hand.

"I hope there ain't no bad news," he said, handing Ralph the brick-coloured envelope.

Ralph tore it open in a moment, and his face grew ashen.

He did not speak for several seconds, but continued to stare with unblinking eyes at the pencilled words.

"Is it bad news?" William questioned at length, unable to restrain his curiosity and his anxiety any longer.

Ralph raised his eyes and looked at him.

"Mother's dead," he answered, in a whisper; and then the telegram slipped from his fingers and fluttered to the floor.

William picked it up and read it.

"Your mother found dead in bed. Send instructions *re* disposal of remains."

"They might have worded the message a little less brutally," William said at length.

"Officialism is nothing if not brutal," Ralph said bitterly.

Then the two men looked at each other in silence. William had little difficulty in guessing what was passing through Ralph's mind.

"If I were in his place," he reflected, "what should I be thinking? Should I like my mother to be put into a parish coffin and buried in a pauper's grave?"

William spoke at length.

"You'd like your mother and father to sleep together?" he questioned.

Ralph's lips trembled, but he did not speak.

"The world's been terribly rough on you," William went on, "but you'll come into your own maybe by and by."

"I shall never get father and mother back again," Ralph answered chokingly.

"We oughtn't to want them back again," William said; "they're better off."

"I wish I was better off in the same way," Ralph answered, with a rush of tears to his eyes.

"She held on, you see, till you came back to her," William said, after a long pause; "then, when she got her heart's desire, she let go."

"Dear old mother!"

"And now that she's asleep, you'll want her to rest with your father."

"But I've no money."

"I'll be your banker as long as you like. Charge you interest on the money, if you'll feel easier in your mind. Only don't let the money question trouble you just now."

Ralph grasped William's hand in silence. Of all the people he had known in St. Goram, this comparative stranger was his truest friend and neighbour.

So it came to pass that Mary Penlogan had such a funeral as she herself would have chosen, and in the grave of her husband her children laid her to rest. People came from far and near to pay their last tribute of respect. Even Sir John Hamblyn sent his steward to represent him. He was too conscience-stricken to come himself.

And when the grave had been filled in, the crowd still lingered and talked to each other of the brave and patient souls whose only legacy to their children was the heritage of an untarnished name.

CHAPTER XXII

A FRESH START

Some people said it was a stroke of good luck, others that it was an exhibition of native genius, others still that it was the result of having a good education, and a few that it was just a dispensation of Providence, and nothing else. But whether luck or genius, Providence or education, all were agreed that Ralph Penlogan had struck a vein which, barring accidents, would lead him on to fortune.

For six months he had worked on the "floors" of St. Ivel Mine, and earned fourteen shillings a week thereat; but as a friendly miner and his wife boarded and lodged him for eight shillings a week, he did not do badly. His savings, if not large, were regular. Most months he laid by a pound, and felt that he had taken the first step on the road to independence, if not to fortune.

As the weeks sped away, and springtime grew into summer, and all the countryside lay smiling and beautiful in the warmth of the sunshine, his spirits rose imperceptibly; the sense of injustice that had burdened him gradually grew lighter, the bitter memory of Bodmin Gaol faded slowly from his mind, his grief at the loss of his parents passed unconsciously into painless resignation, and life, for its own sake, seemed to gather a new meaning.

He was young and strong, and in perfect health. Consequently, youth and strength and hope and confidence asserted themselves in spite of everything. How could he help dreaming bright dreams of the future when the earth lay basking in beauty in the light of the summer sun, and away at the end of the valley a triangular glimpse of the sea carried his thoughts into the infinite?

So strong he felt, so full of life and vitality, that nothing seemed impossible to him. He was not impatient. He was so young that he could afford to bide his time. He would lay the foundation slowly and with care. He had to creep before he could walk, and walk before he could run.

Now and then, it is true, he had his bitter and angry moments, when the memory of the past swept over him like an icy flood, and when a sense of intolerable injustice seemed to wrap the world in darkness and shut out all hope of the future.

One such moment he had when he contracted with William Jenkins to mow down a field of hay on Hillside Farm. He could do this only by working overtime, which usually meant working sixteen hours a day. But he was anxious to earn all he could, so that at the earliest possible date he might get a little home together for himself and Ruth.

He had not seen Hillside for many a month until the day he went to interview William Jenkins. He knew it would cost him a pang, but he could not afford to wait on sentiment or emotion. And yet he hardly realised how deeply the place was enshrined in his heart until he stood knocking at the door of the house that was once his home.

He was glad that nobody heard his first knock. He thought he had got beyond the reach of emotion, but it was not so. Suddenly, as a wave rises and breaks upon the shore, a flood of memory swept over him. He was back again in the dear dead past, with all the hopes of boyhood dancing before his eyes. He saw his father coming up the home-close with a smile upon his face, his mother in the garden gathering flowers with which to decorate the table. He could almost fancy he heard Ruth singing in the parlour as she bent over her sewing.

Then the wave retreated, leaving him cold and numbed and breathless. It was his home no longer. He was standing, a stranger, at the door that once he opened by right. His eyes cleared at length, and he looked out across the fields that he had helped to reclaim from the waste. How familiar the landscape was! He knew every mound and curve, every bush and tree. Could it be possible that in one short year, and less, so much had happened?

He pulled himself together after a few moments, and knocked at the door again. William Jenkins started and looked confused when he saw Ralph standing before him, for he had never been able to shake off an uneasy feeling that he had not done a kind and neighbourly thing when he took Hillside Farm over David Penlogan's head, even though Sir John's agent had pressed him to do so.

Ralph plunged into the object of his visit after a kindly greeting.

"I hear you are letting out your hay crop to be cut," he said, "and I came across to see if I could get the job."

"I did not know you were out of work," Jenkins said uneasily.

"I'm not," Ralph answered. "But I want to put in a little overtime these long days. Besides, you know I'm used to farm work."

"But if you work only overtime it will take you a long time to get down the crop."

"Oh, not so long. It's light till nearly ten o'clock. Besides, we're in for a spell of fine weather, and a day or two longer won't make any difference."

"The usual price per acre, I suppose?" the farmer questioned, after a pause.

"Well, I presume nobody would be inclined to take less," Ralph said, with a laugh.

The farmer dived his hands into his pockets, contemplated the evening sky for several minutes, took two or three long strides down the garden path and back again, cleared his throat once or twice, and then he said—

"Will waant yer money, 'spose, when the job's done?"

"Unless you prefer to pay in advance."

The farmer grinned, and dug a hole into the ground with his heel.

"There ain't too much money to be made out of this place, I'm thinkin'," he said at length.

"Not at the price you suggest," Ralph said, with a twinkle in his eye.

The farmer grinned again.

"I didn't main it that way," he said, digging another hole in the gravel. "I was thinkin' of myself. The farm ain't as good as I took it to be."

"But it will mend every year."

"Ef it don't I shall wish I never see'd it. The crops are lookin' only very middlin', I can assure 'ee."

"Sorry to hear that. But what about the hay-field?"

"I 'spose you've got a scythe?"

"I can get one, in any case."

"Well, 'spose we say done!" And Jenkins contemplated the evening sky again with considerable interest.

Afterwards Ralph wished that he had found work for his spare time almost anywhere rather than on Hillside Farm. There was not a single thing that did not remind him in some way of the past. He would raise his head unconsciously, expecting to see his father working by his side. The flutter of Mrs. Jenkins' print dress in the garden would cause the word "mother" to leap to his lips unbidden, and when the daylight faded, and the moon began to peep over the hill, he would turn his face towards the house, fancying that Ruth was calling him to supper.

He finished the task at length, and dropped his hard-earned silver into his pocket.

"It'll be a dear crop of hay for me, I'm thinkin'," Jenkins said lugubriously.

"It isn't so heavy as it might be," Ralph answered. "A damp spring suits

Hillside best."

"I sometimes wish your father had it instead of me." And Jenkins twisted his shoulders uncomfortably.

"Father is better off," Ralph answered slowly, looking across the valley to a distant line of hills.

"Ay, it's to be hoped so, for there ain't much better off here, I'm thinkin'. It's mostly worse off. And as we get owlder we feel it more 'n more."

"So you regret taking the farm already?" Ralph questioned almost unconsciously.

"I ded'n say so. We've got to make a livin' somehow, leastways we've got to try." And he turned suddenly round and walked into the house.

Ralph walked across the fields to interview Peter Ladock, whose farm adjoined. He struck the boundary hedge at a point where a gnarled and twisted oak made a feature in the landscape. Half-way over the hedge he paused abruptly. This was the point his father had asked him to keep in his memory, and yet until this moment he had never once thought of it.

Not that it mattered: the county was intersected with tin lodes, iron lodes, copper lodes, and lead lodes, and most of them would not pay for the working. And very likely this lode, if it existed—for, after all, his father had had very little opportunity of demonstrating its existence—would turn out to be no better than the rest.

For a moment he paused to draw an imaginary line to the chimney-top, as his father had instructed him, then he sprang off the hedge into Ladock's field and made his way towards his house. Peter, who knew his man, agreed to pay Ralph by the hour, and he could work as many hours as he liked.

To one less strong and healthy than Ralph it would have been killing work; but he did not seem to take any harm. Once a week came Sunday, and during that day he seemed to regain all that he had lost. Fortunately, too, during harvest-time the farmers provided extra food. There was "crowst" between meals, and supper when they worked extra late.

No sooner was the hay crop out of the way than the oats and barley began to whiten in the sunshine, and then the wheat began to bend its head before the sickle.

Ralph quadrupled his savings during the months of June, July, and August, and before September was out he had taken a cottage and begun to furnish it.

Bice had a few things left that once belonged to his mother and father. Ralph pounced upon them greedily, and bought them cheaply from the assistant

147

when Bice was out.

On the first Saturday afternoon he had at liberty he went to St. Hilary to interview his sister. Ruth was on the look-out for him. She had got the afternoon off, and was eager to look into his eyes again. It was nearly three months since she had seen him.

She met him with a glad smile and eyes that were brimful of happy tears.

"How well you look," she said, looking up into his strong, sunburnt face. "I was afraid you were working yourself to death."

"No fear of that," he said, with a laugh; "it is not work that kills, you know, but worry."

"And you are not worrying?" she asked.

"Not now," he answered. "I think I'm fairly started, and, with hard work and economy, there is no reason why we should not jog along comfortably together."

"And you are still of the same mind about my keeping house for you?"

"Why, what a question! As if I would stay a day longer in 'diggings' than I could help."

"Are you not comfortable?" she questioned, glancing anxiously up into his face.

"Yes, when at work or asleep."

"There is still another question," she said at length, with a smile.

"And that?"

"You may want to get married some time, and then I shall be in the way."

He laughed boisterously for a moment, and then his face grew grave.

"I shall never marry," he said at length. "At least, that is my present conviction."

She regarded him narrowly for a moment, and wondered. There came a look into his eyes which she could not understand—a far-away, pathetic look, such as is seen in the eyes of those who have loved and lost.

Ruth was curious. Being a woman, she could not help it. Who was there in St. Goram likely to touch her brother's fancy? Young men who have never been in love often talk freely about getting married.

She changed the subject a few minutes later, and carefully watched the effect of her words.

"I suppose nothing has been heard in St. Goram of Miss Dorothy?"

"No," he said hurriedly. "Have you heard anything?" And he looked at her with eager eyes, while the colour deepened on his cheeks.

"I am not in the way of hearing St. Goram news," she said, with a smile.

He drew in his breath sharply, and turned away his eyes, and for several minutes neither of them spoke again.

Ruth began unconsciously to put two and two together. She had heard of such things—read of them in books. Fate was often very cruel to the most deserving. Unlikelier things had happened. Dorothy was exceedingly pretty, and since her accident she had revealed traits of character that scarcely anyone suspected before. Ralph had been thrown into very close contact at the most impressionable part of his life. He had succoured her when she was hurt, carried her in his arms all the way from Treliskey Plantation to the cross roads. Nor was that all. She had discovered him after his accident, and when the doctor arrived on the scene, he was lying with his head on her lap.

If he had learned to love her, it might not be strange, but it would be an infinite pity, all the same. The cruel irony of it would be too sad for words. Of course, he would get over it in time. The contempt he felt for Sir John, the difference in their social position, and last, but not least, the fact that she had been effectually banished from Hamblyn Manor, and that there was no likelihood of their meeting again, would all help him to put her out of his heart and out of his life. Nevertheless, if her surmise was correct, that Dorothy Hamblyn had stolen his heart, she could quite understand him saying that he did not intend to marry.

"Poor Ralph!" she said to herself, with a sigh. And then she began to talk about the things that would be needed in their new home.

Ruth had saved almost the whole of her nine months' wages, which, added to what Ralph had saved, made quite a respectable sum. To lay it out to the best advantage might not be easy. She wanted so many things that he saw no necessity for, while he wanted things that she pronounced impossible.

On the whole, however, they had a very happy time in spending their savings and getting the little cottage in order. Everything, of course, was of the cheapest and simplest. They attended most of the auction sales within a radius of half a dozen miles, and some very useful things they got for almost nothing.

Both of them were in the best of spirits. Ruth looked forward with great eagerness to the time of her release from service; not that she was overworked, while nobody could be kinder to her than her mistress.

Nevertheless, a sense of servitude pressed upon her constantly. She had lived all her life before in such an atmosphere of freedom, and had pictured for herself a future so absolutely different, that it was not easy to accommodate herself to the straitened ways of service.

Ralph was weary of "diggings," and was literally pining for a home of his own. He had endured for six months, because he had been lodged and boarded cheap. He had shown no impatience while nothing better was in sight, but when the cottage was actually taken, and some items of furniture had been moved into it, he began to count the days till he should take full possession.

He went to bed, to dream of soft pillows and clean sheets, and dainty meals daintily served; of a bright hearth, and an easy-chair in which he might rest comfortably when the long evenings came; of a sweet face that should sit opposite to him; and, above all, of quietness from the noisy strife of quarrelsome and unruly children.

Ruth returned from St. Hilary on the first of October—a rich, mellow day, when all the earth seemed to float in a golden haze. William Menire discovered that he had business in St. Hilary that day, and that it would be quite convenient for him to bring Ruth and her boxes in his trap. He put the matter so delicately that Ruth could not very well refuse.

It was a happy day for William when he drove through St. Goram with Ruth sitting by his side, and a happy day for Ruth when she alighted at the garden gate of their little cottage, and caught the light of a new hope in her brother's eyes.

It was a fresh start for them both, but to what it might lead they did not know —nor even desire to know.

CHAPTER XXIII

THE ROAD TO FORTUNE

No sooner had Ralph got settled in his new home than his brain began to work with renewed energy and vigour. He began making experiments again in all sorts of things. He built a rough shed at the back of the cottage, and turned it into a laboratory. He spent all his spare time in trying to reduce some of his theories to practice.

Moreover, he got impatient of the slow monotony of day labour. He did not grumble at the wages. Possibly he was paid as much as he deserved, but he did chafe at the horse-in-the-mill kind of existence. To do the same kind of thing day after day, and feel that an elephant or even an ass might be trained to do it just as well, was from his point of view humiliating. He wanted scope for the play of other faculties. He was not a mule, with so much physical strength that might be paid for at so much per hour; he was a man, with brains and intelligence and foresight. So he began to look round him for some other kind of work, and finally he took a small contract which kept him and three men he employed busy for two months, and left him at the end twenty-eight shillings and ninepence poorer than if he had stuck to his day labour.

He was nothing daunted, however. Indeed, he was a good deal encouraged. He was afraid at one time that he would come out of his contract in debt. He worked considerably more hours than when he was a day labourer, and he was inclined to think that he worked considerably harder, and there was less money at the end; but he was far happier because he was infinitely more interested.

Ruth, who had been educated in a school of the strictest economy, managed to make both ends meet, and with that she was quite content. She had great faith in her brother. She liked to see him busy with his experiments. It kept him out of mischief, if nothing else. But that was not all. She believed in his ultimate success. In what direction she did not know, but he was not commonplace and humdrum. He was not willing to jog along in the same ruts from year's end to year's end without knowing the reason why. She rejoiced in his impatience and discontent, for she recognised that there was something worthy and even heroic behind. Discontent under certain circumstances and conditions might be noble—almost divine. She wished sometimes that she had more of his spirit.

She never uttered a word of complaint if he gave her less money to keep house upon, never hinted that his experiments were too expensive luxuries for their means. Something would grow out of his enterprise and enthusiasm by and by. He had initiative and vision and judgment, and such qualities she felt sure were bound to tell in the end.

When Ralph had finished his first contract he took a second, and did better by it. He learned by experience, as all wise men do, and gathered confidence in himself as the result.

With the advent of spring rumours got into circulation that a large and wealthy company had been formed for the purpose of developing Perranpool.

A few years previously it had been only a fishing village, distinguished mainly for the quality of its pilchards. But some London journalist, who during a holiday time spent a few days there, took it into his head to turn an honest penny by writing a friendly article about it. It is to be presumed he meant all he said, for he said a great deal that many people wondered at. But, in any case, the article was well written and was widely quoted from.

The result was that the following year nearly every fisherman's wife had to turn lodging-house keeper, and not being spoiled by contact with the ordinary tripper, these worthy men and women made their visitors comfortable with but small profit to themselves.

The next year a still larger number of people came, for they had heard that Perranpool was not only secluded and salubrious, but also remarkably cheap.

That was the beginning of Perranpool's fame. Every year more and more people came to enjoy its sunshine and build sand-castles on its beach. Houses sprang up like mushrooms, most of them badly built, and all of them entirely hideous. A coach service was established between it and the nearest railway station, a company was formed for the purpose of supplying gas at a maximum charge for a minimum candle-power, while another company brought water from a distance, so rich in microbes that the marvel was that anyone drank it and lived.

Since then things have further improved. A branch railway has been constructed, and two or three large hotels have been built, a Local Board has been formed, and the rates have been quadrupled. A "Town Band" plays during the season an accompaniment to the song the wild waves sing, and the picturesque sea-front has given place to an asphalted promenade. At the time of which we write, however, the promenade existed only in imagination, and some of the older houses were threatened by the persistently encroaching sea.

So a company was formed for the purpose of building a breakwater and a pier, and for the purpose of developing a large tract of land it had acquired along the sea-front, and tenders were invited for the carrying out of certain specified work.

None of the tenders, however, were accepted. There was no stone in the neighbourhood fit for the purpose, and to bring granite from the distant quarries meant an expense that was not to be thought of. The directors of the company began to feel sick. The debenture holders were eating up the capital, and the ordinary shareholders were clamouring for a dividend, while the sea threatened to eat up the land.

Meanwhile Ralph Penlogan had been looking at a huge heap of gravel and mica and blue clay which had been accumulating during three generations on the side of a hill some two or three miles inland. Every day and all the year round men pushed out small trucks and tipped their contents over the brow of this huge barrow. Every year the great heap extended its base, engulfing hedges and meadows and even plantations. There was no value in this waste whatever. In fact, it involved the company in a loss, for they had to pay for the land it continued to engulf. Anyone who liked to cart away a few loads for the purpose of gravelling his garden-path was at liberty to do so. The company would have been grateful if the whole mass of it could have been carted into the sea.

Ralph got a wheelbarrowful of the stuff and experimented with it. Then he wrote to the chairman of the company and asked permission to use some of the waste heap for building purposes—a permission which was at once granted. In fact, the chairman intimated that the more he could use the more he—the chairman—and his co-directors would be pleased.

Ralph's next step was to interview a local contractor who was very anxious to build the new sea-wall and pier. The result of that interview was that the contractor sent in a fresh tender, not to build the wall of granite, but with a newly discovered concrete, which could be manufactured at a very small cost, and which would serve the purposes of the company even better than granite itself.

Ralph registered his invention or discovery, got his concession from the Brick, Tile, and Clay Company into the best legal form possible, and then commenced operations.

Telfer, the contractor, who was delighted with the quality of the concrete, financed Ralph at the start, and helped him in every way in his power.

The Perranpool Pier and Land Company, after testing the new material in every way known to them, accepted Telfer's tender, and the great work was commenced forthwith.

In a couple of months Ralph had as many men at work as he had room for. Telfer had laid a light tram-line down the valley, and as fast as the blocks were manufactured they were run down to Perranpool.

Ralph was in high spirits. Having the material for nothing, and water in abundance, he was able to manufacture his concrete even cheaper than he had calculated. In fact, his profits were so good that he increased the wages of his hands all round, and got more work out of them in consequence.

Robert Telfer, however, who was much more of a man of the world than Ralph, was by no means satisfied with the condition of affairs. He foresaw contingencies that never occurred to the younger man.

"Look here," he said to Ralph one day, "you ought to turn out much more stuff than you are doing."

"Impossible," Ralph answered. "I have so many men at work that they are getting in each other's way as it is."

"But why not double your shifts? Let one lot get in at six and break off at two, and the second come in at two and leave off at ten."

"I never thought of that," Ralph answered.

"Well, you take my advice. There's an old proverb, you know, about making hay while the sun shines."

"But the sun will shine as long as you take my concrete."

"Don't be too sure of that."

"How?" Ralph said, glancing up with questioning eyes.

"The raw material may give out."

Ralph laughed.

"Why, there's stuff enough to last a hundred years," he said.

"That may be; but don't be too sure that you will be allowed to use it."

"Do you mean to suggest that the company will attempt to go behind their agreement?"

"More unlikely things have happened."

"Then you have heard something?"

"Nothing very definite. But some of the shareholders are angry at seeing you make money."

"But the stuff has been lying waste for generations, and accumulating year by year. They rather gain than lose by letting me use it up."

"But some of them are asking why they cannot use it themselves."

"Well, let them if they know how."

"You have patented your discovery?"

"I have tried, but our patent laws are an outrage."

"Exactly. And, after all, there's not much mystery in concrete."

"Well?" he said, in a tone of inquiry.

"Well, before you are aware you may have competition, or, as I said just now, the raw material may run out."

"I cannot conceive that honourable men will try to go behind their promise."

"As individuals, no; but you are dealing with a company."

"Well, what is the difference?"

Mr. Telfer laughed.

"There ought to be no difference, I grant. Nevertheless, you will find out as you grow older that companies and corporations and committees will do what as single individuals they would never dream of doing. When men are associated with a hundred others, the sense of individual responsibility disappears. Companies or corporations have neither souls nor consciences. You, as an individual, would not settle a dispute with a revolver, or at the point of a sword. Possibly you think duelling a crime, yet as a member of a community or nation you would possibly applaud an appeal to arms in any quarrel affecting our material interests."

"Possibly I should," Ralph answered, looking thoughtful.

"Then you see what I am driving at?"

"And you advise making the most of my opportunity?"

"I do most certainly. I don't deny I may be selfish in this. I want as much of the stuff as I can buy at the present price. Nobody else can make it as cheaply as you are doing."

"Why not?"

"First, because you are on good terms with your men, and are getting the most out of them. Second, because you have no expenses to pay—that is, you have no salaries to pay or directors to fee."

"I'll think about it," Ralph said, and the interview came to an end.

155

A week later he doubled his shift. He had no difficulty in getting men, for the pay was good and the work was in the open air, and in no sense of the word dangerous.

He was on the spot nearly all the time himself. He left nothing to chance. He delegated none of his own work to other people. Ruth saw very little of him; he was off over the hill early in the morning, and he did not return home till late at night.

She understood he was prospering, but his prosperity made no difference to their style of living. He was too fully occupied to think of anything but his work, and too much of a man to be spoiled by a few months of success.

He had taken Mr. Telfer's advice, and was doubling his output, but he was still of opinion that no attempt would be made to get behind the concession that had been granted to him by the Brick, Tile, and Clay Company.

As the days passed away and grew into weeks and months, and he heard nothing from the chairman or any of the directors, or of any investigation, he was more than ever convinced that Mr. Telfer's fears were entirely without foundation.

It might be quite true that individual shareholders rather resented his making money out of stuff that they threw away as waste. But, on the whole, as far as he was able to judge, people appeared rather to rejoice that the tide had turned in his favour. He had thought rather hard things of some of his neighbours at one time, and it was still true that they were more friendly disposed towards him in his prosperity than in his adversity, but, on the whole, they were genuine, good-hearted people, and none of them appeared to envy him his little bit of success.

Sometimes William Menire took himself to task for not rejoicing as heartily in Ralph's success as he felt he ought to do. But William had a feeling that the more the Penlogans prospered the farther they would get away from him. He pictured to himself, almost with a shudder, a time when they would go to live in a big house and keep servants, and perhaps drive their own carriage; while he, as a village shopkeeper, might be allowed to call round at their back door for orders.

If they remained poor, he might still help them in trifling things and in unnoticeable ways; might continue on visiting terms with them; might have the pleasure now and then of looking into Ruth's honest eyes; might even reckon himself among their friends.

But if they prospered, the whole world might be changed for him. Not that he ever cherished any foolish hopes, or indulged in impossible dreams. Had he been ten years younger, without a mother to keep, dreams of love and matrimony might have floated before his vision. But now——Well, such dreams were not for him.

This is what he told himself constantly, and yet the dreams came back in spite of everything.

So the weeks and months slipped rapidly and imperceptibly away, and everybody said that Ralph Penlogan was a lucky fellow, and that he had struck a vein that was bound to lead on to fortune.

But, meanwhile, directors had been arguing, and almost fighting, and lawyers had been putting their heads together, and counsel's opinion had been taken, and the power of the purse had been measured and discussed, and even religious people had debated the question as to how far a promise should be allowed to stand in the way of their material interests, and whether even a legal obligation might not be evaded if there was a chance of doing it.

Unfortunately for Ralph, time had allayed all his suspicions, so that when the blow fell, it found him unprepared, in spite of his consultation with Mr. Telfer.

CHAPTER XXIV

LAW AND LIFE

"Promises, like piecrust, are made to be broken," so runs the proverb, and the average man repeats it without a touch of cynicism in his tones. If you can keep your promise without loss or inconvenience to yourself, then do it by all means; but if you cannot, invent some excuse and get out of it. Most men place their material interests before everything else. "Seek ye first the kingdom of God and His righteousness," is a saying that few people regard to-day. The children of this age think they have found a more excellent way. "Seek ye first the kingdom of this world and the policy thereof," is the popular philosophy.

Lawyers and statesmen are busily engaged in taking the "nots" out of the Ten Commandments and putting them into the Sermon on the Mount, and this not only in their own interests, but chiefly in the interests of rich clients and millionaire trusts. "The race is not to the swift, nor the battle to the strong," says the Bible. The modern method of interpretation is to take the "not" out. It makes sense out of nonsense, say the children of this world; for anyone with half an eye can see that the "not" must have crept in by mistake, for the race is to the swift, and the strong always win the battle.

"The meek shall inherit the earth," said the Teacher of Nazareth; but the modern interpreter, with the map of the world spread out before him, shakes his head. There is evidently something wrong somewhere. Possibly there is exactly the right number of "nots" in the Bible, but they have been wrongly distributed.

"The meek shall inherit the earth"? Look at England. Look at South Africa. Look at the United States. The meek shall inherit the earth? Take a "not" out of the Ten Commandments, where there are several too many, and put it into the gap, then you have a statement that is in harmony with the general experience of the world.

When Ralph received a polite note from the chairman of the Brick, Tile, and Clay Company, that from that date his directors would no longer hold themselves bound by the terms of the concession they had made, he felt that he might as well retire first as last from the scene; and, but for Mr. Telfer, he would have done so.

Mr. Telfer's contention was that he had a good point in law, and that it would be cowardly "to fling up the sponge" without a legal decision.

Ralph smiled and shook his head.

"I have no respect for what you call the law," he said, a little bitterly. "I have tasted its quality, and want no more of it."

"But what is the law for, except to preserve our rights?" Mr. Telfer demanded.

"Whose rights?" Ralph questioned.

"Why, your rights and mine, and everybody's."

Ralph shook his head again.

"I fear I have no rights," he said.

"No rights?" Mr. Telfer demanded hotly.

"Put it to yourself," Ralph said quietly. "What rights has a poor man; or, if he thinks he has, what chance has he of defending them if they are threatened by the rich and powerful?"

"But is not justice the heritage of the poor?" Mr. Telfer asked.

"In theory it is so, no doubt; but not in practice. To get justice in these days, you must spend a fortune in lawyers' fees—and probably you won't get it then. But the poor have no fortune to spend."

"I'll admit that going to law is a very expensive business; but what is one to do?"

"Grin and abide."

"Oh, but that is cowardly!"

"It may be so. And yet, I do not see much heroism in running your head against a stone wall."

"But is it manly to sit down quietly and be robbed?"

"That all depends on who the robbers are. If there are ten to one, I should say it would be the wisest policy to submit."

"I admit that the company is a powerful one. But it is a question with me whether they have any right to the stuff at all. Their sett extends from the line of Cowley's farm westward; but their tip has come a quarter of a mile eastward. For years past they have had to pay for the right of tipping their waste. In point of law, it isn't their stuff at all. It isn't even on their land—the land belongs to Daniel Rickard."

"That may be quite true," Ralph answered; "but I can't think that will help us very much."

"Why not?"

"Because I heard this morning they were negotiating with Daniel for the purchase of his little freehold."

Mr. Telfer looked grave.

"In any case," he said, "I would get counsel's opinion. Why not run up to London and consult Sir John Liskeard? He is our member, you know, and in your case his charge would not be excessive. You can afford to spend something to know where you stand. I believe in dying game." And with a wave of his hand, Mr. Telfer marched away.

Two days later Ralph got a second letter from the chairman of the Brick, Tile, and Clay Company which was much less conciliatory in tone. In fact, it intimated, in language too plain to be misunderstood, that the company held him guilty of trespass, and that by continuing his work after the previous intimation he was rendering himself liable to an action at law.

Ralph toiled over the fields towards his home in a brown study. That the letter was only bluff he knew, but it seemed clear enough that if he resisted, the company was determined to fight the case in a court of law.

What to do for the best he could not decide. To fight the case would probably ruin him, for even if he won, he would have to spend all his savings in law expenses. To throw up the sponge at the outset would certainly look cowardly. The only other alternative would be to try to make terms with the company, to acknowledge their right, and to offer to pay for every ton of stuff he used.

When he got home he found Mary Telfer keeping his sister company. Mary had been a good deal at the cottage lately. Ruth liked her to come; they had a great deal in common, and appeared to be exceedingly fond of each other. Mary was a bright, pleasant-faced girl of about Ralph's age. She was not clever—she made no pretension in that direction; but she was cheerful and good-tempered and domesticated. Moreover, as the only child of Robert Telfer, the contractor, she was regarded as an heiress in a small way.

Ruth sometimes wondered whether, in the economy of nature, Mary might not be her brother's best friend. Ralph would want a wife some day. She did not believe in men remaining bachelors. They were much more happy, much more useful, and certainly much less selfish when they had a wife and family to maintain.

Nor was that all; she had strong reasons for believing that Ralph had been smitten with a hopeless passion for Dorothy Hamblyn. She did not blame him in the least. Dorothy was so pretty and so winsome that it was perhaps inevitable under the circumstances. But the pity of it and the tragedy of it were none the less on that account. Hence, anything that would help him in his struggle to forget was to be welcomed. For that Ralph was honestly trying to put Dorothy Hamblyn out of his memory and out of his heart, she fully believed.

For months now he had never mentioned the squire or his "little maid." Now and then Ruth would repeat the gossip that was floating about St. Goram, but if he took any interest in it, he made no sign.

Dorothy had never once come back since she was sent away. Whether she was still at school, or had become a nun, or was living with friends, no one appeared to know. Sir John kept his own counsel, and politely snubbed all inquisitive persons.

That Sir John was in a tight corner was universally believed. He had reduced his household to about one-third its previous dimensions, had dismissed half his gardeners and gamekeepers, had sold his hunters, and in several other ways was practising the strictest economy. All this implied that financially he was hard up.

He got no sympathy, however, except from a few people of his own class. He had been such a hard landlord, so ready to take every mean advantage, so quick in raising rents, so slow in reducing them, that when he began to have meted out to him what he had so long meted out to others, there was rejoicing rather than sympathy.

Ralph naturally could not help hearing the talk of the neighbourhood, but he made no comment. Whether he was glad or sorry no one knew. As a matter of fact, he hardly knew himself. For Sir John he had no sympathy. He could see him starve without a pang. But there was another who loved him, who would share his sufferings and be humbled in his humiliation, and for her he was sorry. So he refused to discuss the squire's affairs, either with Ruth or anyone else. He was fighting a hard battle—how hard no one knew but himself. He did his best to avoid everything that would remind him of Dorothy, did his best in every way to forget her. Sometimes he found himself longing with an inexpressible desire for a sight of her face, and yet on the whole he was exceedingly grateful that she did not return to St. Goram. Time and distance had done something. She was not so constantly in his thoughts as she used to be. He was not always on the look-out for her, and he never started now, fancying it was her face he saw in the distance; and yet he was by no means confident that he would ever gain the victory.

If he never saw her in his waking moments she came to him constantly in his dreams. And, curiously enough, in his dreams there was never any barrier to their happiness. In dreamland social distinctions did not exist, and hard and

161

tyrannical fathers were unknown. In dreamland happy lovers went their own way unhindered and undisturbed. In dreamland it was always springtime, and sickness and old age were never heard of. So if memory were subdued in the daytime, night restored the balance. Dorothy lived in his heart in spite of every effort to put her away.

The sight of Mary Telfer's pleasant and smiling face on the evening in question was a pleasant relief after the worries and annoyances of the day. Mary was brimful of vivacity and good-humour, and Ralph quickly caught the contagion of her cheerful temper.

She knew all the gossip of the neighbourhood, and retailed it with great verve and humour. Ralph laughed at some of the incidents she narrated until the tears ran down his face.

Then suddenly her mood changed, and she wanted to know if Ralph was going to fight the Brick, Tile, and Clay Company.

"What would you do if you were in my place?" Ralph questioned, with a touch of banter in his voice.

"Fight to the last gasp," she answered.

"And what after that?"

"Oh, that is a question I should never ask myself."

"Then you don't believe in looking far ahead?"

"What's the use? If you look far enough you'll see a tombstone, and that's not cheerful."

"Then you'd fight without considering how the battle might end?"

"Why not? If you are fighting for principle and right, you have to risk the cost and the consequences."

"But to go to war without counting the cost is not usually considered good statesmanship."

"Oh, isn't it? Well, you see, I'm not a statesman—I'm only a woman. But if I were a man I wouldn't let a set of bullies triumph over me."

"But how could you help it if they were stronger than you?"

"At any rate, I'd let them prove they were stronger before I gave in."

"Then you don't believe that discretion is the better part of valour?"

"No, I don't. Not only isn't it the better part of valour, it isn't any part of valour. Besides, we are commanded to resist the devil."

"Then you think the Brick, Tile, and Clay Company is the devil?"

"I think it is doing the devil's work, and such meanness and wickedness ought to be exposed and resisted. What's the world coming to if gentlemen go back on their own solemn promises?"

"It's very sad, no doubt," Ralph said, with a smile. "But, you see, they are a hundred to one, and, however much right I may have on my side, in the long-run I shall have to go under."

"Then you have no faith in justice?"

"Not in the justice of the strong."

"But if you have the law on your side you are bound to win."

He laughed good-humouredly.

"Did you ever know any law," he said, "that was not in the interests of the rich and powerful?"

"I never gave the matter a thought," she answered.

"If you had to spend a month in prison with nothing particular to do," he laughed, "you would give more thought to the matter than it is worth."

She laughed heartily at that, and then the subject dropped.

A little later in the evening, when they were seated at the supper-table, Ruth remarked—

"Mary Telfer is like a ray of sunshine in the house."

"Is she always bright?" Ralph questioned indifferently.

"Always. I have never seen her out of temper or depressed yet."

"Very likely she has nothing to try her," he suggested.

"It's not only that, it's her nature to be cheerful and optimistic. He'll be a fortunate man who marries her."

"Is she going to be married soon?"

"Not that I'm aware of," Ruth answered, looking up with a start. "I don't think she's even engaged."

"Oh, I beg pardon. I thought you meant——"

"I was only speaking generally," Ruth interrupted. "Mary Telfer, in my judgment, is a girl in a thousand—bright, cheerful, domesticated, and—and ——"

"Gilt-edged?" Ralph suggested.

"Well, she will not be penniless."

That night as Ralph lay awake he recalled his conversation with Ruth, and almost heard in fancy the bright, rippling laughter of Mary Telfer; and for the first time a thought flashed across his mind which grew bigger and bigger as the days and weeks passed away.

Would it be possible to put Dorothy Hamblyn out of his heart by trying to put another in her place? Would the beauty of her face fade from his memory if he constantly looked upon another face? Would he forget her if he trained himself to think continually of someone else?

These were questions that he could not answer right off, but there might be no harm in making the experiment—at least, there might be no harm to himself, but what about Mary?

So he found himself faced by a number of questions at the same time, and for none of them could he find a satisfactory answer.

Then came an event in his life which he anticipated with a curious thrill of excitement, and that was a journey to London. He almost shrank from the enterprise at first. He had heard and read so much about London—about its bigness, its crowds, its bewildering miles of streets, its awful loneliness, its temptations and dangers, its squalor and luxury, its penury and extravagance —that he was half afraid he might be sucked up as by a mighty tide, and lost.

There seemed, however, no other course open to him. He had tried to come to terms with the Brick, Tile, and Clay Company, had offered to pay them a royalty on all the stuff he manufactured, to purchase from them all the raw material he used. But every offer, every suggestion of a compromise, was met with a stern and emphatic negative.

So he decided to take Mr. Telfer's advice, and consult Sir John Liskeard. In order to do this he would have to make a journey to London. How big with fate that journey was he little guessed at the time.

———————————————

CHAPTER XXV

IN LONDON TOWN

Ralph remained in London considerably longer than he had intended. Sir John Liskeard was a very busy man, and the questions raised by Ralph required time to consider. The equity of the case was simple and straightforward enough; the law was quite another matter. Moreover, as Sir John had been asked to give not merely a legal opinion, but some friendly advice, the relative strength of the litigants had to be taken into account.

Sir John was anxious to do his best for his young client. Ralph appeared to be a coming man in the division he represented in Parliament, and as Sir John's majority on the last election was only a narrow one, he was naturally anxious to do all he could to strengthen his position in the constituency. Hence he received Ralph very graciously, got him a seat under the gallery during an important debate in the House of Commons, took him to tea on the Terrace, pointed out to him most of the political celebrities who happened to be in attendance at the House, and introduced him to a few whom Ralph was particularly anxious to meet.

Fresh from the country and from the humdrum of village life, with palate unjaded and all his enthusiasms at the full, this was a peculiarly delightful experience. It was pleasant to meet men in the flesh whom he had read about in books and newspapers, pleasant to breathe—if only for an hour—a new atmosphere, charged with a subtle energy he could not define.

Of course, there were painful disillusionments. Some noted people—in appearance, at any rate—fell far short of his expectations. Great men rose in the House to speak, and stuttered and spluttered the weakest and emptiest platitudes. Honourables and right honourables and noble lords appeared, in many instances, to be made of very common clay.

Ralph found himself wondering, as many another man has done, as he sat watching and listening, by what curious or fatuous fate some of these men in the gathering ever climbed into their exalted positions.

He put the question to Sir John when he had an opportunity.

"Most of them do not climb at all," was the laughing answer. "They are simply pitchforked."

"But surely it is merit that wins in a place like this?"

Sir John laughed again.

"In some cases, no doubt. For instance, you see that short, thick-set man yonder. Well, he's one of the most effective speakers in the House. A few years ago he was a working shoemaker. Then you see that white-headed man yonder, with large forehead and deep, sad-looking eyes. Well, he was a village schoolmaster for thirty years, and now he is acknowledged to be one of the ablest men we have. Then there is Blank, in the corner seat there below the gangway, a most brilliant fellow—a farmer's son, without any early advantages at all. But I don't suppose that either of them will ever get into office, or into what you call an exalted position."

"But why not?"

"Ah, well"—and Sir John shrugged his shoulders—"you see, the ruling classes in this country belong to—well, to the ruling classes."

"But I thought ours was a purely democratic form of government?"

"It is. But the democracy dearly love a lord. They have no faith in their own order. The ruling classes have; so they remain the ruling classes. And who can blame them?"

"Still, when so much is at stake, the best men ought to be at the head of affairs."

"Possibly they are—that is, the best available men. Tradition goes for a good deal in a country like this. Certain positions are filled, as a matter of course, by people of rank. An historic name counts for a good deal."

"But suppose the bearer of the historic name should happen to be a fool?"

"Oh, well, we muddle through somehow. Get an extra war or two, perhaps, and an addition to the taxes and to the national debt. But we are a patient people, and don't mind very much. Besides, the majority of the people are easily gulled."

"Then promotion goes by favour?" Ralph questioned after a pause.

"Why, of course it does. Did you ever doubt it? Take the case of the Imperial Secretary. Does any sane man in England, irrespective of creed or party, imagine for a moment that he would have got into that position if he had not been the nephew of a duke?"

"But isn't he a capable man?"

"Capable?"—and Sir John shrugged his shoulders again. "Why, if he had to depend on his own merits he wouldn't earn thirty shillings a week in any business house in the City."

Ralph walked away from the House of Commons with a curious feeling of elation and disappointment. He had been greatly delighted in some respects, and terribly disappointed in others.

In St. James's Park he sat down in the shadow of a large chestnut tree and tried to sort out his emotions. He had been in London three days, but had scarcely got his bearings yet. Everything was very new, very strange, and very wonderful. On the whole, he thought he would be very glad to get away from it. It seemed to him the loneliest place on earth. On every side there was the ceaseless roar of traffic, like the breaking of the sea, and yet there was not a friendly face or a familiar voice anywhere in all the throng.

Suddenly he started and leaned eagerly forward. That was a familiar face, surely, and a familiar voice. Two people passed close to where he sat—a young man and a young woman. Her skirts almost brushed his boots; her sunshade—which she was swinging—came within an inch of his hand.

Dorothy Hamblyn! The words leapt to his lips unconsciously, but he did not utter them. She passed on brightly—joyously, it seemed to him, but she was quite unaware of his presence. In the main, her eyes were fixed on the young man by her side—a slim, faultlessly dressed young man, with pale face, retreating chin, and a bored expression in his eyes.

Ralph rose to his feet and followed them. His heart was beating fast, his knees trembled in spite of himself, his brain was in a whirl. What he purposed doing or where he purposed going never occurred to him. He simply followed a sudden impulse, whether it led to his undoing or not.

He kept them in sight until they reached Hyde Park Corner. Then the crowd swallowed them up for several moments. But he caught sight of them again on the other side and followed them into the Park. For several minutes he had considerable difficulty in disentangling them from the crowd of people that hurried to and fro, but a large white plume Dorothy wore in her hat assisted him. They came to a full stop at length, and sat down on a couple of chairs. He discovered an empty chair on the other side of the road, and sat down opposite.

He was near enough to see her features distinctly, near enough to see the light sparkle in her eyes, but not near enough to hear anything she said. That, however, did not matter. He was content for the moment to look at her. He wanted nothing better.

How beautiful she was! She was no longer the squire's "little maid," she was a woman now. Nearly two years had passed since he last saw her, and those years had ripened all her charms and rounded them into perfection.

He could look his fill without being observed. If she cast her eyes in his direction she would not recognise him—probably she had forgotten his existence.

His nerves were still thrilling with a strange ecstasy. His eyes drank in greedily every line and curve and expression of her face. In all this great London there was no other face, he was sure, that could compare with it, no other smile that was half so sweet.

She rose at length, slowly and with seeming reluctance, to her feet. Her companion at once sprang to her side. Ralph rose also, and faced them. Why he did so he did not know. He was still following a blind and unreasoning impulse. She paused for a moment or two and looked steadfastly in his direction, then turned and quickly walked away, and a moment later was swallowed up in the multitude.

Ralph took one step forward, then turned back and sat down with a jerk. He had come to himself at last.

"Well, I have played the fool with a vengeance," he muttered to himself. "I have just pulled down all I have been trying for the last two years to build up."

The next moment he was unconscious of his surroundings again. Crowds of people passed and re-passed, but he saw one face only, the face that had never ceased to haunt him since the hour when, in her bright, imperious way, she commanded him to open the gate.

How readily and vividly he recalled every incident of that afternoon. He felt her arms about his neck even now. He was hurrying across the downs once more in the direction of St. Goram. His heart was thrilling with a new sensation.

He came to himself again after a while and sauntered slowly out of the Park. Beauty and wealth and fashion jostled him on every side, but it was a meaningless show to him. Had Ruth been with him she would have gone into ecstasies over the hats and dresses, for such creations were never seen in St. Goram, nor even dreamed of.

Men have to be educated to appreciate the splendours and glories of feminine attire, and, generally speaking, the education is a slow and disappointing process. The male eye is not quick in detecting the subtleties of lace and chiffon, the values of furs and furbelows.

"Women dress to please the men," somebody has remarked. That may be true in some cases. More frequently, it is to be feared, they dress to make other women envious.

Ralph's education in the particular line referred to had not even commenced. He knew nothing of the philosophy of clothes. He was vaguely conscious sometimes that some people were well dressed and others ill dressed, that some women were gowned becomingly and others unbecomingly, but beyond that generalisation he never ventured.

He had begun to dress well himself almost without knowing it. He instinctively avoided everything that was loud or noticeable. Nature had given him a good figure—tall, erect, and well proportioned. Moreover, he was free from the vanity which makes a man self-conscious, and he was sufficiently well educated to know what constituted a gentleman.

He got back to the small hotel at which he was staying in time for an early dinner, after which he strolled into the Embankment Gardens and listened to the band. Later still, he found himself sitting on one of the seats in Trafalgar Square listening to the splash of the fountains and dreaming of home, and yet in every dream stood out the exquisite face and figure of Dorothy Hamblyn.

Next morning, because he had nothing to do, and because he was already tired of sight-seeing, he made his way again into St. James's Park, and found a seat near the lake and in the shadow of the trees. He told himself that he came there in the hope that he might see Dorothy Hamblyn again.

He knew it was a foolish thing to do. But he had come to the unheroic conclusion during the night that it was of no use fighting against Fate. He loved Dorothy Hamblyn passionately, madly, and that was the end of it. He could not help it. He had tried his best to root out the foolish infatuation, and he had almost hoped that he was succeeding. But yesterday's experience had torn the veil from his eyes, and revealed to him the fact that he was more hopelessly in love than ever.

How angry he was with himself he did not know. The folly of it made him ashamed. His presumption filled him with amazement. If anyone else of his own class had done the same thing he would have laughed him to scorn. In truth, he could have kicked himself for his folly.

Then, unconsciously, his mood would change, and self-pity would take the place of scorn. He was not to blame. He was the victim of a cruel and cynical Fate. He was being punished for hating her father so intensely. It was the Nemesis of an evil passion.

He spent most of the day in the Park, and kept an eager look-out in all directions; but the vision of Dorothy's face did not again gladden his eyes. A hundred times he started, and the warm blood rushed in a torrent to his face, then he would walk slowly on again.

On the following morning he met Sir John Liskeard, by appointment, in his chambers in the Temple.

"He had been going into the case," he explained to Ralph, "with considerable care, but even now he had not found out all he wanted to know. He had, however, discovered one or two facts which had an important bearing on the case."

He was careful to explain, again, that in equity he considered Ralph's claim incontestable, while nothing could be more honourable than the way in which he had tried to come to terms with the company. He spoke strongly of the high-handed and tyrannous way in which a rich and powerful company were trying to crush a poor man and rob him of the fruits of his skill and enterprise.

But, on the other hand, there was no doubt whatever that the company would be able to cite a clear case. To begin with, the agreement, or the concession, was very loosely worded. Moreover, no time limit had been set, which might imply that the company retained the right of withdrawing the concession at any moment. It was also contended by some of the shareholders that the company, as a whole, could not be held responsible for mistakes made by the chairman. That, however, he held was a silly contention, inasmuch as the agreement was stamped with the company's seal, and was signed by the secretary and two directors.

On the other hand, there could be no doubt that the concession had been hurriedly made, no one at the time realising that there was any value in the rubbish heap that had been accumulating for the biggest part of a century. On one point, however, the company had cleverly forestalled them. It had purchased, recently, the freehold of Daniel Rickard's farm. This, no doubt, was a very astute move, and mightily strengthened the company's position.

"I am bound, also, to point out one other fact," the lawyer went on. "I have discovered that both Lord Probus and Lord St. Goram are considerable shareholders in the concern. They are both tremendously impressed by what I may term 'the potentialities of the tailing heap.' In fact, they believe there's a huge fortune in it, and they are determined that the company shall reap the reward of your discovery."

"They need not be so greedy," Ralph said bitterly. "They have both far more than they know how to spend, and they might have been willing to give a beginner a chance."

"You know the old saying," Sir John said, with a smile. "'Much would have more.'"

"I've heard it," Ralph said moodily.

"You will understand I am not talking to you merely as a lawyer. There is no doubt whatever that you have a case, and a very clear case. I may add, a very strong case."

"And what, roughly speaking, would it cost to fight it in a court of law?"

Sir John shrugged his shoulders and smiled knowingly.

"I might name a minimum figure," he said, and he did.

Ralph started, and half rose from his chair.

"That settles the matter," he said, after a pause.

"It would be a very unequal contest," Sir John remarked.

"You mean——"

"I mean, they could take it from court to court, and simply cripple you with law costs."

"So, as usual, the weak must go to the wall?"

"To be quite candid with you, I could not advise you to risk what you have made."

"What I have made is very little indeed," Ralph answered.

"I thought you had made a small fortune."

"I could have made a little if I had been given time; but I have spent most of the profit in increasing and improving the plant."

"I am sorry. To say the least, it is rough on you."

"It is what I have been used to all my life," Ralph said absently. "The powerful appear to recognise no law but their own strength."

When Ralph found himself in the street again his thoughts immediately turned towards home.

CHAPTER XXVI

TRUTH WILL OUT

Ralph went back to his hotel with the intention of packing his bag, and returning home by the first available train. He had got what he came to London to get, and there was no need for him to waste more time and money in the big city. He was not disappointed. The learned counsel had taken precisely the view he had expected, and had given the advice that might be looked for from a friend and well-wisher.

He was not sorry he had come. The reasoned opinion of a man of law and a man of affairs was worth paying for. Though he had practically lost everything, he would go back home better satisfied. He would not be able to blame himself for either cowardice or stupidity. His business now was to submit with the best grace possible to those who were more powerful than himself.

It was annoying, no doubt, to see the harvest of his research and industry and enterprise reaped by other people—by people who had never given an hour's thought or labour to the matter. But his experience was by no means peculiar. It was only on rare occasions the inventor profited by the labour of his brains. It was the financier who pocketed the gold. The man of intellect laboured, the man of finance entered into his labours.

As Ralph made his way slowly along the Strand he could not help wondering what his next move would be when he got home. As far as he could see, he was on his beam-ends once more. There appeared to be no further scope for enterprise in St. Ivel or in St. Goram. He might go back to the mine again and work for fourteen shillings a week, but such a prospect was not an inviting one. He was built on different lines from most of his neighbours. The steady work and the steady wage and the freedom from responsibility did not appeal to him as it appealed to so many people. He rather liked responsibility. The question of wage was of very secondary importance. He disliked the smooth, well-trodden paths. The real interest in life was in carving out new paths for himself and other people.

But there were no new paths to be carved out in St. Ivel or in the neighbouring parishes. The one new thing of a generation—born in his own brain—had been taken out of his hands, and there was nothing left but the old ruts, worn deep by the feet of many generations.

He began to wonder what all the people who jostled him in the street did for a

172

living. Was there anything new or fresh in their lives, or did they travel the same weary round day after day and year after year?

The sight of so many people in the street doing nothing—or apparently doing nothing—oppressed him. The side walks were crowded. 'Buses were thronged, cabs and hansoms rolled past, filled, seemingly, with idle people. And yet nearly everybody appeared to be eager and alert. What were they after? What phantom were they pursuing? What object had they in life? He turned down a quiet street at length, glad to escape the noise and bustle, and sought the shelter of his hotel.

Before proceeding to pack his bag, however, he consulted a time-table, and discovered, somewhat to his chagrin, that there was no train that would take him to St. Goram that day. He could get as far as Plymouth, but no farther.

"It's no use making two bites at a cherry," he said to himself; "so I'll stay where I am another day."

An hour or two later he found himself once more in the Park in the shadow of the trees. It was here he first saw Dorothy, and he cherished a vague hope that she might pass that way again. He called himself a fool for throwing oil on the flame of a hopeless passion, but in his heart he pitied himself more than he blamed.

Moreover, he needed something to draw away his thoughts from himself. If he brooded too long on his disappointments, he might lose heart and hope. It was much pleasanter to think of Dorothy than of the treatment he had received at the hands of the Brick, Tile, and Clay Company, so he threw himself, with a sigh, on an empty seat and watched the people passing to and fro.

Most people walked slowly, for the day was hot. The ladies carried sunshades, and were clad in the flimsiest materials. The roar of the streets was less insistent than when he sat there before. But London still seemed to him an inexpressibly lonely place.

He was never quite sure how long he sat there. An hour, perhaps. Perhaps two hours. Time was not a matter that concerned him just then. His brain kept alternating between the disappointments of the past and hopes of the future. He came to himself with a start. The rustle of a dress, accompanied by a faint perfume as of spring violets, caused him to raise his head with a sudden movement.

"I thought I could not be mistaken!"

The words fell upon his ears with a curious sense of remoteness such as one experiences sometimes in dreams.

The next moment he was on his feet, his face aglow, his eyes sparkling with intense excitement.

"Did I not see you two days ago? Pardon me for speaking, but really, to see one from home is like a draught of water to a thirsty traveller." And Dorothy's voice ended in a little ripple of timid laughter.

"It is a long time since you were at St. Goram?" he said, in a questioning tone.

"I scarcely remember how long," she answered. "It seems ages and ages. Won't you tell me all the news?"

"I shall be delighted," he said; and he walked away by her side.

"Father writes to me every week or two," she went on, "but I can never get any news out of him. I suppose it is that nothing happens in St. Goram."

"In the main we move in the old ruts," he answered slowly. "Besides, your father will not be interested in the common people, as they are called."

"He is getting very tired of the place. He wants to get his household into the very smallest compass, so that he can spend more time in London and abroad."

"Do you like living in London?"

"In the winter, very much; but in the summer I pine for St. Goram. I want the breeze of the downs and the shade of the plantation."

"But you will be running down before the summer is over?"

"I am afraid not. To begin with, I cannot get away very well, and then I think my father intends practically to shut up the house at the end of this month."

"And your brother?"

"He will stay with my Aunt Fanny in London—she is my father's sister, you know—or he may go abroad with father for a month or two." And she sighed unconsciously.

For a while they walked on in silence. They had left the hot yellow path for the green turf. In front of them was a belt of trees, with chairs dotted about in the shadow. Ralph felt as though he were in dreamland. It seemed scarcely credible that he should be walking and talking with the daughter of Sir John Hamblyn.

Dorothy broke the silence at length, and her words came with manifest effort.

"I hope my father expressed his regret, and apologised for the mistake he made?"

"Oh, as to that," he said, with a short laugh, "I am afraid I have given him no opportunity. You see, I have been very much occupied, and then I don't live in St. Goram now."

"And—and—your people?"

"You know, I suppose, that my mother is dead?"

"No; I had not heard. Oh, I am so sorry!"

"She died the day after I came back from prison."

"Oh, how sad!"

"I don't think she thought so. She was glad to welcome me back again, of course, and to know that my innocence had been established. But since father died she seemed to have nothing to live for."

Then silence fell again for several minutes. They had reached the shadow of the trees, and Dorothy suggested that they should sit down and rest a while. Ralph pulled up a chair nearly opposite her. He still felt like one in a dream. Every now and then he raised his eyes to her face, and thought how beautiful she had grown.

"Do you know," she said, breaking the silence again, "I was almost afraid to speak to you just now."

"Afraid?"

"You have suffered a good deal at our hands."

"Well?" His heart was in a tumult, but he kept himself well in hand.

"It must require a good deal of grace to keep you from hating us most intensely."

"I am afraid I am not as good a hater as I would like to be."

"As you would like to be?"

"It has not been for want of trying, I can assure you. But Fate loves to make fools of us."

"I don't think I quite understand," she said, looking puzzled.

"Do you want to understand?" he questioned, speaking slowly and steadily, though every drop of blood in his veins seemed to be at boiling point.

"Yes, very much," she answered, making a hole in the ground with her sunshade.

"Then you shall know," he said, with his eyes on some distant object. He had grown quite reckless. He feared nothing, cared for nothing. It would be a huge joke to tell this proud daughter of the house of Hamblyn the honest truth. Moreover, it might help him to defy the Fate that was mocking him, might help to relieve the tension of the last few days, and would certainly put an end to the possibility of her ever speaking to him again.

"You are right when you say I have suffered a good deal, I won't say at your hands, but at the hands of your father, and Heaven knows my hatred of him has not lacked intensity." Then he paused suddenly and looked at her, but she did not raise her eyes.

"You are his daughter," he went on, slowly and bitingly, "his own flesh and blood. You bear a name that I loathe more than any other name on earth."

She winced visibly, and her cheeks became crimson.

"But Fate has been cruel to me in every way. Your very kindness to me, to Ruth, to my mother, has only added to my torture——"

"Added to——"

But he did not let her finish the sentence. His nerves were strung up to the highest point of tension. He felt, in a sense, outside himself. He was no longer master of his own emotions.

"Had you been like your father," he continued, "I could have hated you also. But it may be that, to punish me for hating your father so bitterly, God made me love you."

She rose to her feet in a moment, her face ashen.

"Don't go away," he said, quietly and deliberately. "It will do you no harm to hear me out. I did not seek this interview. I shall never seek another. A man who has been in prison, and whose mother died in the workhouse——"

"In the workhouse?" she said, with a gasp.

"Thanks to your father," he said slowly and bitterly. "And yet, in spite of all this, I had dared to love you. No, don't sneer at me," he said, mistaking a motion of her lips. "God knows I have about as much as I can bear. I tried to hate you. I felt it almost a religious duty to hate you. I fought against the passion that has conquered me till I had no strength left."

She had sat down again, with her eyes upon the ground, but her bosom was heaving as though a tempest raged beneath.

"Why have you told me this?" she said at length, with a sudden fierce light in her eyes.

"Oh, I hardly know," he said, with a reckless laugh. "For the fun of it, I

176

expect. Don't imagine I have any ulterior object in view, save that of self-defence."

"Self-defence?"

"Yes; you will despise me now. My effrontery and impertinence will be too much even for your large charity. I can fancy how the tempest of your scorn is gathering. I don't mind it. Let it rage. It may help to turn my heart against you."

She did not answer him; she sat quite still with her eyes fixed upon the ground.

He looked at her for several moments in silence, and his mood began to change. What spirit had possessed him to talk as he had done?

She rose to her feet at length, and raised her eyes timidly to his face. Whether she was angry or disgusted, or only sorry, he could not tell.

He rose also, but he scarcely dared to look at her.

"Good-afternoon," she said at length; and she held out her hand to him.

"Good-afternoon," he answered; but he did not take her outstretched hand, he pretended not even to see it.

He stood still and watched her walk away out into the level sunshine; watched her till she seemed but a speck of colour in the hazy distance. Then, with a sigh, he turned his face towards the City. He still felt more or less like one in a dream: there seemed to be an air of unreality about everything. Perhaps he would come to himself directly and discover that he was not in London at all.

He did not return to his hotel until nearly bedtime. The porter handed him a letter which came soon after he went out.

It was from Sir John Liskeard, and requested that Ralph would call on him again at his rooms in the Temple on the following morning, any time between ten and half-past. No reason was given why Sir John wanted this second interview.

Ralph stood staring at the letter for several moments, then slowly put it back into the envelope, and into his pocket.

"Perhaps some new facts have come to light," he said to himself, as he made his way slowly up the stairs, and a thrill of hope and expectancy shot through his heart. "Perhaps my journey to London may not be without fruit after all. I wonder now——"

And when he awoke next morning he was still wondering.

CHAPTER XXVII

HOME AGAIN

"I am sorry to have troubled you to call again," was Sir John's greeting, "but there is a little matter that quite slipped my memory yesterday. Won't you be seated?"

Ralph sat down, still hoping that he was going to hear some good news.

"It is nothing about the Brick, Tile, and Clay Company," Sir John went on, "and, in fact, nothing that concerns you personally."

Ralph's face fell, and the sparkle went out of his eyes. It was foolish of him ever to hope for anything. Good news did not come his way. He did not say anything, however.

"The truth is, a friend of mine is considering the advisability of purchasing Hillside Farm, and has asked me to make one or two inquiries about it."

Ralph gave a little gasp, but remained silent.

"Now, I presume," Sir John said, with a little laugh, "if there is a man alive who knows everything about the farm there is to be known you are that man."

"But I do not understand," Ralph said. "I have always understood that the Hamblyn estate is strictly entailed."

"That is true of the original estate. But you may or you may not be aware that Hillside came to Sir John by virtue of the Land Enclosures Act."

"Oh yes, I know all about that," Ralph said, with a touch of scorn in his voice; "and a most iniquitous Act it was."

Sir John shrugged his shoulders, a very common habit of his. It was not his place to speak ill of an Act of Parliament which had put a good deal of money into his pocket and into the pockets of his professional brethren in all parts of the country.

"Into the merits of this particular Act," he said, a little stiffly, "we need not enter now. Suffice it that Hamblyn is quite at liberty to dispose of the freehold if he feels so inclined."

"And he intends to sell Hillside Farm?"

"Well, between ourselves, he does—that is, if he can get rid of it by private treaty. Naturally, he does not want the matter talked about. I understand there is a very valuable stone quarry in one corner of the estate."

"There is a quarry," Ralph answered slowly, for his thoughts were intent on another matter, "but whether it is very valuable or not I cannot say. I should judge it is not of great value, or the squire would not want to sell the freehold."

"When a man is compelled to raise a large sum of money there is frequently for him no option."

"And is that the case with Sir John?"

"There can be no doubt whatever that he is hard up. His life interest in the Hamblyn estate is, I fancy, mortgaged to the hilt. If he can sell Hillside Farm at the price he is asking for it, he will have some ready cash to go on with."

"What is the price he names?"

"Twenty years' purchase on the net rental—the same on the mineral dues."

"There are no mineral dues," Ralph said quickly, and his thoughts flew back in a moment to that conversation he had with his father.

"Well, quarry dues, then," Sir John said, with a smile.

"And is your friend likely to purchase?" Ralph questioned.

"I believe he would like the farm. But he is a cautious man, and is anxious to find out all he can before he strikes a bargain."

"And will he be guided by your advice?"

"In the main he will."

"Then, if you are his friend, you will advise him to make haste slowly."

"You think the farm is not worth the money?"

"To the ordinary investor I am sure it is not. To the man who wants it for some sentimental reason the case is different."

"What do you mean by that?"

"Well, if I were a rich man, for instance, I might be disposed to give a good deal more for it than it is worth. You see, I helped to reclaim the land from the waste. I know every bush and tree on the farm. I remember every apple tree being planted. I love the place, for it was my home. My father died there ———"

"Then why don't you buy it?" interrupted Sir John.

Ralph laughed.

"You might as well ask me why I don't buy the moon," he said. "If I had been allowed to go on with my present work I might have been able to buy it in time. Now it is quite out of the question."

"That is a pity," Sir John said meditatively.

"I don't know that it is," Ralph answered. "One cannot live on sentiment."

"And yet sentiment plays a great part in one's life."

"No doubt it does, but with the poor the first concern is how to live."

"Then, sentiment apart, you honestly think the place is not worth the money?"

"I'm sure it isn't. Jenkins told me not long ago that if he could not get his rent lowered he should give up the farm."

"And what about the quarry?"

"It will be worked out in half a dozen years at the outside."

"You think so?"

"I do honestly. I've no desire to do harm to the squire, though God knows he has been no friend to me. But twenty years' purchase at the present rental and dues would be an absurd price."

"I think it is rather stiff myself."

"Is Sir John selling the place through some local agent or solicitor?"

"Oh no. Messrs. Begum & Swear, Chancery Lane, are acting for him."

An hour later, Ralph was rolling away in an express train towards the west. He sat next the window, and kept his eyes steadily fixed on the scenery through which he passed. And yet he saw very little of it; his thoughts were too intent on other things. Towns, villages, hamlets, homesteads, flew past, but he scarcely heeded. Wooded hills drew near and faded away in the distance. The river gleamed and flashed and hid itself. Gaily-dressed people made patches of colour in shady backwaters for a moment; the sparkle of a weir caught his eye, and was gone.

It was only in after days that he recalled the incidents of the journey; for the moment he could think of nothing but Dorothy Hamblyn and the sale of Hillside Farm. The sudden failure of his small commercial enterprise did not worry him. He knew the worst of that. To cry over spilt milk was waste both of time and energy. His business was not to bewail the past, but to face resolutely the future.

But Dorothy and the fate of Hillside Farm belonged to a different category. Dorothy he could not forget, try as he would. She had stolen his heart unconsciously, and he would never love another. At least, he would never love another in the same deep, passionate, overmastering way. He was still angry with himself for his mad outburst of the previous day, and could not imagine what possessed him to speak as he did. He wondered, too, what she thought of him. Was her feeling one of pity, or anger, or amusement, or contempt, or was it a mixture of all these qualities?

Then, for a while, she would pass out of his mind, and a picture of Hillside Farm would come up before his vision. On the whole, he was not sorry that the squire was compelled to sell. It was a sort of Nemesis, a rough-and-ready vindication of justice and right.

The place never was his in equity, whatever it might be in law. If it belonged to anybody, it belonged to the man who reclaimed it from the wilderness.

No, he was not sorry that the squire was unable to keep it. It seemed to restore his faith in the existence of a moral order. A man who was not worthy to be a steward—who abused the power he possessed—ought to be deposed. It was in the eternal fitness of things that he should give place to a better man.

Ruth met him at St. Ivel Road Station, and they walked home together in the twilight. They talked fitfully, with long breaks in the conversation. He had told her by letter the result of his mission, so that he had nothing of importance to communicate.

"The men are very much cut up," she said, after a little lull in their talk, which had been mainly about London. "Several of them called this afternoon to know if I had heard any news; and when I told them that you were not going to contest the claim of the company, and that the works would cease, they looked as if they would cry."

"I hope they will be able to get work somewhere else," he answered quietly.

"But they will not get such wages as you have been giving them. You cannot imagine how popular you are. I believe the men would do anything for you."

"I believe they would do anything in reason," he said. "I have tried to treat them fairly, and I am quite sure they have done their best to treat me fairly. People are generally paid back in their own coin."

"And have you any idea what you will do next?" she questioned, after a pause.

"Not the ghost of an idea, Ruth. If I had not you to think of, I would go abroad and try my fortune in a freer air."

"Don't talk about going abroad," she said, with a little gasp.

"Yet it may have to come to it," he answered. "One feels bound hand and foot in a country like this."

"But are other countries any better?"

"The newer countries of the West and our own Colonies do not seem quite so hidebound. What with our land laws and our mineral dues, and our leasehold systems, and our patent laws, and our precedents, and our rights of way and all the bewildering entanglements of red-tapeism, one feels as helpless as a squirrel in a cage. One cannot walk out on the hills, or sit on the cliffs, or fish in the sea without permission of somebody. All the streams and rivers are owned; all the common land has been appropriated; all the minerals a hundred fathoms below the surface are somebody's by divine right. One wonders that the very atmosphere has not been staked out into freeholds."

"But things are as they have always been, dear," Ruth said quietly.

"No, not always," he said, with a laugh.

"Well, for a very long time, anyhow. And, after all, they are no worse for us than for other people."

He did not reply to this remark. Getting angry with the social order did not mend things, and he had no wish to carp and cavil when no good could come of it.

Within the little cottage everything was ready for the evening meal. The kettle was singing on the hob, the table was laid, the food ready to be brought in.

"It is delightful to be home again," Ralph said, throwing himself into his easy-chair. "After all, there's no place like home."

"And did you like London?"

"Yes and no," he answered meditatively. "It is a very wonderful place, and I might grow to be fond of it in time. But it seemed to be so terribly lonely, and then one's vision seemed so cramped. One could only look down lines of streets—you are shut in by houses everywhere. The sun rose behind houses, set behind houses. You wanted to see the distant spaces, to look across miles of country, to catch glimpses of the far-off hills, but the houses shut out everything. Oh, it is a lonely place!"

"And yet it is crowded with people?"

"And that adds to the feeling of loneliness," he replied. "You are jostled and bumped on every side, and you know nobody. Not a face in all the thousands you recognise."

"I should like to see it all some day."

"Some day you shall," he said. "If ever I grow rich enough you shall have a month there. But let us not talk of London just now. Has anything happened since I went away?"

"Nothing at all, Ralph."

"And has nobody been to see you?"

"Nobody except Mary Telfer. She has come in most days, and always like a ray of sunshine."

"She is a very cheerful little body," Ralph said, and then began to attack his supper.

A few minutes later he looked up and said—

"Did you ever hear the old saying, Ruth, that one has to go from home to hear news?"

"Why, of course," she said, with a laugh. "Who hasn't?"

"I had rather a remarkable illustration of the old saw this morning."

"Indeed?"

"I had to go to London to learn that Hillside Farm is for sale."

"For sale, Ralph?"

"So Sir John Liskeard told me. I warrant that nobody in St. Goram knows."

"Are you very sorry?" she questioned.

"Not a bit. The squire squeezed his tenants for all they were worth, and now the money-lenders are squeezing him. It's only poetic justice, after all."

"Yet surely he is to be pitied?"

"Well, yes. Every man is to be pitied who fools away his money on the Turf and on other questionable pursuits, and yet when the pinch comes you cannot help saying it serves him right."

"But nobody suffers alone, Ralph."

"I know that," he answered, the colour mounting suddenly to his cheeks. "But as far as his son Geoffrey is concerned, it may do him good not to have unlimited cash."

"I was not thinking of Geoffrey. I was thinking of Miss Dorothy."

"It may do her good also," he said, a little savagely. "Women are none the worse for knowing the value of a sovereign."

For several minutes there was silence; then Ruth said, without raising her eyes
—

183

"I wish we were rich, Ralph."

"For why?" he questioned with a smile, half guessing what was in her mind.

"We would buy Hillside Farm."

"You would like to go back there again to live?"

"Shouldn't I just! Oh, Ralph, it would be like heaven!"

"I'm not so sure that I should like to go back," he said, after a long pause.

"No?" she questioned.

"Don't you think the pain would outweigh the pleasure?"

"Oh no. I think father and mother wander through the orchard and across the fields still, and I should feel nearer to them there; and I'm sure it would make heaven a better place for them if they knew we were back in the old home."

"Ah, well," he said, with a sigh, "that is a dream we cannot indulge in. Sir John Liskeard asked me why I did not buy it."

"And what did you say to him?"

"What could I say, Ruth, except that I could just as easily buy the moon?"

"Would the freehold cost so much?"

"As the moon?"

"No, no, I don't mean that, you silly boy; but is land so very, very dear?"

"Compared with land in or near big towns or cities, it is very, very cheap."

"But I mean it would take a lot of money to buy Hillside?"

"You and I would think it a lot." And then the sound of footsteps was heard outside, followed a moment later by a timid knock at the door.

"I wonder who it can be?" Ruth said, starting to her feet. "I'm glad you are at home, or I should feel quite nervous."

"Do you think burglars would knock at the front door and ask if they might come in?" he questioned, with a laugh.

Ruth did not reply, but went at once to the door and opened it, much wondering who their visitor could be, for it was very rarely anyone called at so late an hour.

It had grown quite dark outside, so that she could only see the outline of two tall figures standing in the garden path.

She was quickly reassured by a familiar voice saying—

"Is your brother at home, Miss Penlogan?"

And then for some reason the hot blood rushed in a torrent to her neck and face.

CHAPTER XXVIII

A TRYING POSITION

William Menire was troubled about two things—troubles rarely come singly. The first trouble arose a week or two previously out of a request preferred by a cousin of his, a young farmer from a neighbouring parish, who wanted an introduction to Ruth Penlogan.

Sam Tremail was a good-looking young fellow of irreproachable character. Moreover, he was well-to-do, his father and mother having retired and left a large farm on his hands. He stood nearly six feet in his boots, had never known a day's illness in his life, was only twenty-six years of age, lived in a capital house, and only wanted a good wife to make him the happiest man on earth.

Yet for some reason there was not a girl in his own parish that quite took his fancy. Not that there was any lack of eligible young ladies; not that he had set his heart on either beauty or fortune. Disdainful and disappointed mothers who had daughters to spare said that he was proud and stuck-up—that they did not know what the young men of the present day were coming to, and that Sam Tremail deserved to catch a tartar.

Some of these remarks were repeated to Sam, and he acknowledged their force. He had a feeling that he ought to marry a girl from his own parish. He admitted their eligibility. Some of them were exceedingly pretty, and one or two of them had money in their own right. Yet for some reason they left his heart untouched. They were admirable as acquaintances, or even friends, but they moved him to no deeper emotion.

He first caught sight of Ruth at the sale when her father's worldly goods were being disposed of by public auction. She looked so sad, so patient, so gentle, so meekly resigned, that a new chord in his nature seemed to be set suddenly vibrating, and it had gone on vibrating ever since. It might be pity he felt for her, or sympathy; but, whatever it was, it made him anxious to know her better. Her sweet, sad eyes haunted him, her tremulous lips made him long to comfort her.

How to get acquainted with her, however, remained an insoluble problem. She was altogether outside the circle of his friends. She had lived all her life in another parish, and moved in an entirely different orbit.

While she lived with Mr. Varcoe at St. Hilary, he met her several times in the streets—for he went to St. Hilary market at least once a fortnight—but he had no excuse for speaking to her. He knew, of course, of the misfortune that had overtaken her, knew that she was earning her living in service of some kind, knew that her mother was in the workhouse, that her brother was in prison awaiting his trial, but all that only increased the volume of his compassion. He felt that he would willingly give all he possessed for the privilege of helping and comforting her.

For a long time he lost sight of her; then he learned that she had gone to keep house for her brother at St. Ivel. But St. Ivel was a long way from Pentudy, and there was practically no direct communication between the two parishes.

Then he learned that William Menire—a second cousin of his—was on friendly terms with the Penlogans; but the trouble was he hardly knew his relative by sight, and he had never made any effort to know him better. In the past, at any rate, the Menires had not been considered socially the equals of the Tremails. The Tremails had been large farmers for generations. The Menires were nothing in particular.

William was a grocer's assistant when his father died. How he had managed to maintain his mother and build up a flourishing business out of nothing was a story often told in St. Goram. The very severity of his struggle was perhaps in his favour. His neighbours sympathised with him in his uphill fight, and patronised his small shop when it was convenient to do so. So his business grew. Later on people discovered that they could get better stuff for the money at William's shop than almost anywhere else. Hence, when sympathy failed, self-interest took its place. As William's capital increased, he added new departments to his business, and vastly improved the appearance of his premises. He turned the whole side of his shop into a big window at his own expense, not asking Lord St. Goram for a penny.

At the time of which we write, William had reached the sober age of thirty-six, and was generally looked upon as a man of substance.

He was surprised one evening to receive a visit from his cousin, Sam Tremail. The young farmer had to make himself known. He did so in rather a clumsy fashion; but then, the task he had set himself was a delicate one, and he had not been trained in the art of diplomacy.

"It seems a pity," Sam said, with a benevolent smile, "that relatives should be as strangers to each other."

"Relationships don't count for much in these days, I fear," William answered cautiously. "Nevertheless, I am glad to see you."

"You think it is every man for himself, eh?" Sam questioned, with a slight blush.

"I don't say it is the philosophy or the practice of every man. But in the main ____"

"Yes, I think you are right," Sam interjected, with a sudden burst of candour. "And, really, I don't want you to think that I am absolutely disinterested in riding over from Pentudy to see you."

"It is a long journey for nothing," William said, with a smile.

"Mind you, I have often wanted to know you better," Sam went on. "Father has often spoken of your pluck and perseverance. He admires you tremendously."

"It is very kind of him," William said, with a touch of cynicism in his tones. "I hope he is well. I have not seen him for years."

"He is first rate, thank you, and so is mother. I suppose you know they have retired from the farm?"

"No, I had not heard."

"I have it in my own hands now. For some things I wish I hadn't. I tried to persuade father and mother to live on in the house, but they had made up their minds to go and live in town, where they could have gas in the streets, and all that kind of thing. If I had only a sister to keep house it wouldn't be so bad."

"But why don't you get married?"

"Well, to tell you the truth, that is the very thing I have come to talk to you about."

And Sam turned all ways in his chair, and looked decidedly uncomfortable.

"Come to talk to me about?" William questioned, in a tone of surprise.

"You think it funny, of course; but the truth is——" And Sam looked apprehensively towards the door. "We shall not be overheard here, shall we?"

"There's no one in the house but myself, except the cook. Mother's gone out to see a neighbour."

"Oh, well, I'm glad I've caught you on the quiet, as it were. I wouldn't have the matter talked about for the world."

William began to feel uncomfortable, and to wonder what his kinsman had been up to.

"I hope you have not been getting into any foolish matrimonial entanglement?" he questioned seriously.

188

Sam laughed heartily and good-humouredly.

"No, no; things are not quite so bad as that," he said. "The fact is, I would like to get into a matrimonial entanglement, as you call it, but not into a foolish one."

Then he stopped suddenly, and began to fidget again in his chair.

"Then you are not engaged yet?"

"Well, not quite."

And Sam laughed again.

William waited for him to continue, but Sam appeared to start off on an entirely new tack.

"I don't think I've been in St. Goram parish since the sale at Hillside Farm. You remember it?"

"Very well!"

"How bad luck seems to dog the steps of some people. I felt tremendously sorry for David Penlogan. He was a good man, by all accounts."

"There was no more saintly man in the three parishes."

"The mischief is, saints are generally so unpractical. They tell me the son is of different fibre."

"He's as upright as his father, but with a difference."

"A cruel thing to send him to gaol on suspicion, and keep him there so long."

"It was a wicked thing to do, but it hasn't spoilt him. He's the most popular man in St. Ivel to-day."

"I remember him at the sale—a handsome, high-spirited fellow; but his sister interested me most. I thought her smile the sweetest I had ever seen."

"She's as sweet as her smile, and a good deal more so," William said, with warmth. "In fact, she has no equal hereabouts."

"I hear you are on friendly terms with them."

"Well, yes," William said slowly. "Not that I would presume to call myself their equal, for they are in reality very superior people. There's no man in St. Goram, and I include the landed folk, so well educated or so widely read as Ralph Penlogan."

"And his sister?"

"She's a lady, every inch of her," William said warmly; "and what is more, they'll make their way in the world. He's ability, and of no ordinary kind. The rich folk may crush him for a moment, but he'll come into his own in the long-run."

"Are they the proud sort?"

"Proud? Well, it all depends on what you mean by the word. Dignity they have, self-respect, independence; but pride of the common or garden sort they haven't a bit."

"I thought I could not be mistaken," Sam said, after a pause; "and to tell you the honest truth, I've never been able to think of any other girl since I saw Miss Penlogan at the sale."

William started and grew very pale.

"I don't think I quite understand," he said, after a long pause.

"Do you believe in love at first sight?" Sam questioned eagerly.

"I don't know that I do," William answered.

"Well, I do," Sam retorted. "A man may fall desperately in love with a girl without even speaking to her."

"Well?" William questioned.

"That's just my case."

"Your case?"

Sam nodded.

"Explain yourself," William said, with a curiously numb feeling at his heart.

"Mind, I am speaking to you in perfect confidence," Sam said.

William assented.

"I was taken with Ruth Penlogan the very first moment I set eyes on her. I don't think it was pity, mind you, though I did pity her from my very heart. Her great sad eyes; her sweet, patient face; her gentle, pathetic smile—they just bowled me over. I could have knelt down at her feet and worshipped her."

"You didn't do it?" William questioned huskily.

"It was neither the time nor the place, and I have never had an opportunity since. I saw her again and again in the streets of St. Hilary, but, of course, I could not speak to her, and I didn't know a soul who could get me an introduction."

"And you mean that you are in love with her?"

"I expect I am," Sam answered, with an uneasy laugh. "If I'm not in love, I don't know what ails me. I want a wife badly. A man in a big house without a wife to look after things is to be pitied. Well, that's just my case."

"But—but——" William began; then hesitated.

"You mean that there are plenty of eligible girls in Pentudy?" Sam questioned. "I don't deny it. We have any amount. All sorts and sizes, if you'll excuse me saying so. Girls with good looks and girls with money. Girls of weight, and girls with figures. But they don't interest me, not one of them. I compare 'em all with Ruth Penlogan, and then it's all up a tree."

"But you have never spoken to Miss Penlogan."

"That's just the point I'm coming to. The Penlogans are friends of yours. You go to their house sometimes. Now I want you to take me with you some day and introduce me. Don't you see? There's no impropriety in it. I'm perfectly honest and sincere. I want to get to know her, and then, of course, I'll take my chance."

William looked steadily at his kinsman, and a troubled expression came into his eyes. He loved Ruth Penlogan himself, loved her with a passionate devotion that once he hardly believed possible. She had become the light of his eyes, the sunshine of his life. He hardly realised until this moment how much she had become to him. The thought of her being claimed by another man was almost torture to him; and yet, ought he to stand in the way of her happiness?

This might be the working of an inscrutable Providence. Sam Tremail, from all he had ever heard, was a most excellent fellow. He could place Ruth in a position that was worthy of her, and one that she would in every way adorn. He could lift her above the possibility of want, and out of reach of worry. He could give her a beautiful home and an assured position.

"I hope you do not think this is a mere whim of mine, or an idle fancy?" Sam said, seeing that William hesitated.

"Oh no, not at all," William answered, a little uneasily. "I was thinking that it was a little bit unusual."

"It is unusual, no doubt."

"And to take you along and say, 'My cousin is very anxious to know you,' would be to let the cat out of the bag at the start."

"Do you think so?"

"Don't you think so, now? There must be a reason for everything. And the very first question Miss Penlogan would ask herself would be, 'Why does this young man want to know me?'"

"Well, I don't know that that would matter. Indeed, it might help me along."

"But when you got to know her better you might not care for her quite so much."

"Do you really think that?"

"Well, no. The chances are the other way about. Only there is no accounting for people, you know."

"I don't think I am fickle," Sam answered seriously.

"Still, so far it is only a pretty face that has attracted you."

"Oh no, it is more than that. It is the character behind the face. I am sure she is good. She appeals to me as no other woman has ever done. I am not afraid of not loving her. It is the other thing that troubles me."

"You think she might not care for you?"

"She could not do so at the start. You see I have been dreaming of her for the last two years. She has filled my imagination, if you understand. I have been worshipping her all the time. But on her side there is nothing. She does not know, very likely, there is such an individual in existence. I am not even a name to her. Hence, there is a tremendous amount of leeway to make up."

"Still, you have many things in your favour," William answered, a little plaintively. "First of all, you are young"—and William sighed unconsciously —"then you are well-to-do; and then—and then—you are good-looking"— and William sighed again—"and then your house is ready, and you have no encumbrances. Yes, you have many things in your favour."

"I'm glad you think so," Sam said cheerfully, "for, to tell you the truth, I'm awfully afraid she won't look at me."

William sighed again, for his fear was in the other direction. And yet he felt he ought not to be selfish. To play the part of the dog in the manger was a very unworthy thing to do. He had no hope of winning Ruth for himself. That Sam Tremail loved her a hundredth part as much as he did, he did not believe possible. How could he? But then, on the other hand, Sam was just the sort of fellow to take a girl's fancy.

"I can't go over with you this evening," William said at length. "They are early people, and I know Ralph is very much worried just now over business matters."

"Oh, there's no hurry for a day or two," Sam said cheerfully. "The great thing is, you'll take me along some evening?"

192

"Why, yes," William answered, slowly and painfully. "I couldn't do less than that very well."

"And I don't ask you to do more," Sam replied, with a laugh. "I must do the rest myself."

William did not sleep very much that night. For some reason, the thought of Ruth Penlogan getting married had scarcely crossed his mind. There seemed to him nobody in St. Goram or St. Ivel that was worthy of her. Hence the appearance of Sam Tremail on the scene intent on marrying her was like the falling of an avalanche burying his hope and his desire.

"I suppose it was bound to come some time," he sighed to himself; "and I'd rather she married Sam than some folks I know. But—but it's very hard all the same."

A week later Sam rode over to St. Goram again. But Ralph was in London, and William refused to take him to the Penlogans' cottage during Ralph's absence.

On the day of Ralph's return, Sam came a third time.

"Yes, I'll take you this evening," William said. "I want to see Ralph myself. I've great faith in Ralph's judgment." And William sighed.

"Is something troubling you?" Sam asked, with a sudden touch of apprehension.

"I am a bit worried," William answered slowly, "and troubles never come singly."

"Is there anything I can do for you?"

"No, I don't think so," William answered. "But get on your hat; it's a goodish walk."

CHAPTER XXIX

A QUESTION OF MOTIVES

William introduced his cousin with an air of easy indifference, apologised for calling at so late an hour, but excused himself on the ground that he wanted to see Ralph particularly on a little matter of business. Sam was welcomed graciously and heartily, for William's sake. William had been almost the best friend they had ever known. In the darkest days of their life he had come to them almost a stranger, had revealed the kindness of his heart in numberless little ways, had kept himself in the background with a delicacy and sensitiveness worthy of all praise, and had never once presumed on the kindness he had shown them.

For a moment or two William saw only Ruth, and he thought she had never looked more charming and winsome. The warmth of her welcome he attributed entirely to a sense of gratitude on her part, and he was very grateful that she counted him worthy to be her friend. When he saw his cousin glance at her with admiring eyes, a pang of jealousy shot through him such as he had never experienced before. He had scarcely troubled till now that his youth had slipped away from him; but when he looked at Sam's smooth, handsome face; his wealth of hair, untouched by Time; his tall, vigorous frame—he could not help wishing that he were ten years younger, and not a shopkeeper.

Sam and Ruth quickly got into conversation, and then Ralph led William into a little parlour which he used as an office.

"I haven't the remotest idea what I am going to do," Ralph said, in answer to a question from William, "though I know well enough what I would do if I only had money."

"Yes?" William questioned, raising his eyes slowly.

"I'd buy the freehold of Hillside Farm."

"It isn't for sale, is it?" William questioned, in a tone of surprise.

"It is." And Ralph informed him how he came by the information.

For several minutes there was silence in the room, then William said, as if speaking to himself—

"But the place isn't worth the money."

"To a stranger—no; but to me it might be cheap at the price."

"Are you so good at farming?"

Ralph laughed.

"Well, no," he answered. "I'm afraid farming is not exactly my forte; but let us drop the subject. As I told Sir John Liskeard, I might as well think of buying the moon."

"But you are fond of the old place?" William questioned.

"In a sense, yes; but I do not look at it with such longing eyes as Ruth does."

"She would like to live there again?" William questioned eagerly.

"She would dance for joy at the most distant hope of it."

"Then it is for your sister's sake you would like to turn farmer?" William questioned, after a pause.

"I have no wish to turn farmer at all," Ralph answered. "No, no, my dreams and ambitions don't lie in that direction; but why talk about impossibilities? You came across to discuss some other matter?"

"Yes, that is true," William said absently; and then a ripple of laughter from the adjoining room touched his heart with a curious sense of pain.

"They are on friendly terms already," he said to himself. "And in a little while he will make love to her, and what will Hillside Farm be to her then? I would do anything for her sake—anything." And he sighed unconsciously.

Ralph heard the sigh, and looked at him searchingly.

"I'm in an awful hole myself," William blurted out, after a long pause.

"In an awful hole?" Ralph questioned, with raised eyebrows.

"It's always the unexpected that happens, they say," William went on, "but I confess I never expected to be flung on my beam-ends as I have been. If it were not for mother, I'd sell up and clear out of the country."

"Why, what is the matter?" Ralph questioned in alarm.

"You know the part I took in the County Council election?"

"Very well."

"Of course, I knew that Lord St. Goram didn't quite like it. He expects every tenant and lease-holder to vote just as he wishes them. Poor people are not supposed to have any rights or opinions, but I thought the day had gone by when a man was to be punished for thinking for himself."

"But what has happened?" Ralph asked eagerly.

195

"I'm to be turned out of my shop."

"No!"

"It's the solemn truth. I had a seven years' lease, which expires next March, and Lord St. Goram refuses to renew it."

"For what reason?"

"He gives no reason at all. But it is easy to guess. I opposed him at the election, you know. I had a perfect right to do it, but rights go for nothing. Now he is taking his revenge. I've not only to clear out in March, but I've to restore the premises to the exact condition they were in when I took them."

"But you've improved the place in every way."

"No doubt I have, but I did it at my own risk, and at my own expense. He never gave his formal consent to my taking out the side of the house and putting in that big window. His steward assured me it was all right, though he hinted that in case I left his lordship might feel under no obligation to grant compensation."

"But why should he want you to restore the house to its original condition?"

"Just to be revenged, that's all. To show his power over me and to give his tenants an object-lesson as to what will happen if they are unwise enough to think for themselves."

"It's tyranny," Ralph said indignantly. "It's a piece of mean, contemptible tyranny."

"You can call it by any name you like," William answered sadly, "and there's no name too bad for it; but the point to be recollected is, I've got to submit."

"There's no redress for you?"

"Not a bit. I've consulted Doubleday, who's the best lawyer about here, and he says it would be sheer madness to contest it."

"Then what will you do?"

"I've not the remotest idea. There's no other place in St. Goram I can get. His lordship professes that he would far rather have twenty small shops and twenty small shopkeepers all living from hand to mouth than one prosperous tradesman selling the best and the freshest and at the lowest possible price."

"Well, I can sympathise with him in that," Ralph answered, with a smile.

"And yet you are no more fond of buying stale things than other people."

"That may be true. And yet the way the big concerns are crushing out the small men is not a pleasant spectacle."

"But no shopkeeper compels people to buy his goods," William said, with a troubled expression in his eyes. "And when they come to his shop, is he to say he won't supply them? And when his business shows signs of expansion, is he to say it shall not expand?"

"No, no. I don't mean that at all. I like to see an honest business man prospering. And a man who attends to his business and his customers deserves to prosper. But I confess I don't like to see these huge combines and trusts deliberately pushing out the smaller men—not by fair competition, mind you, but by unfair—selling things below cost price until their competitors are in the bankruptcy court, and then reaping a big harvest."

"I like that as little as you do," William said mildly. "Every honest, industrious man ought to have a chance of life, but the chances appear to be becoming fewer every day." And he sighed again.

For several minutes neither of them spoke, then William said—

"I thought I would like to tell you all about it at the earliest opportunity. I knew I should have your sympathy."

"I wish I could help you," Ralph answered. "You helped me when I hadn't a friend in the world."

"I have your sympathy," William answered, "and that's a great thing; for the rest we must trust in God." And he rose to his feet and looked towards the door.

William and Sam did not say much on their way back to St. Goram. They talked more freely when they got into the house.

"It's awfully good of you to introduce me," Sam said, when Mrs. Menire had retired to her room. "I'm more in love with her than ever."

William's heart gave a painful thump, but he answered mildly enough—

"You seemed to get on very well together."

"She was delightfully friendly, but I owe that all to you. She said that any friend of yours was welcome at their house."

"It was very kind of her," William answered slowly. "Did she give you permission to call again?"

"I'm not exactly sure. She did say that any time you brought me along I should be welcome, or words to that effect. So we must arrange another little excursion soon."

"Must we?"

"We must; and what is more, you might, you know, in the meanwhile—that is, if you can honestly do so—that is—you know what I mean, don't you?"

"I don't think I do," William answered, in a tone of mild surprise.

"It's asking a lot, I know," Sam replied, fidgeting uneasily in his chair. "But if you could—that—that is—without compromising yourself in any way, speak a good word for me, it would go miles and miles."

"Do you think so?"

"I'm sure of it. She thinks the world of you, and a word from you would be worth a week's pleading on my part."

"I'm not so sure of that," William answered. "I think all love affairs are best managed by those concerned. The meddling of outsiders generally does more harm than good."

"But there are exceptions to every rule," Sam persisted. "You see, I am awfully handicapped by being so much of a stranger. If I can once get a footing as a friend, the rest will be easy."

William smiled wistfully.

"I wouldn't be precipitate, if I were you," he said. "And in the meanwhile I'll do my best."

Sam slept soundly till morning, but William lay awake most of the night. When he did sleep it was to dream that he was young and prosperous, and that Ruth Penlogan had promised to be his wife.

After an early breakfast, he saw his cousin mount his horse and ride away toward Pentudy, and very soon after William climbed into his trap and went out to get orders.

One of his first places of call was Hillside Farm, and as he drove slowly up to the house he looked at it with a new interest. All sorts of vague fancies seemed to float about in his mind. He saw Ruth back there again, looking happier than any queen; he saw himself with some kind of proprietary interest in the place; he saw Ralph looking in when the fancy pleased him; he saw a number of new combinations and relationships, but so vaguely that he could not fit them into their places.

He found Farmer Jenkins in a very doleful mood.

"I wish I had never seen the place," he declared. "I've lost money ever since I came, and I'm going to clear out at the earliest opportunity."

"Do you really mean it?" William questioned.

"I was never more serious in my life. I sent a letter to the squire a week ago, and told him unless he lowered the rent thirty per cent. I should fling up the farm."

"And has he consented to lower it?"

"Not he. He says he'll call soon and talk the matter over with me, and that in the meantime I'd better keep quiet; but I shan't keep quiet, and I shan't stay."

As William drove away from Hillside an idea, or a suggestion, shot through his brain that made him gasp. Before he got to the village of Veryan he was trembling on his seat. It seemed almost like a suggestion from the Evil One, so subtle was the temptation. He had tried all his life to do the thing that was right. He had never, as far as he knew, taken an unfair advantage of anyone. He had aimed strictly to do what was just and honourable between man and man. But if he bought Hillside Farm, would it be fair dealing? Would it be fair to his Cousin Sam? Would it be fair to Ruth?

William tried to face the problem honestly. He would rather Ruth passed out of his life altogether than do anything mean or unworthy. To keep his conscience clean, and his love free from the taint of selfishness, seemed to him the supreme end of life. But if he bought Hillside Farm, what motive would lie at the back of it? Would it be that he wanted the farm, that he wanted to turn farmer? or would it be the hope that Ruth, with her passionate love of the place, would be willing even to accept the protection of his arms?

"All's fair in love and war," something seemed to whisper in his ear.

But William drew himself up squarely, and a resolute look came into his eyes.

"No," he said to himself, "that is false philosophy. Nothing that is mean or selfish or underhand can be fair or right. If the motive is wrong, the transaction will be wrong."

It took William a much longer time than usual to make his rounds that morning. He was so absent-minded—or, more correctly, his mind was so engrossed with other things—that he allowed his horse on several occasions to nibble the grass by the roadside.

He was no more interested in business matters when he got back. He would pause in the middle of weighing a pound of sugar or starch, completely forgetting where he was or what he was doing.

His mother let him be. She knew that he was greatly troubled at Lord St. Goram's refusal to renew the lease of his shop, and, like a wise woman, did not worry him with needless questions.

That evening, when the shutters were put up, he went to St. Ivel again. He would have some further talk with Ralph about the farm. He would be able also to feast his eyes again on Ruth's sweet face; perhaps, also, if he had strength and courage enough, he might be able to speak a good word for his Cousin Sam.

His thoughts, however, were in such a tangle, and his motives so uncertain, that he walked very slowly, and did not see a single thing on the road. Before he reached the cottage he stopped short, and, taking an order-book and a pencil from his pocket, he dotted down in a series of propositions and questions the chief points of the problem. They ran in this order:—

1. I have as much right to love Ruth Penlogan as anyone else.

2. Though I'm only a shopkeeper, and a dozen years her senior, there's nothing to hinder me from taking my chance.

3. If buying Hillside would help me, and make Ruth happy, where's the wrong? Cannot say.

4. But if buying Hillside would spoil Sam's chance, is that right? Doubtful.

5. Am I called upon to help Sam's cause to the detriment of my own? Also doubtful.

6. Is Ruth likely to be influenced by anything I may do or say? Don't know enough about women to answer that question.

7. Have I the smallest chance? No.

8. Has Sam? Most decidedly.

9. Am I a fool for thinking about Ruth at all? Certainly.

At this point William thrust his order-book into his pocket and quickened his pace.

"It's not a bit of use speculating on possibilities or probabilities," he said to himself a little impatiently. "I'll have to do the thing that seems right and wise. The rest I must leave."

A minute or two later he was knocking at the cottage door.

CHAPTER XXX

SELF AND ANOTHER

Ralph had gone to Perranpool to see Robert Telfer, but Ruth expected him back every moment.

"Won't you come in and wait for him?" Ruth questioned, looking beyond him into the gathering twilight.

William hesitated for a moment, and then decided that he would.

"I am sure he will not be long," Ruth said, as she busied herself getting the lamp ready. "Mr. Telfer wanted to settle with him, as—as he can, of course, deliver no more concrete."

"It's an awful shame," William said abruptly, and he dropped into Ralph's easy-chair.

"It seems very hard," Ruth said reflectively; "but I tell Ralph it may be all for the best. Perhaps he was getting on too fast and too suddenly."

"He is not the sort to have his head turned by a bit of prosperity," William said, watching his fair hostess out of the corner of his eye.

"At any rate, the danger has been removed—if it was a danger." And Ruth sighed gently.

For several moments there was silence in the room. Ruth had the lamp to light and the blind to pull down and a fresh cover to lay on the table. William watched her with averted face and half-closed eyes. How womanly she was in all her movements; how dainty in her appearance; how gentle in her manner and speech!

William felt as if he would almost risk his hope of heaven for the chance of calling her his, and yet he had not the courage even to hint at what he felt. Her very daintiness and winsomeness seemed to widen the gulf between them. Who was he that he should dare make love to one who was fit for the best in the land? It seemed to him—so unworthy did he seem in his own eyes— utterly impossible that Ruth should ever care for a man of his type.

William was almost morbidly self-depreciatory when in the presence of Ruth. His love so glorified her that by contrast he was commoner than commonest clay.

"I was so sorry to hear you are to be turned out of your shop," Ruth said at length, taking a seat on the other side of the table.

"Ralph told you?" he questioned.

"We stayed up till quite late last night, talking about it," she replied. "Ralph is very indignant."

"I am very indignant myself," he answered; "but what's the good? Those who have the power use it as they like."

"I am sorry it has happened," she said gently; "sorry for all our sakes. Ralph's reverence for the ruling classes was not great before. It is less now."

"You cannot wonder at that," he said quickly.

"No, one cannot wonder. And yet there is a danger in judging the whole by a few. Besides, if we had real power, we might not use it any more wisely or justly. The best of people, after all, are only human."

"That being so," he answered, with a smile, "it does not seem right that any individual, or any class of individuals, should have so much power. Who made these people rulers and dividers over us?"

"Ah, now you are getting beyond me," she said; "but since things are as they are, should we not make the best of them?"

"And try to mend them at the same time?"

"Oh yes, by all means—that is, if we can."

"But you have not much hope of mending things?" he questioned.

"Not very much. Besides, if you levelled things up to-morrow, they would be levelled down again the day after."

"Isn't that a rather fatalistic way of looking at things?" he questioned, raising his eyes timidly to her face.

"Is it?" she questioned, and a soft blush swept over her face as she caught his glance. Then silence fell again for several moments.

"The chances of life are very bewildering," he said at length, reopening the conversation. "Some people seem to get all the luck, and others all the misfortune. Look at my Cousin Sam."

"Is he very unfortunate?"

William laughed.

"On the contrary, he has all the luck. He has never known what poverty means, or sickness, or hardship. He was born to affluence, and now, at twenty-six, he's his own master, with a house of his own and plenty of money."

"But he may not be a whit happier than those who have less."

"I don't see how he can help it," William answered. "He's never worried about ways and means. He has troops of friends, absolutely wants nothing except a wife to help him to spend his money."

"Then you should advise him to keep single," Ruth said, with a laugh, "for if he gets married, his troubles may begin."

"There's risk in everything, no doubt," William said meditatively. "Still, if I were in his place, I should take the risk."

"You would?" Ruth questioned, arching her eyebrows, "and you a bachelor?"

"Ah, that is my misfortune," William answered, looking hard at a picture on the wall. "But Sam's way is quite clear."

"Is it?"

"He's a good fellow, too, is Sam. Never a word of slander has been breathed against his name since he was born. He'll make a good husband, whoever gets him."

"I did not know you had such a cousin till last evening," Ruth said meaningly.

"Oh, well, no. We've never seen very much of each other. You see, the Tremails have always been rather big people, and then we have lived a long way apart, and I have never cared to presume on my relationship."

"So he has hunted you up?"

"Well, yes. He came to see me just a fortnight ago or so, and he has ridden over once or twice since. Don't you think he's a fine, handsome fellow?"

"Yes; he is not bad-looking."

"Oh, I call him handsome. It must be nice to be young and have so much strength and energy."

"Well, are you not young?"

"I'm ten years older than Sam," he said, a little sadly, "and ten years is a big slice out of one's life."

"Are you growing pessimistic?" she questioned. "You are usually so hopeful."

"There are some things too good to hope for," he replied, "too beautiful, too far away. I almost envy a man like my Cousin Sam. He has everything within his reach."

"You seem to be quite enthusiastic about your cousin," she said, with a smile.

"Am I? Oh, well, you know, he is my cousin, and a good fellow, and if I can speak a good—I mean, if I can appreciate—that is, if I can cultivate a right feeling toward him, and—and—all that, you know, don't you think I ought to do so?"

"Oh, no doubt," Ruth said, laughing. "It's generally well to be on good terms with one's relations—at least so I've been told," and she went to the door and looked out into the darkness.

Ruth came back again after a few moments, and turned the lamp a little higher.

"Ralph is much longer than I expected he would be," she remarked, without looking at William.

"Perhaps Mr. Telfer was out," he suggested.

"I don't think that. You see he went by appointment. I expect it has taken them longer to square their accounts than they thought."

"I hope Ralph will come well out of it," he said musingly. "He's had a rough time of it so far."

"I am sometimes afraid he will grow bitter and give up. He has talked again and again of trying his fortune abroad."

"But if he went abroad, what would become of you?" William asked, with a sudden touch of anxiety in his voice.

"He would send for me when he got settled."

William gave a little gasp.

"Would you like to go abroad?" he questioned.

"I would much prefer to stay here if I could; but you see we cannot always have what we would like best."

"No, that is true," he said slowly and meditatively. "The things we would like best are often not for us. I don't know why it should be so. Some people seem to get all they desire. There is my Cousin Sam, for instance."

"He is one of the lucky ones, you say?"

"It seems so from my point of view. Did he tell you when he first saw you?"

"No."

"He would not like to remind you. It was the day of the sale at Hillside. He was greatly—that is, of course he could not help noticing you. Since then he has seen you lots of times. A fortunate fellow is Sam."

"Perhaps he does not think so."

"Oh, I fancy he does. I don't see how he can help it. He lives in a beautiful old house. It's years since I saw it, but it remains in my memory a pleasant picture. His wife will have a rare time of it."

"How do you know he does not intend to follow your example and remain a bachelor?"

"How? Sam knows better than that. Do you think I would remain a bachelor if —if—but there! You remember what you said just now about the things we want most?"

"I did not know——" Then a step sounded on the gravel outside. "Oh, here comes Ralph." And Ruth sprang to her feet and rushed to the door.

A moment later the two men were shaking hands.

"I hope I have not kept you waiting long," Ralph said. "The truth is, Telfer and I have been settling up."

"So your sister told me."

"And I'm bound to say he's treated me most handsomely. Technically, he might have got the better of me on a dozen points; but no! he's been most fair. It's a real pleasure to come across a man who doesn't want to Jew you."

"Oh, bless you, there's lots of honest people in the world!" William said, with a smile.

"Yes, I suppose there are; the misfortune is one so often tumbles across the other sort."

"Perhaps you will have better luck in the future," William replied.

"I only want fair play," Ralph answered; "I ask for nothing more than that."

"And have you hit upon anything for the future?"

"Not yet. But I don't want to be in a hurry. I've ready money enough to last me a year or two. I really didn't think I had done so well, for I'm a duffer at figures. If I only had about four times as much I'd buy Hillside."

"And turn farmer?"

"No, farming is not my forte." And he turned and looked towards the door of the pantry behind which Ruth was engaged getting supper ready.

"Let's go into my room," he continued, in a half-whisper. "I've something I want to say to you."

William followed him without a word.

"I don't want to awaken any vain hopes in Ruth's mind," Ralph went on. "The thing is too remote to be talked about almost. But you have wondered why I should want Hillside Farm when I've no love for farming?"

"I have supposed it was for your sister's sake."

"No, it's not that exactly. It's my love of adventure, or you might call it my love of speculation."

"I don't quite understand."

"Of course you don't. So I'll explain. You are the best friend I ever had, and I can trust you. Besides, if I ever did anything I should want your help. You are a business man, I'm a dreamer. You are good at accounts, I'm a fool at them."

William's eyes opened wider and wider, but he did not interrupt.

"Now, there's just the possibility of a fortune in Hillside," Ralph went on. "Not on the surface, mind you. The crops raised there will never be a fortune for anybody; but my father believed there was a rich tin lode running through it."

"Why didn't he test it?"

"He had no opportunity."

"Why not? The farm was his as long as the 'lives' remained alive."

"But all the mineral rights were reserved by the ground landlord. So that if my father had discovered a gold mine he would have got nothing out of it."

"So he kept silent?"

"Naturally; for if a mine was started, not only would he get no good out of it, but his farm would be ruined."

William remained silent and thoughtful.

"Now, if I could get the freehold," Ralph went on, "I should be free from every interference. I could sink a shaft for a few fathoms and test the thing. If it proved to be worthless, very little harm would be done. I should still have the farm to work or to let. Do you see my point?"

"I do, but——"

"I know what you would say. I have not the money," Ralph interrupted. "That is quite true. But I've more than I thought I had. And if the Brick, Tile, and Clay Company will take my plant at a fair valuation, I shall have more. Now I want to ask you, as a business man, if you think I could get a mortgage for the rest?"

"Possibly you might," William said slowly, "but there are a good many objections to such a course."

"Well, what are they?"

"We'll take one thing at a time," William answered meditatively. "To begin with: I don't believe Sir John Hamblyn would sell the place to you under any circumstances if he knew."

"Why not?"

"Because he has wronged you, and so he hates you. Nothing would please him better than for you to leave the country."

"Well?"

"If you begin to look round for a mortgage, or for securities——"

"Yes, I see."

"If you are to get the place, your name must not be given at the outset; you must buy through an agent or solicitor. You must be ready with the money on the nail."

Ralph looked thoughtful for several moments.

"I'm afraid it's of no use hoping," he said at length; "though when Robert Telfer handed me over his cheque this evening the world did look bright for a moment."

"But if you bought the farm you might lose everything," William suggested; "and it would be a pity to throw away your first earnings."

"Why so? There's no good in hoarding money. I want to be doing something. Besides, I might find work for half the parish."

"Then you have faith in the tin lode of which your father spoke?"

"I am confident there is a lode there. My father was not likely to be mistaken in a matter of that kind. As a practical miner and mineralogist there was not his equal in the county."

"But he did not test the lode?"

"He had no chance."

"Hence, it may be worthless."

"I admit it. Mind you, my father was confident that it was rich in tin. Of course, he may have been mistaken."

"But you are prepared to risk your all on it?"

"I am. I wish I had ten times as much to risk."

The next moment Ruth appeared, with the announcement that supper was ready.

"Let me sleep over it," William whispered to Ralph; "and to-morrow morning you come up to my shop and we'll see what we can make of it."

And he turned and followed Ruth into the next room.

CHAPTER XXXI

A PARTNERSHIP

It was late when William left Ralph Penlogan's cottage, but he was in no hurry to get to St. Goram. He sauntered slowly along the dark and deserted lane with his hands in his pockets and his eyes nowhere in particular. He tried to comfort himself with the reflection that he had not been selfish—that he had done his best for his Cousin Sam, that he had spoken the good word that he promised.

But for some reason the reward of virtue was not so great as he had hoped. There was no feeling of exultation in his heart at his triumph over temptation; in truth, he was much more inclined to call himself a fool for lending aid to his cousin at all.

This reflection reacted on his spirits in another way. He was more selfish than he could have believed. He was like the man who gave half a crown at a collection, and regretted it all his life afterwards. He had forced himself to speak a good word for his cousin, but there was no virtue in it. Service rendered so grudgingly was deserving of no reward.

"I am like the dog in the manger," he said to himself, a little disconsolately; "I cannot have her myself, and I don't want anybody else to have her."

Then he fell to thinking of Ruth's many attractions. He had never seen anyone before with such a wealth of hair, and he was sure there was no one in the three parishes who arranged her hair so gloriously as Ruth did. And then her figure was just perfection in his eyes. She was neither too short nor too tall, too stout nor too thin. There was not a single line or curve that he would have altered.

And her character was as perfect as her form and as beautiful as her face. William's love shed over her and around her a golden haze which hid every fault and magnified every virtue.

By morning he was able to see things a little more in their true perspective, and when Ralph called he was able to put love aside and talk business, though he was by no means sure that in business matters Ruth did not influence him unconsciously.

Ralph had great faith in William's judgment and sagacity. He always looked at both sides of a question before deciding. If he erred at all, it was on the side of excessive caution.

Ralph could not help wondering what was in William's mind. He had said practically nothing the previous evening. He had asked a few questions, and pointed out certain difficulties, but he had committed himself to nothing, yet it seemed clear that he had some scheme in his mind which he would reveal when he had duly considered it.

For a few minutes they talked generalities, then William plunged into the subject that was uppermost in the thoughts of both.

"I don't wonder that you want to get hold of the freehold of Hillside," he said. "I should if I were in your place. Apart from sentiment, the business side appeals strongly. The discovery of a good tin lode there would be the making of St. Goram——"

"And the ruin of the farm," Ralph interjected.

"Well, the erection of a big engine-house on the top of the hill and fire stamps in Dingley Bottom would certainly not improve the appearance of things from an artistic point of view."

"'There is no gain except by loss,'" Ralph quoted, with a smile.

"True; but we all ought to consider the greatest good of the greatest number."

Ralph laughed.

"Don't credit me with virtues I don't possess," he said. "I confess I'm thinking in the first instance only of myself."

"Well, I suppose that's only natural," William said seriously. "But now to business. If you purchase the farm at the squire's price, how much money will you require beyond what you have?"

Ralph named the sum.

"Is that all?"

"Yes. I told you last night the concrete had turned out well."

"It can be done easily," William said, with a sudden brightening of his face.

"How?"—with an eager look.

"I will advance you all the money you want, either as a loan or on mortgage."

"You really mean it?"

"I do. But on one condition—and that is that you do not say anything to your sister about it."

"But why not? I have no secrets from Ruth."

210

William coloured and looked uncomfortable.

"It's merely a whim of mine," he said. "Women don't understand business, and she might think I was doing you a great favour, and I don't want her to think anything of the kind."

"But you are doing me an immense favour!"

"I'm not, really. The margin of security will be, if not ample, at least sufficient; and if the lode should prove of value, why, you will be able to pay off the loan in no time."

"If the lode should prove of any value, William, you shall go shares!" Ralph said impulsively.

"No, no! If I take no risk, I take no reward. You will risk everything in testing the thing."

"I'm fond of risks," Ralph said, with a laugh. "A little adventure is the very spice of life. Oh, I do hope the farm is not already sold!"

"I don't think it can be," William answered. "We have wasted no time yet. If it is sold, you will have to wait, and hope the buyer will get tired of his bargain."

Ralph shook his head.

"If I can't get it now," he said, "I shall try my fortune beyond the seas."

"Well, we needn't wait an hour longer. You can have my trap to drive to St. Hilary. Let some lawyer whom you can trust act for you."

"Won't you go with me?" Ralph questioned eagerly. "You see, the question of security will come up first thing."

"It would be almost better if you could keep out of sight altogether."

"I know it. Couldn't you see the whole thing through for me?"

"I might try."

Half an hour later Ralph had sent word to Ruth that he would not be home till evening, and was driving away with William Menire in the direction of St. Hilary.

They were both too excited to talk much. Ralph felt as though the whole universe were trembling in the balance. If he failed, there would be nothing left worth considering. If he succeeded, paradise threw open her gates to him.

Far away beyond the hills there was a great city called London, and in that city dwelt one who was more to him than all the world beside. She was out of his reach because he was poor and nameless and obscure. But if he won for himself a position, what was to hinder him from wooing her, and perhaps winning her? Money for its own sake he cared nothing for. The passion for position had never been a factor in his life. He loved beautiful things—art and music and literature—partly from instinct, and partly because he had been educated to appreciate them, but there was not an ounce of snobbery in his composition. He had no reverence for rank as such, or for mere social position, but he had sense enough to recognise their existence, and the part they played in the evolution of the race. He could not get rid of things by shutting his eyes to their existence.

So they drove along the quiet road mainly in silence. Each was busy with his own thoughts. Each had a secret that he dared not reveal to the other.

"I believe you will win," William said abruptly after a long interval of silence. "I always said you would."

"Win?" Ralph questioned absently, for he was thinking of Dorothy Hamblyn at the time.

"Your father was a shrewd man where mineral was concerned."

"Yes. And yet he loved corn and cows far more than copper and tin."

"I wouldn't mind being in your place."

"You would not be afraid of the risk?"

"No. I would like it."

"Then let's go shares!" Ralph said eagerly. "It's what I've wanted all along, but did not like to propose it."

"You really mean it?"

"My dear fellow, it is what I would desire above everything else! You have business capacity, and I haven't a scrap."

"If I were sure I could help you."

"We should help each other; but the gain would be chiefly mine."

"Partnerships don't always turn out well," William said reflectively.

"I'll gladly risk it," Ralph answered, with a laugh.

William dropped his driving whip into the socket and reached across his hand. It was his way of sealing the contract.

Ralph seized it in a moment.

"This is the proudest day of my life!" William said. And there were distinct traces of emotion in his voice.

"I hope you will not be sorry later on," Ralph answered dubiously.

"Never!" was the firm reply. And he thought of Ruth, and wondered what the future had in store for him.

For the rest of the way they drove in silence. There were things in the lives of both too sacred to be talked about.

CHAPTER XXXII

FOOD FOR REFLECTION

There was widespread interest of a mild kind when it became known in St. Goram that Sir John Hamblyn had disposed of the freehold of Hillside Farm. It was an action altogether unprecedented in the history of the Hamblyn family. What it portended no one knew, but it seemed to crystallise into a concrete fact all the rumours that had been in circulation for the last two or three years.

The first news reached Farmer Jenkins in a letter from Sir John. It was brief and to the point:—

"I have this day sold the freehold of Hillside Farm. Your new landlord will no doubt communicate with you shortly.—Yours truly,

"JOHN HAMBLYN."

Farmer Jenkins stared at the letter for a considerable time after he had mastered its contents.

"So-ho!" he said to himself at length. "Now I understand why he wanted the matter of reduction of rent to stand over. 'Cute dog is Sir John. If he's sold the place on the basis of present rental he's swindled somebody. I wonder who the fool is who bought it. Anyhow, I won't stay here after Lady Day." And he pushed the letter into his pocket, pulled a weather-beaten wideawake hat over his bald pate, and started out in the direction of St. Goram.

William Menire was standing behind his desk when Jenkins stumbled into his shop. He laid down his pen at once, and prepared himself to execute the farmer's order.

It was not a large order by any means—something that had been forgotten on the previous day—and when the farmer had stuffed it into one of his big pockets he looked up suddenly and said—

"You ain't heard no news, I expect?"

"What sort of news?" William questioned.

"Oh, any sort."

"Well, no. There doesn't seem to be much stirring at the present time."

"More stirring than you think, perhaps," Jenkins said mysteriously.

"That's possible, of course. Have you been hearing something?"

"Squire's cleared out, ain't he?"

"I hear he has practically closed the Manor for an indefinite period."

"Purty hard up, I reckon."

"Why do you think so?"

"Took to sellin' his estate."

"No!" William said, with a little gasp.

"It's solemn truth. I got a letter from him just now sayin' he'd sold Hillside Farm."

"Sold it?"

"Them's his very words. Here's the letter, if you like to read it."

William took the letter and retired to the window. He did not want the farmer to see his agitation. He had been waiting day after day for nearly a month for some definite news, and here it was in black and white. He wondered what Ralph would say when he heard. Once more his hopes had been blown to the wind. His dream of success, not for the first time or the second, had been dashed to the ground.

"Seems definite enough, don't it?" questioned the farmer, coming nearer.

"Oh yes, there can be no mistake about it," William answered, trying his best to keep his voice steady.

"Well, it don't make no difference to me," the farmer said indifferently. "I've made up my mind to clear out at Lady Day. There ain't no luck about the place. I keep feelin' as though there was a kind of blight upon it."

"Indeed?"

"The way the squire shoved it on to me wasn't square to David Penlogan. I can see it clear enough now, and I've never felt quite comfortable since David died. I keep feelin' at times as though he was about the place still."

"Who—David?"

"Ay. He was terrible fond of the place by all accounts. It was a pity Sir John didn't let him stay on. He might have been livin' to this day if he had."

"Yes, that is quite true; but we must not forget that David is better off. He was a good man, if ever there was one."

"Anyhow, the place don't prosper under me, somehow. And if the new landlord is willin' to lower the rent I shan't stay on. I've got my eye on something I think'll suit me better." And, turning slowly round, the farmer walked out of the shop.

William stood staring at the door long after the farmer had disappeared. He had seen the possibility of the farm falling into other hands from the first, but had never fully realised till now how much that might mean to him. His own future was involved just as much as Ralph's. While there was a prospect of getting the farm he had not troubled about his own notice to quit. Now the whole problem would have to be thought out again. Nor was that all—nor even the most important part. He had seen, in fancy, Ruth installed in the old home that she loved so much; seen how Hillside had called to her more loudly and potently than all the pleadings of Sam Tremail; seen the gulf that now lay between them gradually close up and disappear; seen her advance to meet him till their hands had clasped in a bond that only death could break.

It was a foolish fancy, perhaps, but he had not been able to help it taking possession of him from time to time, and with the passing of the days and weeks the fancy had become more and more vivid and real.

"It is all over now," William said to himself, as he stood staring at the door. "Ralph will go abroad and leave her alone at home. Then will come the choice of going away to a strange country or going to Pentudy, and Sam, of course, will win," and William sighed, and dropped into a chair behind his desk.

A minute or two later the door swung open again, and Ralph Penlogan stalked into the shop.

William rose at once to his feet, and moved down inside the counter.

"Well, William, any news yet?" Ralph questioned eagerly.

William dropped his eyes slowly to the floor.

"Yes, Ralph," he said, in a half-whisper. "We've missed it."

"Missed it?"

"Ay! I've been a bit afraid of it all along. You remember their lawyer told Mr. Jewell that there were several people after it."

"Where's Jewell's letter?" Ralph questioned, after a pause.

"I've not heard from Jewell."

"Then how did you get to know?"

"Jenkins told me. He got a letter from Sir John this morning saying he had sold it."

216

"To whom?"

"He mentioned no name—possibly he didn't know. It went to the man, I expect, who was willing to pay most for it."

"Perhaps Sir John got to know we were after it."

"Possibly, though I don't think Jewell would tell him."

"Oh, well, it doesn't matter, I suppose," Ralph said, in a hard voice. "It's all in the day's work."

"I feel a good deal more upset about it than I thought I should," William said, after a long pause.

"Yes?" Ralph questioned.

"I fancy the spirit of adventure had got a bit into my blood," William answered, with a gentle smile. "I felt ready to speculate all I had. I was itching, as one may say, to be at the lode."

"Such an adventurous spirit needed checking," Ralph said, with a laugh that had more bitterness in it than mirth.

"Perhaps so. Now we shall have to face the whole problem over again."

"I shall try my fortune abroad. I made up my mind weeks ago that if this failed I should leave the country."

"Yes, yes. But it comes hard all the same. There ought to be as much room for enterprise in this country as in any other."

"Perhaps there is, but we are in the wrong corner of it."

"No, it isn't that. It is simply that we have to deal with the wrong people. I grow quite angry when I think how all enterprise is checked by the hidebound fossils who happen to be in authority, and the stupid laws they have enacted."

Ralph laughed.

"My dear William, you will be talking treason next," he said, and then a customer came in and put an end to further conversation.

Ralph went back home, and without saying anything to his sister, began quietly to sort out his things.

"I may as well get ready first as last," he said to himself; "and the sooner I take my departure the better."

He was very silent when he came down to dinner, and his eyes had an absent look in them.

"What have you been doing all the morning?" Ruth asked at length.

"Sorting out my things, Ruth; that's all."

She started, and an anxious look came into her eyes.

"But why have you been sorting them out to-day?" she questioned.

"Because to-morrow will be Sunday," he said, with a smile, "and you are strongly opposed to Sunday labour."

"But still, I don't understand?" she interrogated uneasily.

"I would like to get off on Tuesday morning if possible."

"Do you mean——" she began.

"I shall have to clear out sooner or later, Ruth," he interrupted, "and the sooner the better."

"Then you have decided to go abroad, Ralph?" And her face became very pale.

"What else can I do?" he asked. "I really have not the courage to settle down at St. Ivel Mine at fourteen shillings a week, even if I were sure of getting work, which I am not."

"And I don't want you to do it," she said suddenly, with a rush of tears to her eyes.

"In a bigger country, with fewer restrictions and barbed wire fences, I may be able to do something," he went on. "At worst, I can but fail."

"I hoped that something would turn up here," she said, after a long pause.

"So did I, Ruth; and, indeed, until this morning things looked promising."

"Well?"

"Like so many other hopes, Ruth, it has gone out in darkness."

"You have said nothing to me about it," she said at length.

"No. I did not wish to buoy you up with hopes that might end in nothing."

"What was it you had in your mind, Ralph?" And she raised her soft, beseeching eyes to his.

"Oh, well," he said uneasily, "no harm can come of telling you now, though I did promise William that I would say nothing to you about it."

"Oh, indeed!" she said, in hurt tones. "What has he to do with it?"

"Well, as a matter of fact, he had nearly everything to do with it."

"And he had so little confidence in me that I was not to be trusted?"

"No, sis. William Menire is not that kind of man, as you ought to know by this time."

"Then why was I not to be told? Does he take me for a child?"

"Perhaps he does. You see, he is years older than either of us; but his main concern was that you should not feel in any way under an obligation to him."

"I do not understand."

"William feels very sensitive where you are concerned. The truth is, he was going to advance most of the money for the purchase of Hillside."

"Ralph!"

"It is true, dear; and until this morning we hoped we should get it."

"Well?"

"It has been sold to somebody else."

For a long time no other word was spoken. Ruth made a pretence of eating, but she had no longer any appetite for her dinner. Ralph had given her food of another kind—food for reflection. A dozen questions that had been the vaguest suggestions before suddenly crystallised themselves into definite form.

When the dinner was over, Ralph put on his hat and made for the door.

"I am going down to Perranpool," he said. "I have one or two things I want to talk over with Robert Telfer before I go."

"Don't forget to remember me to Mary," Ruth said, following him to the door.

"Anything else?" he questioned, with a smile.

"Yes. Tell her to come up and see me as soon as ever she is able."

"All right," and, waving his hand, he marched rapidly away.

Ruth sighed as she followed him with her eyes. It seemed to her a thousand pities that his native land had no place for such as he. He was not of the common order. He had gifts, education, imagination, enterprise, and yet he was foiled at every point.

Then for some reason her thoughts travelled away to William Menire, and the memory of her brother's words, "William is very sensitive where you are concerned," brought a warm rush of colour to her cheeks.

Why should William be so sensitive where she was concerned? Why should he be so shy and diffident when in her presence? Why was he ever so ready to sing the praises of his cousin?

She was brought back to herself at length by the sound of horse's hoofs, and a minute or two later Sam Tremail drew up and alighted at the garden gate.

CHAPTER XXXIII

A PROPOSAL

Sam did not wait for an invitation. Flinging the reins over the gate post, he marched boldly up the garden path, and greeted Ruth at the door. She received him courteously, as was her nature, but a more sensitive man might have felt that there was not much warmth in her welcome.

"I was riding this way, and so I thought I would call," he explained. "I hope I don't intrude?"

"Oh no, not at all. Will you come inside?"

"Thank you, I shall be pleased to rest a few minutes, and so will Nero. Is your brother at home?"

"No, he has just gone down to Perranpool."

"Mr. Telfer has nearly finished his contract, I hear."

"So I am told."

"And the company have a mountain of concrete on their hands."

"Ralph says they are charging so enormously for it. Besides, they have not sought out new markets."

"Markets would open if the stuff was not so poor. They managed to hustle your brother out of his rights without getting his secret."

"Is that so?"

"So I am told. I know nothing about the matter myself. I can only repeat what people are saying. By the by, I suppose you have heard that your old home has been sold?"

"Yes."

"St. Goram seems to be quite excited about it. The people in my cousin's shop can talk of nothing else."

"Then you have called on your cousin?"

"Just to say 'How d'ye do?' But Saturday afternoon appears to be a busy day with him. Seems a shame that he has to turn out, doesn't it?"

"It is a shame."

"Of course, in a measure, it's his own fault. He ought not to have opposed Lord St. Goram. A man in business ought not to have any politics, and should keep out of public affairs."

"But suppose he agreed with Lord St. Goram?"

"Oh, that would make a difference, of course. A man ought to know on which side his bread is buttered."

"And principle and conviction should not count?"

"I don't say that. A man can have any convictions he likes, so long as he keeps them to himself; but in politics it is safest to side with the powers that be."

"You think so?"

"I am sure of it. Take the case of my Uncle Ned."

"I never heard of him," Ruth said innocently.

"Oh, well, his late landlord was a Liberal, and, of course, my uncle was a Liberal. Then his landlord became a Unionist, and Uncle Ned became a Unionist also. Well, then his landlord died and his son took possession. He's a Conservative and true blue, and, of course, Uncle Ned is a Tory of the Tories. What is the result? He gets no end of privileges. Moreover, there is no fear of his being turned out of his farm."

"And you admire your Uncle Ned?"

"I think he might be a little less ostentatious. But he knows on which side his bread is buttered. Now my Cousin William goes dead against his own landlord; there's all the difference. Result, Ned remains and prospers; William has notice to quit."

"I'd rather be William than your Uncle Ned."

"You would?"

"A thousand times. A man who places bread and butter before conscience and conviction is a coward, and a man who changes his political creed to please his landlord is too contemptible for words."

Sam turned uneasily in his chair and stared. He had never imagined that this sweet-faced girl could speak so strongly. Moreover, he began to fear that he had unconsciously put his foot into it. He had called for the purpose of making love to Ruth, and had come perilously near to making her angry.

How to get back to safer ground was a work of no small difficulty. He could not unsay what he had said, and to attempt to trim would only provoke her scorn. Neither could he suddenly change the subject without considerable loss of dignity. So, after an awkward pause, he said—

"Everyone has a right to his or her own opinions, of course. For myself, I should not be prepared to express myself so strongly."

"Perhaps you do not feel strongly," she said.

"I don't think I do," he replied, in a tone of relief; "that is, on public questions. I am no politician, and, besides, there is always a good deal to be said on both sides of every question. I try as far as possible, you know, to keep an open mind," and he smiled benevolently, and felt well pleased with himself.

After that conversation flagged. Ruth appeared to be absent-minded, and in no mood for further talk. Nero outside champed at his bit, and was eager to be on the move again. Sam turned his hat round and round in his hands, and puzzled his brain as to how he should get near the subject that was uppermost in his mind.

He started a number of topics—the weather, the chances of a fine day for Summercourt Fair, the outbreak of measles at Doubleday, the price of tin, the new travelling preacher, the Sunday-school anniversary at Trebilskey, the large catch of pilchards at Mevagissey—but they all came to a sudden and ignominious conclusion.

He rose to his feet at length almost in despair, and looked towards the door. For some reason the task he had set himself was far more difficult than he had imagined. In his ride from Pentudy he had rehearsed his speech to the listening hedgerows with great diligence, and with considerable animation. He had rounded his periods till they seemed almost perfect. He had decided on the measure of emphasis to be laid on certain passages. But now, when he stood face to face with the girl he coveted, the speech eluded him almost entirely, while such passages as he could remember did not seem at all fitting to the occasion. The time clearly was not propitious. He would have to postpone his declaration to a more convenient season.

"I'm afraid I must be going," he said desperately.

"Your horse seems to be getting impatient," Ruth replied, looking out of the window.

"It's not the horse I care for," he blurted out; "it's you."

"Me?" she questioned innocently.

"Do you think anything else matters when you are about?" he asked in a tone almost of defiance.

"I fear I do not understand," she said, with a bewildered expression in her eyes.

"Oh, you must understand," he replied vehemently. "You must have seen that I love you."

"No, no!"

"Don't interrupt me, please, now that I've started. Give me a chance—oh, do give me a chance. I've loved you ever since your father's sale. I'm sure it's love I feel for you. Whenever people talk about my getting married, my thoughts always turn to you in a moment. I waited and waited for a chance of speaking to you, and thought it would never come; and now that I've got to know you a bit——"

"But you don't know me," she interrupted.

"Yes, I do. Besides, William has told me how good you are; and then I'm willing to wait until I know you better, and you know me better. I don't ask you to say Yes to-day, and please don't say No. I'm sure I could make you happy. You should have a horse of your own to ride if you wanted one, and I would be as good to you as ever I could, and I don't think I'm a bad sort. Ask my Cousin William, and he'll tell you that I'm a steady-going fellow. I know I'm not clever, nor anything of that sort; but I would look after you really well —I would, indeed. And think of it. You may need a friend some day. You may be left alone, as it were; your brother may get married. There's never any knowing what may happen. But if you would let me look after you and care for you, you wouldn't have a worry in the world. Think of it——"

She put up her hand deprecatingly, for when his tongue was once unloosed his words flowed without a break. He looked very manly and handsome, too, as he stood before her, and there was evident sincerity in his tones.

He broke off suddenly, and stood waiting. He felt that he had done the thing very clumsily, but that was perhaps inevitable under the circumstances.

Ruth looked up and met his eyes. She was no flirt; she was deeply moved by his confession. Moreover, when he spoke of her being alone some day and needing protection, he touched a sympathetic chord in her heart. She was to be left alone sooner than he knew. Already preparations had begun for her brother's departure.

"Please do not say any more," she said gently. "I do not doubt your sincerity for a moment."

"But you are not offended with me?" he gasped.

"No, I am not offended with you. Indeed, I feel greatly honoured by your proposal."

"Then you will think it over?" he interrupted. "Say you will think it over. Don't send me away without hope."

She smiled a sweet, pathetic smile, and answered—

"Yes, I will think it over."

"Thank you so much," he said, with beaming face. "That is the most I could hope for to-day," and he held out his hand to her, which she took shyly and diffidently.

"If you can only bring yourself to say Yes," he said, as he stood in the doorway, "I will do my best to make you the happiest woman in the world."

She did not reply, however. From behind the window curtains she watched him mount his horse and ride away; then she dropped into an easy-chair and stared into space.

It is sometimes said that a woman rarely gets the man she wants—that he, unknowing and unseeing, goes somewhere else, and she makes no sign. Later on she accepts the second best, or it may be the third best, and tries to be content.

Ruth wondered if contentment was ever to be found along that path, if the heart grew reconciled to the absence of romance, if the passion of youth was but the red glare of sunrise which quickly faded into the sober light of day.

Sam Tremail was not a man to be despised. He was no wastrel, no unknown adventurer. He was a man of character and substance. He had been a good son; he would doubtless make a good husband. Could she be content?

No halo of romance gathered about his name. No beautiful and tender passion shook her heart when she thought of him. Life at Pentudy would be sober and grey and commonplace. There would be no passion flowers, no crimson and scarlet and gold. On the other hand, there would be no want, no mean and niggling economies, no battle for daily bread. Was solid comfort more lasting, and therefore more desirable, than the richly-hued vesture of romance?

How about the people she knew—the people who had reached middle life— the people who were beginning to descend the western slope? Had there been any romance in their life? Had they thrilled at the beginning at the touch of a hand? Had their hearts leaped at the sound of a voice? And if so, why was there no sign of it to-day? Did familiarity always breed contempt? Did possession kill romance? Did the crimson of the morning always fade into the grey of noon?

Would it be better to marry without dreams and illusions, to begin with the sober grey, the prose and commonplace, than begin with some richly-hued dreams that would fade and disappear before the honeymoon came to an end? To be disillusioned was always painful. And yet, would not one swift month of rich romance, of deep-eyed, passionate love, be worth a lifetime of grey and sober prose?

Ruth was still thinking when Ralph returned from Perranpool.

Meanwhile Sam was trotting homeward in a very jubilant frame of mind. He pulled up in front of William Menire's shop and beckoned to his cousin.

"I want you to congratulate me, old man," he said, when William stood at his horse's head.

William's face fell in a moment, and his lips trembled in spite of himself.

"Have you—you—been to—to——?" William began.

"I've just come from there," Sam interrupted, with a laugh. "Been there for the last hour, and now I'm off home feeling that I have done a good day's work."

"You have proposed to her?"

"I have! It required a good bit of courage, but I've done it."

"And she has accepted?"

"She has not rejected me, at any rate. I didn't ask for a definite answer right off. But it is all right, my boy, I'm sure it is. Now, give us your hand. You've been a good friend to me. But for you I might never have got to know her."

William reached up his hand slowly and silently.

"It's often been a wonder to me," Sam said, squeezing his kinsman's hand, "that you never looked in that direction yourself; but I'm glad you never did."

"It would have been no use," William said sadly. "I'm not the kind of man to take any girl's fancy."

"Oh, that's all nonsense," Sam said gaily. "I admit that a great many girls like a fellow with a lot of dash and go, and are not particular about his past so long as he has a winning tongue and a smart exterior. But all girls are not built that way. Why, I can fancy you being a perfect hero in some people's eyes."

"You must have a vivid imagination," William said, with a smile; and then Sam put spurs to his horse and galloped away.

William went back to his work behind his counter with a pathetic and far-away look in his eyes. He was glad when the little group of customers were served, and he was left alone for a few minutes.

He had intended going to see the Penlogans that evening, but he decided now that he would not go. While Ruth was free he had a right to look at her and admire her, but he was not sure that that right was his any longer.

He wondered if Sam noticed that he did not congratulate him. He could not get out the words somehow.

He sat down at length with his elbow on the counter, and rested his head on his hand. He began to realise that he had built more on the acquisition of Hillside Farm than he knew. He had hoped in some vague way that the farm would be a bond between him and Ruth. Well, well, it was at an end now; the one romance of his life had vanished. His unspoken love would remain unspoken.

The next day being Sunday, all the characters in this story had time for meditation. Ruth and Ralph walked to Veryan that they might worship once more in the little chapel made sacred to them by the memory of father and mother. Ruth had great difficulty in keeping back the tears. How often she had sat in that bare and comfortless pew holding her father's hand. How she missed him again. How acute and poignant was her sense of loss.

She never once looked at her brother. He sat erect and motionless by her side, but she doubted if he heard the sermon. The thought of the coming separation lay heavy upon him as it did upon her.

On their way back Ruth plucked up her courage and told Ralph of Sam Tremail's proposal the previous afternoon.

Ralph stopped short for a moment, and looked at her.

"Now I understand why you have been so absent-minded," he said at length. "I was afraid you were fretting because I was going away."

"If I fretted, I should try and not let you see," she answered. "You have enough to bear already."

"The thought of leaving you unprotected is the hardest part," he said.

"Would it be a relief to you if I accepted Sam Tremail's offer?" she questioned.

"Supposing you cared for him enough, it would be," he replied. "Sam is a good fellow by all accounts. Socially, he is much above us."

"I have nothing against him," she answered slowly, "nothing! And I am quite sure he meant all he said."

"And do you care for him?"

She shook her head slowly and smiled—

"I neither like him nor dislike him. But he offers me protection and a good home."

"To be free from worry is a great thing," he answered, looking away across the distant landscape; and then he thought of Dorothy Hamblyn, and wondered if love and romance were as much to a woman as to a man.

"Yes, freedom from worry is doubtless a great thing," she said, after a long pause, "but is it the greatest and best?"

But she waited in vain for an answer. Ralph was thinking of something else.

CHAPTER XXXIV

A FRESH PAGE

William Menire got up early on Monday morning and helped to tidy up the shop before breakfast. He was not sorry that the working week had begun again. Work left him very little time for brooding and introspection. He had been twice to church the previous day, but he could not remember a word of the sermons. His own thoughts had drowned the voice of the preacher.

"I hope I shall have a busy week," he said to himself, as he helped his apprentice to take down the shutters. "The less I think the happier I shall be."

During breakfast the postman called. There was only one delivery per day, and during Sunday there was no delivery at all.

William glanced at the letters, but did not open any of them. One, in a blue envelope, was from Mr. Jewell, the solicitor. The postmark bore Saturday's date.

"His news is two days late," William reflected. "We really ought to have two deliveries in a place like this."

Then he helped himself to some more bacon. His mother was not so well, and had her breakfast in bed.

No one called him from the shop, so he was allowed to finish his breakfast in peace. Then he turned his attention to his correspondence. The blue envelope was left to the last.

"I wonder if Jewell knows the name of the purchaser?" he reflected, as he inserted a small paper-knife and cut open the envelope. He unfolded the letter slowly, then gave a sudden exclamation.

"Dear Sir,—I am advised by post this morning that your offer for Hillside Farm has been accepted, and——"

But he did not stop to read any further. Rushing into the passage, he seized his hat, and without a word to anyone, hurried away in the direction of St. Ivel as fast as his legs could carry him.

Ralph was standing in the middle of the room measuring with his eye the capacity of an open portmanteau, when William, breathless and excited, burst in upon him. Ruth was seated at the table, the portmanteau by her side.

"WILLIAM, BREATHLESS AND EXCITED, BURST IN UPON HIM."

"I say, Ralph, we've got it," William cried excitedly, without noticing Ruth.

"Got what?" Ralph said, turning suddenly round.

"Got the farm," was the reply. "We jumped to conclusions too soon on Saturday. Jewell says our offer has been accepted."

"Accepted!"

"Ay. Here is the letter, if you like to read it. Shut up your portmanteau, and take it out of sight. You are not going abroad yet awhile."

Ruth, who had risen to her feet on William's sudden appearance, now ran out of the room to hide her tears.

Ralph seized the lawyer's letter and read it slowly and carefully from beginning to end. Then he dropped into a chair and read it a second time. William stood and watched him, with a bright, eager smile lighting up his face.

"It seems all right," Ralph said at length.

"Ay, it's right enough, but I wish we had known earlier."

"It would have saved us a good many anxious and painful hours."

"Never mind. All's well that ends well."

"Oh, we haven't got to the end yet," Ralph said, with a laugh. "If that lode turns out a frost, we shall wish that somebody else had got the place."

"Never!" William said, almost vehemently.

"No?"

"I shall never regret we've got it, or rather that you have, though there isn't an ounce of tin in the whole place."

"Why not?"

"I don't know. One cannot give a reason for everything. But I have a feeling that this opens up a fresh page in the life of both of us."

"That's true enough, but everything depends on the kind of page it will be."

"I'm not worried about that. The thing that interests me is, the powers that be are not going to shunt us as they hoped. Lord St. Goram meant to drive me out of the parish, but I'm not going——"

"Nor I," Ralph interposed, with a laugh; and he shut up the portmanteau, and pushed it against the wall.

"We shall have to keep dark, however, till the deeds are signed," William said. "We must give Sir John no excuse for going back on his bargain. I'd wager my Sunday coat, if I were a betting man, that he hasn't the remotest idea we are the purchasers."

"Won't he look blue when he discovers? You know how he hates me."

"Ay, he has made no secret of that. It is rumoured, however, that he is going to live out of the country, and so he may not get to know for some time. However, we must walk warily till the thing is finally and absolutely settled. Also"—and William lowered his voice to a whisper—"you'd better say nothing yet to your sister."

"Oh, but she knows," Ralph replied.

William looked blank.

"I told her on Saturday what we had been trying to do. I thought she might as well know when the thing, as we thought, had come to an end. Besides, she heard what you said when you came in."

"I forgot all about her for the moment," William said absently. "Perhaps, after all, it is as well she knows. I hope, however, she will not feel in any way obligated to me."

"My dear fellow, what are you talking about?" Ralph said, with a smile. "Why, we owe nearly everything to you."

"No, no. I couldn't have done less, and so far I have received far more than I gave. But I must be getting back, or things will have got tied into a knot," and putting on his hat, he hurried away.

Ruth came back into the room as soon as William had disappeared. Her eyes were still red and her lashes wet with tears, but there was a bright, happy smile on her lips.

"Oh, Ralph," she said, "isn't it almost too good to be true?"

"It may not be so good as it looks," he said, in a tone of banter.

"Oh, it must be, Ralph; for, of course, we shall go back again to Hillside to live."

"But we can't live on nothing, you know, and the whole thing may turn out a frost."

"But you are quite sure it won't, or you and William Menire would not be so elated at getting it."

"Are we elated?"

"You are. You can hardly contain yourself at this moment. You would like to get on the top of the house and shout."

"Which would be a very unwise thing to do. We must not breathe a word to anyone till the thing is absolutely settled."

"And what will you do then?"

"Begin prospecting. If I can get as much out of the place as father sunk in it I shall be quite content."

During the next few weeks William Menire and the Penlogans saw a good deal of each other. Nearly every evening after his shutters had been put up William stole away to St. Ivel. He and Ralph had so many plans to discuss and so many schemes to mature. Ruth was allowed to listen to all the debates, and frequently she was asked to give advice.

It was in some respects a very trying time for William. The more he saw of Ruth the more he admired her. She seemed to grow bonnier every day. The sound of her voice stirred his heart like music, her smile was like summer sunshine. Moreover, she treated him with increasing courtesy, and even tenderness, so much so that it became a positive pain to him to hide his affection. And yet he wanted to be perfectly loyal to his Cousin Sam. Sam had proposed to her, Sam was waiting for an answer, if he had not already received it, and it would be a very uncousinly act to put the smallest obstacle in the way.

Not that William supposed for a moment that he could ever be a rival to Sam in any true sense of the word. On the other hand, he knew that Ruth was of so generous and grateful a nature that she might be tempted to accept him out of pure gratitude if he were bold enough and base enough to propose to her.

So William held himself in check with a firm hand and made no sign, but what the effort cost him no one knew. To sit in the same room with her evening after evening, to watch the play of her features and see the light sparkle in her soft brown eyes, and yet never by word or look betray the passion that was consuming him, was an experience not given to many men.

He was too loyal to his ideals ever to dream of marriage for any cause less than love. Possession was not everything, nor even the greatest thing. If he could have persuaded himself that there was even the remotest possibility of Ruth loving him, he would have gone on his knees to her every day in the week, and would have gladly waited any time she might name.

But he had persuaded himself of the very opposite. He was a dozen years her senior. While she was in the very morning of her youth, he was rapidly nearing youth's eventide. That she could ever care for him, except in a friendly or sisterly fashion, seemed an utter impossibility. The thought never occurred to him but he attempted to strangle it at once.

So the days wore away, and lengthened into weeks, and then the news leaked out in St. Goram that William and Ralph had gone into partnership and had purchased Hillside Farm. For several days little else was talked about. What could it mean? What object could they have in view? For agricultural purposes the place was scarcely worth buying; besides, William Menire knew absolutely nothing about farming, while most people knew that Ralph's tastes did not lie in that direction.

A few people blamed Ralph for "fooling William out of his money," for they rightly surmised that it was chiefly William's money that had purchased the estate. Others whispered maliciously that William had befriended Ralph simply that he might win favour with Ruth; but the majority of people said that William was much too 'cute a business man to be influenced by anybody, whether man or woman, and that if he had invested his money in Hillside Farm he had very good reasons for doing it. The only sensible attitude, therefore, was to wait and see what time would bring forth.

One of the first things Ralph did as soon as the deeds were signed was to send for Jim Brewer. He had heard that the young miner was out of work, and in sore need. He had heard also that Jim had never forgiven himself for not confessing at the outset that it was he who shot the squire by mistake.

Ralph had never seen the young fellow since he came out of prison, and had never desired to see him. He had no love for cowards, and was keenly resentful of the part Brewer had played. Time, however, had softened his feelings. The memory of those dark and bitter months was slowly fading from his mind. Moreover, poor Brewer had suffered enough already for the wrong he had done. He had been boycotted and shunned by almost all who knew him.

Ralph heard by accident one day of the straits to which Brewer had been driven, and his resentment was changed as if by magic into pity. It was easy to blame, easy to fling the word "coward" into the teeth of a weaker brother; but if he had been placed in Jim Brewer's circumstances, would he have acted a nobler part? It was Brewer's care for his mother and the children that led him to hide the truth. Moreover, if he had been wholly a coward, he would never have confessed at all.

Ralph told Ruth what he intended to do, and her eyes filled in a moment.

"Oh, Ralph," she said, "it is the very thing of all others I should like you to do."

"For what reason, Ruth?"

"For every reason that is great and noble and worthy."

"He played a cowardly part."

"And he has paid the penalty, Ralph. Your duty now is to be magnanimous. Besides——" Then she hesitated.

"Besides what?" he asked.

"I have heard you rail at what you call the justice of the strong. You are strong now, you will be stronger in time, and so you must see to it that you don't fall into the same snare."

"Wise little woman," he said affectionately, and then the subject dropped.

It was dark when Jim Brewer paid his visit. He came dejectedly and shamefacedly, much wondering what was in the wind.

Ralph opened the door for him, and took him into his little office.

"I understand you are out of work?" he said, pointing him to a seat.

Jim nodded.

"You understand prospecting, I believe?"

"Yes."

"Well, I can give you a job if you are prepared to take it, and you can begin work to-morrow if you like."

Brewer looked up with dim and wondering eyes, while Ralph further explained, and then he burst into tears.

"I don't deserve it," he sobbed at length. "I did you a mean and cowardly trick, and I've loathed myself for it ever since."

"Oh, well, never mind that now. It is all over and past, and we'd better try and forget it."

"I shall never forget it," Jim said chokingly, "but if you can forgive me, I shall be—oh, so happy!"

"Oh, well, then, I do forgive you, if that is any comfort to you."

Jim hid his face in his hands and burst into fresh weeping.

"Forgive my giving way like this," he said at length. "I ain't quite as strong as I might be. I had influenza a month agone, and it's shook me a goodish bit."

"Why, bless me, you look hungry!" Ralph said, eyeing him closely.

"Do I? I'm very sorry, but the influenza pulls one down terrible."

"But are you hungry?" Ralph questioned.

Jim smiled feebly.

"Oh, I've been hungrier than this," he said; "but I'll be glad to begin work to-morrow morning."

"I'm not sure you're fit. But come into the next room—we are just going to have supper."

Jim hesitated and drew back, but Ralph insisted upon it; and yet, when a plate of meat was placed before him, he couldn't eat.

"Excuse me," he said, his eyes filling, "but the little ones ain't had nothing to-day, and they can't bear it as well as me. If you wouldn't mind me taking it home instead?"

Ruth sprang to her feet in a moment.

"I'll let you have plenty for the little ones," she said, with trembling lips. "Now eat your supper, and enjoy it if you can." And she ran off into the pantry and quickly returned with a small basket full of food, which she placed by his side.

"That ain't for me?" he questioned.

"For you to take home to your mother and the children."

He laid down his knife and fork and rose to his feet.

"I'd like to go home at once, if you don't mind?" he said brokenly.

"But you haven't half finished your supper."

"I'd like to eat it with the little ones and mother, if you wouldn't mind?"

"By all means, if you would rather," Ruth said, smiling through unshed tears.

"I should feel happier," he said; and he emptied his plate into the basket.

Ralph went and opened the door for him, and watched him as he hurried away into the darkness.

He came back after a few minutes, and sat down; but neither he nor Ruth spoke again for some time. It was Ralph who at length broke the silence.

"He may be a long way from being a hero," he said, "but he has a lot of goodness in him. I shall never think hardly of him any more."

Ruth did not reply for a long time, then she said, "I am glad Brewer is to begin prospecting for you."

"Yes?" he questioned.

"I can't explain myself," she answered, "but it seems a right kind of beginning, and I think God's blessing will be upon it."

"We will hope so, at any rate. Yes, we will hope so."

And then silence fell again.

CHAPTER XXXV

FAILURE OR FORTUNE

Farmer Jenkins was grimly contemptuous. He hated miners. "They were always messing up things," sinking pits, covering the hillsides with heaps of rubbish, erecting noisy and unsightly machinery, cutting watercourses through fruitful fields, breaking down fences, and, generally speaking, destroying the peace and quietness of a neighbourhood.

He told Ralph to his face that he considered he was a fool.

"Possibly you are right, Mr. Jenkins," Ralph said, with a laugh.

"Ay, and you'll laugh t'other side of your face afore you've done with it."

"You think so?"

"It don't require no thinking over. Yer father sunk all his bit of money in this place, in bringing it under cultivation; and now you're throwing your bit of money after his, and other folks' to boot, in undoin' all he did, and turning the place into a desert again."

"But suppose the real wealth of this place is under the surface, Mr. Jenkins?"

"Suppose the sky falls. I tell 'ee there ain't no wealth except what grows. However, 'tain't no business of mine. If folks like to make fools of their selves and throw away their bit of money, that's their own look-out." And Farmer Jenkins spat on the ground and departed.

Jim Brewer pulled off his coat, and set to work at a point indicated by Ralph to sink a pit.

That was the beginning of what Ruth laughingly called "Great St. Goram Mine," with an emphasis on the word "great."

After watching Jim for a few minutes, Ralph pulled off his coat also, and began to assist his employee. It did not look a very promising commencement for a great enterprise.

The ground was hard and stony, and Jim's strength was not what it had been, nor what it would be providing he got proper food and plenty of it; while Ralph could scarcely be said to be proficient in the use of pick and shovel.

By the end of the third day they had got through the "rubbly ground," as Jim called it, and had struck what seemed a bed of solid rock.

Ralph got intensely excited. He had little doubt that this was the lode, the existence of which his father had accidentally discovered. With the point of his pick he searched round for fissures; but the rock was very closely knit, and he had had no experience in rock working.

Jim Brewer, as a practical miner, showed much more skill, and when Ralph returned to his home that evening his pockets were full of bits of rock that had been splintered from the lode.

"Well, Ralph, what news?" was Ruth's first question when she met him at the door. She was as much excited over the prospecting expedition as he was.

"We've struck something," he said eagerly, "but whether it's father's lode or no I'm not certain yet."

"But how will you find out?"

"I've got a sample in my pocket," he said, with a little laugh. "I'll test it after supper," and he went into his little laboratory and emptied his pockets on the bench.

By the time he had washed, and brushed his hair, supper was ready.

"And who've you seen to-day?" he said, as he sat down opposite his sister.

"Not many people," she said, blushing slightly. "Mr. Tremail called this afternoon."

He looked up suddenly with a questioning light in his eyes. Sam's name had scarcely been mentioned for the last two or three weeks, and whether Ruth had accepted him or rejected him was a matter that had ceased to trouble him. In fact, his mind had been so full of other things that there was no place left for the love affairs of Sam Tremail and his sister.

"Oh, indeed," he said slowly and hesitatingly; "then I suppose by this time it may be regarded as a settled affair?"

"Yes, it is quite settled," she said, and the colour deepened on her neck and face.

"Well, he's a good fellow—a very good fellow by all accounts," he said, with a little sigh. "I shall be sorry to lose you. Still, I don't know that you could have done much better."

"Oh, but you are not going to lose me yet," she answered, with a bright little laugh, though she did not raise her eyes to meet his.

"Well, no. Not for a month or two, I presume. But I have noticed that when men become engaged they get terribly impatient," and he dropped his eyes to his plate again.

"Yes, I have heard the same thing," she replied demurely. "But the truth is, I have decided not to get married at all."

"You mean——"

"I could not accept his offer, Ralph. I think a woman must care an awful lot for a man before she can consent to marry him."

"And *vice versâ*," he answered. "Yes, yes, I think you are quite right in that. But how did he take it, Ruth?"

"Not at all badly. Indeed, I think he was prepared for my answer. When he was leaving he met Mary Telfer outside the gate, and he stood for quite a long time laughing and talking with her."

"I did not know he knew her."

"He met her here a fortnight ago."

"Did Mary know why he came here?"

"I don't know. I never told her."

"I am very glad on the whole you have said No to him. Mind you, he's a good fellow, and, as things go, an excellent catch. And yet, if I had to make choice for you, it would not be Sam Tremail. At least I would not place him first."

"And who would you place first?" she questioned, raising her eyes timidly to his.

"Ah, well, that is a secret. No, I am not going to tell you; for women, you know, always go by the rule of contrary."

"If you had gone abroad," Ruth said, after a long pause, "and I had been left alone, I might have given Mr. Tremail a different answer. I don't know. When a good home is offered to a lonely woman the temptation is great. But when I knew that you were going to stay at home, and that Hillside was to be ours once more, I could think of nothing else. Do you think I would leave Hillside for Pentudy?"

"But Hillside is not ours altogether, Ruth."

"It is as good as ours," she answered, with a smile. "William Menire does not want it; he told me so. He said nothing would make him happier than to see me living there again."

"Did he tell you that?"

"He did."

"That's strange. I always understood he did his best to bring about a match between you and Sam Tremail."

"He may have done so. I don't know. He had always a good word for his cousin. On the whole, I think he was quite indifferent."

"William can never be indifferent where his friends are concerned."

"Oh, then, perhaps he will be pleased that I am going to remain to keep house for you."

And then the subject dropped.

Directly supper was over, Ralph retired to his work-room and laboratory, and began with such appliances as he had to grind the stones into powder. It was no easy task, for the rock was hard and of exceedingly fine texture.

Ruth joined him when she had finished her work, and watched him with great interest. His first test was made with the ordinary "vanning shovel," his second with the aid of chemicals. But neither test seemed conclusive or satisfactory.

"There's something wrong somewhere," he said, as he put away his tools. "I must do my next test in the daylight."

Ruth got very anxious as the days passed away. She learned from her brother that he had employed more men to sink further prospecting pits along the course of the lode, but with what results she was unable to discover.

Ralph, for some reason, had grown strangely reticent. He spent very little time at home, and that little was chiefly passed in his laboratory. His face became so serious that she feared for the worst, and refrained from asking questions lest she should add to his anxiety.

William Menire dropped in occasionally of an evening, but she noticed that the one topic of all others was avoided as if by mutual consent. At last Ruth felt as if she could bear the suspense no longer.

"Do tell me, Ralph," she said; "is the whole thing what you call a frost?"

"Why do you ask?" he questioned.

"Because you are so absorbed, and look so terribly anxious."

"I am anxious," he said, "very anxious."

"Then, so far, the lode has proved to be worthless?" she questioned.

"It is either worthless, or else is so rich in mineral that I hardly like to think about it."

"I don't understand," she said.

"Well, it is this way. The tests we have made so far show such a large percentage of tin that I am afraid we are mistaken."

"How? In what way?"

"If there had been a less quantity, I should not have doubted that it was really tin, but there is so much of it that I'm afraid. Now do you understand?"

"But surely you ought to be able to find out?"

"Oh yes; we shall find out in time. A quantity of stuff is in the hands of expert assayers at the present time, and we are awaiting their report. If their final test should harmonise with the others, why—well, I will not say what."

"And when do you expect to hear?"

"I hope, to-morrow morning."

"But why have you kept me in the dark all this time?"

"Because we did not wish to make you anxious. It is bad enough that William and I should be so much on the *qui vive* that we are unable to sleep, without robbing you of your sleep also."

"I don't think I shall be robbed of my sleep," she said, with a laugh.

"Then you are not anxious?" he questioned.

"Not very."

"Why not?"

"Because father was not the man to be mistaken in a matter of that kind. If any man in Cornwall knew tin when he saw it, it was father."

"I am glad you are so hopeful," he said; and he went off into his laboratory. He did not tell her that the possibilities of mistake were far more numerous than she had any conception of, and that it was possible for the cleverest experts to be mistaken until certain tests had been applied.

William Menire turned up a little later in the evening, and joined Ralph in his laboratory. He would have preferred remaining in the sitting-room, but Ruth gave him no encouragement to stay. She had grown unaccountably reserved with him of late. He was half afraid sometimes that in some way he had offended her. There was a time, and not so long ago, when she seemed pleased to be in his company, when she talked with him in the freest manner, when she even showed him little attentions. But all that was at an end. Ever since that morning when he had rushed into the house with the announcement that their offer for Hillside Farm had been accepted, she had been distinctly distant and cool with him.

He wondered if Ruth had read his heart better than he had been able to read it himself; wondered whether his love for her had coloured his motives. He had been anxious to act unselfishly; to act without reference to his love for Ruth. He was not so sure that he had done so. And if Ruth had guessed that he hoped to win her favour by being generous to her brother—and to her—then he could understand why she was distant with him now. Ruth's love was not to be bought with favours.

Unconsciously William himself became shy and reserved when Ruth was about. The fear that she mistrusted him made him mistrustful of himself. He felt as though he had done a mean thing, and had been found out. If by chance he caught her looking at him, he fancied there was reproach in her eyes, and so he avoided looking at her as much as possible.

All this tended to deepen the reserve that had grown up between them. Neither understood the other, and William had not the courage to have the matter out with her. A few plain questions and a few plain answers would have solved the difficulty and made two people as happy as mortals could ever hope to be; but, as often happens in this world, the questions were not asked and the unspoken fear grew and intensified until it became absolute conviction.

Ruth did not join her brother and William in the laboratory. She sat near the fire with a lamp by her side and some unfinished work in her lap. She caught up her work every now and then, and plied a few vigorous stitches; then her hands would relax again, and a dreamy, far-away look would come into her eyes.

Now and then a low murmur of voices would come through from the little shed at the back, but she could distinguish nothing that was said. One thing she was conscious of, there was no note of mirth or merriment, no suggestion of laughter, in the sounds that fell on her ear. The hours were so big with Fate, so much was trembling in the balance, that there was no place for anything but the most serious talk.

"Nothing seems of much importance to men but business," she said to herself, with a wistful look in her eyes. "Life consists in the abundance of the things which they possess. They get their joy out of conflict—battle. We women live a life apart, and dream dreams with which they have no sympathy, and see visions which they never see."

The evening wore away unconsciously. The men talked, the woman dreamed, but neither the talk nor the dreams brought much satisfaction.

Ruth stirred herself at length and got supper ready for three, but William would not stay. He had remained much too long already, and had no idea it was so late.

Ruth did not press him, she left that to her brother. Once or twice William looked towards her, but she avoided his glance. Like all women, she was proud at heart. William was conscious that Ruth's invitation was coldly formal. If he remained he would be very uncomfortable.

"No, I must get back," he said decidedly, without again looking at Ruth; and with a hasty good-evening he went out into the dark.

For a few minutes he walked rapidly, then he slackened his pace.

"She grows colder than ever," he said to himself. "She intends me to see without any mistake that if I expected to win her love by favours, I'm hugely mistaken. Well, well!" and he sighed audibly. "To-morrow morning we shall know, I expect, whether it is failure or fortune," he went on, after a long pause. "It's a tremendous risk we are running, and yet I would rather win Ruth Penlogan than all the wealth there is in Cornwall."

William did not sleep well that night. Neither did Ralph nor Ruth. They were all intensely anxious for what the morrow should bring.

CHAPTER XXXVI

THE PENALTY OF PROSPERITY

By the evening of the following day all St. Goram had heard the news; by the end of the week it was the talk of the county. The discovery of a new tin lode was a matter of considerable importance, not only to the few people directly interested, but to the entire community. It would mean more work for the miner, more trade for the shopkeeper, and more traffic for the railway.

The "out-of-works" straggled into St. Goram by the dozen. Mining experts came to see and report. Newspaper men appeared on the scene at all hours of the day, and wrote astonishing articles for the weekly press. Ralph found himself bombarded on every side. Speculators, financiers, company promotors, editors, reporters, photographers, miners, and out-of-works generally made his life a burden. He would have kept out of sight if he could, and turned William Menire on the crowd. But William was busy winding up his own business. Moreover, his mother was ill, and never seemed happy if he was off the premises.

Ralph almost wished sometimes that he had never discovered the lode. Men came to him for employment who scarcely knew how to handle a shovel, and he often had to take off his coat and show them the way. He was like a beggar who had found a diamond and did not know what to do with it. On all hands people spoke of his good fortune, but after a few weeks he began to be in doubt. Difficulties and worries and vexations began to gather like snowflakes in a winter's storm. Lord St. Goram put in a claim for a certain right of way. The District Council threatened legal proceedings if he interfered with a particular watercourse. Sir John Hamblyn's legal adviser raised a technical point on the question of transfer. The Chancellor of the Duchy sent a formidable list of questions relating to Crown rights, while Farmer Jenkins wanted compensation for the destruction of crops which had never been destroyed.

"I've raised a perfect hornets' nest," Ralph said to William Menire one evening, in his little room at the back of the shop. "Everybody seems to consider me fair game. There isn't a man in the neighbourhood with any real or fancied right who has not put in some trumpery claim or other. The number of lawyers' letters I have received is enough to turn my hair grey."

"Oh, never mind," William said cheerfully, "things will come out right in the end! I am sorry you have to face the music alone, but I'm as fast here as a thief in a mill."

"I know you are," Ralph said sympathetically. "But to tell you the candid truth, I am not so sure that things will come out right."

"Why not?"

"Because everybody is up in arms against us."

"Not everybody."

"Everybody who thinks he can get something out of us. Our little dominion is surrounded by hostile tribes. I never realised till the last few days how completely we are hemmed in. On two sides the Hamblyn estates block our passage, on the third side Lord St. Goram's land abuts, and on the fourth side old Beecham has his fence and his barbed wire, and all these people have struck up a threatening attitude. Sir John is naturally as mad as a hatter that he sold the farm at all. Lord St. Goram is angry that a couple of plebeians should own land in what he regards as his parish; while old Beecham, who regards himself as an aristocrat, sides with his own class, and so between them our fate promises to be that of the pipkin between the iron pots."

"But we need not go beyond the bounds of our own property," William said.

"There you are mistaken," Ralph answered quickly. "Our small empire is not self-contained. There is no public road through it or even to it. Lord St. Goram threatens to block up the only entrance. And you know what going to law with a landed magnate means."

William looked grave.

"Then we must have a 'dressing floor' somewhere," Ralph went on, "and the only convenient place is Dingley Bottom. Water is abundant there. But though God gave it, man owns it, and the owner, like an angry dog, snarls when he is approached."

"Very good," William said, after a pause, "but don't you see we are still masters of the situation?"

"No, I can't say that I do. We are only two very small and very obscure men with a very limited amount of cash. As a matter of fact, I have got to the end of mine. In a battle with these Titans of wealth, what can we do?"

"Sit tight!"

"Easier said than done. Your business life in St. Goram has been terminated. At the present time I am earning nothing. In order to sit tight, we must have something to sit on."

"We can farm Hillside, and live on vegetables."

"Jenkins does not go out till March, and in the meanwhile he is claiming compensation for damages."

"We can easily deal with him. He won't go to law; he is too poor, and has too genuine a horror of lawyers. So he will submit his claim to arbitration."

"But even with Jenkins out of the way, and ourselves installed as farmers, we are still in a very awkward plight. Suppose St. Goram really contests this right of way—which was never hinted at till now—he can virtually ruin us with law costs."

"He would never be so mean as to attempt it."

Ralph laughed bitterly.

"My dear fellow," he said, "I can see clearly enough there is going to be an organised attempt to crush us. As for the question of meanness, that will never be considered for a moment. We are regarded as interlopers who have been guilty of sharp practice. Hence, we must not only be checkmated, but ground into powder."

"They haven't done it yet," William said, with a cheerful smile, "and I'm not going to say die till I'm dead."

Ralph laughed again, and a little less bitterly than before. William's hopefulness was not without its influence upon him.

For a while there was silence, then William spoke again.

"Look here, Ralph," he said; "strength will have to be met with strength. The strong too often know nothing of either mercy or justice. One does not like to say such a thing, or even think it, but this is no time for sentiment."

"Well?"

"You know our hope has been to work the lode ourselves; to increase our plant, as we have made a little money; to employ only St. Goram men, and give each one a share in the concern. It was a benevolent idea, but it is clear we are not to be allowed to carry it out."

"Well?"

"Two courses are still open to us. The first is to fill in the prospecting pits and let the lode lie undeveloped. The second is to let the financiers come in and form a company that shall be strong enough to meet Lord St. Goram and his class on their own ground."

Ralph was silent.

"I know you do not like either alternative," William went on, "but we are

247

pushed up into a corner."

"The first alternative will fail for the reason I mentioned just now," Ralph interposed. "St. Goram will dispute the right of way."

"And he knows we cannot afford to go to law with him."

"Exactly."

"Then we are thrown back on the second alternative, and our little dream of a benevolent autocracy is at an end. Strangers must come in. People who have no interest in St. Goram will find the money. A board of directors will manage the concern, and you and I will be lost in the crowd."

Ralph raised his eyes for a moment, but did not reply.

"Such a plan has its advantages," William went on. "If we had been allowed to carry out our plan, developments would be very slow."

"Not so slow. You must remember that the lode is very rich."

"It would necessarily be slow at the start," William replied. "By letting the financiers come in, the thing will be started right away on a big scale. Every man out of work will have a job, and money will begin to circulate in St. Goram at once."

"That is no doubt true, but—well, it knocks on the head much I had hoped for."

"I know it does; but living in our little corner here, our view may be narrow and prejudiced. There is honest company promoting as well as dishonest. Combination of capital need not be any more wrong than combination of labour. No single man could build a railway from London to Penzance, and stock it; and if he could, it is better that a company should own it, and work it, than a single individual. You prefer a democracy to an autocracy, surely?"

Ralph's face brightened, but he remained silent.

"Suppose you and I had been able to carry out our idea," William went on. "We should have been absolute rulers. Are we either of us wise enough to rule? We might have become, in our own way, more powerful than Lord St. Goram and all the other county magnates rolled into one. Should we have grace enough to use our power justly? We have benevolent intentions, but who knows how money and power might corrupt? They nearly always do corrupt. We complain of the way the strong use their strength; perhaps it is a mercy the temptation is not put in our way."

"Perhaps you are right, William," Ralph said at length, "though I confess I distrust the whole gang of company promoters that have been buzzing about me for the last month."

"Why not consult Sir John Liskeard? He is our member; he is interested in the place. He knows most people, and he would at least bring an unprejudiced mind to bear on the question."

Ralph gave a little gasp. To see Sir John he would have to go to London. If he went to London, he might see Dorothy Hamblyn.

He did not speak for a moment. The sudden vision of Dorothy's face blotted out everything. It was curious how she dominated him still; how his heart turned to her constantly as the needle to the pole; how her face came up before him in the most unexpected places, and at the most unexpected times; how the thought of her lay at the back of all his enterprises and all his hopes.

"It means money going to London," he said at length.

"We must sow if we would reap," William replied, "and our balance at the bank is not quite exhausted yet. Don't forget that we are partners in this enterprise, and in any case we could sell the farm for a great deal more than we gave for it."

"We may be compelled to sell it yet," Ralph said ruefully.

"But not until we are compelled," was the cheerful reply. "No, no; if we don't win this time, it will not be for want of trying."

"My experience has not been encouraging," Ralph answered. "In every struggle so far, I have gone under. The strong have triumphed. Right and justice have been set aside."

"You have gone under only to come to the top again," William laughed.

"But think of father and mother."

"Martyrs in the sacred cause of freedom," William answered. "The rights of the people are not won in a day."

Ralph was silent for a while, then he looked up with a smile.

"Your judgment is sounder than mine," he said. "I will go to London to-morrow."

He had no difficulty in getting an interview with Sir John. The member for the St. Hilary division of the county had his eye on the next election. Moreover, he was keenly interested in the new discovery, and was not without hope that he might be able to identify himself with the concern. He manifested distinct pleasure when Ralph was announced, and gave all his attention to him at once.

Ralph put the whole case before him from start to finish. Liskeard listened attentively with scarcely an interruption. He smiled now and then as Ralph explained his own hope and purpose—his benevolent autocracy, as William called it—and how he had been foiled by the ring of strong men—strong in wealth and social influence—who threatened to strangle all his hopes and schemes.

It took Ralph a long time to tell his story, for he was anxious to leave no point obscure. Sir John listened without the least trace of weariness or impatience. He was too keenly interested to notice how rapidly time was flying.

"I think your partner has the true business instinct," he said at length. "It is almost impossible to carry out great schemes by private enterprise."

"Then you approve of forming a company?"

"Most certainly. I have been expecting to see in the papers for weeks past that such a company had been formed."

"I mistrust the whole lot of them," Ralph said, with a touch of vehemence in his tone. "Everybody appears to be on the make."

"It is of very little use quarrelling with human nature," Sir John said, with a smile. "We must take men as we find them, and be careful to keep our eyes open all the time."

"If someone stronger than yourself ties you to a tree and robs you, I don't see much use in keeping your eyes open," Ralph answered bluntly. "Indeed, it might be a prudent thing to keep your eyes shut."

Liskeard lay back in his chair and laughed heartily.

"I see where you are," he said at length. "Still, there is a soul of honour alive in the world even among business men. Don't forget that our great world of commerce is built on trust. There are blacklegs, of course, but in the main men are honest."

"I am glad to hear it," Ralph answered dubiously. "But now to get to the main point. Will you help us in this thing? William Menire and myself are both inexperienced, both ignorant, both mistrustful of ourselves, and particularly of other people."

"Can you trust me?" Liskeard questioned, with a laugh.

"Yes, we can, or I should not have come to you."

"Then I think I may say I can put the thing through for you."

"It's a good thing," Ralph said warmly. "There is not a lode a quarter so rich in the three parishes. I question if there is anything equal to it in the whole county."

"I have read the assayer's report," Sir John answered.

"And because it is so good," Ralph went on, "I'd like St. Goram to have the first claim, if you understand. If there are any preferences, let them go to the people at home."

"And your share?"

"William and I will leave our interests in your hands. You are a lawyer. All we want is justice and fair play."

"I understand. If you will dine with me at the House to-morrow night I think we shall be able to advance the case a step further."

Ralph got into an omnibus in Fleet Street, and alighted at Westminster. Thence he made his way into St. James's Park. The weather was raw and cold, the trees bare, the paths muddy and deserted. He wandered up and down for the best part of an hour—it was too cold to sit down—then he made his way across Hyde Park Corner and struck Rotten Row.

A few schoolgirls, accompanied by riding masters, were trotting up and down. A few closed carriages rolled by on the macadam road, a few pedestrians sauntered listlessly along under the bare trees.

A few soldiers might be seen talking to giggling nursemaids, but the one face he hungered to see did not reveal itself. He walked almost to Kensington Palace and back again, by which time night had begun to fall. Then with a little sigh he got into a 'bus, and was soon rolling down Piccadilly.

London seemed a lonely place in the summer time; it was lonelier than ever in the winter.

CHAPTER XXXVII

LIGHT AND SHADOW

By the end of the following May, Great St. Goram Mine was in full working order. Ralph was installed as managing director; William was made a director and secretary to the company. Lord St. Goram was in Scotland at the time, and when he applied for shares he was too late. His chagrin knew no bounds. He had imagined that he had Ralph and William in the hollow of his hand. That two country bumpkins, as he was pleased to call them, would be able to float a company had not occurred to him. He knew the project that first occupied their thoughts. He knew that he could make it impossible for them to carry their ideas into effect.

His agent had hinted to William that his lordship would be willing to take the farm off their hands at a price; hence, he believed that by applying gentle pressure, and waiting, he would be able in a very short time to get the whole thing into his hands.

For a few weeks he threatened the company with all sorts of pains and penalties, but the company was not to be bluffed. Private interest had to give way before public convenience. Where the welfare of a whole community was at stake, no petty and niggling contention about right of way was allowed to stand. The company made its own right of way, and was prepared to pay any reasonable damage.

With the company at his back, Ralph laughed in the consciousness of his strength. He had never felt strong before. It was a new experience, and a most delightful sensation. He had never lacked courage or will power, but he had been made to feel that environment or destiny—or whatever name people liked to give it—was too strong for him. Strength is relative, and in comparison with the forces arrayed against him, he had felt weaker than an infant.

When his father was driven from his home, he had bowed his head with the rest in helpless submission. When he was arrested on a false and ridiculous charge, he submitted without protest. When he saw his mother dying in a workhouse hospital, he could only groan in bitterness of spirit. When the Brick, Tile, and Clay Company gave him notice to suspend operations, he had tamely to submit. In fact, submission had been the order of his life. It had been given to others to rule; it had been his to obey.

This would not have been irksome if the rule of the strong had been wise and just. But when justice was thrust aside or trampled under foot, as if it had no place in the social order, when equity was only the shuttlecock and plaything of interested people, when the weak were denied their rights simply because they were weak, and the reward of merit was to be cuffed by the tyrant, then his soul revolted and he grew bitter and cynical in spite of himself.

Now, however, the tables had been turned. For the first time in his life he felt himself among the strong. He need no longer sit down tamely under an injustice, or submit to insults in silence. Success was power. Money was power. Combination was power.

He pulled himself up suddenly at length with a feeling almost of terror. He was in danger of becoming what he had condemned so much in others. The force and subtlety of the temptation stood revealed as in a blinding flash. It was so splendid to have strength, to be able to stalk across the land like a giant, to do just what pleased him to do, to consult no one in the doing of it. It was just in that the temptation and the danger lay. It was so easy to forget the weak, to overlook the insignificant, to treat the feeble as of no account. Strength did not constitute right.

That was a truth that tyrants never learned and that Governments too frequently shut their eyes to. God would hold him responsible for his strength. If he had the strength of ten thousand men, he still had no right to do wrong.

So at length he got to see things in their true proportion and perspective. The strength that had come to him was only an adventitious kind of strength, after all. Unless he had another and a better kind of strength to balance it, it might prove his destruction. What he needed most was moral strength, strength to use wisely and justly his opportunities, strength to hold the balance evenly, strength to do the right, whatever it might cost him, to suffer loss for conscience' sake, to do to others what he would they should do to him.

If he ever forgot the pit out of which he had been digged, success would be a failure in the most direful sense.

He trembled when he saw the danger, and prayed God to help him. He was walking on the edge of a precipice and knew it; a precipice over which thousands of so-called successful men had fallen.

"Ruth," he said to his sister one evening, with a grave look in his eyes, "if you ever see me growing proud, remind me that my mother died in a workhouse."

"Ralph?" she questioned, with a look of surprise on her face.

"I am not joking," he said solemnly. "I was never in more sober earnest. I have stood in slippery places many times before, but never in one so slippery as this."

"Are not things going well at the mine?" she asked, in alarm.

"Too well," he answered. "The shareholders will get twenty per cent. on their money the first year."

"And you are a large shareholder," she said, with a look of elation in her eyes.

"Besides which, there are the dues to the landlord, as well as the salary of the manager. Do you not see, Ruth, that this sudden change of fortune is a perilous thing?"

"To some people it might be, Ralph."

"It is to me. It came to me this afternoon as I walked across the 'floors' and men touched their caps to me."

"But you can never forget the past," she said.

"But men do forget the past," he answered. "Would you ever imagine for a moment that Lord Probus, for instance, was not to the manner born?"

"I have seen him only two or three times," she answered; "but it seems to me that he is always trying to be a lord, which proves——"

"Which proves what?"

"Well, you see, a man who is really a gentleman does not try to be one. He is one, and there's an end of it; he hasn't to try."

"Oh, I see. Then forgetting the past is all a pretence?"

"A man may forget his poverty, but I do not think he can forget his parents. You need not remember where mother died, but how she and father lived; their goodness is our greatest fortune."

He did not make any further reply then, and a little later he put on his hat and said—

"I am going along to see William. He went home poorly this morning."

"Poorly?"

"Caught a chill, I fancy. The weather has been very changeable, you know."

Ruth felt a sudden tightening of the strings about her heart, and when Ralph had disappeared she sat down by the window and looked with unseeing eyes out across the garden.

She was back again in the old home, the home in which she had spent so many happy and peaceful years, and from which she had been exiled so long. She was very happy, on the whole, and yet she realised in a very poignant sense that Hillside could never be again what it had been.

It was bound to be something more or something less. Nothing could restore the past, nothing could give back what had been taken away.

The twilight was deepening rapidly across the landscape, the tender green of spring was vanishing into a sombre black. From over the low hill came fitfully the rattle of stamps which had been erected in Dingley Bottom, and occasionally the creak of winding gear could be faintly heard.

From the front windows of the house there was no change in the landscape, but from the kitchen and dairy windows the engine-house, with its tall, clumsy stack, loomed painfully near. Ralph had planted a double line of young trees along the ridge, which in time would shut off that part of the farm given over to mining operations, but at present they were only just breaking into leaf.

It was at first a very real grief to Ruth that the mine so disfigured the farm. She recalled the years of ungrudging toil given by her father to bring the waste land under cultivation, and now the fields were being turned into a desert once more. She soon, however, got reconciled to the change. The best of the fields remained unharmed, and the man and boy who looked after the farm had quite as much as they could attend to. Ralph did not mind so long as there was a bowl of clotted cream on the table at every meal. Beyond that his interest in the farm ceased.

But the mine was a never-failing source of pleasure to him. Tin was not the only product of those mysterious veins that threaded their way through the solid earth. There were nameless ores that hitherto had been treated as of no account because no use had been found for them.

Ralph began making experiments at once. His laboratory grew more rapidly than any other department. His early passion for chemistry received fresh stimulus, and had room for full play, with the result that he made his salary twice over by what he saved out of the waste.

William Menire's interest in the mine was purely commercial, and in that respect he was of great value. He laboured quietly and unceasingly, finding in work the best antidote to loneliness and disappointment. His mother was no longer with him. She had joined the silent procession of the dead. He was thankful for some things that she did not live to see the winding up of his little business—for it seemed little to him now in contrast with the wider and vaster interests of the company with which he was connected. She had been very proud of the shop, particularly proud of the great plate-glass window her son had put in at his own expense.

The edict of Lord St. Goram to restore the house to its original position had been a great blow to her. She had adored the aristocracy—they were not as other men, mean and petty and revengeful—hence the demand of his lordship shattered into fragments one of her most cherished illusions.

She did not live to hear the click and ring of the trowel, telling her that a brick wall was taking the place of the plate glass. On the very last day of her life she heard as usual the tinkle of the shop bell and the murmur of voices below.

When William had laid her to rest in the churchyard he disposed of his stock as rapidly as possible, restored the house to its original condition as far as it was possible to do it, and then turned his back upon St. Goram.

The little village of Veryan was much nearer the mine, much nearer the Penlogans, and just then seemed much nearer heaven. So he got rooms with a garrulous but godly old couple, and settled down to bachelordom with as much cheerfulness as possible.

That he felt lonely—shockingly lonely at times—it was of no use denying. He missed the late customers, the "siding up" when the shutters were closed, the final entries in his day-book and ledger. Big and wealthy and important as the Great St. Goram Tin Mining Company was, and exacting as his labour was in the daytime, he was left with little or nothing to do after nightfall. The evenings hung on his hands. Books were scarce and entertainments few, and sometimes he smoked more than was good for him.

He went to see Ralph as often as he could find a reasonable excuse, and always received the heartiest welcome, but for some reason the cloud of Ruth's reserve never lifted. She was sweet and gentle and hospitable, but the old light had gone out of her eyes and the old warmth from her speech. She rarely looked straight into his face, and rarely remained long in his company.

He puzzled himself constantly to find out the reason, and had not the courage to ask. He wanted to be her friend, to be taken into her confidence, to be treated as a second brother. Anything more than that he never dared hope for. That she might love him was a dream too foolish to be entertained. He was getting old—at any rate he was much nearer forty than thirty, while she was in the very flower of her youth. So he wondered and speculated, and got no nearer a solution of the problem.

Ralph was so engrossed in his own affairs that he never noticed any change, and never guessed that Ruth was the light of William's eyes.

The idea that William Menire might be in love occurred to no one. He was looked upon as a confirmed bachelor, and when the public has assigned a man to that position he may be as free with the girls as he likes without awaking the least suspicion.

Ruth sat by the window until it had grown quite dark, and then a maid came in and lighted the lamp. She took up her work when the maid had gone, and tried to centre her thoughts on the pattern she was working; but her eyes quickly caught a far-away expression, and she found herself listening for the footfall of her brother, while her hands lay listlessly in her lap.

Several times she shook herself—metaphorically—and plied her needle afresh, but the effort never lasted very long. An unaccountable sense of fear or misgiving stole into her heart. She grew restless and apprehensive, and yet she had no tangible reason for anxiety.

William Menire was more her brother's friend than hers, and the fact that he had caught cold was not a matter of any particular moment. Of course a cold might develop into something serious. He might be ill—very ill. He might die. She caught her breath suddenly, and went and opened the door. The stars were burning brightly in the clear sky above, and the wind blew fresh and strong from the direction of Treliskey Plantation. She listened intently for the sound of footsteps, but the only noise that broke the silence was the rattle of the stamps in Dingley Bottom.

Somehow she hated the sound to-night. It grated harshly on her ears. It had no human tone, no note of sympathy. The stamps were grinding out wealth for greedy people, careless of who might suffer or die.

She came in and shut the door after a few moments, and looked apprehensively at the clock. Ralph was making a long call.

The house grew very still at length. The servant went to bed. The clock ticked loudly on the mantelpiece; the wind rumbled occasionally in the chimney.

Suddenly the door opened, and her brother stood before her. His face was flushed, and there was a troubled look in his eyes.

"You are late, Ralph," she said, scarcely daring to look at him.

"William is very ill," he said, as if he had not heard her words, "dangerously ill."

"No!"

"Pneumonia, the doctor fears. He is terribly anxious."

"Who—the doctor?"

"Yes. If William dies I shall lose my best friend."

CHAPTER XXXVIII

LOVE AND LIFE

Ruth lay awake long after she had retired to rest. The fear which had been expressed by Ralph increased her own a thousandfold. If William should die, not only would her brother lose his best friend—there was a more terrible thought than that, a thought which need not be expressed in words, for nobody understood.

Somebody has said that a woman never loves until her love is asked for; that though all the elements are there, they remain dormant till a simple question fires the train. But love—especially the love of a woman—is too subtle, too elusive a thing to be covered by any sweeping generalisation.

William had never spoken his love to Ruth, never even looked it, yet the fire had got alight in Ruth's heart somehow. When it began she did not know. For long she had no suspicion what it meant. Later on she tried to trample it out; she felt ashamed and humiliated. The bare thought of loving a man who had never spoken of love to her covered her with confusion.

Sometimes she tried to persuade herself that it was not love she felt for William Menire, but only gratitude mingled with admiration. He had been the best friend she and her brother had ever known. All their present prosperity they owed to him, and everything he had done for them was without ostentation. He was not a showy man, and only those who knew him intimately guessed how great he was, how fine his spirit, how exalted his ideals.

She had never thought much about love until Sam Tremail proposed to her; but when once the subject stared her in the face she was bound to look at it. And while she was looking and trying to find what answer her heart gave, William came with the announcement that the farm was theirs, and theirs through his help and instrumentality. From that moment she knew that it was not Sam Tremail she loved. Of course, she had known all along that Sam was not the equal of his cousin in any sense of the word. But Sam was young and handsome and well-to-do, while William was journeying toward middle life, and had many of the ways of a confirmed bachelor.

It came to her as in a flash that all true love must be built on reverence. Youth and good looks might inspire a romantic attachment, a fleeting emotion, a passing fancy, but the divine passion of love grew out of something deeper. It was not a dewdrop sparkling on a leaf. It was a fountain springing out of the heart of the hills.

With knowledge came pain and confusion. She had not the courage to look William in the eyes. She was in constant dread lest she should reveal her secret. She would not for the world that he should know. If he should ever guess she would die of shame.

From that day onward she had a harder battle to fight than anyone knew— perhaps the hardest of all battles that a woman is called upon to wage. William came and went constantly; helped them when they removed to Hillside, and was never failing in friendly suggestions. Ralph was so full of the mine that such small details as wallpapers and carpets and curtains never occurred to him, and when they were mentioned he told Ruth to make her own choice. It was William who came to the rescue in those days, and saved her an infinity of trouble and anxiety.

Ruth thought of all this as she lay awake, listening to the faint and fitful rattle of the stamps beyond the hill. Was this brave, unselfish life to be suddenly quenched—this meek but heroic soul to be taken away from earth?

She was pale and hollow-eyed when she came downstairs next morning, but Ralph was too absorbed to notice it. He too had been kept awake thinking about William, and directly breakfast was over he hurried away to Veryan to make inquiries.

Ruth waited till noon for news—waited with more impatience than she had ever felt before. She had no need to ask Ralph if William was better. She knew by the look in his eyes that he was not. After that, the hours and days moved with leaden feet. Ralph went to Veryan twice every day, and sometimes three times. Ruth grew more and more silent. Her task became more painfully difficult. Other people could talk about William, could praise his qualities, could recount the story of his simple and heroic life, but she, by her very love for him, was doomed to silence.

She envied the nurse who could sit by his bedside and minister to his needs. She felt that it was her place. No one cared for him as she did. It seemed a cruel thing that her very love should keep her from his side, and shut her up in silence.

Ralph came in hurriedly one evening, and sat down to table; but after eating a few mouthfuls, he laid down his knife and fork, and pushed his plate from him.

"I suppose you know William is dying?" he said, without raising his eyes.

She looked at him with a startled expression, but did not speak. She made an effort, but the words froze on her tongue.

"One should not doubt the Eternal wisdom," he went on huskily, "but it seems a huge mistake. There are a hundred men who could be better spared."

"God knows best," Ruth tried to say, but she was never sure that the words escaped her lips.

"He seems quite resigned to his fate," Ralph continued, after a pause. "The doctor told him this morning that if he had any worldly affairs to settle he should put them in order without delay. He appears to be waiting now for the end."

"He is not afraid?" Ruth questioned, bringing out the words with a great effort.

"Not a bit. He reminds me of father more than any man I have ever known. His confidence is that of a little child. By-the-bye, he would like to see you before he goes."

"See me, Ralph?"

"He expressed himself very doubtfully and timidly, and asked me if I thought you would mind coming to say good-bye."

"There could be no harm in it, Ralph?"

"Not a bit. He has been like an elder brother to us both."

"Yes—yes." And she rose from the table at once, and went upstairs to get her hat and jacket.

"What, ready so soon?" he questioned, when she appeared again.

"I may be too late as it is," she answered, in a voice that she scarcely recognised as her own.

"I will go with you," he said, "for it will be dark when you return."

For awhile they walked rapidly and in silence, but when the village came in sight they slackened their pace a little.

"It is hard to give up hope," Ralph said, as if speaking to himself. "He was so healthy and so strong, and he has lived a life so temperate and so clean that he ought to pull through anything."

"Does the doctor say there is no hope?"

"He has none himself."

William was listening with every sense alert. He knew by some subtle instinct, some spiritual telepathy, that Ruth was near. He caught her whisper in the hall, he knew her footstep when she came quickly up the stairs, and the beating of his heart seemed to get beyond all bounds.

He was too weak to raise himself in bed, but his eyes were strained toward the door.

"You will leave me when she comes," he said to the nurse as soon as he heard Ruth's voice in the hall, and directly the door was pushed open the nurse disappeared.

Ruth walked straight up to the bedside without faltering. William feebly raised his wasted hand, and she took it in both hers. She was very composed. She wondered at herself, and was barely conscious of the effort she was making.

He was the first to break the silence, and he spoke with a great effort, and with many pauses.

"Will you not sit there, where I can see you?" he said, indicating a chair close to the bedside. "It is very good of you to come. I thought you would, for you have always been kind to me."

The tears came very near her eyes, but she resolutely raised her hand to hide them from William.

"You and your brother have been my dearest friends," he went on. "Ralph is a noble fellow, and I do not wonder that you are proud of him. It has been a great joy to me to know him—to know you both."

"That feeling has been mutual," Ruth struggled to say; but William scarcely waited to hear her out. Perhaps he felt that what he had to say must be said quickly.

"I thought I would like to tell you how much I have valued your friendship— there can be no harm in that, can there?"

"Why, no," she interposed.

"But that is not all," he went on. "I want to say something more, and there surely can be no harm in saying it now. I am nearing the end, the doctor says."

"Say anything you like," she interrupted, in a great sob of emotion.

"You cannot be angry with me now," he continued. "You might have been had I told you sooner. I know I have been very presumptuous, very daring, but I could not help it. You stole my heart unconsciously. I loved you in those dark days when you lived in the little cottage at St. Goram. I wanted to help you then. And oh, Ruth, I have loved you ever since—not with the blind, unreasoning passion of youth, but with the deep, abiding reverence of mature years. My love for you is the sweetest, purest, strongest thing I have ever cherished; and now that I am going hence the impulse became so strong that I could not resist telling you."

She turned to him suddenly, her eyes swimming in tears.

"Oh, William——" Then her voice faltered.

"You are not angry with me, Ruth?" he questioned, almost in a whisper.

"Angry with you? Oh, William——But why did you not tell me before?"

"I was afraid to tell you, Ruth—afraid to put an end to our friendship."

She knelt down on the floor by his bedside and laid her face on his hand, and he felt her hot tears falling like rain.

For awhile neither of them spoke again; then she raised her head suddenly, and with a pitiful smile on her face she said—

"You must not die, William!"

"Not die?" he questioned.

"No, no! For my sake you must get better," and she looked eagerly and earnestly into his eyes, as though she would compel assent to her words.

"Why for your sake?" he asked slowly and musingly.

"Why? Oh, William, do you not understand? Can you not see——"

"Surely—surely," he said, a great light breaking over his face, "you cannot mean that—that——"

"But I do mean it," she interrupted. "How could I mean anything else?"

He half rose in bed, as if inspired with new strength, then lay back again with a weary and long-drawn sigh. She rose quickly to her feet, and bent over him with a little cry. A pallor so deathly stole over his face that she thought he was dying.

After a few moments he rallied again, and smiled reassuringly. Then the nurse came back into the room.

"You will come again?" he whispered, holding out his hand.

She answered him with a smile, and then hurried down the stairs.

She gave no hint to Ralph of what had passed between them, and during the journey home through the darkness very little was said; but she walked with a more buoyant step than during the outward journey, and in her eye there was a brighter light, though Ralph did not see it.

She scarcely slept at all that night. She spent most of the time on her knees in prayer. Before Ralph got down to breakfast she had been to Veryan and back again. She did not allude, however, to this second journey. William was still alive, and in much the same condition.

For nearly two days he dwelt in the valley of the shadow, and no one could tell whether the angel of life or of death would prevail. The doctor looked in every few hours, and did all that human skill could do. William, though too spent to talk, and almost too weak to open his eyes, was acutely conscious of what was taking place.

To the onlookers it seemed as if he was passing into a condition of coma, but it was not so. He was fighting for life with all the will power he possessed. He had something to live for now. A new hope was in his heart, a new influence was breathing upon him. So he fought back the destroying angel inch by inch, and in the end prevailed.

There came a day when Ruth again sat by his bedside, holding his hand.

"I am getting better, sweetheart," he said, in a whisper.

"Yes, William."

"Your love and prayers have pulled me through."

"I could not let you go," she said.

"God has been very merciful," he answered reverently. "Next to His love the most wonderful thing is yours."

"Why should it be wonderful?" she asked, with a smile.

"You are so beautiful," he answered, "and I am so unworthy, and so——"

But she laid her hand upon his mouth and smothered the end of the sentence.

When once he had turned the corner he got better rapidly, but long before he was able to leave the house all St. Goram knew that Ruth Penlogan had promised to be his wife.

Ralph saw very little of his sister in those days, she spent so much of her time in going and coming between Hillside and Veryan. Fortunately the affairs of the mine kept his hands occupied and his thoughts busy, otherwise he would have felt himself neglected and alone.

It was not without a pang he saw the happiness of William and his sister. Not that he envied them; on the contrary, he rejoiced in their newly found joy; and yet their happiness did accentuate his own heartache and sense of loss.

A year had passed since that memorable day in St. James's Park when he told Dorothy Hamblyn that he loved her. He often smiled at his temerity, and wondered what spirit of daring or of madness possessed him.

He had tried hard since, as he had tried before, to forget her, but without success. For good or ill she held his heart in bondage. What had become of her he did not know. Hamblyn Manor was in possession of the gardener and his wife, and one other servant. There were rumours that some "up-the-country" people had taken it furnished for a year, but as far as he knew no one as yet had appeared on the scene. Sir John, it was said, was living quietly at Boulogne, but what had become of Dorothy and her brother no one seemed to know.

One afternoon he left Dingley Bottom earlier than usual, and wandered up the long slant in the direction of Treliskey Plantation. His intention was to cross the common to St. Goram, but on reaching the stile he stood still, arrested by the force of memory and association.

As he looked back into the valley he could not help contrasting the present with the past. How far away that never-to-be-forgotten afternoon seemed when he first came face to face with Dorothy Hamblyn! How much had happened since! Then he was a poor, struggling, discontented, ambitious youth, without prospects, without influence, and almost without hope.

Now he was rich—for riches are always relative—and a man. He had prospects also, and influence. Perhaps he had more influence than any other man in the parish. And yet he was not sure that he was not just as discontented as ever. He was gaining the world rapidly, but he was still unsatisfied. His heart was hungering for something he had not got.

He might get more money, more power, more authority, more influence. What then? The care of the world increased rather than diminished. It was eternally true, "A man's life consisteth not in the abundance of the things he possesseth."

His reflections were disturbed at length by the clicking of the gate leading into the plantation. He turned his head suddenly, and found himself face to face with Dorothy Hamblyn.

CHAPTER XXXIX

PERPLEXING QUESTIONS

There was no chance of withdrawal for either. If Ralph had caught a glimpse of Dorothy earlier, he would have hidden himself and let her pass; but there was no possibility of that now. He could only stand still and wait. Would she recognise him, or would she cut him dead? It was an interesting moment—from his point of view, almost tragic.

Wildly as his heart was beating, he could not help noticing that she looked thin and pale, as though she had recovered from a recent illness. She came straight on, not hesitating for a moment, and his heart seemed to beat all the more tumultuously with every step she took.

If in the long months that had elapsed since he saw her last he had grown for a moment indifferent, his passion flamed up again to a white heat at the first glimpse of her face. For him there was no other woman on earth. Her beauty had increased with the passing of the years; her character, strengthened and ennobled by suffering, showed itself in every line of her finely expressive face.

It was a trying moment for both, and perhaps more trying for Dorothy than for Ralph. For good or ill she knew that this young man had affected her whole life. He had crossed her path in the most critical moments of her existence. He had spoken words almost at haphazard which had changed the whole current of her thoughts. He had dared even to tell her that he loved her, when influence was being brought to bear on her to bestow her affection in another direction.

There were moments when she felt half angry that she was unable to forget him. He was out of her circle, and it seemed madness to let his image remain in her heart for a single moment, and yet the fascination of his personality haunted her. He was like no other man she had ever met. His very masterfulness touched her fancy as nothing had ever done before. If only he had been of her own set she would have made a hero of him.

When she left him in the Park after that passionate outburst of his, she made up her mind that she must forget him—utterly and absolutely. The situation had become dangerous; her heart was throbbing so wildly that she could scarcely bear it; the tense glow and passion of his words rang through her brain like the clashing of bells; her nerves were tingling to her finger-tips.

"Oh, what madness all this is," she said to herself—"what utter madness!" And yet all the while her heart seemed to be leaping exultantly. This clever, daring, handsome democrat loved her—loved her. She lingered over the words unconsciously.

Lord Probus had said he loved her, and had tempted her with a thousand brilliant toys; Archie Temple—with whom she had walked in the Park more than once—had professed unbounded and undying devotion; but her heart had never leaped for a moment in response to their words. The only man who moved her against her will, and sent the blood rushing through her veins like nectar, was this son of the people, this man who hated her class and tried his best to hate her.

Nevertheless, her resolve was fixed and definite. She must forget him. Unless she put him out of her thoughts he would spoil her whole life. Socially, they belonged to different hemispheres. The fact that her father was hard pressed for money, and was living abroad in order to economise, did not alter their relative positions. A Hamblyn was still a Hamblyn, though he lived in an almshouse.

It was easier, however, to make good resolves than to carry them into effect. Events would not allow her to forget. As the companion and private secretary of the Dowager Duchess of Flint, she had to read the papers every day, and not only the political articles, but the commercial and financial. The success of the Great St. Goram Mine was talked of far and wide, and the new discoveries of Ralph Penlogan, the brilliant young chemist and mineralogist, were the theme of numberless newspaper articles. Dorothy found herself searching all the papers that came her way for some mention of his name, and her heart seemed to leap into her mouth every time she saw it in print.

The dowager often dabbled in stocks and shares for want of something better to do. She liked to have what she called a "flutter" now and then, and she managed to pick up a few Great St. Goram shares at eighty per cent. premium.

It came out one day in conversation that Dorothy knew the exact locality of Great St. Goram Mine, knew the young man who had made the discovery, knew all about the place and all about the people, in fact. The dowager's interest grew. She began to make inquiries, and finally decided to rent Hamblyn Manor for a year. Dorothy was in a transport of excitement. To go back again to the dear old home would be like heaven, even though her father and Geoffrey were not there.

But that was not all. She would see Ralph Penlogan again—that would be inevitable. It seemed as though the Fates had determined to throw them together. The battle was not ended yet, it was only beginning.

The second day after their arrival at Hamblyn Manor she went for a long walk through the plantation. It was a lovely afternoon. The summer glory lay upon land and sea. She stood still for several moments when she came to the spot where she had found Ralph Penlogan lying senseless. How vividly every circumstance came up before her, how well she remembered his half-conscious talk. She did not see Ralph leaning against the stile when she pushed open the gate, and yet she half expected he would be there. It was the place where they first met, and Fate, or Destiny, or Providence, had a curious way of bringing them together, and she would have to face the inevitable, whatever it might be.

She was not in the least surprised when she caught sight of him, nor did she feel any inclination to turn back. Life was being shaped for her. She was in the grasp of a power stronger than her own will.

She looked at him steadily, and her face paled a little. He had altered considerably. He looked older by several years. He was no longer a youth, he was a man with the burden of life pressing upon him. Time had sobered him, softened him, mellowed him, greatened him.

Ought she to recognise him? For recognition would mean condoning his daring, and if she condoned him once, he might dare again, and he looked strong enough and resolute enough to dare anything.

She never quite decided in her mind what she ought to do. She remembered distinctly enough what she did. She smiled at him in her most gracious and winning manner and passed on. She half expected to hear footsteps behind her, but he did not follow. He watched her till she had turned the brow of the hill toward St. Goram, then he retraced his steps in the direction of his home.

He too had a feeling that it was of no use fighting against Fate. Events would have to take their course. She was not lost to him yet, and her smile gave him fresh hope.

He found the house empty when he got home, save for the housemaid. Ruth was out with William somewhere.

Ralph threw himself into an easy-chair and closed his eyes. His heart was beating strangely fast, his hands shook in spite of himself. The sight of Dorothy was like a match to stubble. He wondered if her beauty appealed to other people as it did to him.

Then a new question suggested itself to him, or an old question came up in a new form. To tell Dorothy Hamblyn that he loved her was one thing, to make love to her was another. Should he dare the second? He had dared the first, not with any hope of winning her, but rather to demonstrate to himself the folly of any such suggestion. But circumstances alter cases, and circumstances had changed with him. He was no longer poor. He could give her all the comforts she had ever known. As for the rest, her name, her family pride, her patrician blood, her aristocratic connections, they did not count with him. To ask a woman reared in comfort and luxury to share poverty and hardship and want was what he would never do. But the question of ways and means being disposed of, nothing else mattered. He was a man and an Englishman. He had lived honestly, and had kept his conscience clean.

He believed in an aristocracy, as most people do, but the aristocracy he believed in was the aristocracy of character and brains. He did not despise money, but he despised the people who made it their god, and who were prepared to sell their souls for its possession. To have a noble ancestry was a great thing; there was something in blood, but a man was not necessarily great because his father was a lord. The lower orders did not all live in hovels, some of them lived in mansions. All fools did not wear fustian, some of them wore fur-lined coats and drove motor-cars; the things that mattered were heart and intellect. A man might drop his "h's" and be a gentleman. The test of worth and manhood was not the size of a man's bank balance, but the manner of his life. Sir John Hamblyn boasted of his pedigree and was proud of his title, and yet, to put it in its mildest form, he had played the fool for twenty years.

Ralph got up from his seat at length and walked out into the garden. He had not felt so restless and excited for a year. The affairs of Great St. Goram Mine passed completely out of his mind. He could think only of one thing at a time, and just then Dorothy Hamblyn seemed of more importance than anything else on earth.

Up and down the garden paths he walked with bare head and his hands in his pockets. Now and then his brows contracted, and now and then his lips broke into a smile. The situation had its humorous as well as its serious side.

"If she had been the daughter of anybody else!" he said to himself again and again.

But outweighing everything else was the fact that he loved her. He could not help it that she was the daughter of the man who had been his greatest enemy. He could not help it that she belonged to a social circle that had little or no dealings with his own. Love laughs at bolts and bars. He was a man with the rights of a man and the hopes of a man.

Before Ruth returned he had made up his mind what to do.

Meanwhile, Dorothy was sauntering slowly homeward in a brown study. She felt anything but sure of herself. She hoped she had done the right thing in recognising Ralph Penlogan, but her heart and her head were not in exact agreement. The conventions of society were very strict. The Jews had no dealings with the Samaritans.

"If only Ralph Penlogan had been in her circle," and her heart leaped suddenly at the thought. How handsome he was, how resolute, how clever! Unconsciously she compared him with her brother Geoffrey, with Archie Temple, and with a number of other young men she had met in the drawing-rooms of London society.

The duchess had urged her to be friendly with Archie Temple. He was such a nice young man. He was well connected, was, in fact, the nephew of an earl, and was in receipt of a handsome salary which a generous Government paid him for doing nothing. He was a type of a great many others, impecunious descendants, many of them, of younger sons—drawling, effeminate, shallow-pated nobodies. Socially, of course, they belonged to what is called society printed with a capital S, but that was the highest testimonial that could be given them.

Dorothy found herself unconsciously revolting against the conventional view of life and the ethics of the social Ten Commandments. Were the mere accidents of birth the only things to be considered? Was a man less noble because he was born in a stable and cradled in a manger? Did greatness consist in possessing an estate and a title? Was worth to be measured by the depth of a man's pocket?

Measured by any true standard, she felt instinctively that Ralph Penlogan overtopped every other man she had met. How bravely he had fought, how patiently he had endured, how gloriously he had triumphed. If achievement counted for anything, if to live purely and do something worthy were the hall-marks of a gentleman, then he belonged to the world's true aristocracy, he was worth all the Archie Temples of London rolled into one.

Before she reached Hamblyn Manor another question was hammering at her brain—

"Did Ralph Penlogan still love her?"

She looked apprehensively right and left, and was half afraid lest her thoughts should take shape and reveal themselves to other people.

What would people think if they knew she had put such a question to herself? Had she forgotten that she was the daughter of Sir John Hamblyn?

No, she had not forgotten; but she was learning the truth that true worth is not in title, or name, or fortune; that neither coronet nor crown can make men;

that fools clad in sables are fools still, and rogues in mansions are still rogues.

The love of a man like Ralph Penlogan was not a thing to resent. It was something to be proud of and to be grateful for.

She retired to rest that night with a strange feeling of wonder in her heart. She was still uncertain of herself.

"Suppose Ralph Penlogan still loved her, and suppose——" She hid her face in the bedclothes and blushed in spite of herself.

He was fearless, she knew, and unconventional, and had no respect for names, or titles, or pedigrees as such. Moreover, he was not the man to be discouraged by small obstacles or turned aside by feeble excuses, and if he chose to cross her path she could not very well avoid him. The place was comparatively small, the walks were few, and during this glorious weather she could not dream of remaining indoors.

She had encouraged him that afternoon by recognising him. She had smiled at him in her most gracious way; and so, of course, he would know that she had forgiven him for speaking to her as he had done when last they met. And if he should seek her out; if, in his impetuous way, he should tell her he loved her still; if he should ask for an answer, and for an immediate answer. If—if——

She was still wondering when she fell asleep.

CHAPTER XL

LOVE OR FAREWELL

With Ralph Penlogan, resolution usually meant action. Having made up his mind to do a thing, he did not loiter long on the way. In any case, he could only be rebuffed, and he preferred to know the truth at once to waiting in doubt and uncertainty. A less impetuous nature would have seen many more lions in the way than he did. For a son of the masses to woo a daughter of the classes was an unheard-of thing, and had he taken anyone into his confidence he would have been dissuaded from the enterprise.

In this matter, however, he did not wear his heart upon his sleeve. So carefully had he guarded his secret, that even Ruth was under the impression that if he had ever been in love with Dorothy Hamblyn, he had outgrown the infatuation. Her name had not been mentioned for months, and she had been so long absent from St. Goram that it scarcely seemed probable that a youthful fancy would survive the long separation.

Ralph did not tell her that the squire's "little maid" had once more appeared on the scene. She would hear soon enough from other sources. He intended to keep his own counsel. If he failed, no one would ever know; but in any case, failure should not be due to any lack on his part either of courage or perseverance.

He was very silent and self-absorbed that evening, and had not Ruth been so much taken up with her own love affair, she would not have failed to notice it. But Ruth was living for the moment in a little heaven of her own—a heaven so beautiful, so full of unspeakable delights, that she was half afraid sometimes that she would wake up and find it was all a dream.

William was growing stronger every day, and expected soon to be as well as ever. Moreover, he seemed determined to make up for all the years he had lost. Ruth to him was a daily miracle of grace and beauty, and her love for him was a perpetual wonder. He did not understand it. He did not suppose he ever would. He accepted the fact with reverent gratitude, and gave up attempting to fathom the mystery.

He was very shy at first, and almost dubious. He felt so unworthy of so great a gift, but comprehension grew with returning strength, and with comprehension, courage. He believed himself to be the luckiest man on earth, and the happiest. The most difficult thing of all to believe was that Ruth could possibly be as happy as he.

Conviction on that point came through sight. It was not what Ruth said; it was the light that glowed in her soft brown eyes. A single glance meant volumes. A shy glance darted across the room stirred his heart like music.

Ralph watched their growing intimacy and their deepening joy with a sense of keen satisfaction. William was the one man in the world he would have chosen for his sister if he had been called upon to decide, and he was thankful beyond measure that Ruth had recognised his sterling qualities, and, without persuasion from anyone, had made her choice.

As the days passed away, Ralph had great difficulty in hiding his restlessness from his sister. It seemed to him that Dorothy purposely avoided him. He sought her out in all directions; lay in wait for her in the most likely places; but, for some reason or other, she failed to come his way. He spent hours leaning against the stile near Treliskey Plantation, and on three separate occasions defied the notices that trespassers would be prosecuted, and boldly marched through the plantation till he came in sight of the gables of the Manor; but neither patience nor perseverance was rewarded. He had to return disconsolate the way he had come.

Had he been of a less sanguine temperament, he would have drawn anything but hopeful conclusions. Her avoidance of him could surely have but one meaning, particularly as she knew the state of his feelings towards her.

But presumptions and deductions did not satisfy Ralph. He would be content with nothing short of actual facts. He was not sure yet that she purposely avoided him, and he was sure that she had smiled when they met, and that one fact was his sheet anchor just now.

He went to St. Goram Church on the following Sunday morning, much to the surprise of the vicar, for both he and Ruth were unswervingly loyal to the little community at Veryan, to which their father and mother belonged. Deep down in his heart he felt a little ashamed of himself. He knew it was not to worship that he went to church, but in the hope of catching a glimpse of Dorothy Hamblyn's face.

The Hamblyn pew, however, remained empty during the whole of the service. If he had gone to church from a wrong motive, he had been deservedly punished.

He began to think after awhile that Dorothy had paid a flying visit just for a day, and had gone away again, and that consequently any hope he ever had of winning her was more remote than ever. This view received confirmation from the fact that he never heard her name mentioned. Ruth had evidently not heard that she had been in St. Goram. Apparently she had come and gone without anyone seeing her but himself—come and gone like a gleam of sunshine on a stormy day—come and gone leaving him more disconsolate than he had ever been before.

For two days he kept close to his work, and never went beyond the bounds of Great St. Goram Mine. For the moment he had been checkmated, but he was not in despair. London was only a few hours away, and he had frequently to go there on business. He should meet her again some time, and if God meant him to win her he should win.

It was in this hopeful spirit that he returned late from the mine. Ruth brewed a fresh pot of tea for him, and put several dainties on the table to tempt his appetite, for it had recently occurred to her that he was not looking his best.

"What do you think, Ralph?" she said at length.

He looked up at her with a questioning light in his eyes, but did not reply.

"Dorothy Hamblyn is at the Manor."

"Indeed," he said, in a tone of apparent indifference. "Who told you that?"

"She has been there a fortnight!"

"A fortnight?"

"Dr. Barrow told William. He has been attending her."

"She is ill, then?"

"She has been. Caught a chill or something of the kind, and was a good deal run down to start with, but she is nearly all right again now. I wonder if she will come to see me here as she used to do at the cottage?"

"Possibly."

"I hope she will. It would be so nice to see her again. Her father may be a tyrant, but she is an angel."

Ralph gave a short, dry laugh.

"You do not seem very much interested," Ruth continued.

"Why should I be?" he questioned, looking up with a smile.

"I thought you used to like her very much."

"Oh, well, I did for that matter. But—but that's scarcely to the point, is it?"

"Well, no, perhaps it isn't. Only—only——"

"Yes?"

"Well, I sometimes wonder if you will ever do what William has done."

"Oh, I fell in love with my sister long before he did."

"Your own sister doesn't count."

"She does with William—counts too much, I'm afraid. He's no eyes for anything else."

"Oh, go along!"

"Not till I've had my tea. Remember, I'm hungry."

Then a knock came to the door, and William entered. He was still thin and pale, but there was a light in his eyes and a glow on his cheeks such as no one ever saw in the old days.

On the following afternoon Ralph made his way up the slant again in the direction of Treliskey Plantation. It was a glorious afternoon. The hot sunshine was tempered by a cool, Atlantic breeze. The hills and dales were looking their best, the hedges were full of flowers, the woods and plantations were great banks of delicious green. At the stile he paused for several minutes and surveyed the landscape, but his thoughts all the time were somewhere else. Hope had sprung up afresh in his heart, and a determined purpose was throbbing through all his veins.

After awhile he left the stile and passed through the plantation gate. He was a trespasser, he knew, but that was a matter of little account. No one would molest him now. He was a man of too much importance in the neighbourhood. He hardly realised yet what a power he had become, and how anxious people were to be on good terms with him. In himself he was conscious of no change. So far, at any rate, money had not spoiled him. Every Sunday as he passed through the little graveyard at Veryan he was reminded of the fact that his mother had died in the workhouse. If he was ever tempted to put on airs—which he was not—that fact would have kept him humble.

The true secret of his influence, however, was not that he was prosperous, but that he was just. There was not a toiler in Great St. Goram Mine who did not know that. In the past strength had been the synonym for tyranny. Those who possessed a giant's strength had used it like a giant. But Ralph had changed the tradition. The strong man was a just man and a generous, and it was for that reason his influence had grown with every passing day.

Yet he was quite unconscious of the measure of his influence. In his own eyes he was only David Penlogan's son, though that fact meant a great deal to him. David Penlogan was an honest man—a man who, in a very real sense, walked with God—and it was Ralph's supreme desire to prove worthy of his father.

But it was of none of these things he thought as he walked slowly along between high banks of trees. The road was grass-grown from end to end, and was so constructed that the pedestrian appeared to be constantly turning corners.

"I think she will walk out to-day," he kept saying to himself. "This beautiful weather will surely tempt her out."

He had made up his mind what to do and say in case they did meet. For good or ill, he was determined to know his fate. It might be an act of presumption, or a simple act of folly—that was an aspect of the question that scarcely occurred to him.

The supreme factor in the case, as far as he was concerned, was, he loved her. On that point there was no room for doubt. The mere social aspect of the question he was constitutionally incapable of seeing. A man was a man, and if he were of good character, and able to maintain the woman he loved, what mattered anything else?

He came face to face with Dorothy at a bend in the road. She was walking slowly, with her eyes on the ground. She did not hear his footsteps on the grass-grown road, and when she looked up he was close upon her. There was no time to debate the situation even with herself, so she followed the impulse of her heart and held out her hand to him.

"I thought I should meet you to-day," he said. "I am sorry you have been ill."

"I was rather run down when I came," she answered, glancing at him with a questioning look, "and I think I caught cold on the journey."

"But you are better now?"

"Oh yes, I am quite well again."

"I feared you had returned to London. I have been on the look-out for you for weeks."

She looked shyly up into his face, but did not reply.

"I wanted to know my fate," he went on. "You know that I love you. You must have guessed it long before I told you."

"But—but——" she began, with averted eyes.

"Please hear me out first," he interrupted. "I would not have spoken again had not circumstances changed. When I saw you in London I was poor and without hope. I believed that I should have to leave the country in order to earn a living. To have offered marriage to anyone would have been an insult. And yet if I had never seen you again I should have loved you to the end."

"But have you considered——" she began again, with eyes still turned from his face.

"I have considered everything," he interrupted eagerly, almost passionately. "But there is only one thing that matters, and that is love. If you do not love me—cannot love me—my dream is at an end, and I will endure as best I am able. But if your heart responds to my appeal, then the thing is settled. You are mine."

"But you are forgetting my—my—position," she stammered.

"I am forgetting nothing of importance," he went on resolutely. "There are only two people in the world really concerned in this matter, you and I, and the decision rests with you. It is not my fault that I love you. I cannot help it. You did not mean to steal my heart, perhaps, but you did it. It seems a curious irony of fate, for I detested your father; but Providence threw me across your path. In strange and inexplicable ways your life has become linked with mine. You are all the world to me. Cannot you give me some hope?"

"But my father still——" she began.

"You are of age," he interrupted. "No, no! Questions of parentage or birth or position do not count. Why should they? Let us get back to the one thing that matters. If you cannot love me, say the word, and I will go my way and never molest you again. But if you do love me, be it ever so little, you must give me hope."

"My father would never consent," she said quickly.

"That is nothing," he answered, almost impatiently. "I will wait till he does give his consent. Oh, Dorothy, the only thing I want to know is do you love me? If you can give me that assurance, nothing else in the world matters. Just say the little word. God surely meant us for each other, or I could not love you as I do."

She dropped her eyes to the ground and remained motionless.

He came a step nearer and took her hand in his. She did not resist, nor did she raise her eyes, but he felt that she was trembling from head to foot.

"You are not angry with me?" he questioned, almost in a whisper.

"No, no; I am not angry," she said, almost with a sob. "How could I be? You are a good man, and such love as yours humbles me."

"Then you care for me just a little?" he said eagerly.

"I cannot tell how much I care," she answered, and the tears came into her eyes and filled them to the brim. "But what does it matter? It must all end here and now."

"Why end, Dorothy?"

"Because my father would die before he gave me to you. You do not know him. You do not know how proud he is. Name and lineage are nothing to you, but they are everything to him."

"But he would have married you to Lord Probus, a—a bloated brewer!" He spoke angrily and scornfully.

"But he had been made a peer."

"What does that matter if Nature made him a clown?"

"Which Nature had not done. No, no; give him his due. He was commonplace, and not very well educated——"

"And do these empty social distinctions count with you?" he questioned.

"I sometimes hate them," she answered. "But what can I do? There is no escape. The laws of society are as inflexible as the laws of the Medes and Persians."

"And you will fling love away as an offering to the prejudices of your father?"

"Why do you tempt me? You must surely see how hard it is!"

"Then you do love me!" he cried; and he caught her in his arms and kissed her.

For a moment she struggled as if to free herself. Then her head dropped upon his shoulder.

"Oh, Ralph," she whispered, "let me love you for one brief minute; then we must say farewell for ever!"

CHAPTER XLI

THE TABLES TURNED

Three days later Ralph paused for a moment in front of a trim boarding-house or pension on the outskirts of Boulogne. It was here Sir John Hamblyn was "vegetating," as he told his friends—practising the strictest economy, and making a desperate and praiseworthy effort to recover somewhat his lost financial position.

Ralph told no one what he intended to do. Ruth supposed that he had gone no farther than London, and that it was business connected with Great St. Goram Mine that called him there. Dorothy, having for a moment capitulated, had been making a brave but futile effort to forget, and trying to persuade herself that she had done a weak and foolish thing in admitting to Ralph Penlogan that she cared for him.

Love and logic, however, were never meant to harmonise, and heart and head are often in hopeless antagonism. Dorothy pretended to herself that she was sorry, and yet all the time deep down in her heart there was a feeling of exultation. It was delightful to be loved, and it was no less delightful to love in return.

Almost unconsciously she found herself meditating on Ralph's many excellences. He was so genuine, so courageous, so unspoiled by the world. She was sure also that she liked him all the better for being a man of the people. He owed nothing to favour or patronage. He had fought his own way and made his own mark. He was not like Archie Temple, who had been pushed into a situation purely through favour, and who, if thrown upon the open market, would not earn thirty shillings a week.

It was an honour and a distinction to be loved by a man like Ralph Penlogan. He was one of Nature's aristocracy, clear-visioned, brave-hearted, fearless, indomitable. His handsome face was the index of his character. How he had developed since that day he refused to open the gate for her! Suffering had made him strong. Trial and persecution had called into play the best that was in him. The fearless, defiant youth had become a strong and resolute man. How could she help loving him when he offered her all the love of his own great heart?

Then she would come to herself with a little gasp, and tell herself that it was her duty to forget him, to tear his image out of her heart; that an attachment such as hers was hopeless and quixotic; that the sooner she mastered herself the better it would be; that her father would never approve, and that the society in which she moved would be aghast.

For two days she fought a fitful and unequal battle, and then she discovered that the more she fought the more helpless she seemed to become. She had kept in the house lest she should discover him straying in the plantation.

On the third day she went out again. She said to herself that she would suffocate if she remained any longer indoors. Her heart was aching for a sight of Ralph Penlogan's face. She told herself it was fresh air she was pining for, and a sight of the hills and the distant sea. She loitered through the plantation until she reached the far end. Then she sighed and pushed open the gate. She walked as far as the stile, and leaned against it. How long she remained there she did not know; but she turned away at length, and strolled out across the common and down into the high road, and so home by way of the south lodge.

The air had been fresh and sweet, and the blue of the sea peeped between the hills in the direction of Perranpool, and the woods and plantations looked their best in their summer attire, and the birds sang cheerily on every hand. But she heard nothing, and saw nothing. The footfall she had listened for all the time failed to come, and the face she was hungering to see kept out of sight.

He had evidently taken her at her word. She had told him that their parting must be for ever, that it would be worse than madness for them to meet, and she had meant it all at the time; and yet, three days later, she would have given all she possessed for one more glimpse of his face.

The following day her duties were more irksome than she had ever known them. The dowager wanted so many letters written, and so many articles read to her. Dorothy was impatient to get out of doors, and the more rapidly she tried to get through her work the more mistakes she made, with the result that it had to be done over again.

It was getting quite late in the afternoon when at length she hurried away through the plantation. Would he come to meet her? She need not let him make love to her, but they might at least be friends. Love and logic were in opposition again.

She lingered by the stile until the sun went down behind the hill, then, with a sigh, she turned away, and began to retrace her steps through the plantation.

"I ought to be thankful to him for taking me at my word," she said to herself, with a pathetic look in her eyes. "Oh, why did he ever love me? Why was I ever born?"

Meanwhile Ralph Penlogan and Sir John Hamblyn had come face to face. Ralph had refused to send up his name, hence, when he was ushered into the squire's presence, the latter simply stared at him for several moments in speechless rage and astonishment.

Ralph was the first to break the silence.

"I must apologise for this intrusion," he said quietly, "but——"

"I should think so, indeed," interrupted Sir John scornfully. "Will you state your business as quickly as possible?"

"I will certainly occupy no more of your time than I can help," Ralph replied, "though I fear you are not in the humour to consider any proposal from me."

"I should think not, indeed. Why should I be? Do you wish me to tell you what I think of you?"

"I am not anxious on that score, though I am not aware that I have given you any reason for thinking ill of me."

"You are not, eh? When you cheated me out of the most valuable bit of property I possessed?"

"Did we not pay the price you asked?"

"But you knew there was a valuable tin lode in it."

"What of that? The property was in the market. We did not induce you to sell it. We heard by accident that you wanted to dispose of it. If there had been no lode we should have made no effort to get it."

"It was a mean, dishonest trick, all the same."

"I do not see it. By every moral right the farm was more mine than yours. I helped my father to reclaim it. You spent nothing on it, never raised your finger to bring it under cultivation. Moreover, it was common land at the start. In league with a dishonest Parliament, you filched it from the people, and then, by the operation of an iniquitous law, you filched it a second time from my father."

Sir John listened to this speech with blazing eyes and clenched hands.

"By Heaven," he said, "if I were a younger man I would kick you down these stairs. Have you forced your way in here to insult me?"

"On the contrary, it was my desire rather to conciliate you; but you charged me with dishonesty at the outset."

"Conciliate me, indeed!" And Sir John turned away with a sneer upon his face.

"We neither of us gain anything by losing our tempers," Ralph said, after a pause. "Had we not better let bygones be bygones?"

Sir John faced him again and stared.

"It is no pleasure to me to rake up the past," Ralph went on. "Probably we should both be happier if we could forget. I don't deny that I vowed eternal enmity against you and yours."

"I am glad to hear it," Sir John snorted.

"Time, however, has taken the sting out of many things, and to-day I love one whom I would have hated."

"You love——?"

"It is of no use beating about the bush," Ralph went on. "I love your daughter, and I have come to ask your permission——"

He did not finish the sentence, however. With blazing eyes and clenched fist Sir John shrieked at the top of his voice—

"Silence! Silence! How dare you? You——"

"No, do not use hard words," Ralph interrupted. "You may regret it later."

"Regret calling you—a—a——" But no suitable or sufficiently expressive epithet would come to his lips, and he sank into a chair almost livid with anger and excitement.

Ralph kept himself well in hand. He had expected a scene, and so was prepared for it. Seizing his opportunity, he spoke again.

"Had we not better discuss the matter without feeling or passion?" he said, in quiet, even tones. "Surely I am not making an unreasonable request. Even you know of nothing against my character."

"You are a vulgar upstart," Sir John hissed. "Good heavens, you!—you!—aspiring to the hand of my daughter."

"I am not an upstart, and I hope I am not vulgar," Ralph replied quietly. "At any rate, I am an Englishman. You are no more than that. The accidents of birth count for nothing."

"Indeed!"

"In your heart you know it is so. In what do you excel? Wherein lies your superiority?"

For a moment Sir John stared at him; then he said, with intense bitterness of tone—

"Will you have the good manners to take yourself out of my sight?"

"I will do so, certainly, though you have not answered my questions."

"If I were only a younger man I would answer you in a way you would not quickly forget."

"Then you refuse to give your permission?"

"Absolutely. I would rather see my child in her coffin."

"If you loved your child you would think more of her happiness than of your own pride. I am sorry to find you are a tyrant still."

"Thank you. Have you any further remarks to make?"

"No!" And he turned away and moved toward the door. Then he turned suddenly round with his hand on the door knob.

"By-the-bye, you may be interested to know that I have discovered a very rich vein that runs through your estate," he said quietly, and he pulled the door slowly open.

Sir John was on his feet in a moment.

"A very rich vein?" he questioned eagerly.

"Extraordinarily rich," was the indifferent reply. "Good-afternoon."

"Wait a moment—wait a moment!" Sir John cried excitedly.

"Thank you, but I have no further remarks to make." And Ralph passed out to the landing.

Sir John rushed past him and planted himself at the head of the stairs.

"You are not fooling me?" he questioned eagerly. "Say honestly, are you speaking the truth?"

"Do you wish to insult me?" Ralph asked scornfully. "Am I in the habit of lying? Please let me pass."

"No, no! Please forgive me. But if what you say is true, it means so much to me. You see, I am practically in exile here."

"So I understand. And you are likely to remain in exile, by all accounts."

"But if there is a rich vein of mineral that I can tap. Why, don't you see, it will release me at once?"

"But, as it happens, you cannot tap it, for you don't know where it is. I am the only individual who knows anything about it."

"Exactly, exactly! Don't go just yet. I want to hear more about it."

"I fear I have wasted too much of your time already," Ralph said ironically. "You asked me just now to take myself out of your sight."

"I know I did. I know I did. But I was very much upset. Besides, this lode is a horse of quite another colour. Now come back into my room and tell me all about it."

"There is really not very much to tell," Ralph answered, in a tone of indifference. "How I discovered its existence is a mere detail. You may be aware, perhaps, that I occupy most of my time in making experiments?"

"Yes, yes. I know you are wonderfully clever in your own particular line. But tell me, whereabouts is it?"

"You flatter me too much," Ralph said, with a laugh. "To tell you the truth, it was largely by accident that I discovered the lode I am speaking of. Unfortunately, it is outside the Great St. Goram boundary, so that it is of no use to our shareholders."

The squire laughed and rubbed his hands.

"But it will be of use to me," he said. "Really, this is a remarkable bit of luck. You are quite sure that it is a very valuable discovery?"

"As sure as one can be of anything in this world. The Hillside lode is rich, but this——"

"No, no," Sir John interrupted eagerly. "You don't mean to say that it is richer than your mine?"

"I shall be greatly surprised if—if——" Then he paused suddenly.

"Go on, go on," cried Sir John excitedly. "This bit of news is like new life to me. Think of it. I shall be able to shake off those Jewish sharks and hold up my head once more."

"I don't think it is at all necessary that you should hold your head any higher," Ralph replied deliberately and meaningly. "You think far too much of yourself already. Now I will say good-afternoon for the second time."

"You mean that you will tell me nothing more?"

"Why should I? If your justice had been equal to your greed, I might have been disposed to help you; but I feel no such disposition at present."

"You want to bargain with me?" Sir John cried angrily.

"Indeed, no. What I came about is too sacred a matter for bargaining." And, slipping quickly past Sir John, he hurried down the stairs and into the street.

The squire stared after him for several minutes, then went back into the room and fetched his hat, and was soon following.

When he got into the open air, however, Ralph was nowhere visible. He ran a few steps, first in one direction, then in another. Finally, he made his way down into the town. He did not go to the wharf, for no boat was sailing for several hours; but he loitered in the principal streets till he was hungry, and then reluctantly made his way toward his temporary home. He was in a state of almost feverish excitement, and hardly knew at times whether he was awake or dreaming.

What his exile in France meant to him, no one knew but himself. But his financial affairs were in such a tangle, that it was exile or disgrace, and his pride turned the scale in favour of exile. Now, suddenly, there had been opened up before him the prospect of release—but release upon terms.

He tried, over his lonely dinner, to review the situation; tried to put himself in the place of Ralph Penlogan. It was a profitable exercise. The lack of imagination is often the parent of wrong. He was bound to admit to himself that Ralph was under no obligation—moral or otherwise—to reveal his secret, or even to sell his knowledge.

"No doubt I have behaved badly to him," Sir John said to himself, "and badly to his father. He has good reason for hating me and thwarting me. By Jove! but we have changed places. He is the strong man now, and if he pays me back in my own coin, it is no more than I deserve."

Sir John did not make a good dinner that evening. His reflections interfered with his appetite.

"Should I tell if I were in his place?" he said to himself. And he answered his own question with a groan.

Under the influence of a cigar and a cup of black coffee, visions of prosperity floated before him. He saw himself back again in Hamblyn Manor, and in more than his old splendour. He saw himself free from the clutches of the money-lenders, and a better man for the experiences through which he had passed.

But his visions were constantly broken in upon by the reflection that his future lay in the hands of Ralph Penlogan, the young man he had so cruelly wronged. It was a hard battle he had to fight, for his pride seemed to pull him in opposite directions at the same time.

Half an hour before the boat started for Folkestone he was on the wharf, eagerly scanning the faces of all the passengers. He had made up his mind to try to persuade Ralph to go back with him and stay the night. His pride was rapidly breaking down under the pressure of unusual circumstances.

He remained till the boat cast off her moorings and the paddle-wheels began to churn the water in the narrow slip, then he turned away with a sigh. Ralph was not among the passengers.

CHAPTER XLII

COALS OF FIRE

Ralph returned home by way of Calais and Dover, and on the following day he came face to face with Dorothy outside the lodge gates. He raised his hat and would have passed on, but she would not let him.

"Surely we may be friends?" she said, extending her hand to him, and her eyes were pleading and pathetic.

He stopped at once and smiled gravely.

"I thought it was your wish that we should meet as strangers," he said.

"Did I say that?" she questioned, and she turned away her eyes from him.

"Something to that effect," he answered, still smiling, though he felt as if every reason for smiles had passed from him.

"I have been expecting to see you for days past," she said, suddenly raising her eyes to his.

"I have been from home," he answered. "In fact, I have been to Boulogne."

"To Boulogne?" she asked, with a start, and the blood mounted in a torrent to her neck and face.

"I went across to see your father," he said slowly.

"Yes?" she questioned, and her face was set and tense.

"He was obdurate. He said he would rather see you in your coffin."

For a moment there was silence. Then she said—

"Was he very angry?"

"I am sorry to say he was. He evidently dislikes me very much—a feeling which I fear is mutual."

"I wonder you had the courage to ask him," she said at length.

"I would dare anything for your sake," he replied, with averted eyes. "I would defy him if you were willing. And, indeed, I cannot see why he should be the arbiter of your fate and mine."

"You must not forget that he is my father," she said quietly and deliberately.

"But you defied him in the case of Lord Probus."

"That was different. To have married Lord Probus would have been a sin. No, no. The cases are not parallel."

"Then you are still of the same mind?" he questioned.

"It would not be right," she said, after a long pause, "knowing father as I do, and knowing how keenly he feels all this."

"Then it is right to spoil my life, to fling all its future in shadow?"

"You will forget me," she said, with averted eyes.

"Perhaps so," he answered a little bitterly; "time is a great healer, they say," and he raised his hat again and turned away.

But her hand was laid on his arm in a moment.

"Now you are angry with me," she said, her eyes filling. "But don't you see it is as hard for me as for you? Oh, it is harder, for you are so much stronger than I."

"If we are to forget each other," he replied quietly and without looking at her, "we had better begin at once."

"But surely we may be friends?" she questioned.

"It is not a question of friendship," he answered, "but of forgetting, or of trying to forget."

"But I don't want to forget," she said impulsively. "I could not if I tried. A woman never forgets. I want to remember you, to think of your courage, your —your——"

"Folly," he interrupted.

She looked at him with a startled expression in her eyes.

"Is it folly to love?" she questioned.

"Yes, out of your own station. If I had loved anyone else but you——"

"No, no! Don't say that," she interrupted. "God knows best. We are strengthened and made better by the painful discipline of life."

He took her outstretched hand and held it for a moment, then raised it to his lips. So they parted. He could not feel angry or resentful. She was so sweet, so gentle, so womanly, that she compelled his reverence. It was better to have loved her and lost, than to have won any other woman on earth.

On the following afternoon, on reaching home, Ruth met him at the door with a puzzled expression in her eyes.

"Who do you think is in the parlour?" she questioned, with a touch of excitement in her voice.

"William Menire," he ventured, with a laugh.

"Then you are mistaken. William has gone to St. Hilary. But what do you say to the squire?"

"Sir John Hamblyn?"

She nodded.

"He's been waiting the best part of an hour."

For a moment he hesitated, then he strode past her into the house.

Sir John rose and bowed stiffly. Ralph closed the door behind him and waited for the squire to speak.

"I went down to the boat, hoping to catch you before you left Boulogne," Sir John began.

"I returned by way of Calais," was the quick reply.

"Ah, that explains. I was curious to have a little further talk with you. What you said about the lode excited me a great deal."

"I have little doubt of it."

"I own I have no claim upon you," Sir John went on, without heeding the interruption. "Still, keeping the knowledge to yourself can do you no good."

"That is quite true."

"While to me it would be everything."

"It might be a bad thing. In the past, excuse me for saying it, you have used your wealth and your influence neither wisely nor well. In fact, you have prostituted both to selfish and unworthy ends."

"I have been foolish, I own, and I have had to pay dearly for it. You think I pressed your father hard, but I was hard pressed myself. If I hadn't allowed myself to drift into the hands of those villainous Jews I should have been a better man."

"But are you not in their hands still?"

"Well, yes, up to a certain point I am. At present they are practically running the estates."

"And when will you be free?"

"Well, I hardly know. You see they keep piling up interest in such a way that it is difficult to discover where I am. But a rich lode would enable me to clear off everything."

"I am not sure of that. If during your lifetime they have got a hold on the estates, how do you know they would not appropriate the lode with the rest?"

Sir John looked blank, and for several moments was silent.

"Do you know," he said at length, "that I have already paid three times more in interest than the total amount I borrowed?"

"I can quite believe that," was the answer. "Would you mind telling me the amount you did borrow?"

Sir John named the sum.

Ralph regarded him in silence for several moments.

"It is a large sum," he said at length, "a very large sum. And yet, if I am not greatly mistaken, it is but a trifle in comparison with the value of the lode I have referred to."

"You do not mean that?" the squire said eagerly.

"But it would be folly to make its existence known until you have got out of the hands of those money-lenders," Ralph went on.

"They would grab it all, you think?"

"I fear so. If all one hears about their cunning is true, there is scarcely any hope for a man who once gets into their clutches. The law seems powerless. You had better have made yourself a bankrupt right off."

"I don't know; the disgrace is so great."

Ralph curled his lip scornfully.

"It seems to me you strain at a gnat and swallow a camel," he said.

"I have been hard pressed," the squire answered dolefully.

For several seconds neither of them spoke again. Ralph was evidently fighting a hard battle with himself. It is not easy to be magnanimous when it is more than probable your magnanimity will be abused. Why should he be kind to this man? He had received nothing but cruelty at his hands. Should he turn his cheek to the smiter? Should he restrain himself when he had the chance of paying off old scores? Was it not human, after all, to say an eye for an eye and a tooth for a tooth? Was not revenge sweet?

They were facing each other in the very house from which he and his mother and Ruth had been evicted, the house in which his father had died of a broken heart. Did not every stone in it cry out for vengeance? This man had shown them no mercy. In the hour of their greatest need he had been more cruel than any fabled Shylock. He had insisted upon his pound of flesh, though it meant beggary to them all. He had pursued them with a vindictiveness that was almost without a parallel. And now that the tables had been turned, and the tyrant, bereft of his power, was pleading for mercy, was he to kiss the hand that before had struck him?

Moreover, what guarantee was there that if this man were restored to his old position he would be any better than he was before? Was not his heart what it had always been? Was he not a tyrant by nature?

Sir John watched the look of perplexity gather and deepen on Ralph's face, and guessed the struggle that was going on within him. He felt very humble, and more penitent than Ralph knew.

The younger man lifted his head at length, and his brow cleared.

"I have been strongly tempted," he said slowly, "to mete out to you what you have measured to us."

"I have no claim to be considered," Sir John said humbly.

"You have thwarted me, or tried to thwart me, at every stage of my life," Ralph went on.

"I know I have been no friend to you," was the feeble reply.

"And if I help you back to power, I have no guarantee that you will not use that power to thwart me again."

The squire let his eyes fall to the ground, but did not reply.

"However, to play the part of the dog in the manger," Ralph went on, "is not a very manly thing to do, so I have decided to tell you all I know."

"You will reveal the lode to me?" he questioned eagerly.

"Yes. It will be good for the neighbourhood and the county in any case."

The squire sat down suddenly, and furtively wiped his eyes.

"But the money-lenders will have to be squared first. Will you allow me to tackle them for you? I should enjoy the bull-baiting."

"You mean——"

"I mean that in any case they must not be allowed to get the lode into their hands."

"I don't know how it is to be avoided."

"Will you leave the matter to me and William Menire?"

"You mean you will help me?"

"We shall be helping the neighbourhood."

Sir John struggled hard to keep the tears back, but failed.

"And you impose no condition?" he sobbed at length.

"No, I impose no condition. If the thing is to be done, let it be done freely."

"You unman me altogether," the squire said, with brimming eyes. "I did not expect, I really didn't. I have no claim, and I've been beastly hard on you. I know I have, and I'm sorry, real sorry, mind you; and if—if——"

"We'll let the 'ifs' go for the present, if you don't mind," Ralph said, with a dry laugh. "There are a good many present difficulties to be met. I should like to see your agreement with the money-lenders."

"You shall see everything. If you can only get me out of this hole you will make me the most thankful man alive!"

Ralph smiled dubiously.

"When can I see the papers?" he asked.

"To-day if you like. They are at the Manor."

"Very good. I will walk across after tea, or will you fetch them here?"

"If it would not be troubling you to walk so far——"

"I will come with pleasure."

The squire felt very chastened and humble as he made his way slowly back to the Manor, through Treliskey Plantation. Magnanimity is rarely lost on anyone, kindness will melt the hardest heart. The squire's pride was being slowly undermined, his arrogance seemed almost a contemptible thing.

By contrast with Ralph's nobler character he began to see how mean and poor was his own. He had prided himself so much on his name and pedigree, and yet he was only beginning to see how unworthy he had proved of both. What, after all, was the mere accident of birth in comparison with moral greatness? Measured by any right standard, Ralph Penlogan was an infinitely better man than he. He had not only intellect, but heart. He possessed that true nobility which enabled a man to forgive his enemy. He was turning in a very literal sense his cheek to the smiter.

Sir John entered the house with a curious feeling of diffidence. His home, and yet not his. The dowager made him welcome, and placed the library and a bedroom above at his disposal for as long as he might care to stay.

Dorothy was delighted to have her father with her again, and yet she was strangely puzzled as to the object of his visit. She was puzzled still more when a little later Ralph Penlogan was shown into the room where she and her father sat.

She rose to her feet in a moment, while a hot blush swept over her neck and face. For a second or two she stood irresolute, and glanced hastily from one to the other. What was the meaning of it all? Her father, instead of glaring angrily at his visitor, received him with the greatest cordiality and even deference, while Ralph advanced with no sign of fear or hesitation.

Neither of them appeared for the moment to be conscious of her presence. Ralph did not even look towards her.

Then her father said in a low voice—

"You can leave us for a little while, Dorothy."

She hurried out of the room with flaming cheeks and fast-beating heart. What could her father want with Ralph Penlogan? What was the mystery underlying his hurried visit? Could it have any reference to herself? Had her father relented? Had he at last come to see that character was more than social position—that a man was great not by virtue of birth, but by virtue of achievement?

For the best part of an hour she sat in her own room waiting and listening. Then the dowager summoned her to read an article to her out of the *Spectator*.

It grew dark at last, and Dorothy sought her own room once more, but she was so restless she could not sit still. The very air seemed heavy with fate. Her father and Ralph were still closeted in the library. What could they have to say to each other that kept them so long?

When the lamps were lighted she stole out of her room and waited for a few moments on the landing. Then she ran lightly down the stairs into the hall. The library door was still closed, but a moment later it was pulled slightly open. She drew back into a recess and pulled a curtain in front of her, though why she did so she hardly knew.

She could hear distinctly a murmur of voices, then came a merry peal of laughter. She had not heard her father laugh so merrily for years.

Then the two men walked out into the hall side by side, and began to converse in subdued tones. She could see them very distinctly. How handsome Ralph looked in the light of the lamp.

The squire went with his visitor to the front door, and opened it. She caught

Ralph's parting words, "I will see to the matter without delay. Good-night!"

When the squire returned from the door he saw Dorothy standing under the lamp with a look of inquiry in her eyes.

CHAPTER XLIII

SIR JOHN ATONES

Dorothy did not see Ralph again for nearly a month, and the hope that had animated her for a brief period threatened to go out in darkness. Her father, much to her surprise, remained at the Manor, he and the dowager having come to terms that appeared to be mutually satisfactory. But for what purpose he had returned to St. Goram, and why he remained, she did not know, and more puzzling still was why he had held that long and friendly interview with Ralph Penlogan.

More than once she had tried to get at the truth. But her father was completely on his guard against every chance question. He had never been in the habit of taking Dorothy into his confidence in business matters. He was of opinion that the less girls knew about matters outside the domestic realm the better. Moreover, until he was safely out of the clutches of the money-lenders, it would not be safe to take anyone into his confidence. So to Dorothy, at any rate, he remained a mystery from day to day, and the longer he remained, the deeper the mystery seemed to grow.

There was, however, one compensation. He was more cheerful and more affectionate than he had ever been since her refusal to marry Lord Probus. What that might mean she was unable to guess. There appeared to be no particular reason for his cheerfulness. For the moment he was living on charity, for of course he could not dream of paying the dowager for his board and lodgings. He did not appear to be engaged on any gambling adventure or business enterprise. No one came to see him. He went nowhere, except for an occasional long walk after dark, and he scarcely ever received a letter.

One evening he was absent several hours, and did not return till after midnight. Dorothy waited up for him, and had begun to be greatly concerned at his non-arrival. She was standing at the open door listening when she caught the sound of his footsteps, and she ran a little way down the drive to meet him.

"Oh, father, wherever have you been?" she cried out anxiously.

"Why, little girl, why are you not in bed?" he answered, with a laugh.

"Because I waited up for you, and I expected you an hour ago. I have been terribly anxious."

"Nobody is likely to run away with me," he said, bending over and kissing her.

"But it is so late for you to be out alone. If there was anyone you have been in the habit of visiting, I should not have worried, but I feared you had been taken ill, or had met with an accident."

"I did not know you cared for your old father so much," he said, with a note of tenderness in his voice that was new to her.

"But I do care," she answered impulsively, "and care lots and lots more than I can tell you."

He kissed her again, and then taking her arm, he led her into the house. Bolting the front door, he followed her into the library.

She was standing against the fireplace when he entered, and she noticed that his eyes were unusually bright.

"I have been to Hillside Farm," he said, and a broad smile spread itself over his face.

"To Hillside Farm?" she questioned.

"Young Penlogan has had some business affairs of mine in hand, and to-night we have settled it."

She stared at him with a look of wonder in her eyes, but did not reply.

"It's been a ticklish task, and, of course, I have said nothing about it. But I've been in high hopes ever since I came back. Penlogan is really a remarkable fellow."

"Yes?" she questioned, wondering more than ever.

"It's a curious turn of the tables," he went on; "but he's behaved splendidly, and there's no denying it. He might have heaped coals of fire on my head at every point. He might—but—well, after one straight talk—not another word. He's behaved like a gentleman—perhaps I ought to say like a Christian. No conditions! Not a condition. No. Having made up his mind to do the straight thing, he's carried it through. It's been coals of fire, all the same. I've never felt so humbled in my life before. I could wish—but there, it's too late to wish now. He's spared me all he could. I'm bound to say that for him, and he's carried it through——"

"Carried what through, father?"

He started, and smiled, for his thoughts had evidently gone wandering to some distant place.

"I'm afraid it's too long a story to tell you to-night."

"No, no, father. I'm quite wide awake. And, indeed, I shall not sleep for the night, unless you tell me."

"I'm wide awake myself," he said, with a laugh. "By Jove! I feel as if I could dance. You can't imagine what a relief it is to me. Life will be worth living again."

"But what is it all about, father?"

"Oh, that clever dog, Penlogan, discovered a rich vein of ore in my ground, and he's given me all the benefit of the discovery. I've been hard up for a long time, as you know; been in the hands of sharks, in fact. I feel ashamed to tell you this, though I expect you have guessed. Well, thanks to Penlogan, I've shaken them off, got quite free of them. Now I'm free to go ahead."

"And has Ralph Penlogan done all this for nothing?"

"Absolutely. He wanted you when he came to see me at Boulogne, but I told him I'd see you buried first. Good heavens! I could have wrung his neck."

She smiled pathetically, but made no answer.

"He's a greater man than I knew," Sir John went on, after a pause. "He was strongly tempted to be even with me—he told me so—but the finer side of him conquered. Good heavens! if only Geoffrey were such a man, how proud I should be."

"Geoffrey has been trained in a different school."

"There may be something in that. Some natures expand under hard knocks, are toughened by battle and strife, greatened by suffering, and sweetened by sorrow."

She looked up into his face with a wondering smile.

"Ah, my Dorothy," he said, with a world of tenderness in his tones, "I have learned a great deal during the last few weeks. In the past I've been a fool, and worse. I've measured people by their social position. I've set value on filigree and embroidery. I've been proud of pedigree and name, and I've tried to put my heel upon people who were my superiors in every way. Good heavens! what vain fools we are in the main. We value the pinchbeck setting and kick the diamond into the gutter."

"Then you have finished with Mr. Penlogan now?" she questioned, after a long pause.

"Finished with him? Why so? I hope not, anyhow."

"But you have got all you want out of him."

"I never said so. No, no. We shall have to form a company to work the new lode, and he will be invaluable."

"And he will get nothing?"

"I don't know that he wants anything. He has plenty as it is."

She made no reply, and for a moment or two they looked at each other in silence. Then Sir John said, with a chuckle—

"A penny for your thoughts, Dorothy!"

"A penny for yours, father."

"Do you really care very much for the fellow?"

"For the fellow?"

"I mean for Penlogan, of course. Mind you, I'm not surprised if you do. He's the kind of fellow any girl might fall in love with, and, to be quite candid, I shouldn't object to him for a son-in-law."

"Oh, father!" and she ran to him and threw her arms about his neck.

"Then you do care for him, little girl?"

But the only answer he got was a hug and a kiss.

"Oh, very good," he went on. "I'll let him know to-morrow morning that he may come along here and see you if he likes. I don't expect he will lose very much time. What! crying, little girl? Come, come, you mustn't cry. Crying spoils the eyes. Besides, it is time we were both in bed."

She kissed him more than once, and then ran hurriedly out of the room.

On the following afternoon she went for a walk through the plantation alone.

"He will come this way," she said to herself. "He will be sure to come this way. He knows it is my favourite walk."

She walked slowly, but with every sense alert. She knew that her father had been to see Ralph, and, of course, he would be impatient to see her. If he were half as impatient as she was he would be on his way now.

She espied him at length a long way down the road, and she drew back a little in the shadow of the trees and waited. Her heart was beating very fast, and happy tears kept welling up into her eyes.

She was looking away from him when at length he came upon her.

"Dorothy!" he said, in a voice that thrilled her like a strain of music.

"Yes, Ralph," and she turned her perfect face full upon him.

"Your father said I might come."

"Yes, I know," and she placed both her hands in his.

"I have waited long for this day," he said.

"We are the happier for the waiting."

"You are satisfied?"

"I am very happy, Ralph."

He gathered her to himself slowly and tenderly, and kissed her. There was no need for many words just then. Silence was more eloquent than speech.

That evening the dowager came to the conclusion that she would have to look out for a new companion and secretary.

Lightning Source UK Ltd.
Milton Keynes UK
UKHW040826030822
406784UK00002B/430